Maya did not know w̶... ...ing so swiftly, with her and the injured boy as captive. By all rights, they should have rested after raping her and looting her camp. Did they suspect that her mate, Black Caribou, might return and wreak vengeance on them? At least that meant they had not killed Caribou as she feared. Or was it what the thin one, Dag, had seen when he had been about to plunge his knife into her and she turned her eyes upon him? The eyes that might make him worship her as a goddess or slay her as a Demon. Her blue and green eyes.

Dag had done neither. Instead he carried her along with the boy toward an unknown shaman. When Maya looked at the boy, she understood. For not only had he uttered words in her own language—the pure Spirit Tongue—his green and blue eyes ...

His eyes. He had green and blue eyes. . . .

KEEPER OF THE STONE

KEEPER OF THE STONE

A Novel
by
Margaret Allan

A SIGNET BOOK

SIGNET
Published by the Penguin Group
Penguin Books USA Inc., 375 Hudson Street,
New York, New York 10014, U.S.A.
Penguin Books Ltd, 27 Wrights Lane,
London W8 5TZ, England
Penguin Books Australia Ltd, Ringwood,
Victoria, Australia
Penguin Books Canada Ltd, 10 Alcorn Avenue,
Toronto, Ontario, Canada M4V 3B2
Penguin Books (N.Z.) Ltd, 182–190 Wairau Road,
Auckland 10, New Zealand

Penguin Books Ltd, Registered Offices:
Harmondsworth, Middlesex, England

First published by Signet,
an imprint of Dutton Signet,
a division of Penguin Books USA Inc.

First Printing, August, 1994
10 9 8 7 6 5 4 3 2

BOOK ONE

BEGINNINGS

It is fear that first brought gods into the world.
—Petronius

Never to be cast away are the gifts of the gods.
—Homer

The gods cannot be trusted.
—Traditional

CHAPTER ONE

One she would keep, the other send away
Till joined once again, they bring the new day.

1

The maddening rhyme ticked round Maya's already churning thoughts, a distracting little ditty because, for some odd reason, it made her think of death. Her death. *One she would keep . . .*

Who would keep? Keep *what*?

Maya sighed and snapped her fingers in irritation. It was time. She couldn't wait any longer. She was frightened of the anticipated confrontation, and that fear, when she should have felt only confidence, frightened her even more.

She had dressed in a robe cut from the skin of an albino caribou and decorated with drawings of power. Around her neck she draped a necklace of teeth from the jaws of a mother lion. From her wrists and ears dangled treasures carved of mammoth tusk. With a grimace—for it was hot and heavy—she donned a headdress fashioned from the skull of a doe caribou. Finally she unwrapped her most prized possessions—a rattle carved out of an unblemished length of maple, and a mammoth sculpted from a bit of pink quartz.

When she finished she looked through the slit at the edge of the door of the Spirit House. Her nostrils twitched at the smoke from the herbs burning in the Sacred Fire. She listened to the hum of conversation as the Tribe gathered at the Hearth. She gave her robe a final shake, tilted her head back, and inhaled deeply.

I will die soon, she thought. *Well, why not?*

Her fingers curled at her sides. They itched for the Mammoth Stone, but that was gone long ago. The pink quartz figurine she'd carved to replace it was beautiful, but its power was weak.

She no longer dreamed the Great Dreams. That had seemed a blessing. It had meant freedom, and a future for her and Black Caribou. Now the future had arrived, and she missed the Stone desperately.

What will the Mother do? she wondered.

She hadn't seen Her in thirty full turns of the seasons. But the small dreams had come. Tiny messages that added up to a warning. From the Mother? If not Her, then whom? The Other, He of Snakes and Fire? But that Dark Lord had nothing to do with her, Shaman who was only a vessel. Or did He?

The rhythm of the drums quickened. She watched the drummers, young men naked but for the hide clouts, their sweaty faces vacant as they pounded the magical cadence.

She sighed. Soon all questions would be answered. Would she still be Shaman? Or a pariah, cast out to die alone, while Buffalo Daughter wore the robe of white caribou?

Oh, Mother!

She paused, but the Mother made no reply. She had abandoned Her daughter. As Her daughter had abandoned Her?

The carving was slick in her palm as she pushed through the door. The sunlight smote her like a hammer. She blinked, straightened her shoulders, and marched toward the Hearth of Testing. Voices fell silent, then resumed in whispers after she passed.

The Mammoth Stone!

But it was too late for futile regrets. She walked to face this judgment alone—for the Mother was fickle, and worked Her own purposes. *Never my purposes,* she thought. *How can I forget that?*

She stopped at the fire, her face grim, and glanced at those gathered to watch the challenge. Most of them she'd counted as friends. But as she examined their features with the newfound clarity of dread, she saw their fear and understood why this testing must now take place.

Lines marked the faces of the adults, sunken bellies disfigured many of the children, and hungry wailing sounded from the infants. She knew they blamed her. The Shaman was the health of her People, and their tribulations were her own.

It had been a moon since the hunters had killed a stringy bison whose meat was barely enough for soup. Since then her magic had remained barren. Her People were hungry and frightened. Never in all the years of trekking had they gone so long without fresh meat.

A stir beyond the fire drew her attention. At first she couldn't see Buffalo Daughter for the crowd that surrounded her. Buffalo Daughter's extended family was by far the largest in the Tribe. It seemed all of them had chosen to support the young woman by escorting her to the challenge. Maya saw her own family—Black Caribou, her mate, along with Young Wolf and Little Caribou, her two sons, and their wives and children—gathered a few feet away, watching her. Black Caribou offered a nervous smile that didn't come off.

She understood. Caribou remembered too much. Though he never spoke of it, she knew he'd seen the truth on that day she'd defeated her enemies, the Shamans Ghost and Broken Fist. Her spine shivered as she recalled the appalling force the Great Mother had channeled through the Mammoth Stone into the destruction of the two Shamans. She knew that if she held that Stone today, she would have nothing to fear from this confrontation. But the Stone was gone. She must face Buffalo Daughter's challenge alone.

She stared across the fire at Buffalo Daughter. So be it, then. If the Mammoth Stone was denied to her, it was also denied to her challenger. They would meet on equal ground, without the aid of the Great Powers who ruled the World. She, born a vessel for those Powers, understood Them better than anyone still living. Sometimes, when pity for Ghost stole into her thoughts, she was grateful that the Stone had been left behind. Ghost's terrible fate reminded her of the destiny of vessels, after their usefulness was over.

"Ho, Shaman!" the woman's voice called sharply. "Are you Dreaming now?"

Maya smiled. "No, Buffalo Daughter, I am not. I awaited your arrival." She glanced at the shadows that had lengthened past high noon. "You are late, I see."

"Perhaps you should not be in such a hurry," Buffalo Daughter replied.

The woman who stood beyond the fire was about Maya's height. She possessed a full, rounded figure. Her hair and eyes were black as chips of obsidian.

Maya regarded her silently, her thoughts envious.

She has never known the pain of difference. She was never mocked because of the way she looked. She grew up loved and cared for.

Once again Maya felt loneliness, as she recalled her own childhood, so full of fear.

Does she know? Does she understand what it is she seeks so fiercely?

Buffalo Daughter wore a robe like Maya's, but made from the skin of her own namesake. It fell in soft folds from her shoulders to her feet. She had pounded into the cured bison hide a mixture of dried berries and certain roots, so that her garment was red as blood. She had etched magical runes of power on the skin with charcoal. A rack of antlers topped Buffalo Daughter's head. On her face she'd smeared a mask of red clay, which made her eyes flash like coals at the bottom of a fire.

Altogether fearsome for one so young, Maya thought, and decided, with grudging admiration, that Buffalo Daughter had learned her lessons well. *I taught her everything she knows. But did I teach her everything I know?*

Maya spread her arms. "Buffalo Daughter, why do you come to face me now?" She spoke slowly. Her words quieted the crowd. The drummers paused. Into the silence came only the hiss and spit of the fire.

The younger woman stood proudly erect. Her red clay mask remained rigid as she spoke. Only her lips moved. The effect was eerie, as if Buffalo Daughter had become a doll, controlled by something else.

Perhaps she is, Maya thought.

"The great animals disappear," Buffalo Daughter said. "Your magic no longer finds them or calls them. The hunters return with empty hands. The People cry out with empty bellies. Soon the children will begin to die. We are cursed with evil Spirits. Why have you not driven these Spirits away? Have you lost your magic, Shaman?"

There it was. The challenge, finally spoken aloud, hung

in the air between them. She felt the weight of her People's gaze on her as they waited for her answer.

It was true. She had sought in the half-world of Dream for the Spirits of mammoth, caribou, and great-horned bison, but for many moons she had found nothing. In the gray light of worried mornings, she had asked herself the same question. Her People depended on her for their survival. If she could no longer guarantee their safety, perhaps it was better to find out now. To lay down her burden, and pass on to the fate that awaited a fallen Shaman. She sighed. In a way, this confrontation was a relief.

"I have not lost my Powers, Buffalo Daughter," she said. "If you choose to match your Dreams against mine, you will know the truth. Do you so choose?"

Buffalo Daughter didn't flinch. "I do."

Maya nodded. "Very well. Make ready."

A murmur swept across the crowd. Buffalo Daughter intended to overturn their history. Only Black Caribou among them had ever seen magic faced against magic, though the battle he'd witnessed was far different from what would now ensue.

And a good thing, Maya thought. At least this contest would not involve the cold Powers that ruled them all. Or so she hoped.

She watched as Buffalo Daughter spread out a rug made of the skin of her namesake. On this the woman settled herself and arranged her robe around her.

Maya gestured, and her youngest son's second wife, White Fox, spread out a mammoth hide, its fur combed softly. Maya sank down, wincing at the pains in her knees. She was too old for this. Why did she have to face such a challenge at the twilight of her life? Hadn't she served the Mother faithfully? This should have been a time to cherish her children and grandchildren, not a time of sorrow and hunger and fear.

Oh, Mother, why me? Why now?

But she knew the answer. The Mother used Her tools as She chose—She didn't ask their permission. *And that is all I am,* Maya thought. *All I ever was. A tool.*

It was a desolate thought.

"Are you ready, Shaman?" Buffalo Daughter called.

Buffalo Daughter's image shimmered through waves of

heat above the fire, so that the younger woman seemed to float above the earth.

"I'm ready," Maya replied. "Let us begin."

Buffalo Daughter lifted a clay bowl and scooped out a fingertip's worth of yellow paste. She put the finger to her lips, licked, and swallowed. Then, carefully, she replaced the clay bowl at her side.

Maya opened the pouch at her waist and took out a handful of dried brown berries. They tasted sharp, bitter. Each woman used her own elixir, but the effect would be the same. A gateway to Dreams.

Dream matched against Dream, and to the more powerful Dream, victory. When this contest was done, the People would still have a Shaman. Only the name of that Shaman was now in doubt.

Calmly, Maya gazed across the fire at her challenger. As if sensing her attention, Buffalo Daughter's own eyes locked with hers. Maya felt the dark current pulsing between them.

Everything stopped. Maya smelled the herbal essence of the fire, tasted the bitterness of the berries she'd swallowed, heard the sigh of the wind, felt the hard earth beneath her buttocks, and looked into Buffalo Daughter's dark, burning eyes. Growing larger, larger . . .

The Dream took her and the world fell away.

2

In the darkness, Maya saw two points of light—the eyes of Buffalo Daughter, locked in confrontation, sharing the same Dream. It was true, then. This battle was ordained. Two could share a single Dream only by the leave of those Spirits who ruled the Dream World. For an instant all hung motionless. Then, slowly, the dark began to clear.

Maya's mind convulsed in shock as the Dream World sprang into existence around her. She stood on a vast and rolling green plain. Nearby, a grove of trees bent to the breeze. The air sparkled like clear water, and made the range of white-topped mountains in the distance seem near enough to touch.

She knew where she was, though she hadn't been here in

more than fifty seasons. It was a Great Dream, for she had returned at last to the World of the Mother Herself!

Triumphantly she faced Buffalo Daughter, who stood a few steps away. "Now you see my Power," Maya said. "This is the World of the Mother I have brought you to."

But Buffalo Daughter's lips curled into an enigmatic smile. "You have brought *me* here, Shaman? I think not." The younger woman raised her right hand toward the trees. "Look, Shaman! Your doom approaches."

Maya turned. At first she saw nothing. Then, slowly, the figures began to resolve in the gemlike light. Again, almost forgotten, the huge beasts. A mammoth mother, tall as a tree. A great caribou, and pacing alongside in perfect harmony, the gigantic mother lion Maya remembered so well. Yet something was different. In the forefront walked the old woman who was the Mother's handmaiden. She led at the front of the pack a mighty golden buffalo.

The group approached, slowed, halted. The Mother's servant took hold of one of the buffalo's long, curving horns and led her away from the main group. Not once did the old woman turn her varicolored eyes on Maya. Instead, without hesitation, she guided the huge beast to Buffalo Daughter's side.

"Here, Daughter, is your sign. Mount up and ride." The old woman's voice shivered with the sound of suddenly rising wind. For an instant Maya felt the awesome electric presence of the Mother Herself, like the tremorous aftershock of a bolt of lightning.

Buffalo Daughter vaulted onto the buffalo, which received her patiently. Once settled, the young woman gazed down at Maya's face. There was a whisper of regret in her next words.

"This is my Dream, O Shaman, not yours. And this is my Power as well. Do you doubt it?"

Maya stood dumb, unable to answer. Buffalo Daughter sat atop her giant mount, at whose head waited the woman who served the Mother in all things. Maya stared at the ancient handmaiden. An unspoken plea moved her lips.

"Your time is over, Daughter," the old woman said. Maya heard pity in her voice, but iron decision as well. "Now another will take your place." The old woman looked up at Buffalo Daughter and smiled. "Welcome, Daughter," she said.

"No!" Maya was startled by the harsh cry, even more startled to realize it had come from her own throat. Yet she couldn't stop herself. The words tumbled heedlessly in a jumble of outrage. *"I have served faithfully!"*

Maya felt her cheeks burn with shame, with rage, with helplessness. *"It isn't fair!"*

The older woman waited patiently until she was sure Maya was done. Then, as if nothing had been said, she turned back to Buffalo Daughter. "Go with Her blessing," she said softly. Once again, Maya felt the harsh lightninglike quiver that signaled the nearness of the Great Mother.

Bleakness chilled her heart. She wanted to grab Buffalo Daughter and shake her, make her realize how meaningless such promises were. To tell her how once the same promise had been made to her, on this same gentle plain. And how false that promise had become, now that her own time had ended. But it was futile. The younger woman, who had never felt the essence of the Mother, the endless raging well of Power, would not—could not!—understand. Only time would teach her, as it had taught Maya, that the Gods could not be trusted. The Gods—for the Mother didn't rule alone, something else Buffalo Daughter would someday discover—used Their tools however They would, and when They were done with them . . .

When They were done.

"The Dream is over," Maya said softly.

With infinite compassion, the old handmaiden regarded her. "Yes," she replied. "It is."

Maya bowed her head and let the dark sweep her away.

3

"Maya!"

It was Black Caribou. It took her a moment before she recognized the voice and felt his hand on her shoulder. She opened her eyes.

"Yes, Caribou," she said. "I'm here."

Worry colored his voice as he whispered in her ear. "Maya, what has happened? Look at Buffalo Daughter!"

Maya glanced across the fire. The sacred flames had

burned down to coals. Buffalo Daughter stood silently, staring at her. There was a new majesty to the younger woman, evident in the straightness of her spine, and in the way her nostrils flared as she held her head high, waiting for Maya to awaken.

"Yes, Caribou." She patted her husband's hand. "I know. Here, help me up."

She grunted as Caribou lifted her. She swayed only a moment. Then, knowing what remained, she faced her nemesis.

"Maya," Buffalo Daughter said.

Hushed exclamation erupted from the crowd. No one missed Buffalo Daughter's use of the Shaman's name without her title. But this was nothing to the roar that swelled up when Maya replied, "Yes, Shaman?"

Buffalo Daughter's smile told the rest of the story, but the ritual had to be completed.

"Do you yield your Power to me?"

"I yield, Shaman."

Buffalo Daughter paused an instant to savor the moment of her ascension. Only a few terrible words were left, to seal her new office. Yet before she spoke them, her black eyes flickered.

Does she see her own future? Maya wondered.

Perhaps Buffalo Daughter saw *something,* for her voice lost its iciness, and quavered a bit.

"You are cast out, Maya. You must leave the People, for another serves them now!"

Caribou's breath-squeezing hug about her waist startled her, but she managed to reply, "Yes, Shaman."

A stir at the edge of the crowd turned heads. Men pushed their way to the fire, their voices full of joy, their eyes alight.

"Buffalo!" one shouted. "A small herd, less than half a day away!"

All eyes swept from Maya to the new Shaman, whose Power was now made convincingly evident. Maya felt something gritty in her left hand. She opened her fingers and looked down. A handful of pink grains were all that remained of the tiny quartz mammoth. They fell in a glittering shower to the ground.

"I will leave tomorrow," Maya said.

So began the greatest journey of the Bearer of the Stone.

CHAPTER TWO

1

He woke beneath a tangle of bushes, the cries of birds in his ears. He ran his tongue over scabbed lips, tasted salt, and winced as he turned his head. The smell of wild onions and dirt filled his nostrils. Heat baked on his skull, and itched in the wounds crusted on his chest and arms. When he pushed himself up, the deep muscles in his back moved stiff as an old hide.

A flapping cloud of wings exploded from a nearby tree, the sound shockingly loud. He put out one hand to steady himself and gasped at the spike of pain that blurred his vision.

Thirsty!

Then—*What is my name? I can't remember my name!*

In panic he sank back down. The fluttery rush of his heart filled his ears. His eyelids flickered and fell. A bit later the birds returned. Nothing moved in the clearing to disturb them. They ignored the shape huddled beneath the clump of berry-laden bushes as they pecked busily at the bright red morsels.

They left the boy alone because his chest still faintly lifted, fell, lifted again. Should that movement cease, they would take his eyes as easily as the berries—but not yet.

That was the first day.

2

"I am Serpent. My name is Serpent."

The sound startled him awake. His eyes popped open in darkness.

"My name is Serpent."

Disoriented, it was a moment before he realized the sound came from his own battered lips, his own arid voice box.

"Serpent?" he said. "Is that my name?"

But it must be. He couldn't remember another. He could recall everything else—the beatings and the burnings, the horrible promises, the tortures small and large—oh, yes, he could remember all *that*. But the only name he knew was the one he spoke again, softly, against the night.

"Serpent. My name is Serpent."

The whole tidal wave of pain, thirst, fear that had been walled up behind the sweet fortress of sleep hit him then.

"Unnnggh."

There was no force to his soft moan, only an exhaustion that seemed to creep from his bones, spread to muscles, nerves, heart. He lay still, trying to push all this away, to ignore it, and finally his thoughts achieved a certain order.

First: *I'm hurt, badly injured. This time was the worst of all.* Then: *I have to help myself, or I will die.* Inexorably, this led to a greater question: *Do I care?*

A part of him whispered seductively, *No, you don't care, so easy to lie back, sink into the waiting darkness, rest . . .*

Then, clearly, a single picture. Black birds digging at his naked eyes, bits of flesh spattering on desiccated cheeks. The face of a skull. His face.

He sat bolt upright, ignoring the flash of agony the effort cost. Listened to the heavy thud of his heart. Smelled the clean oak scent of the forest that surrounded him. In the middle distance something coughed. From farther away came a low, bubbling scream of reply.

He turned his head, realizing suddenly that he could see. Somewhere above the forest canopy was a moon and stars. Enough light filtered down for him to make out shapes.

So thirsty.

He cocked his head and listened for the nocturnal sounds of beasts. The beasts would help him. At night the great animals went to drink. They would lead him to water. They would assuage his thirst.

He trusted the beasts. He understood them. Not men, he didn't trust or understand *those* torturers, but he knew beasts. Nor did he fear them, though he didn't understand why that was so.

Sipping air in painful bursts, he staggered to his feet. Off to his left, something trumpeted. Not anger, pleasure. He could tell the difference.

Water lay—that way.

Limping badly, he set off.

That was the first night.

                                3

The sun rose dim above a white haze, so that the clearing he found seemed filled with a luminous, all-pervasive glow. Carefully Serpent parted a screen of low scrub, its thick leaves shiny green, and peered out at the tiny pond in the center of the clearing. A wide, much trampled path led off into deeper forest, but the muddy verge of the watering hole was deserted. The great beasts, their fighting and feeding done for the night, had slunk off to sleep.

He took a deep breath, nerving himself, and stepped into the open. The smell of water filled his nose and caution flew. Limping, shambling, grunting at the pain, he flung himself across the matted grass until he lay in the mud, his face splashing down, up, down again into the precious liquid.

Too much, too fast. He sputtered and gagged as fluid filled his nose, choked the back of his throat. He pushed himself up on one elbow, began to scoop with his palm. Eventually he slowed, his terrible thirst finally brought under control. He sighed and patted his sunken belly, rolled over onto his bony butt—and stared into the vast emerald eyes of the huge cat that had padded silently into the clearing behind him and now sat on massively coiled haunches, watching him.

He laughed. It was a strange, dry sound in the silence, as if that particular noise was foreign to his tongue. "Did you come to watch me? Or to eat me?"

The tawny cave lion cocked her broad head, a perplexed, almost quizzical expression stealing across her muzzle. Her jaws opened wide, fangs as long as his arm flashing white in the pink cave of her mouth as she yawned.

Serpent found this so comical he laughed again. Then, slowly, he stood, and extended one hand toward the formidable beast. "I'm too small even for your breakfast, Mother. Go away and leave me alone."

The she-cat had very poor eyesight. Her nose was superb, though, and she smelled the acidic odor of blood wafting from the freshly opened wounds on the small thing in front of her. Yet, oddly, the scent aroused no blood lust. In fact, she was bored. She coughed once, yawned again, and hitched herself lazily to her feet. Padded past the boy, stuffed her muzzle into the pond, drank. When she finished, she ambled onward, entered the path on the far side, and continued on her way.

"Good-bye, Mother," Serpent called, but she didn't look back.

The confrontation filled him with a strange kind of joy. He was free at last. No men—no *man*—could hurt him if he couldn't be found, and he had no intention of letting that happen. No, not ever. Not even if it cost him his life.

Once again he chuckled, though the sound was lower and uglier than it had been before. His life? He was thirteen years old. His life had been leaking out as long as he could remember. The animals might kill him, but they wouldn't torture him.

He knew beasts, all right. The true beasts walked on two legs—and the worst of them served the God.

He jerked a ragged breath into his lungs, flinching as a sheet of pain rippled across the web of cuts on his chest. *Have to do something about that,* he thought.

He stepped away from the pond. The quality of the light in the clearing had slowly changed. The foggy luminescence yielded to a harder, clearer glow. He knelt carefully and examined the muddy ground around the water.

Mosses had been trampled into the earth and a mulch of leaves. His nostrils twitched as he put his face close to the ground, searching with his nose instead of his eyes. On his hands and knees he slowly quartered the area until he found what he sought—a particular patch of mush that stank of herbs and rot.

He scooped up a handful of the noxious stuff and carefully smeared it on his chest. It felt cool and warm at the
same time. He waited until he was certain the poultice had
begun to leach the fever from his flesh. Then he covered
his chest, the festering bruises on his leg, and the burns on
his arms and shoulders. He couldn't reach the lacerations
on his back, and so he lay down and wallowed in the muck
until the pain began to dull there, as well. When he finished, he resembled some sort of painfully slender, bony
ghost made of slime. Had he been able to see himself he
would have laughed again.

Instead, he luxuriated in the cessation of pain. Overhead,
shafts of golden sunlight began to penetrate the green, turn
the water to sapphire, and strike chips of crystal from its
surface.

He sighed and moved slowly away. He would have to
sleep now. The mud would harden, flake off, have to be replaced. He'd been running for a long time. Now he would
rest. But he would rest in freedom, for the first time in his
young life. That was something.

That was the second day.

4

Serpent awoke with a gasp, arms instinctively clutched
round his knotted belly. A slow balloon of pain floated
there, inchoate, unquenchable. But when he looked down,
he saw nothing but brown skin, unmarked by any wound.
He shook his head as another ladder of cramps twisted his
gut. Finally he understood.

"Hungry . . ." he mumbled through thick lips.

He hadn't eaten in three days. He sat up slowly, feeling
dried mud flake away in a puff of dust. The burrow he'd
fashioned beneath a thicket of prickly scrub screened his
view of the watering hole. It was late in the morning. Flies
and gnats buzzed over his scabs, which itched intolerably.
The throbbing in his belly subsided a bit, though his tough,
scrawny muscles still groaned at movement. He licked his
lips—the swelling had gone down—and slowly clambered
up, swaying a bit until he got his bearings.

More dried mud cracked away as he pushed through the

green barriers into the clearing. He shambled clumsily to the water, knelt, and drank. His belly filled with coolness and the pain almost disappeared, but a little remained in a hard knot of hunger.

Serpent rose and looked around. There were several bushes heavy with red berries, but those berries were bad to eat. He sighed and pushed a flop of long black hair out of his eyes, then trudged back toward the edge of the clearing. He avoided the beckoning ease of the broad animal trail and instead went into the forest past one of the berry bushes, pushing creepers and stringy branches out of the way. Grunting faintly at his various aches and pains, he forced himself to concentrate on the terrain as he negotiated the slowly rising forest floor.

Birds flew heedlessly above, cawing and screeching. Insects buzzed in his ears, and deeper croaks sounded from the profuse brush that grew low and sun-starved beneath the trees. He saw a flash of brown movement off to his left. Rabbit, he guessed.

He angled in that direction and discovered a moderately sized fallen tree trunk twice his own length, half rotted, with a copper-red trail of busy ants angling down one side. The spot would do, he decided.

He set himself to the task as well as he could, but it took him almost two hours to locate stones of the proper size to construct a small deadfall trap. He baited the trigger stone with a bit of moss smeared with his own blood.

When he finished, he rose and looked around. Nothing to do now but wait. Wearily he trudged back toward the water hole. Most of the healing mud poultices had flaked from his various wounds. When he arrived at the clearing, he examined himself in the light. The cuts on his chest appeared to be forming scabs, and what he could see of his burned shoulders, likewise. Since he had a vast experience of such minor wounds, he guessed that two or three days would see full scabs formed with healthy flesh growing beneath.

The bruise and wound on his thigh was a different story. He hadn't noticed the hole in the center of one spreading purple-yellow bruise but now it was plain, a deep penetration from which ugly, honey-colored pus had begun to ooze.

It worried him. The pus signaled the presence of a malevolent Spirit that, unless exorcised, might eat his entire leg. He sighed. There wasn't much he could do at the moment but continue with the poultices, drink water, rest, and hope his trap bore something more than another trail of ants attracted by the smell of his bloody moss.

It took him several minutes to repack fresh mud on his cuts and burns. Carefully he pinched the swollen flesh around the puncture on his thigh, and grunted as more pus squirted out. He shook his head. Whatever the Spirits willed.

He slowly crawled into his burrow and settled into the leaves he'd piled the night before. The makeshift bed crackled softly beneath him and sent up a pleasant-smelling cloud of dust. He watched the golden motes flicker in the light. After a while his eyelids drooped, then closed.

5

He knew it was the Dream even as he entered it. He'd had it many times before, although he never consciously recalled it upon awakening. It always started the same. He would find himself walking across a broad green meadow toward a strand of trees. In the distance a range of vast peaks sketched themselves in stone and ice against the vague horizon. The light came from everywhere—it seemed a molten thing, part of the air, part of the earth. It filled space to its limits that, he sensed, were without limit. The light was all. Somehow he understood this, and wasn't frightened by it.

Now, just as many times before, he saw the figures emerge from the trees and move slowly forward to meet him. As always they were dim and slow to resolve in the limpid, crystalline light, but after a time he could see clearly: the man, the woman, the beasts.

A wave of warmth rolled over him, filled him up, seemed almost to lift a part of him out of himself. Yet the two said nothing, and the beasts remained silent. "Who are you?" he whispered, knowing he'd asked the question a hundred, no, a thousand times before, and as before, there was no reply. But the man smiled.

Had he done that before? Serpent couldn't remember. Now the man raised his right hand and motioned toward himself, beckoning. Serpent shook his head. That was new. Wasn't it?

Nodding and smiling, the man continued to urge him toward the group, and now the woman stepped away, so the man stood alone. The man seemed familiar, almost as if—

No. He couldn't remember.

His legs recalled something, though. Without any thought to drive them, they lifted, came down on the soft glowing greensward, pulled Serpent forward.

The man's eyes—his eyes!—seemed to dance with approval, and Serpent heard his own voice shouting, *"Yes, yes, yes!"* as he flew across the grass to—

Darkness.

Gone like that, just that quick. Nothing there, no light, no strange, light-soaked place, no—hope. Gone.

Awake.

His teeth rattled in his head. Sweat exploded on his brow. His lungs clenched like fists, unclenched, knotted again. Someone was driving a sharp stick into his leg, pushing into the tender flesh, twisting, and he *screamed*!

It was the sound from his own raw throat that brought him fully awake, his eyes wild and rolling. "Who—what?"

In the distance a thin whistling shriek, descending. Serpent listened to it until he understood. The death cry of some small beast, a fox, a possum, a—rabbit?

The trap!

As always, the Dream left him like a ghost, erasing all trace of its memory. He staggered to his feet, wracked with fever, and lurched into the woods. Ahead, the thin screech tapered into a whine, a low hiss, silence. Serpent labored forward as quickly as he could, branches slapping across his face and chest, the green world slipping into haze as sweat dripped into his eyes until he could blink them clear again.

He stumbled to a halt and stood grinning at his handiwork. The trigger stone was barely visible where it poked out from beneath the much larger hammer stone—but better than that, something else also showed in the line between stone and earth: a small red paw.

Fox, he guessed, though the color was not quite right. It didn't matter. Whatever it was, he could eat it. All at once his mouth filled with saliva, and his stomach humped in anticipation. Suddenly awash with hunger, he leaned over—the world swayed dizzily—and pushed at the hammer stone. With a faint sucking sound it rolled away to reveal a mush of hair and splintery white bone and crushed pink flesh. Near one side of the mess a single black eye stared up at him, empty and perfect as a pearl.

Rabbit!

He'd never seen one that color before, and he was mildly surprised that such an animal had been attracted by bait made only of moss and blood. But it had, and now he could eat!

With clawed fingers and tearing teeth, he did.

The still-warm flesh was wet and rubbery at the same time, like chewing clotted spit. But the juices helped, and the blood was a salty joy. For a time everything faded as he ripped and tore and crammed and jawed, until at last nothing was left but hanks of hair and gnawed bones. He spat the hair and cracked the tiny bones and sucked the marrow out until nothing was left and only then did he sink back and rub his belly and sigh.

Never had any food tasted so good, not even—

But he didn't remember that, did he?

No, he didn't.

Face smeared with fresh blood, he reset his trap. In his feeding frenzy, most of the poultices he'd applied to his wounds had cracked and broken off again, like some insect shedding its carapace to reveal raw pink flesh beneath. His wounds felt on fire, but a still-sane part of him could recognize the difference between the heat of healing and the darker, more lascivious conflagration that rose from the hole in his thigh, brought to the surface in a slow up-welling of thick yellow fluid.

Blotchy red lines had begun to creep from the wound, extending up toward his crotch, down toward his knee. The thigh itself was swollen and very tender, and hot to his probing touch.

An evil Spirit, no doubt. His father knew many roots and leaves and berries, some of which were good for just this kind of deadly Spirit. But in his fever Serpent couldn't remember all of them, and had seen none of the ones he did recall.

He checked the trap one final time, then dragged himself

back onto his feet. The effort cost him greatly, and he wondered if he could make it back to the watering hole. He gritted his teeth and set out, and, after some indeterminate time, knelt by the pool. He scooped the clear, spring-brought liquid until his thirst had, for at least a while, been defeated.

Then, once again, he slathered the greenish-brown goo on his chest and arms, and on his leg as well, though he suspected the Spirit had lodged too deep within the puncture wound for him to reach it with a simple poultice. There was another alternative, he knew, but that was so horrifying he wouldn't let himself think of it. Not yet.

When he finished, he felt sleep screaming behind his eyelids, and staggered in a daze back to his burrow. Fell straight down like a string-chopped puppet and slept like a stone. When he awoke it was still light, but the sun was of a new day.

6

He lay still and sodden with sweat, too exhausted to even turn his head. It felt as if his leg had turned into a swollen, fever-filled balloon, though there wasn't much pain. He didn't think that was a good sign—pain was an indication of healing, and the lack of it signaled some kind of irreparable destruction. In fact, it was very likely that the demon in his thigh would kill him.

The sun had turned his burrow into a tiny oven and he lay within, basted in his own juices. His teeth ticked silently in his jaws, but he took no notice; the fandango of fever and chill had gone on for so long it seemed natural. For a moment he simply lay still, curled on his side, a small, hideously wounded boy staring at a blade of grass only a few inches from his eyeball.

Up the blade of grass crawled a tiny red ant. It moved with jittery purpose, tiny legs delicately grasping the green surface, until it reached the very tip and hung a moment, swaying. Serpent watched it, wondered what had caused it to climb the blade when there was nothing for it at the end of its journey.

As if sensing his thoughts, the ant turned and began its

downward trek, going a bit faster as it descended. When it reached the ground it paused, turned as if confused, then marched resolutely off into the tangle of ground cover.

Serpent wondered what the world of the ant was like, where blades of grass were like tall trees, and almost everything was bigger and more dangerous than it was.

Like my world, he realized suddenly. And that was the moment he understood that, for the first time in his thirteen years, he was free, truly *free*. When this revelation swept over him, he felt as if blinders had been ripped from his eyes, as if something lumpy and gray in the very center of his heart had dissolved. But he didn't move. He couldn't, he was too worn out. Even in his sleep his body had fought the Demon, and his body was losing that battle.

His father would have known what to do. His father, even now, could have saved him. Serpent was absolutely certain of *that*, for his father, Gotha the Shaman, was as expert in the art of healing as he was in the equally arcane craft of torture. The two, in fact, went together in Serpent's case, for he would have died long before from the practice of the second, if not for Gotha's skill in the first.

Gotha. Father.

The pain that filled Serpent's eyes then had nothing to do with the agonies of his body. In that instant his tortured soul peeped out, and it was weeping with the anguish of loss.

Loss? How could he feel *loss*? The idea was preposterous! He niggled at it, trying to understand why, even as the hour of his doom approached, that was precisely what he felt. Something ripped away, never to be replaced, some essential part of him blasted from his heart by the revelation of freedom.

Free? But I will never *be free!*

A chilly little voice deep inside his pain whispered, *Oh, yes you will. You will be dead, and that most certainly is freedom, my fine lad.*

It all came back to Gotha, came back to Father, to THE SHAMAN. As if hypnotized by the single blade of grass still slowly waving before his eyes, Serpent sank into the festering swamp of memory, searching for some unknowable reeking bottom and the hard, unexplainable kernel of loss he knew was hidden there.

That was the fourth day.

CHAPTER THREE

1

Gotha woke to find the Speaker gone.

At first a blind fiery rage clogged his vision. He stood near the post where the Speaker had been tethered, his big hands knotted on the blood-dark wood, holding tight for fear of falling over in the dizziness of his anger. After a time the seizure passed, and his mind began to function in its usual chilly manner—for he was Chief and Shaman of the People of Fire and Ice, and his gift and power was to know the ways of both.

Slowly he lowered himself to his knees in the ring of pale ashes and examined the thick leather thong that had bound the Speaker. He brought the end of it up close to his eyes and grunted softly. The fresh teeth marks in the ancient leather were plain enough to read. The boy had gnawed his way to freedom.

Gotha tossed the useless binding aside and stood. Around him the soft bustle of morning began to fill the encampment as the women stoked up cookfires. He glanced at the sky, which was a featureless gray haze, and guessed there would be rain as warm as blood by noon.

The omens, he decided, weren't good.

He picked up the thong and examined it again. The ancient leather was tough as iron. He grinned without humor. It must have taken the boy most of the night to chew his way through it. Gotha shook his head. Where had the Speaker found the strength? The Speaking had been long and hard, the Speaker almost used up at its finish.

Gotha had been careful, but in the final frenzy, the Crone had poked a sharp stick deep into the Speaker's thigh before the Shaman could stop her. It was that wound that had

brought Gotha from his bed so early in the morning, for the
boy would need special treatment to prevent an evil Spirit
from eating his body from the inside out. Nor was it in the
Shaman's interest to let such a thing happen, for the
Speaker was the seat and symbol of his power, and without
him—

Gotha didn't want to think about it. No, far better to
think about how to find the Speaker and bring him back.
The sooner the better, for that wound had looked ugly. It
would need Gotha's knowledge soon, lest it putrefy and the
Speaker die. A dead Speaker was no good to anybody, least
of all Gotha.

He spat into the ashes and turned away, a tall man with
black hair shimmering in a fall to his slender waist. His
eyes, hooded, smoldered like dark crystal in his face, his
bleak gaze bisected by the bridge of a nose as sharp as the
stone hatchet that dangled from his belt.

"Dag! Ulgol! Wake your lazy asses up!"

2

"He can't have gotten far," Dag said. The tracker picked
up one of the rocks from the Speaking Circle and offered
it to Gotha. "Look. This blood is fresher than the rest. He
started bleeding again when he crawled away."

Gotha took the rock and turned it over in his hands.
"Crawled?" he said.

Dag grunted and pointed to a pair of long indentations in
the dust not far away from the Circle. "There. On his hands
and knees."

Gotha sighed. "Well, tracker. Do you think you and
Ulgol can find one small boy who is crawling on his hands
and knees and dripping blood like rain?"

Dag grinned. "Of course."

The Shaman's face changed then, without any muscles
there moving at all. It was as if his skin became suffused
with stone, and the grin fell from Dag's lips as if someone
had slapped him. "Then do it, tracker, and do it quickly.
Bring him back to me."

Dag jumped hastily to his feet. "Yes, Shaman." He

turned, slapped Ulgol on one broad shoulder, and began to trot away.

"Dag?"

"Yes?"

"Do not harm him."

There was such a threat in Gotha's words that Dag felt the flesh of his thighs shudder as his balls pulled into tight knots in his crotch. "No, Shaman, I won't."

"Good. Be off with you then. And hurry!"

Without another word the two men loped away from the camp. Only Ulgol, whose brains, Dag sometimes thought, were half-scrambled, paused for a final look back.

"What's the matter?" Dag asked. He noted with relief that Gotha had turned away and didn't see this small lapse.

"I didn't get any breakfast." Ulgol's flat nose twitched at the rich smells of meat and greens now rising from the fires.

"Idiot. Didn't you hear the Shaman? We'd better find that Demon-ridden brat if we ever want to eat around our own fires again."

"Yes, Dag," Ulgol said.

"Well, then. Let's go."

3

Gotha stumped moodily back to his house. Already sweat was dripping from his high, fine-boned brow. The dead embers of rage sat like stones in his gut. His hands twitched. He wanted to strangle something.

The Crone poked her raisin face out of her own tent and cackled at him. "Ho, Gotha. A fine morning."

He rounded on her. "A pox on you, witch. May your face rot on your bones! May your withered tits swell with poison! May your—"

She drew back from his anger for a moment, then cackled again. "Your mood isn't so good this morning, Shaman? Perhaps"—she tittered slyly—"it was something you ate?"

Gotha glared at her, clenching and unclenching his fists. Why hadn't he killed the old hag long ago? He didn't think it was only because she was his mother. There *must* have been some other reason. But he forced himself to calm down. Now was not the time to rechew old mysteries. And maybe the dried-out bag of bones could be of help.

"Mother, come to my house. We have a . . . problem."

The Crone scrabbled out her door like a skinny spider emerging from a hole in the ground. Her dirty white hair twitched leadenly with the movement, and a patch of it suddenly stood straight out from the side of her bony skull. Gotha grimaced.

I came from that? he asked himself for the thousandth time.

"A problem, sonny. Well, tell it to the Crone. Mother can make it better, oh, yes she can."

"I doubt *that*," Gotha replied. "But come anyway." He glanced sharply at her face. "Your eye is leaking again. Wipe it off. Why must you be so disgusting?"

With the ease of long practice, the Crone reached up and flicked a gob of greenish ooze from the empty socket of her left eye. "Wait till you get old, sonny. Just you wait!"

His bowels heaved. It wasn't a subject he liked to pursue with her. "Move your bones," he grunted. "I haven't got all day."

Another horrifying peal of rusty croaks erupted from her toothless gullet. She lurched forward and snapped one wrinkled claw around his wrist. "Help me along, Shaman. The Crone is tired this morning, after so much work at the Speaking."

And mad, Gotha thought as he led her toward his house. But she managed her Demon well enough. *Thank the God for that!*

4

Dag entered the woods full of hope for a quick end to the Shaman's quest, but after a half hour of thrusting his slender body through a wall of scrub that seemed mostly thorns, he began to worry. At first the trail was plain enough. The boy must still have been crawling along, for the signs lodged in crushed leaves and the occasional scribbles of dried blood were easy to read. But then, as the scrub grew thicker and thornier in the cathedral silence of the tall trees, the trail began to dissipate.

As time slid along toward high noon, Dag raised one hand and brought Ulgol to a halt. Sweat itched and stung in a hundred tiny wounds on the tracker's limbs. His belly griped with emptiness, and his head swirled with irritations like a cloud of mosquitoes. Nor was his mood lightened any by the sight of an unscathed Ulgol, who had escaped all injury by clumping along as close to Dag's butt as he could, thus avoiding, by virtue of Dag's path breaking, any hurt to himself.

"You stupid pig," Dag muttered under his breath—but only under his breath, for Ulgol, though placid enough, was awesome when aroused by some elemental emotion— like rage. The big man was just smart enough to dislike being called stupid.

"Huh? What, Dag?"

"Why don't you go first?" Dag said.

Ulgol smiled sweetly. "Because I can't track like you, Dag. You always tell me so."

Dag sighed. Ulgol was his best friend, despite Dag's occasional urge to brain the oaf with a handy rock. "You're right, Ulgol. Sorry."

Ulgol stared down at his whippetlike compatriot. "Will you find the brat in time for midday meal, do you think?"

This question kindled Dag's irritation all over again, for the question was precisely what was becoming a worrisome thorn in his skull.

"I don't know," he said at last.

"Why? What's the matter?"

Dag thought about it. "Back there apiece. Remember when I said, 'He stood up here,' and showed you the spot?"

Ulgol nodded. "Yes. That bush, you showed me how the twigs were broken where he pulled himself up."

Dag grinned. Ulgol's slow earnestness was endearing. "That's right. I thought he would fall down again as he grew weaker, but he hasn't. So his trail is harder to find. Also, his wounds must have scabbed over, because he's quit bleeding."

Ulgol regarded his friend doubtfully. "Then we can't find him before the women cook for evening?"

"Tcha!" Dag spat, narrowly missing Ulgol's foot. "Don't you ever think about anything but food?"

"No, not much," Ulgol said seriously. "Sometimes I think about fighting." His face brightened. "Or fucking. I think about that, too."

Dag turned away, shaking his head. "Well, we'd better think about finding that brat, or the Shaman will use *us* for the next Speaking, and then we won't think about anything at all."

The threat evidently penetrated the slow rise and fall of Ulgol's thoughts, because he squinted in alarm. "Do you think so, Dag? But we don't have the Voice. What good would we be for a Speaking?"

Dag sighed. "I don't know, my friend. But Gotha would do it anyway. And enjoy it, too!"

The two men stared at each other until Dag pushed into a thicket where spiderwebs swayed softly beneath the many feet of their tiny masters.

"If it rains, *then* it will get hard. But we'll find the little beast, Ulgol. Don't worry."

"I think it's going to rain," Ulgol said, following.

5

The Crone gazed at the inside of her son's house, her one eye as sharp for detail as that of a hunting hawk—and as pitiless.

"Where's the Speaker?"

Gotha settled himself cross-legged and waited until the Crone, accompanied by a chorus of faint cracks and pops, had done likewise.

"Gone."

Her eye sparked at him. "Oh? Gone where?"

He glared at her. "How should I know? Gone, that's all." He snorted. "Miserable brat."

"Eh, heh, heh. Forgot how to tie a knot, did you? I thought I taught you better."

"No, he did not untie the knots. He gnawed through the thong. I am not stupid, Mother."

She snorted. A brownish-green bubble dripped from her right nostril. Gotha looked away.

"It doesn't matter anyway," he continued. "The brat's gone. I sent Dag and Ulgol after him. He can't have gotten far. They'll bring him back."

"Dag is a good tracker," she said. "Ulgol couldn't find his own ass unless you tied a haunch of buffalo to it."

Gotha eyed her dubiously. "Have you had any ... Dreams?"

"About what? The Speaker?" She shook her head. "I haven't had any Dreams at all. Not for moons." Her sly cackle filled the small hut. "Why? Worried about something?"

"Why would he run away? He's never tried to run away before."

She shrugged. "Who knows? He's growing up. He's not really a child anymore. Maybe he just decided he'd had enough of the Speakings."

In some strange way this frightened Gotha deeply, and he lashed at her. *"If you hadn't tried to murder him with that stick, maybe none of this would have happened!"*

She sighed. "Oh, Shaman. Sonny—"

"And don't call me that!"

"I'm still your mother, whether you like it or not. Rant and rave all you want, but you know I can't help myself when the Goddess takes me. I tried to murder the brat? How?"

"You don't remember?"

"I just told you."

"Mmph. Well, right at the end—he'd just finished Speaking—you just ran up to him and jabbed him in the leg with a sharp branch. Made a pretty deep hole, it looked like. And come to think about it, I'm not sure he was finished." He paused, considering. "Yes. He'd opened his mouth again, and his eyes hadn't lost that glazed look he gets."

"It's simple enough, then. Did he stop when I jabbed him?"

"Yes."

"Then the Goddess didn't want him to Speak whatever it was he was about to say."

"The God Speaks through him. The Mother has no power over the Lord of Snakes."

The Crone fixed her eye on him. *"Oh, She doesn't? Then where is your precious Speaker, my fine Shaman?"*

His smile was strained. "Probably being dragged back here right now by Dag and Ulgol."

The Crone lifted her withered head and sniffed. "I think it's going to rain," she said. She leaned over and massaged her knees. "I know it's going to rain."

The tent flap suddenly began to slap against the bentwood door frame. A moment later the first roll of thunder boomed in their ears.

"It's harder to track in the rain, isn't it?" she remarked.

"Oh, shut up."

"There is something odd about all this. You only tie him for a Speaking, and that's to keep him close at hand, lest he try to escape the pain. Otherwise, he always runs free. But he's never disappeared before." She stopped, licked her lips. "I think if you get him back, this will happen again. Once the brat has developed a taste for real freedom, he won't stop trying to taste it again."

"I'll get him back," Gotha said grimly, "and when I do, there won't be any more escapes."

"Oh? And how can you be so certain of that?"

"Because it's very hard for a boy to run when he has no feet to run on."

"Ahh," she said. "I see." She rocked back and forth and cackled so hard he had to slap her three times to make her stop.

6

The storm came first as a gust of cold wind billowing through the forest canopy, stirring the vast roof of green and fluttering the scrubland below. Not long after, a thunderous drumroll accompanied by an eye-boiling splash of light brought Dag to a halt.

"We'd better take shelter," he said. "It's going to be a bad one."

Ulgol nodded slowly. "Very bad," he agreed.

Dag squinted around, suddenly worried. Ulgol wasn't good for much on a track, but his weather sense was far better than Dag's own. "How bad?" he asked the larger man.

Ulgol shrugged. "Lots of water. Lots of wind."

"Wonderful," Dag said in disgust. "Just when we'd picked up the brat's trail again. This could make a mess of things."

They'd lost the trail sometime back, and wasted two hours circling until Dag had spotted a single footprint in a patch of moss. The boy was being clever, stepping carefully and taking care of what he touched. It showed that he was neither delirious nor too injured to hide effectively. The footprint had been a stroke of luck, and Dag hadn't yet found any other sign to point a direction with.

He examined his surroundings carefully. Not far away he spotted what he was looking for.

"Over there," he said. Then he jumped as another bolt of light shivered the dim green silence. "Come on, grease butt. Get a move on."

He led them toward the shelter he'd seen, and was pleased to find it was better than he'd hoped for. Propped against the trunk of one mighty giant was the rotting bole of another, fallen over in some ancient storm, but still broad and dry beneath. A screen of scrub on either side made a snug and woody cave where they could ride out the downpour.

They had just settled themselves when the first hard sheets of water began to pelt about them.

"Whew, I told you. A bad one," Ulgol said.

Dag thought about the storm, about the Speaker—and about the Shaman. He shivered suddenly.

"Did you bring anything to eat?" he asked.

Ulgol rummaged in his belt pouch, then withdrew two chunks of what looked like bark.

"Some dried deer meet," he said.

"Well, hand it over. I'm hungry."

They ate while Ulgol listened to the storm and Dag listened with increasing discomfort to his own thoughts.

7

The thorns of doubt that had been prickling Gotha ever since he discovered the Speaker had run away now suddenly bloomed into a full-blown crown of worry. When the

Crone's paroxysm had finally sputtered out in a trail of drool, he shook her shoulder harshly.

"Mother, what did you mean when you asked me where the Speaker was?"

Her single eye transfixed him knowingly. She wiped away the drool, the pink marks of his palm fresh and hot on her wrinkled cheeks. "It was just a question, sonny."

He shook his head. "No, I said the Goddess had no power over the Lord, and you laughed and asked me where the Speaker was. Do you mean the Goddess had something to do with this?"

Now it was her turn to look puzzled. "I did?" For a moment her full age showed in the confusion on her face. She shook her head. "I didn't—I mean, I don't think I meant anything." Her single eye sharpened then. "Did you see any signs?"

"Signs?"

"That it might have been She who spoke?"

He stared at her, trying to remember. It had only seemed a bit of conversation, until the ominous implication had penetrated his own thoughts a minute later. What, exactly, had she said?

Oh, She doesn't? Then where is your precious Speaker, my fine Shaman?

But her voice had been clear enough, and her features had shown none of the rictus she always displayed when the Goddess took her.

Nevertheless, the possibilities were more than threatening. It was a strange thing to say to him—almost a warning. The Great Ones moved in mysterious ways, and . . .

It hit him then. He leaned forward. "It wasn't Her, it was Him!"

"What? What are you talking about?"

"The God spoke to me through you. He warned me. The Bitch Goddess is behind all this. Of course She is." He slapped his chest, hard. "Why didn't I see it right away?"

Her mouth fell open. "Shaman? Has your mind flown away like a bird? I belong to Her. Lord Big Dick has nothing to do with me—nor could my tongue be profaned with His words." She shook her head in disgust. "That is left to your brat and his Speakings."

The inspiration slowly ebbed to reveal a cold beach of certainty in his mind. "The God rules the World, Mother,

whether you like to admit it or not. If He chooses you for
His warning, then you are chosen."

"Sonny, I think you are making a mistake. He has never
Spoken through me before."

"The brat has never run away before!"

She rocked once, but made no other reply.

"Mother, I want you to seek a Dream. Use your herbs,
your . . . ways, whatever you need. But seek the Bitch. Try
to find out if She's behind this."

"You profane Her!"

His eyelids lifted, unbanking the fires of rage that never
entirely died behind them. "Mother," he said softly, "you
will do this thing, or I will tie you down and dose you with
the herbs myself—pray I don't jam too many of them down
your worthless throat and you never waken."

She shivered, then whined, "Gotha, Son—"

"Just do it."

"I killed for you, have you forgotten?"

"Nor forgiven!"

In that moment she feared what was in his voice, and
turned away. "Very well," she said. "I will do it. But"—
and a bit of spirit strengthened her, and she sat up
straighter—"be warned! If you arouse Her, Her wrath will
be terrible."

He shrugged. "Goddess She is, but still a woman. I worship the greater. Just do it."

Outside, the rain began to fall.

8

The rain had finally stopped as dusk first began to tint the
leafy roof with shades of gray and pink. The whole forest
sweated in a fog of hot moisture.

Dag armed his slick brow, his eyes stinging with the
salty water that kept him blinking constantly. His vision
was already blurry; now, with the sun making its way
slowly from the World, the shadows lengthened, and the
vital details he needed to follow were harder and harder to
find.

He paused, then slowly turned his head from side to
side. "I don't know," he said at last.

"Have you lost the trail again, Dag?"

The tracker exhaled. "Yes. Snake fry that rain, it washed everything away. I don't know." Tension thrummed tiredly in his voice.

Ulgol patted the smaller man's shoulder with surprising gentleness. "Well, don't worry. We'll just start circling again." He shook the pouch at his waist. "I've got enough dried meat for several days, if we're careful." He looked up at the forest canopy and squinted in the failing light. "Do you think we should make camp?"

Dag cocked his head. Somewhere . . . "I hear a stream. Yes. Let's find it and settle for the night. It will be drier tomorrow." He glanced round at his friend. "This may take a while. No hot dinner for you, Ulgol."

"It doesn't matter," the big man replied mournfully. "I wasn't expecting it anyway." Then, slowly, another question washed across his broad features. "What will the Shaman do if we don't find the brat, Dag? Will he be very angry?"

"Yes," Dag said softly. "Very angry."

9

It took three more days of plodding in ever-widening circles, and then it was only an accident that made it happen. Ulgol, the now-empty pack slapping softly against his thigh, had pressed too close and one of his big feet got tangled in between Dag's legs just as the smaller man struggled to climb over a fallen tree trunk.

"Ooahh!" Dag whistled as he pitched headfirst the rest of the way over the log. He splatted face first into a pile of moldy leaf rot on the other side and lay there a moment chewing dirt. His right knee stung unmercifully where he'd scraped it in his passage. As he sprawled, Ulgol clambered over and planted one heavy foot square in the middle of his back, crushing him down again.

That moment seemed to crystallize all the frustrations and torments of the previous three days, and Dag turned his head enough to scream, "*You clumsy hog. You great stupid*—" And stopped.

His eyes widened slowly.

Ulgol leaned over and started to hoist him up, mumbling sullenly, "I'm not stupid, Dag, you shouldn't call me *stupid* . . ."

"Put me down!"

Obediently, Ulgol released his meat-hook grip, and Dag splashed back down—but hardly noticed in his excitement. On hands and knees he scrabbled hastily toward the crimson glint he'd seen marking a single leaf close to the ground. Yes!

"Ulgol! Here! Come look!"

Ulgol lumbered over. "What, Dag?"

"Here!" Dag swallowed, then went on more slowly. "Fresh blood. On this leaf." He leaned forward, ran his tongue over the trace. "Very fresh. No more than an hour. The brat's around here somewhere, Ulgol."

Quickly he scrambled to his feet, his nostrils widened as he searched for the boy's scent. But after a moment the light faded a bit in his eyes. "Around here *somewhere,* but not *right* here."

He slapped his compatriot on one knotted biceps. "Close, though. Come on, let's find him."

Dag's excitement was contagious. Slowly his new air of confidence infected the bigger man, who offered a slow grin in reply. "I'll follow you, Dag," he said.

"Of course you will. Come on."

But Dag didn't explain the true source of his joy. That blood had been *fresh.* Which meant the brat was still alive.

Dag had not looked forward at all to returning to Gotha with nothing but a corpse for his efforts. Dead brats didn't Speak. But if the boy had survived this long, he would probably make it the rest of the way.

And but for Ulgol tripping him up, he would never have seen the mark at all. *Thank the God!*

10

They crouched near the leafy hollow Serpent had found.

"This is where he's burrowed up," Dag said. "See. All this blood. Some old, only a little new. He's healing. And all the footprints in the mud by the pond. He's got to be—"

Stopped. "Shhh, not a word!" he whispered.

A sudden slide and rattle of leaf on stem, not the wind.
A small animal, a—
Flash of white, over—
"There! There he is! Get *him, Ulgol. Go get him!"*

CHAPTER FOUR

1

The nightmare had shattered her sleep like a thunderbolt.

Now Maya shivered and hugged herself against the morning cold. The sandy riverbank was quiet in the silver half-light of approaching dawn. Birds cried somewhere above the mist. The rock on which she sat poked her bony rump. She stood and walked across the sand to the rolling brown water. The smell of mud and rotting vegetation saturated her nostrils.

I will die soon, she thought again, suddenly. Had she been made of frailer stuff, she might have quailed before that knowing. She paused for a moment, holding herself, suddenly conscious of her body. Slowly she ran her hands down across her breasts, her belly, her thighs. Her fingers felt thin and cold, her fingertips extraordinarily sensitive. The flesh beneath her touch was loose and sagging, yet beneath the ravages of time she could still sense the hot juices that had once burned there, when she was young and the world was sweet. The years had eroded that heat, damped it with childbirth, and yet . . . the ghost of that rich warmth still lived within her aging body and yearned for what might have been, of what, perhaps, still could be.

"Oh, Caribou," she whispered. "How have you loved me for so long? Do you still love me?"

Not many dreams of any kind came to her lately, but each that did was more frightening than the last. The dreams spoke of doom. One such horror had awakened her before dawn and now she shivered, for despite everything, it was the little pains that bothered her the most. On damp chilly days her cheekbones and the long bones of her arm ached miserably—reminders of long healed wounds that plagued her more as she grew old and brittle. But the aches were only aches and she had endured far worse. Pain wouldn't stop her. It never had before.

> _One she would keep, the other send away_
> _Till joined once again, they bring the new day!_

The rhyme! That wretched rhyme!

She sighed and started back to the camp at the edge of the sand. She felt slow and clumsy and bloated with dread. She realized that for the first time in her life she actually _missed_ the Mammoth Stone.

"Maya!"

Caribou's baritone shout boomed above the dull rumble of the water. She looked up, startled.

"Over here!"

She had to squint to make out his hulking form far down the bank, crouched near the edge of the river. Even her strange, miscolored eyes had begun to dim. At least, thank the Mother, her hearing was still good—one of the only good things left in her suddenly disintegrating life.

Caribou waved again and she paused, staring at him. He was still a very big man—his form looked as solid and unchanged as the boulders on which he squatted. Nor was the resemblance to his younger self in any way illusory—he had led the Tribe since they'd departed from the Green Valley so many years before, and his hunting prowess was still regarded with awe by the young men. His hair had grizzled until it looked like a permanent roof of snow overtopping his heavy brow, but his arms, when he held her at night, felt as if they were stuffed tight with large, smooth rocks.

Suddenly a pang of love for him as sharp and pure as a mountain stream shot through her, and she realized she was trembling with need of him, of his hard huge chest, of the safe binding circle of his arms.

I can't leave him! And as she continued to stare at him, her vision wavering now behind a curtain of unshed tears, she finally perceived the depth of her loss from the confrontation with Buffalo Daughter—not only her position in the Tribe, but her family, her husband, her very _life_.

A part of her understood the necessity of exile. No Tribe could survive with two Shamans—only the Shaman could

speak for the Goddess and the Spirits, but *two* Shamans—
perhaps speaking different, even contradictory words—
would destroy the Tribe as surely as no Shaman at all.

And yet . . . and yet—

One she would keep . . .

The damned rhyme! *Why* did it hum and buzz in her
mind like a persistent mosquito, its endless drone falling,
then rising once again in her mental ear?

What did it mean?

"Maya, come down!"

She shook her head once, fiercely, as if to dislodge the
tenacious little ditty, then pushed her fingers through her
white-streaked hair. Her feet reluctantly began to move. *I
don't want to go down there and face him, speak to him.
Look into his eyes and know the truth, no matter what he
says. This is his life, too. He is Chief. He leads the Tribe.
It is all he wants to do, that and follow the great herds.
Can I—do I even have the right to ask him to give that up?*

*Would he do it if I begged? And if I begged, would he
come with me?*

She felt her own agitation increase. What if his answer
was yes, but his eyes said no? Could she live with that?

Her long fingers rubbed at her throat gently, nervously,
as if coaxing the necessary words up into her mouth.

"Maya!" He stood now, motioning her toward him, toward a far worse confrontation, she now realized, than the
one of the previous day.

"I'm coming," she called back to him as a dreadful res-
ignation settled over her.

I'm a selfish woman, she thought. *I'll beg.*

2

Her feet—without any help, it seemed, from her mind—
traveled the final yards along the bank to where he waited.
One moment she watched him from a distance, and the
next he was *right there* in front of her, his arms folded
across his chest, his formidable shoulders bunched and
tense.

She wanted nothing more, right then, than to throw herself on him, to feel his arms around her, to hear his warm

breath in her ear as he comforted her. But, as the ghosts of memory suddenly crowded close about her, she saw it in his eyes—he was afraid.

She trembled.

For one tiny instant a bleak future stretched out in the limitless vistas of her imagination—the departure, the lonely wandering, and, eventually, the slow cold slide into starvation and death. And none of it would matter, because he wouldn't be there.

Alone. Always and forever alone.

The price she must pay . . . *for what*?

Anger warmed her then, suffused the desolate vision with a hot penumbra of hate. She had suffered—*oh, how she had suffered*—for the Mother, and now, without a backward glance, the Goddess had turned away. And in that hot crystal moment, the iron that was in her, had always been in her, stiffened to her aid.

Caribou was afraid? No doubt. He feared losing what he had, giving up his own life, and for what?

For a vagabond woman he'd once found, who turned out to Speak for a God, and murdered for Her.

Had he ever forgotten that terrible day before the fire, when the Mother had used Maya to boil Broken Fist's brains inside his own skull? Maybe the fear she saw in his eyes reflected nothing more than his long-buried fear of her.

And still the anger burned. *Very well, husband, if that is the way it will be, then let it start here. My love for you will never end, but I was wrong. I* will not beg! *I may be a tool, but my Wielder is a Goddess!*

She folded her arms across her breasts. They stood and stared at each other in silence across a gray gulf that suddenly seemed unbridgeable, while she watched the fright glow in his eyes like the vague balls that sometimes floated over marshy places.

At last she could bear the separation no longer, and tore her gaze from him. It was one of the hardest things she'd ever done, but she forced herself to speak softly, kindly. "It's all right, Caribou. I understand your choice. How could I not? Who knows me"—and here the tiniest dollop of her own self-loathing crept into her voice, she couldn't help it—"better than me? I don't blame you, husband. I understand you."

His mouth dropped open as she turned away to begin the long walk that could end only in her death. In a way it was a relief that she could no longer see his face and the fear that twisted it into a mask that came near to breaking her heart.

As she walked she straightened her shoulders and thrust her head forward, her bitter pride gall in her throat, and the words she was thinking slipped out without any realization.

"And I love you."

The sound that hammered at her back was the most terrifyingly mournful thing she'd ever been forced to hear. Half howl, half throat-tearing scream, it filled her ears until she thought her head would burst.

"Mayaaa! Don't leave me, Mayaaa! Don't leave me alooooone!"

3

She nestled in his arms, feeling almost childlike, beneath a shady green canopy of willow, the river rolling beyond them like a great brown snake.

"I was scared, Maya, so scared. I know you. You'd try to take it all on yourself, go off and leave me. To spare me, some crazy womanish thought. But you're stronger than me that way. I knew I couldn't stop you if you decided, and I was *so* afraid you had. When you turned away, I—I . . ."

He shook his shaggy head, then leaned down and nuzzled her neck. She sighed, still aghast at the terrible mistake she'd almost made.

Of course he'd been afraid. She hadn't mistaken the fear she'd seen in his black eyes, only the reason for it. He hadn't feared leaving the People—only that she would depart without him. How could she have been so stupid?

So untrusting, she amended. *But I have reason not to trust, don't I?* that bitter part of her amended.

Not him, the honest part replied. *Not Caribou, who has never wavered, not in our entire lives together.*

Then she put it away. The mistake avoided, the choice not made.

Thank the Goddess!

Then it struck her. For a woman whose life had been supposedly destroyed by the Mother, she'd had cause to thank Her twice in less than an hour.

One she will keep . . .

Is that you, Mother? Is that you making a rhyme?

"It will be all right," Caribou soothed. "Everything will be all right." His great arms encircled her, and for a moment she felt small, safe, protected. He thought his strength could keep her from harm. He would try, at least, and for that she thought her heart would burst from her chest with the joyous agony of loving him. *Could* he keep her safe? She didn't think so. But it didn't matter, because he would try, and *that,* in the end, was reason enough for love.

She felt his rough, callused fingers on her breasts, and for a moment all fear fled, and she felt young again. The old heat burned within her, filled her belly, and bubbled in her loins like melting honey. Slowly she turned to face him, feeling the hard rod of his cock against her thigh. She put her hand on the hot, swollen head of it and squeezed and felt him shudder against her. Her fingers went slippery as his pre-come gushed into her palm. She hoisted herself up and lowered herself down on him, gasping as he penetrated her. Then, rocking gently, they burned away the cold morning mist with a fire hotter than that the Gods had given with their lightning bolts.

The human fire. The fire of love.

4

They took down their tent together and loaded it onto travois poles. The sky finally cleared into a dome of high blue through which flashed the occasional hawk. It turned hot. Maya sweated as she worked, and thought about almost nothing. Occasionally people came by, to whisper things into her ear that she knew she wouldn't remember later. There was a furtiveness about these leave-takings, even those from her sons and daughters and their families. She knew what it was. It was fear. An old Shaman and now a new Shaman, and what did it all mean? They were frightened of the change, and wondered what it meant for them.

Already Maya was fading from their lives, the vanquished Shaman going into exile.

The only real surprise was that Caribou had chosen to share that exile, and she suspected that was the more worrisome problem to the average leave-taker. They had a new Shaman—but who would take the place of their mighty hunter?

She snagged the last of the binding cords tight and stood up and squinted into the sun. Plenty of daylight left. They would make good time if they left soon.

Then it hit her. Good time to go *where*? Where were they going?

She paused, her mind stuck in that meaningless groove. She had no idea what came next. It had been hard enough to cross the first hurdles, the confrontation and then the question of Caribou. Having passed them, she was at a loss.

Exile. What did it mean? At the moment all she could think of was that it meant *away*. And she was amazed to find a great release in the thought, as if her life with the Tribe had become a trap, from which only now was she free.

Caribou touched her shoulder and she jumped. "Oh. Caribou."

He grinned at her. Something about him looked different. Younger, almost. She smiled back, and touched his chest gently.

"All done here," she said.

"Good. If we leave right away, we can be well upriver before dark. We'll camp by the water. I know a good spot."

"Caribou, why upriver? Where are we going?"

His broad features crinkled in surprise. "How else would we go back to the Green Valley?"

And that was all right, she knew it was all right.

It was the answer she'd been waiting for, after moons of dreams and questions.

"Well, yes," she said. "Of course."

The old life became the new, and only change remained the same.

One she would keep. Maybe the Mammoth Stone could break that riddle, too, now that its call ached in every bone of her body.

It is meant, she thought as her mouth fell open. *I am*

only a tool, and now, once again, I turn toward my purpose.

"Shouldn't we hurry?"

He patted her shoulder. "Yes, Maya. We will hurry." And so they did.

5

Maya was astounded at the joy that filled her like clear water as they marched along the riverbank. Caribou, perhaps wrestling with his own thoughts, spoke little, but he would turn and smile brightly at her every now and then. The worst of the heat passed by the middle of the afternoon, and a fine slow breeze danced across their sweating shoulders.

She felt renewed, and for a time, all thoughts of death retreated. They dragged the travois together, he silent, she enjoying the stretch of muscle against bone, even though she knew the old aches would greet her in the morning. It was an in-between time, when the past was gone and the future yet to come.

Near to evening, with the sun splashing streaks of red and lavender glory along the horizon, they made a hasty camp. She stoked up the fire in the small hearth and boiled some of their dried rations in a skin pot. The smell intermingled with honeysuckle, oak, and the river water, filling her with delicious laziness.

After they had eaten, she stretched luxuriously and thought that perhaps she wouldn't ache that badly the next morning. "Caribou?"

"Mmm?"

"How did you know we would go back to the Green Valley?"

He arched one eyebrow. "Where else would we go?"

Of course. So obvious. Why hadn't she thought of it before? *Because I wasn't meant to think of it?*

A tendril of disquiet snaked through her chest. *Tools don't think, do they?*

"I wonder if Old Berry is still alive."

He shrugged. "She'd be a very old berry if she was." He chuckled softly.

They waited in silence as dusk grew smoky around them. Her last thought before sleep was simple.

Let it be all right.

It wasn't quite a prayer, not exactly. She didn't know whom she prayed for. She didn't think it was herself, though.

6

By the third day she was well settled into the long, pleasant rhythms of the trek; they marched briskly, but not so strenuously that her aches plagued her any more than usual in the morning, and even those twinges faded quickly once she took her place on the travois pole next to Caribou. It was coming up noon on the third day when she noticed the thrumming.

It wasn't a sound, exactly, though she began to turn her head this way and that, trying to catch it with her ears. Nor was it precisely a vibration. It was as if the whole world had begun to hum a long, low tone, in the earth, in the air, in the very light.

"You hear it?" she asked.

Caribou clumped to a halt and let the pole fall with a leafy crunch. "Uh huh. It's the rivers."

Then she remembered. Several months before, early spring with winter's back only freshly broken, the Tribe had meandered slowly past a place where the river they'd more or less followed for years had met an even greater torrent. She could see it still, and was surprised at the vividness of the images that flooded her memory.

The river, which had been their path breaker, was mighty enough, a broad sweep of dark green water that swept along with a hollow smooth hissing sound, but the deluge into which it finally emptied seemed to her a Mother of Waters so wide it was hard to see across to the far shore. She had stood on the bank with her mouth open and listened to that great joining, her eyes drinking in the sight of it, so slickly powerful, and had felt obscure surges from her groin to her gut. Somehow that melding had seemed overwhelmingly feminine, almost frighteningly so. It was almost as if the Mother Herself were present in that place, bound up in the power of it.

Now, once again she heard that deep-throated thrumming, and for a moment she saw in her mind's eye the golden mists that had clothed the joining of the waters.

The joining.

Till joined once again they bring the new day.

"Let's camp near it. Can we make it that far by sundown?"

Caribou cocked his face at the sky, rubbed his chin thoughtfully.

"A hard march, but maybe."

"Let's try."

He grunted, reshouldered the travois poles, and set off. She gritted her teeth at the pace, but hid her pains. Something called to her, something important.

She wondered what it was.

7

Twilight had already purpled toward night when they finished setting up camp on a bluff overlooking the confluence of the two great rivers. Stare though she might, Maya was unable to see anything, though the dark trembled endlessly with the force of that coalescence. The words *Mississippi, Ohio,* and *Cairo, Illinois,* would not be heard in the world for eons, but something bone deep inside her understood that this was a place of lasting importance.

She built a small fire against a low wall of stone where they made their bed for the evening, and after they ate, they settled against the rock that still held heat from the day. She felt keyed up, full of nervous energy, riven with expectation.

"Caribou?"

"What?"

"Do you remember how you met me?"

He laughed softly. "I didn't meet you. I found you."

"Yes. I wish I could remember it. Everything changed then."

"I've told you about it before."

"I know. It's just that *I* can't remember it. All I have is your memories." She paused. The fire put off a glow and a fragrant sweetness of the dried wood she'd burned. The rivers rumbled, happy in their eternal congregation.

"A long time ago," he remarked. "A lot has happened since."

She nodded in the dark, the fireglow burnishing her cheeks. She felt suspended in the dark, balanced delicately between past and future, pregnant with discovery.

Something was about to happen. *What?*

"Hold me, Caribou."

He moved closer and she put her head on his chest and listened to his heart. When she woke that sound was still in her ears and the past had fallen away. Dawn flamed above the bluffs.

I will die soon, she thought, *but I will live long enough.* Long enough for what?

To do what is necessary.

8

"I'm going to hunt. There," Caribou said, and pointed down the bluff toward the deepening forest beyond the river verge. "I think I saw deer. We're low on meat."

She nodded. "We can stay here awhile. I can dry what we don't eat."

"That's a good idea." He brightened. "If I get a deer, would you make me a new coat?"

She thought of the sharp bone needles in her pack. "Of course." It would take a while, but not too long. Curing the hide would be the hardest part.

He glanced at her. "You were in such a hurry yesterday. Why not today?"

How could she explain the feelings singing in her muscles? She shrugged. "There's no rush, is there? We've got all summer, before it turns cold and the snows start. The Green Valley will wait for us."

He sensed something in her words, perhaps the words unspoken, but his wife was a strange one. The years had taught him that, and also taught him when not to question that strangeness. He unfolded himself and stood. "I won't go far," he said.

"Do you want breakfast?"

He shook his head. "I'll take a bit of dried meat with me. Better not to hunt on a full stomach. Slows me down."

She smiled at him. "Mother's luck, husband."

"Thank you."

She watched him until he dwindled and disappeared in the green darkness of the forest. Then she turned to her own pack, to the needles and scrapers, and to a mental inventory of the curing process. A part of her waited, for what it knew not.

Coming. Something coming.

CHAPTER FIVE

1

If the dark fever in his leg hadn't worked its way up until it filled his eyes with hazy fire, Serpent would never have stumbled into them the way he did. But the murky blanket had covered his normal alertness so thickly he'd been reduced to a rote floundering between his hideaway and the rude trap he'd constructed. His hours had become a slowly changing lattice of light and dark, sleep and a dim kind of wakefulness.

The wound on his leg was worse; he'd taken the final step he knew, and found a sharp bit of stone and made two deep slices across the puncture wound. Blood and a foul-smelling yellowish ooze had burst from the swollen place, and for a time he'd felt a little better. But now the edges of the new wounds had turned the color of badly dried meat, and the mud poultices only seemed to make the swelling worse.

If Dag hadn't shouted, he would have walked right into them, but the sudden cry, so unexpected, galvanized him from his stupor.

His eyes bulged in their sockets as he recognized Ulgol's lumbering form thrashing through the scrub toward him. His last fleeting glimpse before he turned and ran was of Dag, far more dangerous, passing Ulgol, his nostrils flaring with the thrill of the chase.

2

Maya puttered about until the sun approached high noon, aware that she was puttering. Every once in a while she paused, her head lifted as if smelling the air for some scent she'd almost forgotten. The rivers played their organ chords for her.

All morning she'd felt it growing, inside her and outside as well. What it was she had no idea, and once or twice she wondered if the whole thing wasn't a mistake, if her mind wasn't playing tricks on her in her old age.

But that wasn't it, either, was it? For a long time she'd thought of herself as old, but now, with the sun playing yellow in her unbound hair, she felt—if not exactly young again—at least no longer quite on her deathbed. It was, perhaps, the change in her life. Ruts could age you just as much as time, for boredom and age walked the same paths, hand in wrinkled hand. And she had certainly been thrown out of her rut, hadn't she?

Nevertheless, it was joy singing in her veins, despite her exile, despite the bad dreams. Joy and a growing sense of anticipation—would it be today? Later this afternoon, as the sun sank toward the treetops?

Would it be now?

What? *What?*

She stopped then and pushed her hair back out of her face, feeling a slick rime of sweat on her skin. She was a good distance from their camp now, near where the scrub began to thicken and rise into woods. The sun beat on the water like a great, silent bell. In the woods a bird cried raucously, once, twice.

A small cloud of wings exploded.

The boy staggered out just after the birds, lurching blindly. He fought through the brush. She could see fresh, livid scratch marks on his chest.

Now, she thought. *Now!*

She ran toward him, as if he were calling her forward, but his eyelids were screwed tight-shut, and she could hear only the harsh bellows of his lungs.

He slammed into her and knocked her over. He fought her as she tried to gather him into her arms. They thrashed for a moment in a wild tangle. He screamed thinly, desperately.

She struggled to control him, a cold part of her thinking, *He's hysterical, I have to be careful or he'll hurt himself worse,* when Ulgol clumped up panting and clouted her on the side of her head.

White sparks in darkness, then nothing.

3

Most of her bad dreams of late had been inchoate, dark choking things with only a hint of form, full of nameless and threatening Spirits. But occasionally, like a spoiled berry in rancid pemmican, there would be other nightmares, and the most ghastly was the one that despite her mostly successful efforts at daylight repression still haunted her fifteen years after the event.

Just after she'd become a woman in the Green Valley the new Shaman, Ghost, in token of his ascension to office, had beaten and raped her. Maya had no concept of rape, that is, an act of forcible sex judged to be immoral or simply wrong. Such morals did not yet exist, and right was judged by physical might in such matters. Men were stronger and women dependent on them and their hunting skills, so if a man chose to satisfy his lust with any woman who took his fancy, he might do so with impunity. Protest, if it came at all, would come either from the Shaman, for spiritual reasons, or from the man to whom the woman belonged. If she belonged to nobody, then she was helpless.

Ghost had beaten her savagely in the process of raping her, and the pain was forever tied into the act, freezing it in nightmare silence within the confines of her skull. In the rotten and decayed dreams that sometimes assaulted her sleep Ghost replayed the act, occasionally as she had seen him last—his body literally tearing itself apart, him chewing off his own tongue and spitting it in a gout of blood through torn lips.

Always she remembered the weight of him, the stench of him, the relentless pain of him, and at first she thought it was a nightmare again.

"Off . . ." she muttered, "get *off* me," and pushed at the

matted chest that rolled and heaved against her breasts, but Ulgol paid no attention and continued to thrust into her with long, agony-filled strokes. The stink of him clogged her nostrils; the right side of her head throbbed, and her eye on that side seemed to be stuck almost shut with pink slime.

It *was* a nightmare, but one made real. Something in the back of her mind nagged, *The boy, where is the boy*?

With a mighty heave Ulgol ejaculated into her, and for an instant she felt she must have split wide open down there. Then he collapsed his full weight on her, breathing like a gaffed fish, and, finally, rolled off her. A bit of breeze crossed her naked body like a blessing and she turned her head away from the sun blazing overhead and blinked her good eye, trying to distinguish the hazy shape that loomed above her.

"Me, now," Dag whooped. "My turn now!"

Instinctively she tried to curl into a ball. She felt rough hands reach into her crotch and pry her legs apart. She kicked out and felt her heel strike thin flesh, hard bone.

Dag cried out.

A moment later his own foot crashed into her ribs with a dull thudding smack, and a bloom of agony froze her lungs. Her next breath dragged in as a soft wheeze, exploded out in a scream. Dag grunted with ugly pleasure. Then he fell on her.

This time she came around with a coldly silent snap, an inner awareness that great danger had stalked and found her. Was this the inner prophesy that had worried her these many moons? Was this the hour, perhaps even the minute of her death?

Slowly, stifling the moan that pushed at her lips, she rolled onto her side. The movement sent blurry waves across her field of vision, but after a moment they passed, and she took in the scene.

A few yards away the boy lay facing her, trussed like a captured rabbit, his hands bound behind him to his ankles, the unnatural, bowlike bend of his back making his ribs stand out like thin sticks beneath his stretched and lacerated flesh.

His eyes were closed, but he didn't look dead. She concentrated, and managed to make out a faint rise, an almost imperceptible flexing of muscle over his lungs. Not dead, then. For some reason this seemed important—that he wasn't dead, that there was still hope.

Why in Mother's name should *that* be important?

With a weird kind of irritation she pushed the thought away. At least they hadn't tied her up. The two men, one hulk almost as big as Caribou, the other a skinny, rope-muscled man whose head seemed pinched at the top, crouched facing equidistant from both her and the boy. The thin man gestured, said something that sounded tantalizingly familiar, then pointed over the other man's shoulder. The big man grunted. The thin man moved both hands urgently, making a wringing motion. Maya winced. She could guess who—and what—might get wrung.

Caribou.

She moved her head inch by slow inch—*Don't do anything to attract their attention*!—and examined the tree line. Shadows had begun to gather there, darkening the spaces between the huge old trunks, and she realized she must have been unconscious for quite a while. It was getting on toward late afternoon. Where was Caribou?

Suddenly she seemed to see him, a cloudy day vision that fogged her mind, him creeping slowly behind a white-tailed deer, his hunter's mind concentrated. And behind him two other men, one big, one smaller, their spears clutched in knotted fists—until they rushed forward and stabbed, and stabbed, and stabbed—

No!

She closed her eyes and waited until the horrible figment dissolved. Then she opened her eyes and scanned the forest again. Darker there—and no Caribou.

Maybe there was truth in her vision. And maybe not, but she would have to proceed as if it *was* true. She couldn't count on her husband rescuing her, though a part of her thought that Caribou, veteran of a thousand hunts, might not be so easily surprised as her day-mare had suggested.

Nevertheless. Better to assume, for whatever reason, help might not arrive in time. (She didn't allow herself to think the word *never*.) Moving only her eyes, she turned back to the two men who still crouched, arguing.

Their voices were low, but there was passion evident in them. They were in disagreement about something. But what? If there was a wedge between them made possible by their argument, she had to know the substance of it.

And now, as she concentrated her hearing—still the strongest of her physical senses—she made out words. But the language, though temptingly familiar in spots, was foreign to her.

It was a soft, guttural tongue, with lots of clicking stops and harsh, breathy endings. But there was a rhythm to it, almost as if they were chanting. She sipped air and forced herself to think. Where had she heard chanting that sounded like that speech?

Certainly not with the People, or with the Tribe she'd left in the Green Valley—wait a minute. Not the Tribe exactly, but when Broken Fist, the Snake Shaman, had made his awful pact with the Shaman Ghost, he'd done so in the tongue of the Spirits. This sounded something like that, and though she'd had no cause to speak that tongue for fifteen years, she still rustily remembered it.

Once she realized what she was listening to, she was able to pick up a word here and there. Spirit talk shared much, but each tribal Shaman spoke it differently. And these men didn't seem to be Shamans. How did they know the Spirit words?

The boy moaned faintly, then subsided. She glanced at him, distracted by his presence. She had no idea how he fitted into this, except he'd been running from them. Were they enemies? Had they captured him from another Tribe? It was plain enough he'd been tortured. Although there were fresh scratches on his body, they were minor compared to the pattern of scabs and bruises that covered almost all of his body. Even scars—yes, those were old scars, so many of them they were like fine pink netting beneath the newer injuries.

Tortured for a long time, then. A very long time. He'd escaped from somewhere—no need to wonder why, just look at him—and these two had come to fetch him back.

Just her bad luck to be in the wrong place at the wrong time. Well, it wasn't anything new—Maya knew from her past that when her luck turned sour, it took no half measures. Her nightmares had portended disaster. From the boy's appearance, capture by these men, whoever they were, was nothing less than that. She wondered why he hadn't tried to escape before his body had been turned into a patchwork of scar tissue, then realized she had no way of knowing how many times he'd fled these monstrous people who spoke a broken and degraded Spirit Tongue.

She pushed this from her thoughts. None of it would help at the moment. Her primary task was to stay alive until either Caribou could rescue her, or until she could escape. Such was her nature that she gave only short consideration to rescue. If it were to happen, well and good. But Caribou's actions were out of her hands. He might even be dead. Better to make her own way if she could—at least it would be something she could control.

If she could stay alive. The thin man made a single chopping motion with his right hand, stood up, and took a stone knife from his pouch. His face was empty of emotion as he walked slowly toward her. He didn't seem disturbed that she was awake. And why should he be? There was no place for her to run.

Nevertheless, if this was death, she would face it on her feet. She gritted her teeth as she got her feet under her, then stood up, fighting dizziness all the way. The man paused, staring at her. She blinked; the coagulating blood in her left eye blurred her sight. She would see her fate clear-eyed, she decided. Carefully, she scraped away the clot and with two fingers pried up her eyelid.

The thin man's forehead wrinkled suddenly. She smiled at him. Did he fear her eyes, those strange green and blue orbs? Good. Let him think it was a demon he faced. Perhaps it would slow his knife.

She raised her right hand, palm out, and said in the language of the Spirits, *"Stop. Go away now, or I will slay your Spirit and leave it to wander in the dark forever!"*

4

Dag had been more annoyed with Ulgol before, though he couldn't remember when. But there were times—like now—when he would have cheerfully buried his foot to the ankle in the big lunk's asshole. What in Snake's name was he thinking about, wanting to bring this foreign woman back with them? It had taken him half an hour of fervent argument before he'd been able to convince Ulgol how stupid—without ever using the word *stupid*—it was to even think about such a thing.

First, he'd shown Ulgol the small camp, and pointed out to him the packs and the travois. Too much for one woman to carry. Therefore, someone else—most likely her man—was around somewhere. Second, it was extremely rare for only two or three people to travel by themselves, so perhaps others of this strange tribe were about. Third, their job wasn't to bring back captives and perhaps draw attention to their own People; it was to bring back the brat. They'd been hunting him a long time; no doubt Gotha would be in a terrible mood. Fourth, and most important, was the boy himself. He was in awful shape, wasted to near bones, feverish, and Dag didn't like the look of that festering, fly-blown sore on his leg at all. In fact, he thought they'd be very lucky to get him back alive—and the last thing they needed was a captive who had to be watched, perhaps even carried, slowing them down.

The answer was simple enough, obvious to anybody. Anybody but big, ugly, *stupid* Ulgol. So he'd wasted half an hour, when they could have already sliced the bitch's throat and been on their way, no one the wiser, least of all whoever it was who'd been traveling with her.

He noted she was awake. As he walked toward her, she sat up, then, slowly, tottered to her feet and faced him. He stopped and stared at her. Not bad at all, for an old woman—and not all *that* old, either. For an instant he wondered what she was doing out here by herself, but brushed the thought away. It didn't matter, anyway. In a few seconds nothing at all would matter to her, but he paused. There was something about her . . .

Despite the beating she'd taken, she faced him fearlessly. Her right eye was swollen and obscured by a crust of drying blood, but her left eye sparked at him as blue as a deep-winter pond flecked with ice. He'd seen blue eyes before, perhaps not as proud, or as threatening, as this, but her gaze pinned him.

He felt a chill as she wiped the rind of gore from her other eye and forced it wide. *What was this!*

As he gasped at the sudden revealing of the emerald in her left eye socket, she spoke. He didn't understand the words, but then he wouldn't. Only Gotha spoke her tongue, the Tongue of the Lord of Snakes. And she bore His signs!

Dag felt his stomach clench with queasiness. His teeth clicked together.

What have I got myself into now?

5

Caribou—former mighty hunter of People of the Bison, then Chief and mighty hunter of the Two Tribes, and now simply Caribou, hot, exasperated, and mosquito-bitten frustrated hunter—wiped sweat from his wide brow, honked a wad of snot from his flattened nose, and spat softly onto the humus-soft earth next to the fallen tree trunk he was crouching behind.

At first it had seemed the perfect deer-blind, situated somewhat higher than a small stream about thirty yards from his position, and abutting a narrow but seemingly well-used game trail that led down to the place where the stream pooled as it swerved around a huge pile of boulders.

Now, as late afternoon began to puddle into dusk, his haunches had begun to quiver from the strain of crouching behind the log all day, both his spear and his bow near to hand. For the past few hours he'd been regretting his choice of game—surely by now he could have brought down a brace of rabbits or even some kind of bird—but this seemingly perfect spot had been just too good to pass up.

He armed more sweat from his brow—the deep woods had begun to seem like bathing in one of the pools next to the Lake of Smokes back in the Green Valley—and wondered whether to give up now, or wait another hour to see if anything showed up to drink in the twilight before full dark.

He sighed unconsciously while he thought. The Lake of Smokes reminded him of the Green Valley, and that reminded him of the reason for this journey in the first place. He'd never much been interested in Maya as Shaman; he only thought of her as Maya his woman. Not a stupid man, merely not very introspective, he seldom considered the reasons for this curious division, and when he did, it was an even rarer occurrence for him to recollect what was probably the true source of his lack of interest in the public half of her life. Yet, every couple of years or so, like a lost but importuning ghost, the memory would return and pluck at the hem of his consciousness.

He suspected that Maya knew he'd seen more that long-ago day than he'd ever admitted to her, but she'd never questioned him on it, perhaps sensing that he'd come to some accommodation that was better left undisturbed, for both their sakes.

And she was right, he reflected. If, in the early years after the incident, he'd allowed himself to understand the full implication of that horrifying day, he now knew none of his life with her would have been possible. Had he accepted what he'd seen with his own eyes and, more important, what he'd *felt* with a sense he no more understood now than he had then, he might have gone mad.

Even now, fifteen years after, those cataclysmic moments when *something else, something huge* had shouldered into the World and done battle, the memory of it made him blink his eyes and try to think of anything else.

Sometimes, the memory wouldn't let him do it, and it seemed today was one of those times. Very well, then. Think about it. He'd about given up on getting any game today, anyway.

The woman he'd found, carried, saved, eventually taken for his own. Or had he? Perhaps it was the other way around. *Something* had cast her from her own People, sent her wandering broken and delirious down the paths toward the mouth of the Green Valley where he'd found her that first time. Oh, yes, sometimes in the warm darkness before sleep, when they lay wrapped in soft fur and companionship, she had spoken of the time before. But not much, and with not much detail. He knew that the Shaman Ghost had broken her, but he never fully understood the reasons for that breaking—and since the Shaman Ghost was as hideously dead as he could be (*I saw that, didn't I?*), the Shaman Ghost would never be able to tell him the truth of the matter.

Something to do with the Mammoth Stone, he supposed. No, he *knew* it, though how he *knew* it he wasn't entirely certain. Perhaps in the same way he'd *known* when those ghastly forces had broken the foundations of the World— *Maya had been the Key, hadn't she?*—and pushed the smallest part of Themselves into the ken of man. One man. Him.

He knew more than he knew, did Caribou, and that knowing made him very nervous, for it seemed now that his life was being changed by something as mysterious as whatever it was that had changed Maya's own, so many years ago. They hadn't spoken of it yet, but he knew she dreamed bad dreams. Sometimes he woke to find her thrashing silently, her teeth and fists clenched. Then he would hold her slick-sweat body and whisper soothing words into her ear, though he doubted she heard them. The dreams had become more frequent and worse of late, and he guessed they had something to do with her decision to face Buffalo Daughter.

For it hadn't been necessary. Buffalo Daughter could issue any challenge she wanted to, but unless Maya agreed to accept the challenge, it was to no avail. And there certainly wasn't any precedent for acceptance—a Shaman might lay down a Shaman's Power only if the Shaman chose to do so. Yet Maya had so chosen, and now they were exiles, and Maya had spoken of none of this to him.

Yet he knew. He'd known even before she had, perhaps, for she'd seemed startled when he'd assumed the Green Valley was their destination. The Green Valley and what awaited her there.

The Key to her life, whether she would admit it or not. She thought she'd left it behind, escaped it for good, but he knew she hadn't. It had allowed her a time of respite, but only a time. Now it wanted her back.

He was afraid of that wanting, but he knew he could no more oppose it than she could. And so he went, because he understood one other thing: He loved her. So he would go, and hope for the best, even though he'd seen the worst.

He grunted and shifted his position. His right leg had gone to sleep, and pins and needles danced in the numb flesh with his movement.

It was almost fully dark. He sighed again and climbed slowly to his feet. There would be no haunch of deer for the fire tonight, nor meat to dry and mix with grease and berries for the journey.

He grinned at nothing in particular. Mighty hunter, huh. But when he set off he tramped briskly. Memories and Mammoth Stone or not, the workings of Maya's fate were too much for him. He was only along for the journey, but he would travel it with her to the end.

Whatever questions must be answered, let her do it. He would love her anyway.

6

Heat lightning flickered soundlessly beyond the horizon. Overhead, a sudden burst of shooting stars, like a handful of flung sparks, scratched their way across the night. The sky was bright, but without a moon, the earth lay dark beneath her stumbling feet.

She went on as carefully as she could, though her hands were bound behind her back, and a longer cord—*Cut from my own tent,* she thought bitterly—was tied around her neck like a leash, leading to the big man's hand. He jerked her along, only pausing to snarl at her if she tripped up and fell.

Dag led them swiftly on. The big man—she thought his name might be Ulgol—carried the boy across his shoulders like freshly slaughtered game.

Oh, Caribou. Are you still alive? Will you be able to find me?

The thin man, whose name she was certain was Dag, had reacted to her words far beyond expectation. She really had no idea beyond frightening him, making him pause. Instead, after staring goggle-eyed at her for several seconds, he seemed to come to some conclusion, and leapt forward. She cringed against his expected blow, but he didn't strike her. Not then. He merely grabbed her arm, barked some order to Ulgol, and proceeded to drag her away.

They paused at her camp only long enough to rifle the small remaining store of food there and cut the rude thongs that bound her. During all of this Dag kept glancing about, the picture of frightened alertness. His watchfulness gave her a certain forlorn hope. If his fear was of the return of her mate, then most likely the men hadn't killed Caribou. *Such watchfulness is wise,* she thought grimly, *for they have good reason to fear him, whether they know it or not.*

They'd moved out quickly after that, and her initial hope that they might camp after the sun went down was quickly dashed. Dag simply kept them going, almost running at times, never slower than a quick trot. *He knows*, Maya thought. *Caribou is coming.*

She still didn't know why he'd reacted as he did. At first she'd thought it was her eyes. She'd deliberately shown him her mismatched colors, aware of the deadly gamble— would he kill her for a Demon, or worship her for a Goddess? It seemed he would do neither, and for the second time in her life she found herself being carried toward the unknown.

Toward an unknown Shaman, she guessed. For she had seen and heard something that had changed everything in those instants when Dag had been frozen in shock. She'd glanced down at the boy just after she'd spoken.

His eyes had popped open. There was delirium in them, and she doubted he saw the world at all. But he saw *something*, that was certain, for he'd mumbled a few words before his eyes had snapped shut again. Words in her own Shaman's language, the pure Spirit Tongue.

And now she knew why her life had changed, and now she knew what had been coming, for it had arrived.

His eyes. His green and blue eyes.

Oh, Mother! What have you done to me now?

CHAPTER SIX

1

THE GREEN VALLEY

Just beyond the small lake called First Lake, into which emptied the springs that bubbled from the great rock wall above Home Camp, was a meadow abutting the scattered paths and houses of Second Camp. From her perch atop the piled boulders of the Jumble, amid the crystal sound of the springs, the meadow reminded White Moon of a soft green pillow. Spring had come early to the Green Valley, and the knee-high grass on the meadow rippled gently as invisible fingerlets of wind caressed it in long, vagrant patterns.

Several young men leapt and rolled and shouted at each other in the meadow, their game with a straw-stuffed ball of skin occupying all their attention. One in particular stood out on this fine spring morning; he was taller than the others, his muscles more finely knit, his black eyes brighter and more piercing. Like the others he wore only a clout of skin over his genitals, and his sweating body gleamed in the sun as if it had been oiled. One of the other young men tried to take the ball from him, but he danced lithely away, the muscles in his stomach contracting into hard-etched cords as he laughed at his would-be tormentor.

His teeth were white as first-fallen winter snow. His name was Sharp Knife, and White Moon's belly felt warm and somehow weak as she watched him—while another part of her whispered quietly, *He knows. He knows you're watching.*

And so he did. She could see it in the way his bright glance would dart in her direction—*See what I did!*—whenever he accomplished some particularly athletic feat, but he would somehow turn away precisely one instant before their gazes locked and he would have to acknowledge his awareness of her on her rocky seat.

What Sharp Knife couldn't see, even if he looked, was the way her skin tingled as she watched him. And what he might have seen as only maidenly dreaminess was something far sharper and more specific. As she watched him, she remembered a time at dusk not long before, when the shadows had cloaked them as they drifted beneath the soft branches of spring trees.

She loved everything about him, but most of all, she loved his cock. It was the memory of *that* that had painted the dreamy look across her high-cheekboned features. She smiled as she remembered it. Sharp Knife's penis was not as big as that of his friend, Long Snake, and he didn't insist on showing it to everybody, the way Long Snake did. But it was nicely shaped, fitting the curve of her palm perfectly. Her hand clenched as she remembered the way the veins stood out on it in small hard knots, the way it jerked and quivered when she stroked it.

She loved to rub it against the soft skin of her cheek, feeling the film of sticky moisture that coated the head of it, while the hot musky smell of his balls filled her nostrils.

He would moan when she touched the small hole with the tip of her tongue, and his ass would clench tight as a rock when she trailed her lips up from the curly hair to the soft-hard bands of muscle on his belly.

She shivered faintly as she recalled the way her skin seemed to melt against his as he lay on top of her, the hair on his chest scraping with delicious pain on the tenderness of her nipples, and the sweet agony of him inside her, bucking and groaning while she bit at the flesh of her neck. His blood tasted of salt, and the memory of it made her lick her lips as she watched him play.

She shifted slightly, aware of her cunt, hot and slippery and full of juice. In a way it was funny, watching him like this with the vision of his cock plain in her mind's eye, but she couldn't help herself. She couldn't tear her gaze from him. Her fascination with him was endless. Her eyes traced his every move, the smooth play of muscle beneath his golden skin, the way his thighs bunched up so powerfully (*I remember those thighs,* she thought, and quivered), the liquid grace that characterized his every movement, his laughing, expressive features.

He was playing for her, she knew, even though he pretended otherwise. She was certain he was as aware of her as she was of him, though his boyish pride wouldn't allow him to show his love so openly. Well, she amended, not a boy any longer, though *that* had only occurred recently. But he was a man now, closely related to the vanished Chief, Black Caribou, and someday to be the leader of the Bison Clan.

Most times, though, she still thought of him as a boy, and herself only as a girl, and the new thoughts and worries that had crept into her mind of late would be pushed far away.

Unconsciously she shook her head, as if an invisible mosquito had buzzed in her ear. No, she didn't want to think about any of that, not now, not on so perfect a spring day, when even the air seemed washed with light.

What she really wanted to do was run down to the meadow and take Sharp Knife's hand and pull him, laughing, down the forest paths to the place they both knew quite well, and fall into his arms until the laughter was stilled by the sweet silence of his heartbeat beneath her ear. And so she sat, thinking of that sweet silence, while red-throated blackbirds darted over her head and the springs chuckled at her feet, and the cries of the young men vanished softly into the morning air.

"White Moon! Where *are* you, you dratted girl?"

The cracked and raucous shout cut through the noise of the game like a badly chipped knife through soft fat. White Moon sat up straight, the dreamy haze gone out of her eyes. Two spots of red burned suddenly on her high cheekbones.

"Oh, my," she whispered as she pulled her fingers through her long black hair, straightening it as well as she could. She pulled and patted her skin tunic into a semblance of order and then, when she was satisfied with the neatness of her appearance, looked toward Second Camp across the lake and called, "I'm here, Berry! I'm coming!"

An enormously fat shape, supported at each elbow by a younger woman, waddled slowly into view. It seemed to take the monstrously obese woman hours to lumber up to lakeside. The young men fell away from her as if she were a stampede of bison. A very slow stampede.

Sharp Knife now faced White Moon directly and smiled. "Have fun!" he shouted and then, with a final mocking grin, turned and ran.

"Men!" White Moon muttered to herself. "Cowards, all of them!"

But she understood. Old Berry frightened everyone, including herself. Even her father, Wolf, Chief of the Two Tribes, and Muskrat, the Shaman, deferred to the immense old lady, who wielded her power with all the querulous abandon of a summer storm.

Late, White Moon thought. *I was to walk with her this morning, and it's almost noon. She'll eat me.*

With this not-so-improbable image dominating her thoughts, she jumped lightly to her feet and began to negotiate the sawtooth rocks of the Jumble as nimbly as a mountain goat. A moment later she reached Old Berry's side. The ancient woman glared at her, though her two escorts, Red Hair and Running Doe, both seemed calm enough.

"I'm sorry, Aunt," White Moon said. "I forgot. It was such a wonderful morning, and I—"

"And you're such a silly girl," Old Berry rumbled. "You were supposed to walk with me today, but you forgot. You'd rather sit in the sun and watch the young men." Her eyes, still sharp as new-chipped flints, rolled like marbles. She heaved an enormous sigh. "Well, I was young once. I think. I'll let you get by with it this time."

"Oh, Auntie, I'm sorry. I promise I'll do better."

"Yes, you will. You'd better. Or I'll *eat* you!" But the glare Berry tried to summon dissolved in twinkling merriment as the old woman stared fondly at her charge. "Ah, girl, it is a fine day, isn't it?"

"Yes, Auntie. Do you want me to walk with you now?"

"Well, even a sprat like you would be better than these two old crows," Berry replied. "I swear, Red Hair gets grumpier every day."

Red Hair, undisturbed, said, "Old Berry has walked already, dear. She wants to talk with you a moment. We'll let you get to it, and when you're done, you can walk the old bag back to her house."

"Hmmph! See. The older she gets, the meaner. Why can't she be sweet, like me?"

A smile twitched White Moon's lips. "She's very sweet, Aunt. Just like you. Aren't you, Red Hair?"

"Yes, dear. If I was sweet like your aunt, the grass under my feet would be withering at this very moment." She patted Berry's broad, humped shoulder affectionately. "We'll be off, then. Call if you need us."

Berry watched her two companions depart. "Crows," she muttered. "Two old black crows." She raised her walking stick and thumped it smartly on the ground. "Let's go over there, Niece, where it's shadier. This hot sun hurts my eyes."

White Moon took hold of Berry's elbow and together the two women walked to a spot where a huge sycamore tree arched out over First Lake. Several fallen trees had been piled in this spot, their boles worn smooth by the rear ends of years of placid sitters. When, with much puffing and grunting, Berry was settled, she patted the spot next to her and said, "Sit down close to me, niece." She lowered her voice. "It's time we had a talk, you and I." Her gaze took in White Moon's slender waist, shapely thighs, and swelling breasts. She sighed. "Far past time, actually."

White Moon sat. It seemed to her that a cloud passed over the morning, though when she looked up, the sky was as empty as the eye of a bird. She thought she knew what Berry wanted to discuss, and the old woman was right. It *was* time for a talk.

Had her aunt somehow found out about Sharp Knife? Well, it had to come out sometime. But White Moon had made up her mind, and that mind was quite determined. She was *not* going to allow some dusty old legends to interfere with her and Sharp Knife. No, not even if Old Berry herself demanded it.

"I dreamed of Great Maya last night," Berry said.

Something in White Moon's chest flipped, then flopped. "Oh?" she said.

"Yes," said Berry. "It was a strange dream. I didn't understand it."

White Moon cocked her pretty head. Great Maya, vanished long these many years, was her true aunt, the sister of her father, Wolf, but White Moon had never known Maya. Her illustrious relative had disappeared with a portion of the People into the vast prairies shortly after White Moon's birth, leaving behind only the token of her Power in trust for her niece. It should have been an uncomplicated bit of history, but White Moon suspected that Maya's influence had guided her own life in ways she'd never been able to understand.

The older people in the Green Valley had known her aunt, but they spoke little of her to the girl. From childhood White Moon had known the odd silence in a conversation when she approached, and suspected it had to do with the legacy of Maya's Power, although White Moon had only the foggiest notion of what that Power might be. She had thought one of those who'd known Maya best, Old Berry, Wolf, or Muskrat, might assuage her curiosity as she grew older, but aside from a few casual references, even those worthies had remained mostly silent.

She stared at Berry and wondered if the old woman had decided that it was now time for questions, and even for answers. Berry was certainly staring at her strangely enough, her gaze oddly intense, so that White Moon shrugged uncomfortably.

"What was the dream about, Auntie?"

Berry made a shooing motion with her hands. "Maybe nothing, niece. It made no sense. It was as if Maya were lost, and calling for me, but I couldn't see her. In the dream I called back, but my voice was taken from me. There were winds and darkness and then, right before I woke up, there was a spark that grew into a mighty fire." She moved her hands again and seemed about to speak further, but then her eyes narrowed and she said, "That was all."

White Moon had never dreamed of her aunt Maya, nor had she Dreamed, either. The transcendental plunge into direct communication with the Gods of the World was still a mystery, though of late Muskrat had made increasing reference to it, and questioned her closely about any normal dreams she happened to experience.

She rubbed her chin thoughtfully, aware that Berry was still staring at her. What did the old woman want her to say? White Moon felt a momentary flash of irritation; this wasn't the first time the elderly Spirit Woman had seemed to expect something of her, and she felt the same guilt as she had before.

What do you want of me? she thought, wanting to shout

the words aloud. *I didn't know my aunt, I don't have Dreams. What are you waiting for?*

And that was it, wasn't it? Everybody seemed to be *waiting* for something, for her to do something or become something, and she had not the slightest idea what that *something* might be. Not for the first time she wished she'd been born of a different father, dark-eyed and without the marks of legend that both exalted her and set her apart—although in her secret heart she had to admit she rather enjoyed the uniqueness of her status. What young woman would not? To be different, to be special, to be both loved and—she wasn't certain it was so, but she suspected it—secretly feared?

Yet it was all still a mystery to her, and since Sharp Knife had entered into her life so completely, perhaps now was the time to put those old stories to rest and take up her real life with the man she was determined would be her mate.

"Aunt Berry, I don't understand your dream. Did you think I would?"

Berry sighed heavily, and the watchfulness went out of her gaze. "No, child, I guess not." She paused, glanced at the now-empty meadow, and shook her head slightly. "You know, dear, you're a remarkably normal girl."

It was a strange thing to say. Why wouldn't she be normal? Her parents loved her and took care of her. She'd never lacked for friends, shelter, food, or any of the other good things in life. The old stories? Well, that was all they were, just dusty stories, and White Moon had long since discarded any thought of their relevance to her.

She made up her mind all at once. She was a woman now; the bleeding had begun six months before. Other girls her age were mated and growing fat bellies. It was time she did so, too. It was also time Old Berry and Muskrat gave up whatever odd notions they had about her—and her future.

But she hesitated. *Was* this really the right time? Old Berry seemed to sense some of her confusion, for she patted White Moon's hand and said, "Don't worry, dear. The dream wasn't about you, as far as I could tell."

White Moon shook her head. "Oh, Auntie, I'm not worried about your dream."

"Well, then, what are you worried about? Something is

eating at you, isn't it? You've been acting strange lately—or is that just an old lady's imagination?"

White Moon took a deep breath. "No," she said. "It isn't."

"So what is it?"

"It's Sharp Knife. We love each other. I want to be his mate." *There,* she thought, sudden relief flooding her, *I've said it. Now we'll see.*

But Old Berry's reaction was the last thing she'd bargained for. She'd expected some sort of remonstrance, a scolding, perhaps. Something along the lines of "White Moon, you know better things are planned for you." Or, conversely, smiling acquiescence, though she found it hard to imagine Berry acquiescing to anything without at least one argument. But the old woman did nothing, said nothing. She just stared at the girl, and to White Moon, it seemed that something had just died beneath Berry's wrinkled skin, so still did she become.

"Aunt, what's wrong? Is it so terrible that I love Sharp Knife?"

But Berry remained silent. The moment stretched between them until White Moon felt herself grow cold. She glanced up at the sky, but there were no clouds. Where had the chill come from? She searched Old Berry's seamed features, but there was nothing there, no answers in her blank stare.

"Auntie . . . ?"

Berry's lips parted slightly. The strangest sound White Moon had ever heard softly filled the space between them. Half moan, half intensely controlled shriek, it turned the marrow of her bones to ice.

"Ahhh, ahhhhh!"

"Berry, what's *wrong*?"

The old woman began to rock slowly forward, then back. Tears leaked from her eyes. She wept with her eyes open, as the old weep, and White Moon understood that her aunt cried for something larger than either of them, something old, something dark.

But then the moment passed. Berry sniffed, wiped her nose, wiped her eyes. At last she spoke. "Oh, Niece. Oh, you poor, poor girl. It's all my fault. I've been so *stupid*!"

And Berry lifted one meaty hand and slapped herself hard across her cheek, once, twice, three times.

2

Berry decided to walk after all. White Moon held her arm tightly as they stumped slowly along the well-trodden stream path that connected the lakes of Green Valley. Berry's weight seemed to have grown—or, White Moon thought, the old woman was simply leaning more heavily on her than usual.

"Have you slept with him?" Berry asked. "Did you fuck him—you know, let him put his cock in you?"

"Yes, Aunt. I love him, and he wanted it. I did, too."

Berry grunted. It was as she'd expected, but she couldn't see how it helped matters any. If anything, it made the situation worse, even harder to unravel.

It meant that White Moon and Sharp Knife had already mated, but no leave had been given to their joining. The problems were obvious and plentiful.

The first, and least important, was political. The Bison Clan had been much more numerous than the Mammoth when the Two Tribes joined together after Maya's over-whelming victory over Broken Fist, but because Maya had entrusted the Mammoth Stone to White Moon, the Mammoth Clan had remained ascendant. And though the Two Tribes had lived together since, a division still remained. Berry knew Wolf had plans for his beautiful daughter that did not include mating with the most likely youth of the Bison People. Such an outcome would dilute the power that the Mammoth Clan enjoyed over the Bison People. In fact, Wolf's plan—which was seconded by Muskrat, although Berry herself had doubts—didn't call for White Moon to mate at all.

The second problem was deeper, for nobody understood White Moon's true destiny. Berry suspected that the only person who might answer that misty question was still wandering the steppe with her husband, Caribou—and Maya didn't seem likely to return anytime soon. *Drat her,* she thought, *why did she run off and leave us with so many mysteries?* Although Berry understood Maya's reasoning better than anyone else, she still wasn't sure she approved.

Nothing Berry knew about the Power of the Stone pro-hibited White Moon from taking a mate—but nothing encouraged it, either. It would have been far easier if the girl had even once shown any aptitude or understanding for her great obligation, but she hadn't. In her hands the Mammoth Stone might as well have been nothing more than a shapeless chip of tusk. Maya had felt the Power at an early age, though she hadn't understood it—but White Moon, at least as she told it, felt nothing. And Berry, who had made it her business to know her niece better than anyone else, was certain she would know a lie if White Moon spoke it.

Finally, and most important, was White Moon's own status. She was Keeper of the Stone, so designated by Great Maya herself and thus, presumably, the handmaiden and channel of Mother's limitless power. In the end, all their thoughts, plans, and worries might amount to nothing.

Berry had not been present when Maya wielded the Stone against the Shamans Ghost and Broken Fist, but she had questioned closely those who had.

She, alone of those still living, had plotted Maya's upbringing with Old Magic, the dead Shaman of the Mammoth People, and much of *that* she'd kept secret. Muskrat suspected she knew more than she told, but had no proof. Nor did she understand herself why she'd kept so much to herself, but she thought it might have something to do with this love-besotted girl at her side.

What it all came down to was a hard truth. White Moon belonged to the Mother, and She would do as She wished with her, when She wished to do it. Perhaps there was nothing to be done at all—but Maya had told Berry something else, after she had taken the full Power of the Stone into herself. She said there had been a choice, and she had made that choice before the Mother, in the place of Dream, beyond the World—and that until she'd made the choice, the Power of the Stone had been denied to her.

Did White Moon have a choice to make? Berry had no idea. But to allow her the freedom to choose without the knowledge necessary to make such choices might destroy not only the girl, but all of the People, Bison and Mammoth, as well. Berry recalled the devastation the Mother had wrought on the Mammoth Clan—a plague that had wiped nine of every ten away in less than a single winter—with clear-eyed dread. The Great Goddess was not to be trifled with. But it was so hard to *understand* Her intentions.

It was so hard to understand the wishes of *any* of the Spirits, from the greatest to the smallest. And the fact remained that she knew nothing about White Moon or her destiny, and anything she did or said might be horribly wrong. It was this fear, shared by both Wolf and Muskrat, that had led them to raise the girl as they had—telling her only a little of the history that had preceded her, training her in some lore, but not all, and hoping that the Mother would give them a sign of Her desires for the Keeper of Her Stone.

Have we waited too long?

She had wept from fear, Berry realized. Fear of the Mother, fear of the Power, but mostly fear for White Moon. This first love between the two youngsters, though they might think it all-consuming, was but a bright springtime dance, a childish little play perhaps doomed to utter destruction before the ancient, cold Power that ruled them all.

If it is the wrong choice. Berry sighed aloud, her huge, flabby breasts rising once, then falling as she exhaled raspingly, which caused White Moon's eyes to widen. *But how can we know?*

In the end, Berry made her own choice, a human choice colored by human emotions—though she didn't know that it was a choice, and one given to her by the Power that gives all such choices. *I can't know,* she thought, *so I will deal with what I do know. I love this girl. I will help her if I can.*

So she would try, unaware that even as she decided, far out in the world, beyond the endless steppe, the spark of her dream had already begun to grow into the fire to come.

BOOK TWO

THE HUNTERS AND THE HUNTED

Dreams, which beneath the hovering shades of night
Sport with the ever-restless minds of men,
Descend not from the gods. Each busy brain
Creates its own.

—Thomas Love Peacock

Religions are such stuff as dreams are made of.
—H. G. Wells

CHAPTER SEVEN

1

Black Caribou started his greatest hunt on his hands and knees in the dark, his nostrils filled with the reek of urine. *They pissed on what they couldn't take,* he thought. *After they pay for everything else, they will pay for that, too.*

He crawled like a crab through the wreckage of his camp, learning what he could with his fingers and his nose. His ears had no bearing on this—whoever they were, they were far away by now, long out of earshot—and his eyes were near useless in the moonless dark. But he could run the slashed remains of his tent through his fingers well enough, and his nose spoke clearly of the rest of the damage.

The only thing that gave him hope, even as frustration bubbled like thick porridge in his skull, was that he couldn't smell blood, not in any quantity. So if Maya was dead, her corpse wasn't nearby.

Which was only the smallest shred of hope, of course. It was too dark for him to search the area around the camp. That would have to wait till morning. In the meantime, he decided to salvage what he could. There might be need for journeying with the dawn, and if so, every moment he saved tonight would be one he could spend tomorrow.

Eventually he ceased his efforts, exhausted and filled with dread. He knew he would have to sleep if he could, for he would need every bit of his strength. But that was a long time ago. He was still an immensely powerful man, but no longer the nearly superhuman warrior who had slain the mighty fighter of the Mammoth People, Spear, with a single stroke. Age had both toughened him and made him wiser in the ways of his own body. He had learned to pace himself on the hunt, to use his brain instead of simply bulling through obstacles. He had discovered all the aches and pains of growing older, how to avoid them if he could, and how to ignore them if he couldn't.

He knew that if he could get at least a few hours of sleep tonight, he would be a far more effective tracker when dawn came—but he also thought that sleep, much as he wanted it, much as he *needed* it, might be the one quarry beyond even his hunter's skills this disastrous night.

Maya!

Caribou squatted in the wreckage, that single word reverberating in his mind like the slow thunder of the Ice Wall north of the Green Valley. A bitter wind had begun to blow, and he shivered uncontrollably. His teeth clicked together and he hugged himself. He had no coat—Maya had kept his old one as a pattern, and the intruders—*the killers?*—had ruined it. It was too dark to know for sure, but he suspected he had nothing left but the tiny pack he'd carried on his belt, his knife, his bow and arrows, his spear, and the few skins on his back.

He settled down cross-legged. Overhead the stars burned in mystic conflagrations. The wind died for a moment and he heard the rivers, and wondered if he would have to cross one of them. He hoped not. He didn't know how to swim.

Finally he coughed, stretched himself out on the ground, and closed his eyes. Thoughts swirled in his head—in the morning he would have to search the area to make sure that Maya's body wasn't rolled beneath a stand of scrub or dragged off by animals. If the raiders had taken her, he would follow. And when he found them? (He wouldn't let himself think of the alternative.) When he found them . . .

The promise to himself burned redly in the embers of his mind.

Kill them all!

For many years, Caribou had lived with Maya, who was always ready to soothe his more extravagant tempers. But before he'd met her and been healed by her, his tongue had tasted human flesh. He never forgot that.

The intruders had attacked the wrong man. Gently, he thought to himself that he would show them so. After a time the wind died down and the stars grew dim, and he slipped into dreamless sleep.

The bad dreams would come later.

2

Dawn came subtly, with a rime of pink above an invisible horizon, gradually brightening till the sun emerged in a teardrop of crimson splendor. Caribou came awake with a start, sat up, and groaned at the symphony of aches in his night-chilled muscles. He stared stupidly at the dull brown earth, then shook his head to clear it of the sleep-fogs. Like stones in a rattle, with the shake came a profusion of memories. He stood up and stretched, deliberately avoiding any visual examination of his surroundings.

He didn't want to see what he was afraid he might find. He screwed his eyes shut and yawned hugely, but it was no good. Though he feared to know, he had to look sometime. Slowly he opened his eyes and, even more slowly, turned in a full circle, swinging his arms as he did so.

Yes, they had destroyed the camp. Over there, the two travois poles, splintered and broken. A soggy mound of skins, hastily ripped into tatters. Their food bags, already rifled, now flat and shredded. The stink of stale piss hung around him in invisible shrouds, made heavier by the morning mist that still hazed the middle distance.

His massive shoulders, which had been rigidly—and unconsciously—tense, sagged then, as relief made his knees go weak. He saw his ruined camp, but he didn't see his ruined wife. For which he glanced at the ruby sun and uttered a silent prayer of thanks, to whom he wasn't quite sure. The Lord of Snakes, the God of his youth? Or the Mother, who had ruled his life since?

He thought his gratitude might be aimed at He of Breath, the God of Snakes and Fire, for despite all the years of gentling from Maya, he suspected he would need the aid of that dread Power more than any other. There would be killing to come, and the Lord of Snakes understood killing.

Caribou bowed his head once, as if acknowledging some unheard benediction, and began to get what was left of his possessions together. The sun broke through the mists, burned them away, and warmed his stiff muscles. He still had to make a search, and it would rob him of precious time, but in his deep thoughts he was certain he wouldn't find her. They had taken her, whoever they were, and why not?

Hadn't he once done the same thing himself?

3

Caribou found the trampled spot where Maya had been raped about an hour after the sun came up. He read the signs easily enough—only two men. They hadn't taken any care to disguise their tracks. *In a hurry,* he thought. Then, *They were lucky.*

He hadn't allowed himself to think of that. To think of the "ifs" that hadn't happened. If he hadn't decided to go hunting. If he hadn't stayed out so long. If he'd stayed closer to camp. If he'd found a deer quickly, or if he hadn't decided to hunt deer at all.

Caribou had only the flimsiest concept of fate. His world was full of capricious Spirits, tiny and great Spirits, all of them vying, it sometimes seemed to him, to make human life an incomprehensible jumble. He didn't think of fate, or doom, or any great sweep of divine planning. On the other hand, he didn't consider that his quest, because of this plethora of Spirits, was impossible. In the end, his hunter's practicality overrode any less mundane considerations—a hunter asked for the help of the Spirits, but it was still the hunter's arm that hurled the spear.

He trusted his own right arm, just as he trusted his eyes and nose and the strength in his hamlike hands. Those simple skills would have to be enough. He couldn't influence the Spirits. He wasn't Maya, nor was he a shaman. He was a hunter, and pragmatic enough to understand that he was a very good one.

He would hunt men now, that was all. Nothing wily like deer or rabbit. Men. The danger in men wasn't that they would escape him. It was that they could fight him.

Well, that was all right. He could fight, too. They would find that out.

And so, with that grimly silent promise still echoing in

his head, he set off. He carried a somewhat larger pack than before, pieced together out of remnants and smelling of piss. He had his weapons and his skills.

He marched away without a backward glance, his black eyes narrowed to scan the horizon. The rivers drummed around him, but he no longer noticed the sound. He didn't notice much of anything, except for the occasional careless track in the soft earth along the riverbank.

The party was heading north. He went that way, too.

4

By noon Caribou was coated with sweat. His tongue felt swollen, and much of his rage had baked off beneath the greater heat of the sun. The trail had taken him far away from the river, and he'd come across no streams or springs. The territory had turned arid, consisting of long, faintly rolling swells of brownish grass with a few lonely stands of trees dotted here and there. At the moment he stood wiping his brow midway between two such oases. He glanced back and forth, considering the possibilities.

The trail was still plain enough, although it had grown a bit confusing. At first he'd followed three sets of tracks, but seemingly out of nowhere a fourth spoor had appeared. These footprints were even smaller than Maya's, and he guessed them a child's marks or those of a very tiny man.

Whatever, this procession had not been hard to trace. At times the prints seemed so fresh he stopped, shaded his brow, and peered ahead, expecting to see tiny dark forms in the distance. But he saw nothing in the heat that shimmered above the parched prairie land.

He grunted and unslung his pack. It would do for a marker. Then, moving briskly, his breath rasping between his clenched teeth, he set off for one of the scraps of timber. There would be water there somewhere, he guessed— the trees themselves promised that.

The dusty smells of the grassland gave way instantly to a damper, darker odor, blessedly cool, as he stepped beneath the trees. Here lay a mulch from years worth of fallen leaves, soft beneath the calluses of his feet. The effect was seductive, and the only thing that kept him from sinking to his haunches and resting a moment was the clear call of water wafting from the inner recesses of the miniature forest. It took him only a few moments to locate the spring, which welled slowly into a transparent pool no more than twice his length. The pool had no outlet that he could see. The earth simply absorbed it, though he guessed the sandy bottom hid some kind of outlet.

Less wary than usual, driven by his thirst, Caribou stepped into the pool. His right foot went down into the sand and kept on going. He lurched forward, using his other leg to regain his balance, and then flailed with both hands as he toppled the rest of the way into the shallow water. But his legs were still in the muck, and when he tried to stand again, he couldn't.

Quicksand, he thought. *You fool, it's quicksand.*

He had seen other men eaten by such bogs, but a few had survived similar mishaps. He tried to remember what had saved those survivors, but it was hard to focus his mind. The water soaked through his skins. Immediately, their weight dragged him down. Unable to swim, his natural instinct was to lash about wildly, but the more agitated he became, the farther he seemed to sink. His mind whirled—panic clouded his thoughts.

Drowning! I'm drowning!

And then—*Maya.*

It was as if a gentle hand had been drawn across his forehead. His fevered brain cooled, and for a moment he stopped moving entirely. For some reason, it seemed to him that she was there, standing at the edge of the pool, calmly guiding him.

Husband, she said. *Don't move about. Turn your head to the side and let the water support you.*

Caribou had faced mighty warriors, great beasts, long treks, death in a hundred forms. To follow this advice from what might only be a ghost of his imagination was as hard a thing as he'd ever done, but somehow, he managed to do it. And when he forced his arms to stop their wild flailing he discovered that his chest was indeed buoyant. He floated facedown, then slowly turned his face to the right and sipped air.

He could breathe!

The voice in his mind spoke again. *Don't move your*

legs, but gently—gently!—paddle with your hands until you are close to the bank.

He moved his fingers first, then began to flutter his hands. His body screamed in protest at the measured movement. An older part of him shrieked for a fury of energy, a heaving surge, and it was all he could do to restrain his rebellious nerves. But he still sensed the calming presence nearby and he managed to persevere. And the grassy verge, inch by sluggish inch, grew closer.

At last his forward progress ceased. The slight hand movements could not pull his legs from the sand. But even gingerly reaching as far forward as he could, he couldn't touch the bank. The tips of his fingers fell inches short of the grass.

Immediately the dark clouds of panic welled again in his skull. But before his body could respond, the presence blanketed him with calm.

Slowly take off your shirt. Slowly . . . see the tree stump.

He saw the stump. Some ancient hickory had collapsed, but it had fallen backward, leaving a tangle of thick, broken roots in a shallow hole. Frighteningly, though, even the closest root was almost a foot beyond the edge of the pool. Yet the voice had gotten him this far. He was certain it was Maya's voice, though he couldn't understand how he heard it—which didn't surprise him. There was much about Maya he didn't understand.

Carefully nipping air into the side of his mouth, he removed his sodden jacket. It seemed to weigh as much as a small deer, and he found himself floating a bit higher in the water after he was done.

Hold on to one end of your shirt. Throw the other end of it at the roots.

His eyes widened. So simple! And he thought it would work—but he would get only one chance.

He whipped his arm forward. For a moment it seemed the shirt was too heavy. It wouldn't come away from the surface of the pond—but as his fist, knotted in one end of the garment, hooked forward, the rest followed. The other end of the wet skin landed square in the center of the nest of roots.

Pull slowly, softly, husband. An inch at a time.

The soggy leather stretched, but held firmly, caught in the tangle. It seemed to take forever. The sand fought to hold him, but as he tugged, he felt it loosen its grip on his thighs. Grass passed beneath his hand, but he resisted the urge to sink his clawed fingers into the soft bank. It wouldn't hold him.

Finally, as sweat poured into his eyes and mingled with the waters, he touched the tough, springy wood. Wrapped his fingers around the thickest part. The pent-up frenzy inside his muscles exploded and with a single colossal jerk he dragged himself up and out.

For a time he lay panting, his face half-buried in the roots. A bright sliver of pain ticked above his left eye and he rolled away. He sprawled on his back and stared up at the trees. Black birds flew from branch to branch, disturbed by his presence, cawing harshly.

He realized he was shaking, and it wasn't from the cold. *Thank you, Maya,* he thought. *Thank you, wife.*

She was gone. Yet his heart sang. Somehow, somewhere, she was still alive and watching over him.

He stood and stripped off the rest of his skins. He found a long stick and used it to test the bank until he found a solid spot. Then he knelt, drank, and rinsed the sand from his clothes. He wrung as much water from the hides as he could, then put them back on wet. The heat on the prairie would dry them soon enough, and the motion of his hiking would keep them from stiffening up.

He refilled his water bag from the pond that had almost killed him. He grinned. To take the water was an act of defiance.

Ho, water Spirit, he spoke silently. *You tried to steal my life, but now I steal from you.*

He walked from the deadly copse, a sprig of hope singing in his veins. Maya was out there somewhere. For the first time since returning to their ruined camp, he knew he would find her. It wasn't fate, exactly, but it was as close as he could come.

The Lord of Snakes understood vengeance, too.

CHAPTER EIGHT

1

They didn't cross the river. That was what had worried her at first, that her abductors had come from the other side of the broad waters. Just after the forced march had begun, Maya had remembered Caribou couldn't swim. If Dag and Ulgol had some way of getting across the torrent, Caribou might lose their trail entirely. But to her great relief she realized, even in the dark, that they had turned away from the water, and if her judgment of the stars was correct, they were moving rapidly toward the northeast.

Their pace was brutal. Dag led them at jog-speed, so that in the dark she wasn't able to make out details right under her feet—and Ulgol had no patience with her when she fell. He simply jerked on her leash until she was upright again, and then the cruel trek would resume.

Occasionally she heard soft, high-pitched groans, and understood that the boy on Ulgol's shoulders was having no easier time of it than she was. Worse, probably—she'd noted the fly-blown, swollen wound on his thigh, and knew from her own experience in treating such injuries that the pain must be nearly unbearable. The child would need help soon; without such help he would die, his soul eaten by the ravenous Spirit that infested his flesh.

She could help. She was certain of it—just as she was certain that this boy was the reason her life had taken such an inexplicable turn. Her knowledge of the Great Powers was both bitter and comprehensive. She was only a tool, and if the Mother decided to use her, then use her She would. If that meant using any others, She would do that also. Sometimes Maya wondered if the Mother had any idea what She did—or if She cared. She suspected that the

Mother understood, but didn't care. She worked Her own purposes, vast cold things beyond the ken of the implements She selected to carry them out.

But the boy ... what did the boy mean? What *was* he, with his eyes that matched her own, the marks of Power? Had she been guided to him, or had he been sent to her? And if ...

"Oh!"

The sudden dip took her completely by surprise. She tumbled in midthought, instinctively putting her hands out in the dark to catch herself. But one arm got tangled in her leash, and she heard the sharp crack of bone in her left forearm as she struck the ground hard.

Ulgol, still lumbering mindlessly forward, didn't realize she'd fallen until the leather thong sharply jerked him to a halt. He turned and went back, grunting harshly. It had seemed a good idea to take the woman at first. In his dim way he thought he could have her for himself, after they had returned. A little reward for a job well done. But now, forced to drag her along while they fled from unknown pursuers, it was plain she was a burden. Especially since he'd been forced to carry the brat. Maybe Dag had been right—it would have been better to have cut her throat and left her where they'd found her. But Dag had changed his mind, and though he hadn't bothered to explain his reasons, Ulgol knew his own mental limitations. Dag was the smart one. It was better to let Dag make decisions. Besides, thinking made Ulgol's head hurt.

But when he realized, after touching the prone woman's body in the dark, that she'd knocked herself unconscious, Ulgol wondered if Dag hadn't made the same mistake he had. He knew he couldn't carry both of them, not for any distance. They would have to stop and wait for her to recover.

"Dag!"

"What?"

"The woman fell down."

"Well, get her up."

"I can't. I think she's hurt."

"Oh, *Snakes*," Dag sighed. He loomed over Ulgol's shoulder, peering down. "Look at her arm. I think it's broken."

Ulgol stared in the graying gloom. Yes, there was an

ugly swollen place on her left forearm. He couldn't see any bone splinters sticking out, but something was definitely wrong there.

Slowly, he let the body of the unconscious boy slide to the ground. "What do we do now, Dag?"

Dag hunkered down beside the bigger man and placed one hand gently on Ulgol's shoulder. There had been a childlike plaintiveness in the other's question, and once again Dag understood how much Ulgol depended on him. Something in him responded, and he spoke: "We'll have to camp, I guess."

He glanced over his shoulder. "It will be dawn soon. We've come a long way. Maybe we've thrown off anybody chasing us."

Ulgol checked the horizon, which was showing a tinge of silver-gray. Overhead there were fewer stars than before, though the morning star burned like a green jewel not far above the line of silver. Even as he watched, the demarcation between night and dawn grew brighter.

"We must be halfway home, Dag."

Dag shrugged. "Probably. I hope the brat makes it."

Ulgol was doubtful. He'd been carrying the boy's dead weight for hours, listening to his moans grow ever weaker. And he'd felt the wasted flesh burn hotter against his own as the fever devoured the boy whole.

"What will Gotha do, if the brat dies?"

Dag was silent a moment. Then he gestured at the unconscious woman. "That's why I brought her."

Ulgol glanced at her. "Why?"

"She has the brat's eyes, the marks. And she Speaks the Tongue. Maybe Gotha can use her instead."

Now Ulgol paused, trying to work it out. "How is that, Dag? How can she Speak?"

"I don't know. Maybe the Shaman will."

"I hope he's not angry."

"I hope not, too." Dag stood up. "Well, let's find a spot. It will be hot today. When it gets light, we can check her arm."

Ulgol rose as well, and felt the gentle predawn breeze ruffle his hair. The air smelled of prairie, of dust and dry grass and the faint tang of distant water.

The woman stirred, and groaned once, then fell silent again.

Ulgol felt his hopes rise. "At least she's not dead, Dag."

Dag stared at him. "Let's try to keep it that way."

They set to it.

2

Dag tried to ignore the slobbering, grunting sounds from Ulgol, sound asleep beside him. He was unable to drop off himself. His body ached. His mind felt soft and fuzzy. He craved sleep, but it wouldn't come. Thoughts like a flock of tiny bats whirred and banged against the inside of his skull, and their constant battering denied him the rest he needed.

He tried to put his situation into some kind of order. At first it had seemed simple enough: find the boy and bring him back. But the trail had been twisted and obscure, and they'd spent too much time before they finally found him. Was it too late now? They would bring the boy to Gotha, yes, but as a speaker or as a corpse?

He sighed and glanced over at the tiny form. The brat didn't exactly sleep—but he was by no means conscious. Instead, he sprawled bonelessly, locked in a delirium in which his eyes, sometimes open, sometimes closed, saw nothing. Even as he watched, the boy's eyes popped open, and he exhaled a low moan—but after a moment he subsided, and his eyelids slid down again.

Dag estimated they had another day's trek under the best of conditions—and these were definitely not the best. They had to carry the boy, and now the woman was in bad shape as well. She'd awakened from her swoon shortly after she'd fallen, but her arm was swelling badly. She'd examined herself as they watched, and tried to speak to them while she pointed at the grotesquely distended bruise, but neither of them had been able to understand what she wanted. Dag thought she'd uttered two different tongues—at least they'd sounded different. The Spirit Tongue was unmistakable to his own ears, even though its meaning was a total mystery to him. He suspected she wanted them to help her do something, but he was afraid to try. He was, in fact, afraid of *her*, and growing more suspicious by the hour of the circumstances of their meeting with her. It stank of the work of the God, and Dag was more than content to leave such things to those who were qualified to deal with them—which meant Gotha the Shaman. But Gotha wasn't here, and Ulgol was less than no help at all.

Yet his problem remained. In fact, it had grown worse, and if his grim guess was correct, this might be only the beginning. He hadn't forgotten the camp where he'd found the woman. There had been at least one other, no doubt her mate, and if the tracks he'd examined had been any indication, that mate was at least as big as Ulgol. The thought of a pursuer so formidable did nothing to help him sleep, and he was certain they would be pursued. He, too, would follow in similar circumstances.

Indeed, everything had turned into a fine mess. Once again he thought of at least a partial solution; the woman, if she were unable to travel, would slow them down, but the boy could be carried. Moreover, as long as the woman was with them, she would draw pursuit. If he killed her and left her here, perhaps the giant who followed would end his chase. Rescue was one thing, revenge quite another.

But what would Gotha say? Ulgol had seen the woman's eyes and had heard her Speak. The big man might try to keep the secret—if Dag told him to—but in time his tongue would slip and the truth would come out that Dag had murdered this potential treasure.

What a tangle!

The solution, when it came to him, stretched his thick lips into a joyous smile. The woman was the problem, he couldn't murder her without Ulgol giving him away to Gotha eventually, but Ulgol was asleep! Right next to him, snorting and hiccuping away, a regular fountain of slobber. And if, when the sleeping giant awoke, he found the woman dead, who was there to contradict Dag's version of things?

Nobody, that's who. It would be but the work of a moment to crawl to her side and wrap his strong hunter's fingers around her defenseless throat. There might be a bruise or two, but he doubted Ulgol had the wits to examine her closely enough to find any telltale marks.

For a moment the thought of handling the boy in the same way crossed his mind, but he couldn't see any further advantage in that. Besides, from the look of him, murder wouldn't be necessary. His death would be natural and, like his life, no doubt painful as well.

Dag felt no sympathy, only irritation. However he twisted it, bringing the corpse of the Speaker back to the Shaman would somehow be blamed on the bearer. Of course, in the final analysis he could kill them all, even Ulgol . . .

He shook his head. That would be the ideal solution, but also the most risky. Strangling sleeping women and delirious children was one thing, but testing the strength of his hands against the rind of muscle on Ulgol's neck was an entirely different breed of rabbit. Even using his knife or spear didn't guarantee success—he thought Ulgol entirely capable of snapping his spine like a dry stick, even with a shaft clean through his chest.

Besides, he liked the big hulk. No, on the whole, a simple bit of murder offered the most likely reward. Well, then, and quick done the better. No sense in waiting . . .

Moving carefully, he edged forward to his knees. Ulgol uttered a cacophonous snort, whimpered softly, then subsided again. When Dag was certain his compatriot was sleeping soundly, he rose to a crouch and began to creep toward the sleeping woman. He flexed his long fingers as he moved, feeling the knuckles pop, imagining the feel of her soft flesh in his strangler's grip.

As he advanced, the oddest feelings began to overcome him. It was as if all his senses had suddenly become disquietingly keen, and distinct. He heard a flap of loud wings overhead, and glanced up. Sweat had begun to drip from his narrow brow—the sun, not far above the horizon, abruptly scorched the top of his head—and his vision blurred, then lurched into a moment of painful clarity. A flock of fat sparrows, eerily silent, flew in a ragged circle above him. As he watched, the dance tightened into a single whirling clot of feathers, so near to the ground he could make out the glitter of a thousand avian eyes.

He froze, paralyzed. Surely these weren't natural birds—he'd never seen birds behave so strangely, or so fearlessly. The flock boiled not more than the height of a man above him, silent except for the beat of their pinions.

Suddenly he was seized with the certainty that these weren't birds at all, but some species of evil Spirit come to protect the witch-woman. With horrid clarity he could visualize them descending, their tiny wings beating against his face, their sharp beaks tearing at the slick white flesh of his eyes.

He cowered, unable to turn away from the spectacle. He could even *smell* them, a dry, feathery odor that reeked of death. Slowly he raised his right arm to shield his face. The movement seemed to agitate the birds, and the flock suddenly moved as one toward him. He almost screamed then, but out of the corner of his eye he caught a flash of sharper movement.

The great hawk plunged in utter calm, its yellow eyes intent, its claws spread wide. One moment it was but a black dot on high, growing. The next instant the swirling mass exploded in gouts of blood and torn feathers.

It was done as quickly as that. When Dag armed the sweat from his vision the birds—all of them—were gone, and nothing looked back at him but a sky so blue and empty it made him feel as small as some insect, and as helpless.

Sweat erupted from his entire body. His heart began to pound, and even hunkered down as he was, a wave of dizziness threatened to lay him flat on the ground. He licked his lips—seemingly the only dry part of him—and tried to remember what it was he'd been about to do.

The . . . woman. Strangle her. All at once he understood the meaning of the birds, and a wave of relief shuddered his flesh. It had been the God, He of Snakes and Fire, who had sent His emissary to His servant's rescue. The hawk and the eagle were His, just as the fat chattering sparrows belonged to Her, His great enemy. But He was the stronger, and had just proved it.

Dag inhaled sharply. He was terribly frightened, but now it seemed clear enough what he was supposed to do. He'd never imagined that he might play a role in the doings of the God, but evidently that most unlikely fantasy was precisely what was happening to him. It seemed to him horribly unfair—he was a *hunter,* not a Shaman. And were these feelings that turned his bowels to water and scoured his skull with fever what Gotha the Shaman took as a matter of course? If so, Gotha was a far braver man than Dag had ever imagined. No wonder the Shaman was often in such bad temper.

If it were me, Dag thought, *I'd be slaughtering people right and left.*

With that thought his original intention bloomed again, this time reinforced with a writ of divine intervention. Full of purpose now, he returned his concentration to the woman and gasped.

She stared back at him, as silent as the birds had been, but fully awake and, he judged, fully alert as well.

Stalemate—no, worse.

Defeat!

3

Maya wasn't certain what had awakened her, but her first sight was of a cloud of sparrows instants before a single hawk exploded in their midst. Her second view was of Dag's face, a twisted map upon which terror and murder fought their own private war.

Some instinct warned her to keep still. Whatever torturous thoughts boiled inside the hunter's skull, she was quite certain that none of them bode well for her. Yet the man squatted like a stone unmoving, and she was reluctant to do anything that might break his stasis.

As she watched, Dag's face almost seemed to melt beneath the strain he was suffering—and suffering was what she knew she watched. She tried to imagine what was causing the awful spectacle. *What was going on in his mind?*

He screwed his eyes shut and slowly began to shake his head back and forth. His breath lurched out in choking gasps. Finally, the slow-motion seizure began to fade. Dag's chest jerked once, twice, then relaxed. He opened his eyes. He twisted his lips into a smile that showed teeth.

"You win," he said softly, and shook his head again.

She couldn't understand his words, but the emotion in them was plain enough. It almost sounded like submission. Maya watched him carefully, but whatever furious decision he'd made had calmed him. He sighed once, stood up, and turned away. He returned to his place beside Ulgol and settled down. He closed his eyes. A minute or so later, he began to snore.

Maya felt her own tired muscles unkink. *That was close,* she thought, although she couldn't know how near death had come to touching her.

But she suspected. *Caribou,* she thought, near despair. *I need you, my love.* But she sent no plea to the Mother. She knew it wouldn't do any good.

4

Ulgol was first awake, yawning and stretching as a gaudy sunset painted itself across the western sky. He stirred slowly, unaware of the struggle Dag had fought with himself, and only after a round of scratching and grunting did he recall his circumstances.

"Uh ... huh," he mumbled. He glanced over at the woman who still slept, bound, a few feet away. The boy was just beyond, boneless and pale. At first Ulgol thought he was dead, but no—there was the faintest movement of his chest to betray how tenaciously he still clung to life.

In his own stolid way Ulgol possessed something that might almost be termed imagination. He didn't know the nervous colors that plagued Dag's dreams, and he certainly wasn't party to the surreal worlds of Gotha the Shaman, but he did, in some tenebrous manner, dream his stodgy dreams. Fighting, fucking, food, he'd said to Dag, and these three were indeed the farthest limits of his emotional stretch. But the woman impinged on all three. If she were indeed being followed by the hunter whose tracks Dag had descried, then there might be fighting. As for fucking, he'd already spent himself once on the woman, and hoped to do so again. Food was only a vague, tenuous worry—if they made too many mistakes and angered the Shaman, would he allow Ulgol the freedom of the cooking fires, or banish him forever from the People of Fire and Ice?

Though he could sense these questions, Ulgol was unable to distill from them anything more than an inarticulate cloud of worry. He stood up and, with physical action, as always, much of the bothersome cloud disappeared. A sunny smile, painful in its brute innocence, transfigured his features. Let Dag worry. He was better at it, anyway. In the meantime, the thought of fucking had aroused him. Dag had decided they must bring the Speaking woman to Gotha. Very well, that was easy. And nobody had said Ulgol might not indulge himself along the way.

The thought was very sweet. He would take his pleasure slowly this time, savoring each stroke. Like many whose higher powers were somewhat limited, Ulgol was something of a sensualist. The florid paint of wordless sensation, feelings experienced without examination, was his milieu, though the triggers of sensation were mundane. But he didn't question any of this. It was enough that his cock got hard and there was a handy soft place to stick it into.

She awakened, of course, as soon as he touched her. He could see the panic in her miscolored eyes. She tried to fend him off, evidently forgetting her shattered forearm, and when she pushed at him she uttered a soft gasp of agony. He spread his broad paw across her lips and squeezed, choking off the sound. With his other hand he undid his clothing and settled ponderously on her. Almost gently he took her bound wrists and pushed them aside as she straddled her. She stared at his cock that hung over her face, a single clear drop trembling on its reddened tip.

She tried to bite his palm, but the skin there was calloused and hard as old leather. He only laughed, and lowered himself, and forced his way between her legs.

"Ahhhh!"

He'd intended restraint, planned to take her slowly, to relish the sensation of his overheated skin piercing her, to *wallow* in her until he was spent—but as soon as he penetrated her, she did something completely unexpected. She relaxed her thighs so that he slid into her flesh almost as one welcomed. And then, when he was fully inside her, she tightened her muscles in a long, rhythmic shudder so that, totally against his will and his intentions, he found himself shooting his load of semen into her belly. A moment later, flaccid, he withdrew.

He stared at her. The panic had departed her gaze. In its place was a placid kind of triumph, the certain knowledge of her strength, the strength possessed by all women when confronted by man's mindless lust.

You have penetrated me, but I have swallowed you, her eyes seemed to say. *And I have drained you of your essence.*

Suddenly he was terribly afraid. He raised his right hand

to strike her, but the impulse passed immediately. He rolled off her. He could feel her eyes on him as he shambled away. Wounded, bound, and alone, she had defeated him. He couldn't put that into words, even in his own mind, but the deep part of him understood.

He had faced mystery, and been vanquished by it.

He turned and spat. "Bitch demon!"

But she only smiled at him, a tiny smile with teeth as sharp as knives, and he couldn't face her anymore.

"Having fun?" Dag asked.

Ulgol mumbled something inarticulate. Dag laughed. "Let's get moving," he said. "We'll be home soon."

He was as wrong as Ulgol had been, though he didn't know it. But he would discover his error soon enough, far sooner, in fact, than he'd possibly imagined.

5

Caribou, watching the scene through narrowed, sleep-starved eyes from his hiding place several yards away, saw them break camp, and hissed to himself when Ulgol tied the leash around Maya's neck and jerked her roughly to her feet. But he was a great hunter, and his instincts told him the time was not yet ripe.

Nevertheless, he made his initial decision. He would kill the big one first. It was only fitting, and he would enjoy it *so* much.

CHAPTER NINE

1

THE GREEN VALLEY

Sharp Knife sat by himself on a log just outside the Men's Mystery House. Though he was now fully qualified to enter the low, sod-walled structure, he knew the interior was smoke-stenched and stuffy, and he preferred the brightness of midday for his musings.

So many things had changed in his young life, and so quickly! It seemed like only days since he'd undergone his initiation ceremonies before the gathered hunters inside the House at his back, though it had been six moons past. Then had come his first hunt, and his first kill—a spectacular coup upon a huge bison. One of the older hunters told him his kill was as impressive as that accomplished by the Chief, Wolf, on his own first hunt long ago.

This pleased Sharp Knife to no end, for the hunter who spoke had been of the Bison Clan, and his approval had been radiantly evident. On the other hand, the Mammoth Clan hunters who had witnessed his success had offered congratulations that seemed curiously restrained. But Sharp Knife thought he understood. The Mammoth Clansmen had reason to be leery of his success.

In fact, for some time now he'd had a fair idea of the key role others had planned for him within the power structure of the Two Tribes—a role that some of the Mammoth hunters might not welcome.

He knew that older heads still regarded him as a boy in many ways, but he knew he was destined for greater things, both by birth and by his own talents. True, only recently had this destiny become clear in his own mind, and even now he sometimes had doubts. Nevertheless, he was becoming convinced his fate was a simple one: to become Chief of the Two Clans in the Green Valley.

Considering this, he stretched slowly, enjoying the smooth play of muscle beneath his sleek skin. His golden hide soaked up the sun, which made him feel deliciously lazy, but this mind still clicked along as sharp as the sound of a rattle full of stones.

He thought of his father, Rooting Hog, so named because of his flattened nose. Despite the humorous name, Rooting Hog was an esteemed hunter and, more importantly, the youngest brother of the legendary Black Caribou, who had once been Chief of the Bison Clan, as well as the closest friend of Shaggy Elk, the current leader of the Clan.

This blood of heroes is mine, Sharp Knife thought. It was a reassuring conceit, one more piece of a puzzle he'd been assembling in the secrecy of his own mind for years, ever since he'd first thought the future might hold more in store for him than the simple existence of a hunter.

Many times in those youthful days he'd wondered if he was fooling himself, if his dreams were anything more than the flimsy fantasies his friends chattered about to each other.

"I will kill all the mammoths in the World," his friend Jumping Beetle had announced just after his tenth birthday, and they'd all applauded. They had laughed when Long Snake, who had matured early and been the first one to both plumb the mysteries of masturbation and show the rest of them how to do it, announced that he would mate with every woman of both Tribes, even Old Berry. But they hadn't laughed at Sharp Knife's dream, for he'd never told them of it. Some innate understanding had warned him, even so young, that wisdom included silence, and so he'd kept his own counsel.

Now he wondered if it was time to speak, to acknowledge to certain men of the Bison Clan his awareness of their plans for his future. It was a thorny question. He sighed and leaned back against the wall of the Mystery House, but before he could consider further, a shadow fell across his outstretched feet.

"I found a new way to do it," Long Snake said.

"Do what?" Sharp Knife looked up at his friend and

couldn't resist grinning. Something about Long Snake's rubbery features and ever-present mournful expression—he always seemed about to burst into tears—was irresistibly funny, given his friend's rather joyful obsession with sex.

"Make my snake spit."

Despite himself, Sharp Knife felt his interest piqued. He was fourteen years old, and the doings of the cock between his legs occupied a great deal of his attention. In fact, it had gotten worse since he and White Moon had finally gotten together. It seemed that whenever he thought of her, his snake would respond, and he thought of her—and their few meetings—constantly. And while he would dearly have loved to assuage his hunger with White Moon herself, that just wasn't possible, not in their present circumstances.

"Oh, really?" Sharp Knife said. He grin grew wider. Long Snake was, in his own circumscribed way, an artist.

"Uh-huh. See, what you do is—"

Sharp Knife listened, his eyes growing wider as Long Snake's explanation became both complicated and unlikely. Finally, when his friend finished, Sharp Knife said, "Are you sure? That sounds . . . *impossible.*"

"Oh, no, not at all. I've tried it several times, and it works just fine. Here, you want me to show you?" With which Long Snake thrust his hand into his clout and made to exhibit the object of demonstration.

"No! I mean . . . you can show me later. We'll go down by Second Lake."

Looking slightly crestfallen, Long Snake withdrew his hand. "Well, if you're not interested in *that,* I've got something else you might want to know. It's about . . ." He let his voice trail off in an exaggerated show of reluctance.

Sharp Knife ignored the spurious drama. He was used to it. Everything was dramatic to Long Snake. He shrugged. "Well? Are you going to tell me or not?"

Long Snake rolled his eyes. "White Moon," he whispered.

Long Snake was the only one of his friends who knew about the secret romance. His friend had bragged to him that he was setting his sights on the girl, and strangely frightened, Sharp Knife had blurted out the truth, after swearing Long Snake to utter silence. Since then, Long Snake had delighted in bearing every tidbit of information about White Moon's doings—he was an incurable gossip, and his connections inside the Girl's House were excellent—to Sharp Knife.

"What about White Moon?"

"Berry's found out about you and her."

Sharp Knife sat up straight. This was news—if it was true, that is.

"How do you know that?"

Long Snake grinned. "Red Hair's daughter heard the old bag talking to her mother. Oh, don't worry, your name wasn't mentioned. But Berry said that White Moon had gotten herself in an awful pickle with one of the young men, and since I figure the young man had to be somebody we both know . . ."

"Oh, you bison's butt!" Sharp Knife leapt to his feet. "This is *important*. What else did you hear?"

Startled, Long Snake stepped back. "Well, uh, not much, really," he stammered. "I mean—"

"What is the old hag going to do?"

Long Snake's mournful expression returned full force. Sharp Knife's vehemence had surprised him, and not pleasantly. Of course, he had no way of knowing how his announcement had so coincidentally shattered his friend's afternoon musings of destiny, nor did he understand how crucial a role White Moon played in those musings.

"I—uh—I don't *know*!" Long Snake licked his lips and stared bug-eyed at his friend. "What's the matter, Sharp Knife? She's only a girl, after all. So what if everybody finds out about you and her? You're going to take her for a mate anyway, aren't you?"

Sharp Knife exerted a tremendous effort and brought his feelings under control. It would do no good for anybody to know how *much* this all meant to him. Slowly he lowered his right hand, which he'd unconsciously curled into a fist. He reached forward and put both hands on Long Snake's shoulders and squeezed. Long Snake, he noted, was covered with sweat.

"Oh, friend," he said. "She's the Chief's daughter. I wasn't ready yet to have everybody know. What if Wolf doesn't think I'm good enough?" And while he mouthed this ever-so-plausible explanation for his sudden explosion, something even more disquieting jabbered at the back of his skull. *She's the Keeper of the Stone!*

"Oh," Long Snake said. He blinked. "I see." He stepped

forward and hugged Sharp Knife, then stepped away and regarded him fondly. "You're an idiot, you know."

"What are you talking about?"

"That 'not good enough' mammoth dung. I mean, the rest of us know, even if you don't."

"Know what?" Sharp Knife found himself genuinely curious. For all his dreams of destiny, for all the half-baked plans he wrought and discarded, he had little idea what his friends, let alone his elders, really thought of him.

"You'll be the leader of the Bison Clan one day. I mean, your uncle was Black Caribou, and your father is Shaggy Elk's closest friend. And you're the best of our lot, even if you are an idiot."

Long Snake punched Sharp Knife gently on the chest. "I know what's going to become of me," he continued. "I'll end up mated to about fifty women and fuck myself to death, but you, my friend, are bound for better things. Well, sort of better—you don't like fucking as well as I do, so I *guess* they are better." And with that, he burst out laughing. "You ought to see your face, Sharp Knife. You look just like one of those fish the women catch, with its mouth going boop-boop-boop."

Sharp Knife couldn't think of any answer to this, and so he did the only thing he could think of to end the conversation. He lunged forward and wrapped his arms around Long Snake's waist and flung him to the dirt. An instant later both young men were covered in dust, wrestling like maniacs, all deep thoughts forgotten.

Until later, of course.

2

Muskrat regarded the old woman calmly. "Are you sure about this?" he said at last.

"She told me herself."

"Mmpph." He sat silent for several moments, his round face thoughtful. The Shaman had put on a great deal of weight since those long-gone days when Great Maya had taken up the hasty training of a scrawny Shaman's apprentice who had so unexpectedly become Shaman himself. He was not, to be sure, so hugely grotesque as the ancient woman who balanced ponderously on a broad wedge of log especially flattened to take her bulk, which he'd placed in front of the Spirit House long before when he'd understood she wasn't able to negotiate his doorway any longer. Once the sight of the two of them, their heads together as they conversed, had drawn stares. But after so many seasons, it was simply another sight in Home Camp, and no one even paused unless they had business with one or the other. Now, even though they were in the open air, their conversation was as private as if they spoke behind the drawn flap door of the Spirit House itself.

"This could be a problem," Muskrat the Shaman finally remarked. His voice was mellifluous and assured—the years had treated him well, despite the added flesh on his bones. He no longer bore any resemblance to the skinny frightened boy the Shaman Ghost had plucked from the remnants of the Mammoth Clan to train in the Spirit Mysteries.

But he remembered those days. Despite all the years of good living in between, Muskrat the Shaman remembered, perhaps better than anyone else in the Green Valley, the horror that had spawned his adult life. He had *lived* with the Shaman Ghost and the caldron of madness the Shaman Ghost had become. Muskrat had learned his first rudimentary lessons at the hand of a man whose Dreams were as full of poison as the venom of a pit viper. He had sensed that the Shaman Ghost was *wrong,* but he hadn't known how *wrong* he truly was. Not until the end, when something had shouldered the smallest part of its endless bulk into the World and snuffed the Shaman Ghost as easily as dousing the last dawn flicker of a burned-out campfire.

The Shaman Ghost had screamed as he died—at least, had screamed until he'd bitten out his own tongue—and Muskrat had watched it happen. The memories were seared into him in scars so deep they could never be erased. And then, of course, he'd met Maya.

Or Great Maya, as legend now recalled her. But she hadn't seemed great then, not to him. Just Maya, a woman with deep lines over the bridge of her nose, and streaks of gray already appearing in her hair, full of patience with the new Shaman who was still a boy and understood nothing of what he'd seen, except that he had seen it.

He had changed so much since those days. Sometimes

he wondered if Maya had changed. Sometimes he wondered what had driven her away from the Green Valley. He was certain that she hadn't left merely to follow the herds with her mate, Caribou. She had told him that was the truth, that Caribou wanted to go, and she wanted to go with him. But she had left the Mammoth Stone behind, in the Keeping of her niece, who was still an infant at the time.

Why had she done this?

Muskrat thought that the true answer to this question might be the key that would unlock all the other riddles that swirled about him these days. But how could he discover the answer? Maya was not here to ask, and if she had been, there would have been no question.

Was she still alive somewhere?

Again, a question without an answer. He had tried to Dream of her, but without any success. He hadn't seen her for more years than he had fingers, and in the meantime, she had become something greater in the memories of the Two Tribes than she had been in real life. Or had she?

He realized suddenly that he knew nothing of Maya's true nature or of her real Power. He had seen, but he had not Seen—or had he?

The questions!

He reached up and tapped his forehead gently with the knuckles of his right hand. Berry cocked an eye. "Your head hurt?"

He grinned faintly. "Too many memories."

She nodded somberly. "I know the feeling. So, Shaman What are we to do about the Keeper of the Stone?"

He glanced away. Three sparrows fluttered to the ground and began pecking a few foot lengths down the path from the Spirit House. Omen? He had no idea.

"Do? I don't know. She doesn't want it, does she?"

"Doesn't want the Stone? I suppose not. Sometimes I wonder if she has a brain in her empty head."

"If not, who is responsible but us? Us and our fear?"

Berry nodded. She took his point. If White Moon acted out of ignorance of her own destiny—whatever that might be!—whose fault was it? They had told her nothing, and trusted to the Powers of the Stone. "What were we to do?" Berry asked. "Only Maya really understood the Mammoth Stone. And even she claimed she didn't know everything.

All we have is what she told us. If she didn't tell us enough, then what guilt do we bear? We have done our best."

Muskrat stared at her for several moments, his brown eyes thoughtful. Finally he said, "And there are all the other questions, too."

Berry grunted. "Men's doings." She sounded disdainful.

Muskrat sighed. "Berry, the doings of men are the doings of the World we live in."

She snorted. "Men do what the Spirits demand of them."

Muskrat shook his head slowly. "You know that isn't true. Oh, the Spirits Speak, in one way or another, and they do things we either think we understand, or don't, but men live all the time, not just when the Spirits tell them to."

"How do you know that?"

"How do we know *anything*?" the Shaman riposted. And there it was, the question that underlay all, even unto the Powers Themselves. "I can't answer the question," he continued. "Nor can you, nor, do I think, can Maya. Unless the Mother tells her, and I don't think She has. So it is left to us, to struggle along with what we *think* we know, because we have to live until we die. And in that living, the doings of men are important."

Berry gummed the tip of one wrinkled finger. "And I suppose you think the doings of women have nothing of importance in them?"

He raised both hands. The movement startled the sparrows, who paused to stare at him with bright, empty eyes. "I don't want to argue with you, Berry. You are too wise for me. But in this matter, it will be the men who decide. Your mystery ends at birth, when men leave you and enter the World."

"The Mother rules us still."

He shrugged. "Does She? Sometimes I wonder."

"Be careful," she said.

"Yes," he replied. "I will."

The sparrows flew suddenly, leaving the tiniest puff of dust in their wake. He blinked, as if their departure had been a signal for the end of whatever reverie had suddenly possessed him.

"There is a division between the Two Tribes," he said.

Berry made to speak, then paused. Suddenly she felt the full weight of her years fall on her. All those memories, all that knowledge. She was well aware of what she knew—

her mind, if not her body, had retained its sharpness. At that moment she felt as if the past and the future were both somehow centered upon the lore she held locked in her skull. Only she had known Old Magic and his plots. Only she had seen the Shaman Ghost grow to power and madness. Only she had known Maya before Maya even knew herself. And only she had shepherded this new Shaman from callow youth to uncertain maturity.

Why me? she thought, with more than a bit of resentment—until she remembered Maya crying out that very same question.

Maya had told her the answer. Tools had no choice. There *was* no answer to the question. She might as well ask why the Mother, why the Stone, why the World itself.

Only the Powers need not face the riddle, for They were the true answer to it.

Why?

Because We say so!

"The Tribes have always been divided," she replied, and felt a tendril of fear twitch at the backs of her hands.

"Only the Stone and its Keeper have kept the peace," Muskrat said.

"Not exactly," Berry replied. "White Moon has done nothing herself, except behave like the silly girl she is. I doubt she's even touched the Stone in many summers. It is the fact that she, who is the daughter of the Chief of the Mammoth People, is the Keeper. Just the fact, not any action on her part. She is only a representative of the Power, not the Power Itself."

"Yes, I understand that," Muskrat replied, sounding a bit testy. Old Berry had always been given to lecturing on the obvious, and after so many years, he thought he could be forgiven for finding her, on occasion, just a bit tiresome.

As if she sensed his exasperation, Berry forestalled his reply with a gesture. "Think, Muskrat! What exactly is the Power which White Moon supposedly Keeps?"

It was an odd question. He had seen what he had seen on the day the Bison Tribe had been defeated and two mighty Shamans destroyed, but had others?

It was a fine point, but very real, especially as it related to their problems now. The men of the Two Tribes who schemed for the Chiefdom were mostly younger than those who had been present when Maya wielded the Stone—and what *had* they seen? Now that he thought about it, he suspected they'd seen little—certainly not what he had seen. The Shaman Ghost had not selected him as apprentice merely on a whim. He had some talent, some ability in the Spirit World himself, and Ghost had recognized it.

So perhaps what he'd seen then was his alone. Maya had worked with her eyes wide open, of course, but she was gone. So what it boiled down to was that the aura of Power rested on legend alone, on the stories men told to each other around hunters' fires, and on the whispers told and retold among the women as they worked and gossiped.

The power also rested on the reality of defeat. Somehow the Bison Clan and their Shaman, Broken Fist, had been subdued by the Mammoth People and their orphan who had only become Great Maya after she had departed from them. Moreover, in the terrible season preceding this cataclysm, almost nine of every ten people of the Mammoth had died of some terrible Spirit sent to make them cough up their lungs in agony. Maya had told Berry this was a judgment upon her sin by the Mother, and so both Tribes had good reason to fear such judgments.

But what had been Maya's sin? Simply that she had rejected the Stone, had given it over to the male hands of the Shaman Ghost, whose touch was blasphemy. Ghost had sent the Stone away, though it had somehow found its way back to Maya, and according to Berry, the Mother Herself had offered Maya a second chance. A second choice, actually.

"I wonder if White Moon is rejecting the Stone?" he murmured.

Berry's dark eyes flashed. "She is a silly girl! She doesn't know enough to do such a thing. How can she reject something she knows nothing about?"

"So we come full circle. We haven't taught her, she knows nothing, she can make no choice. Simple, eh? Do *you* think it's that simple, Berry?"

She shook her head. "No, it's not that simple."

He tilted his face back and closed his eyes to catch the sun. Hard to believe how hot it was. Even with the high-walled protection of the Green Valley, the winters hereabouts were long and bitter, and beyond the valley, out on the tundra, nothing human could survive the worst months. In those times, the far-flung hunting parties retreated to the safety of the valley camps to wait out the snows—which accounted for the half-deserted feeling of Home Camp itself. With spring the hunters and their families ranged as far as a hundred miles from the valley, hunting, butchering, preserving and storing meat against the long winter interlude. Now Muskrat felt little pressure, for most of the troublemakers were gone or, if not, too busy to spin their plots. But he feared the coming dark time, only a few short moons away, when ice would wrap the valley in a shroud of boredom, into which fertile soil the seeds of madness might once again sprout.

He glanced at Berry. "Some of the young Bison men make secret sacrifices to the Lord of Breath, He of Snakes and Fire."

Berry's wrinkled features twitched. Her eyes slid sideways, regarded him with an odd mixture of shock and slyness. "How do you know this?"

Muskrat shrugged. "I am Shaman. I know many things."

"You Dreamed?"

"No." He shook his head. "I hear. I see. I have found places were the evidence was unmistakable. Fires and . . . bodies."

Berry gasped. She had heard rumors, but this! It was far worse than she'd imagined. She was an old woman, but not a stupid one. The Bison People had worshiped the Lord of Fire—Old Big Dick, she sometimes thought of Him— through all their history. She supposed it was too much to expect Him to be utterly vanquished simply because the Mother had crushed His Shaman.

"This is bad news, Shaman," she whispered.

"Worse. I have reason to believe that some of the hunting bands openly sacrifice to Him outside the valley, where they think they are unobserved."

"He has no Shaman," she said.

"Not yet," Muskrat replied. "But it is all of a piece, I'm afraid. The maneuvering between the leaders of the Two Tribes, the reappearance of the Snake, the omens . . ."

Berry raised her head sharply. "What omens?"

Muskrat steepled his long fingers beneath his fleshy nose. "You don't think this news you bring about White Moon and Sharp Knife is an omen?"

Berry had hunched forward tensely, awaiting his reply. Now she relaxed. "That! Only a springtime love affair.

White Moon will come to her senses soon enough. I will see to *that*!"

Muskrat regarded her steadily. "Will she?"

Berry made no answer. The two of them sat in silence for a long time.

3

Wolf welcomed them at the doorway of his large house. Inside, the sound of babies squalling was answered suddenly by a woman's voice trilling a soft song. Wolf grinned.

"Welcome, friends. Why the long faces on such a fine day?" His tone was light, bantering, but Berry noticed fresh lines deeply carved into his forehead. *What does he know? What has he heard?* she wondered.

Muskrat spoke first. "Chief, we have brought you a problem, I'm sorry to say."

Wolf's features shifted into a solemn expression in response to the formal address of his title. This was business, then, and not very promising business, from the sound of it.

"Inside?"

Berry shook her head. "Let's sit here. It's peaceful enough."

The babies began to squall again. "Noisy," Wolf remarked.

"All the better," Muskrat said. "Hard to listen."

Wolf nodded. "Join me." He gestured to the rude log benches in front of his house. There were several, for the Chief spoke to many people, and often held informal gatherings on the spot.

"Thank you," Berry said. "If you could help me a bit?"

The two men took her by the arms and lowered her. When she was settled, they took seats on either side of her.

Berry studied Wolf, who sat on her left. She had known him since his birth, in fact had cut the cord that had connected him to his mother on the bloody day of that woman's death. It wasn't a pleasant memory, and much had begun on that terrible day—for Wolf's sister, Maya, had passed between those same bloody thighs, and all Berry's lore hadn't been enough to save their mother.

But Wolf had surely grown to fulfill his early promise. He sat easily, his finely knit body still muscular, his dark eyes alive with intelligence. He wore his dark hair long and plaited, dressed with grease so that it shone in the sunlight. She thought he'd been a wise Chief, but wondered what might happen if he were to be strongly tested—for his life had been as charmed as Maya's was cursed. Only once, when he'd been captured by the Bison Clan, had he faced the danger that the Stone encompassed, and Maya had saved him then. Since that time, his problems had been mostly mundane, and easily solved.

She wondered if he were truly a Chief for hard times, but then shook her head. Only those hard times, if they came, would answer her questions.

Wolf returned her gaze steadily. After a moment, almost as if he could read her thoughts, he took one of her swollen hands in his own and patted it gently. "Don't worry, Auntie. I am Chief, and I will help you if I can. Tell me what troubles you."

But it was Muskrat who replied. "I think," he said slowly, "that the problem is not ours, but yours." And with that, he informed the Chief of his daughter's doings with Sharp Knife.

Wolf listened intently, his eyes never straying from the Shaman's face. When Muskrat had finished, Wolf sat silent for a time. Finally he nodded. "I had feared this was so. I have heard certain things . . ."

Berry leaned forward. "You knew, then?"

Wolf shook his head. "Not for certain, but there has been gossip."

"Well, what do you plan to do about it?" Muskrat interjected sharply.

"Shaman, be calm. Is it such a disaster? Sharp Knife is a handsome boy—well, a man now. Why would he be such a terrible choice for White Moon?"

Berry and Muskrat glanced at each other. Was it possible the Chief didn't understand the issues involved? Could he be so stupid?

Berry took the lead. "Wolf, it's not just a question of her mate. If that were it, we'd do the ceremony tomorrow, and all of us would cheer for their happiness."

Wolf nodded. He spread his hands. "What, then?"

Now Berry stared at him openly. "The Mammoth Stone, nephew. What about the Mammoth Stone?"

His face didn't change. "Very well, Aunt. What *about* the Mammoth Stone?"

Berry felt a thrill of shock quiver in her old veins. What could Wolf be thinking? The Stone had been a central part of all their lives, and merely by its existence, it still was the focus of plots and counterplots, Dreams and destinies. How could this man, whose very *life* had been shaped by the Stone and its Power, seem to dismiss it so easily? But before she blurted out all this in a dismayed jumble, Wolf forestalled her.

He laughed.

"You should see your face, Old Berry. And you, too, Muskrat. You must think an evil Spirit has possessed me, and taken all my thoughts away."

Muskrat shrugged uncomfortably. "Chief, we think—"

Wolf raised one hand. "I know what you think. And no, I haven't taken leave of my senses. Nor am I so stupid I haven't considered the riddle of the Stone. For it *is* a riddle, you know."

Berry exhaled. She hadn't realized she'd been holding her breath until she let it go. "I know it is a riddle, boy," she said tartly. "And it is a riddle I have struggled with—me and Old Magic—since before you were born. So don't daddle with me. If you have any thoughts on the matter, tell me. I'm too old for games. Games make my guts rumble and give me gas."

Something twitched at the corners of Wolf's lips. "Well, we wouldn't want that to happen, would we?" He settled himself more easily on his seat. "Berry, I am not a fool. Of course I have pondered about the Stone. Maybe as much as you have. Maybe more—for the Keeper is, after all, my daughter, and she who wielded the Stone my sister. You might almost call it a family riddle. My family."

Berry narrowed her eyes, concentrating on every word. "Go on," she said.

But Wolf paused. When he continued, he spoke slowly, carefully. "I have never told you this—never told anyone—but Maya spoke to me when she handed the Mammoth Stone to me on the day of her departure."

Berry lifted her head. "I saw her speak. I thought she merely said good-bye."

"Oh, she said that, too. She said she loved me, and I believe she did. But she said other things, as well."

Muskrat couldn't stand it. "*What* did she say, Chief?"

Wolf squinted at nothing in particular. "Mm. She handed over the Stone to me and said, 'Here. For your daughter. Its home is here, with her.' And it frightened me, and I asked her if she was sure, because White Moon was so young, only a baby, and she said, 'It doesn't matter. If she needs it, she will understand when the time comes.'"

Berry closed her eyes. "That's what she said?"

Wolf nodded. "One other thing, but I won't speak of that."

"Why not?" Muskrat asked.

"Because it doesn't have anything to do with our present dilemma."

"How can you be sure?" Muskrat's tone was suddenly querulous, demanding.

Wolf straightened his shoulders, as if bearing up to the mantle of authority that abruptly seemed to rest on them. "Shaman, you will have to trust me. It is a decision I have made, and it is final."

"Oh." He seemed to deflate a bit. "If you're sure . . ."

"I am sure. Anyway, what do you make of Maya's words to me?"

Berry had ignored everything after Wolf's speaking of Maya's parting benediction, if that is what it had been. Now she spoke up. "I don't know. Was it a prophecy?" She sounded very old, and very tired.

Wolf glanced from her to Muskrat, whose own features betrayed only puzzlement, and back again. "I would have asked you that," he said finally. "If anybody would know, I would have thought that you would. You know more about the Stone than anybody, don't you?"

"*I know nothing!*" As if startled by the vehemence of her own outburst, Berry leaned back and took a deep breath. "Wolf, what did she mean? She said that if White Moon needed the Stone, she would understand when the time came. But how? Why? Will the Stone tell her? Omens? The Mother Herself?"

"I don't think it matters how," Muskrat said. "Maya said she would understand, and if we believe her, then we have to believe that, too."

They all stared at each other. The common thought, unspoken though it was, rested in their uneasy expressions. White Moon was, indeed, a silly girl—or so they thought. But had they thought wrong? Each of them had known her from birth, and no matter how hard they tried, it was difficult to match two very different images—the picture of White Moon herself, uncaring, even disdainful of the Mammoth Stone that was in her Keeping, and the dark and bloody history of that Stone itself, and what that might mean for the Keeper.

"You asked me earlier if Sharp Knife might not be an omen," Berry said at last. "Perhaps you are right. Perhaps their coming together, in this time, without our knowledge or sanction, is precisely that." She paused. "Quite often it seems to me that *She* prefers to use Her tools so."

"She?" asked Wolf.

"The Mother," Berry replied. "Whose every working is a mystery beyond our Worldly knowing."

Wolf sighed. "Then if we can't know Her will, perhaps it doesn't matter. Perhaps whatever we do will end up advancing Her plan, whatever it is. If it is. Maya certainly didn't tell me any details."

"What do we know?" Muskrat interjected. His round features had come alive, as if he were in the grip of some profound notion. "We know that Maya left the Stone for White Moon. We know she said that if White Moon needed the Stone, she would understand when the time came. We know that White Moon has decided on her own she wishes to mate with Sharp Knife. And we all know what problems that can bring."

He licked his lips. "What we *don't* know is what the Mother plans, or if She plans at all. So perhaps the wisest course is simply to proceed on what we do know, and let the Mother take care of everything else Herself." He turned his hooded eyes on Berry. "She will anyway, you know."

Wolf stretched slowly, as if to ease the stress from his muscles. "We also know that if White Moon mates with Sharp Knife it will ease certain . . . tensions between the Two Tribes—perhaps even end them for good."

Berry glanced at him in new surprise. Wolf evidently knew much more than she'd given him credit for. "He is Caribou's nephew, after all."

Wolf nodded. "I told you I have thought much of this. I had even thought of Sharp Knife *before* I began to hear the rumors. We all know that one of the reasons I have been Chief for so long a time—and unchallenged, at that—is because the Keeper is my daughter, and everybody is terrified of the Stone. But those who witnessed its one act of Power grow old and forgetful, and the fear of it grows less, as well. Meanwhile, the divisions between the two Peoples widen—especially the Spirit differences." He cocked one sharp eye upon the Shaman. "Is that not so, Muskrat? Even if you haven't seen fit to inform me of your fears?"

The Shaman seemed to squirm. "I—uh—it was a Spirit matter, Chief."

"Did you think I wasn't aware of certain ... discoveries? Perhaps the same discoveries you have made?"

"Sacrifices," Muskrat confirmed glumly.

"They will tear us apart," Wolf said.

"You know, then?"

"Of course I know. And I know that some of the hunter families no longer recognize the authority of the Mother at all. They have reverted to other Powers."

"Lord Big Dick," Berry muttered ominously.

"What?"

"Just a name," she replied. "But I believe you are right, Chief." Her voice echoed her newfound respect for him. "You have no male children, either. Just daughters. Isn't that strange? Almost as if it were intended that no one of your family should follow you as Chief ..."

"I have given thought to that, as well. You may be right—again, if so, it is the hand of the Mother at work, for who else gives us our children? And again, there is nothing I can do about it. What I can do, though, is try to end the danger I see for all of us here in the Green Valley if the old ways come again. Our Two Tribes first met in war, and that could come again. Especially if I do nothing now to try to stop it. Yet I think I can do much, and perhaps White Moon's choice is an omen. Perhaps she knows something without actually knowing it, if you understand what I mean."

"You mean the Mother is at work in her choice?"

"Yes," Wolf said simply. "Mating her to Sharp Knife would solve a lot of problems."

"It would bind the Two Tribes, and it would pretty much assure that Sharp Knife would succeed you as Chief."

"That, and it would give me new authority over the Bison People while I am *still* Chief. Perhaps enough authority to root out those who would worship He of Breath, who is our ancient enemy."

A glow appeared in Muskrat's eyes. "Yes," he whispered, "that might be so. Especially if Sharp Knife agrees."

Wolf turned a mild stare on him. "If he wants to mate with White Moon as much as she with him, he will agree to anything, don't you think?"

Berry said, "If that's what he wants, yes." She thought she had seen something in Sharp Knife the others had not, something perhaps Sharp Knife himself had not seen. She thought Sharp Knife might not lust after White Moon as much as the girl desired him, but he craved what she represented.

Perhaps White Moon alone might not be sufficient to bind him, but the rest of the package would do the trick. Unless she was wrong, Sharp Knife wanted to be Chief more than he wanted anything else in life. Including White Moon.

"We can ask him if that's what he wants," she said.

CHAPTER TEN

1

Caribou could not remember ever being so tired, even on the longest of hunts. How long had he been without sleep? Almost two days and nights, he reckoned. And this, the second night, was now drawing to an end. He had tracked them by sound and smell, staying close behind in the darkness. Occasionally the two hunters he followed exchanged short, grunting conversations, but for the most part he trailed the sound of their harsh breathing. They were moving very quickly for night trekking. Caribou tried not to think of Maya being jerked along by the leash around her neck. Instead, he entertained himself with the bloody details of the fate he planned for her two abductors.

Bit by bit the plan had taken shape in his mind as he tracked the small party. He understood why they traveled at night. They feared him—well, not precisely him, but whoever might follow. He had gained a bit of respect for the brains of the skinny one; the big one was as stupid as he looked, but the smaller one reminded him a bit of his old friend Little Rat, who had almost been too smart for his own good.

At any rate, the night trekking offered them twofold protection. They would be harder to spot from a distance, and it was almost impossible to track well in the dark. Caribou knew it was a good trick, for if he hadn't found them as soon as he had, he might never have found them at all. But the trick wouldn't work if your pursuer was close enough to hear the wheeze of your breathing.

No doubt they would make another camp with the dawn, and Caribou had every intention of letting them do so. In fact, he intended to sleep just as soon as they did. The only difference was he planned to wake sooner—and see to it that they never woke at all.

Animals were very hard to surprise in sleep. Only men slept deeply enough to be vulnerable. Caribou grinned to himself in the dark.

Toward the east the darkness began to gray.

A little bit longer, Maya. Then I will come to you. And to them . . .

2

Maya's limbs felt as heavy as lead. The man who dragged her along had the strength of a bull bison, and was young as well. He paid her gasps no heed, unless she stumbled. At such times, alerted by the slack in the leash that bound her, and mindful of her already wounded arm, he would stop and wait a moment till she collected herself. Then the ceaseless trek resumed.

She smelled the change in the air before she heard the sound. Their trail had arced far away from the rivers, but now it returned, though the drumming of the place where the two great waters met was not repeated. But the odor of fast-moving water was unmistakable, and soon enough she felt the vibrations in the night, so deep as to be almost beyond even her sharp ears.

As if this change signaled some other event, Dag spoke suddenly, and the pressure of the leash around her neck ended as Ulgol plodded to a halt. She almost ran into the back end of him before, in her befuddled exhaustion, she realized they had stopped.

She stood like a dumb animal, hair hanging in her face, breath rasping in her throat, and waited. Dag spoke again, and Ulgol replied. The tone of their words seemed happy, and she wondered what it was that had lifted their spirits.

Perhaps it was the oncoming dawn. She raised her head and stared toward the east, where the endless blanket of stars had begun to fade a bit as the horizon turned the faintest shade of gray. Had they been trekking all night? It seemed so, though she had little recollection of time passing. Everything had melted into a blur of stumbling, loping horror. Even her thoughts had seemed to go vague and mushy, but now, faced with the onset of a new day, her mind gave a small hiccup and began to function once again.

Escape!

Perhaps today would be the day. They would bind her again, while they slept, but it was the big one who did the fetters, and she had discovered his handiwork was not as tight as it might be. She hadn't really tested her bonds, saving that for a better chance at freedom—which she hoped would come with day while the men slept.

Then Dag rustled through the low grass and came to her. His features were shadowed in the darkness, but light from the fading stars caught the whites of his eyes. He spoke to her, a long rumble of sound, but she shook her head. Again she heard tantalizing familiarity in the rhythm of his words, but the meaning seemed to dance just beyond the grasp of her mind. He turned and spoke to Ulgol, who grunted a short reply. Finally Dag extended his hand toward the leash at her neck. Maya flinched, but his touch was gentle as he traced the length of knotted thong and the abraded flesh beneath.

He pointed at the earth, shrugged, swept his arm in an outward motion, looked into her eyes, then touched the leash again. He repeated the dumb show twice before Maya finally understood. He was asking her if she could continue. Slowly she shook her head.

Dag nodded, as if he had expected this reply. He motioned for her to turn around. When she did, he carefully checked the length of the cord used to tie her wrists together.

Weariness suddenly flooded her limbs and filmed her eyesight. Her knees buckled and she sank gratefully to the ground, her half fall cushioned by the springy grass. A moment later she slept.

Dag stood over her several moments, his face intent. Behind him, Ulgol puttered with the making of a trekker's camp, preparing rude beds out of piles of grass. He placed the boy, whose limbs were limp as wet leaves, onto one, and sighed as he relinquished the weight he'd carried for hours.

"They both sleep deeply, Dag," he said.

"I wonder what she thinks?" Dag replied.

"Who cares? We'll be home this morning. A little rest now, and the cookfires by high sun." Ulgol's voice resounded with enthusiasm for the first time in days, Dag thought. He wouldn't mind a little fresh meat himself.

It had been his decision to call a halt. He wanted time to rest, to hone his story a bit. He knew he brought a mystery to Gotha, and wanted to be sure he painted himself in the best possible light. All during the trek his first concern had been to escape pursuit, but now, so close to the Home Camp, he needed to set his thoughts in order. Gotha was unpredictable, and the Crone just plain crazy. This woman's wakefulness had stayed his hand, and prevented one solution to his dilemma. He hadn't been able to simply murder her without a witness to his deed. Perhaps she didn't know she'd saved her own life—and certainly Ulgol had no inkling of what he'd almost done. Which was all to the good.

For a moment he thought fleetingly of the woman's mate, or whoever might have followed, but with safety so near, he judged it no longer a problem. Moreover, each step they'd taken had distanced them from their unseen pursuers. Dag, no mean tracker himself, knew just how hard it was to hunt in the dark, particularly when your quarry knew it was being hunted. He thought that after two days the chances of capture were almost nonexistent.

"Are you going to keep hold of her leash, Dag?"

"Mm? Yes, I'll guard her. What about the brat?"

"He's not going anywhere. It's a good thing we're so close to home. He might actually make it."

"Good. Go ahead and rest, my friend. I know you're tired."

"He's little, but he got heavier, Dag . . ." Ulgol's voice faded, and a moment later his stentorian snores began to fill the silvery dawn light.

Dag returned his contemplation to the woman. He squatted on his haunches and rubbed his chin. His examination of the leash around her neck hadn't been simple concern. Once again he was faced with a choice—a bit more complicated, to be sure, but essentially the same decision he had almost settled the day before. This time he was more certain he would have the freedom to choose.

The lacerations around the woman's neck were extensive—more than enough to hide any bruises his strangler's fingers might cause. Or he could simply jerk the collar of the leash tight, and pretend that she'd somehow tangled herself in it while they slept. He doubted she would awaken and foil him this time. In any event, from the sound of Ulgol's snoring, even her screams wouldn't rouse the other hunter.

In the rapidly brightening light he saw the shadows beneath her eyes, and noted the deepness of her breathing. Exhaustion had taken its toll. If he desired it, this was sleep from which she would not wake.

If he desired it. Did he? That was the question he now had to decide. "Who are you, woman?" he whispered softly, his features slack with puzzlement. But she didn't reply, and he knew that even if she had, he wouldn't be able to understand her. And as he thought this, he realized he had nothing to decide. He'd already decided the day before, and though she'd foiled him then, his decision had not changed. She was simply more trouble than she was worth. The only new wrinkle was their nearness to Home Camp—Gotha might wish to see for himself the corpse of the strange woman Dag would tell him about. Well, that was a small matter. Bodies couldn't dispute accounts of their death.

Dag sighed and rocked forward on his haunches. He came to his knees beside her and placed his fingers smoothly on her neck. He paused, but she didn't even stir.

He took a deep breath. Only a moment more—

The rustling of the dune grass distracted him. He turned, and Caribou's charge distracted him further.

3

Caribou had concealed himself less than three body lengths from their rude camp, behind a boulder cracked almost in half by the scrub that had sprouted in its crevices and split it like an egg.

He was surprised they'd stopped before first light, though full dawn was not far away. Perhaps they had finally tired of their frantic journey? He had planned to sleep himself, but this was too good an opportunity to let pass. The dimness before dawn would be his shield, let him get so close before he struck that no resistance would be possible.

He licked his cracked lips and gripped the shaft of his long spear more tightly, imagining the sharp point of it ripping into the big one's chest and exploding out his back in a gout of hot blood.

Caribou had no illusions. He was older now, far too old to fight hand to hand with the young giant. He would have to kill him first, and quickly, then turn to deal with the weaker of the two, the thin man who seemed to be in charge.

He shifted uneasily on his aching legs as he crouched, listening to the muted conversation between the two men. He watched as the shadowy forms separated, the larger of the two retreating into darkness bearing the boy on his shoulders, the other approaching Maya and reaching for her neck.

Caribou almost charged then, but some sixth sense made him wait. Dag spoke to Maya, but she only shook her head. He made her turn around, and after a moment allowed her to sink to the ground, where he stood, watching her. In the predawn dimness, Caribou couldn't make out the expression on the man's face, but something in the set of his shoulders betrayed confusion. Now he hunkered down and sat that way until Ulgol called something.

Dag replied, but didn't leave his post. Caribou heard Ulgol begin to snore, and still Dag crouched. Was this the time? Caribou hefted his spear silently. If it was now, it wouldn't go as he had planned it. He would have to kill the skinny one first, because he was still awake. Which might wake up the big one before Caribou was ready to deal with him.

He rolled his shoulders, trying to relax the muscles there. Then all plans vanished from his mind as Dag, clearly visible now, sighed, leaned forward, and almost lovingly took Maya's slender neck in his hands. His intent in that moment was unmistakable, and Caribou went mad.

He'd never felt a surge of killing rage like this! He didn't notice when his powerful thighs bunched up and launched him forward, his heavy spear gripped and balanced in both hands with the unconscious ease only a hunter on a charge can understand. He knew his charge had alerted Dag when the other man turned, eyes widening, mouth falling open in sudden terror. He threw up one hand in a warding gesture and cringed backward, and this involuntary reflex saved his life.

Caribou's spear point took Dag high on his right shoulder, rather than in his throat as Caribou had intended. The bladed edge sliced skin, tendon, and bone, and Dag *screamed*! The force of the blow lifted him up and flung him across Maya, spraying her in a fountain of blood as her eyes popped open.

Her screams echoed his own as she tried to push him off her. Fuddled, she wasn't at first able to figure out what was going on, but after a moment she recognized Caribou, who stood over Dag, his spear raised for the death thrust.

The flurry of movement beyond him caught her eye and a fist of ice squeezed her heart.

"Caribou, look out! Behind you!"

Her husband paused, momentarily confused, then lowered his spear and turned barely in time to meet Ulgol's berserker rush.

Ulgol sighed as he settled onto his crude bed, but tired as he was, even the flimsy pile of grasses was as welcoming as his own bed of furs back in Home Camp. A few moments later his lips twitched as he sank into sleep and a mélange of exhausted dreams about two of his favorite things. It seemed only instants before a chorus of screams and shouts brought him awake to face the third of his favorite pastimes: fighting.

Ulgol was not bright in any sense, but he had native reflexes that made him a formidable foe. Despite all his bulk he was fast as a striking snake, and his killer's instincts, honed by years of the hunt, were second to none. When he'd lain down to sleep, tired as he was, he'd drifted away with his right hand clasped firmly on the shaft of his spear, and now, responding to his abrupt arousal, he came to his feet in a single fluid motion, and took in the scene before him with one swift glance.

The strange hunter stood over Dag with his spear already rising into a killing arc. Ulgol lumbered forward, intending to split the intruder's spine with a single thrust backed up with all his weight, but the woman screamed, and the invader paused.

By this time Ulgol had closed half the distance between

them. Seemingly in slow motion he watched Caribou turn, crouch, and raise his own spear.

His instincts measured distances without conscious thought. The other man—he was older, but almost as big as himself, Ulgol noted—bore a spear twice as long as his own weapon. If he continued on his present path, he would spit himself on the point like a helpless rabbit. But his own momentum carried him forward even as he sought to turn. He raised both his arms and swung his spear in a wide arc, trying to bat Caribou's weapon aside, but was only partly successful. His powerful arms shivered as he caught the haft a glancing blow, but the sharp edge of the point sliced his side open in a long, gaping wound.

The pain blinded him momentarily, but the force of his charge had shoved Caribou to one side, and when the older man sought to turn again, he stepped on Dag's ankle and stumbled forward. The butt of Ulgol's spear caught him straight in the solar plexus and knocked all the breath out of him.

Momentarily stunned, Caribou did the only thing he could do, with Ulgol so close to him. He flung his spear aside, lunged forward, wrapped his arms around the bigger man's waist, and heaved. The frenzy of his own fear lent him added strength, and he heard ribs crack softly beneath Ulgol's muscled hide. The bigger man groaned in sudden agony, but managed to brace the shorter length of his own spear against the back of Caribou's neck. Then, for a moment, all motion ceased, as the two giants measured strength against strength.

Once, Caribou would have laughed at such a contest, but the years had taken their toll. A red haze swam slowly across his vision, slowly turning to star-shot black as Ulgol exerted all his own might, slowly pressing the hardened wood of his spear haft deep into Caribou's neck.

He'll break it! Caribou thought suddenly, and redoubled his efforts, but despite another snapping sound from deep within Ulgol's chest, the pressure only increased.

He gritted his teeth and tried to lift the other man off his feet, but it was like trying to move a boulder, and in that moment, Caribou knew he had lost. Somehow Ulgol understood this, for even in his own agony, he suddenly let out a wild howl of triumph.

Caribou felt the last of his strength begin to ebb away. *Is this how it ends . . . ?*

Maya lay tangled in Dag's thrashing limbs, his weight pressing her down, his blood blinding her, his frantic random floppings, like a gaffed fish, sending jagged waves of pain up her injured arm. For an instant the side of his head lay against her face, his rough beard tearing at her skin, and she opened her mouth and bit down hard on his ear. Her teeth clicked through skin and cartilage and she growled deep in her throat as she tore the lobe and most of the bottom half away. She spat out the lump of flesh as Dag screeched like a woman and somehow rolled off her.

Blindly she pitched over on her belly, then got her knees under her and levered herself up. She tasted blood in her mouth and wondered if it were her own or Dag's. A frantic scratching came from behind her and she turned and saw the skinny hunter scrambling off into the brush, his body coated slickly with red.

The chorus of grunts in front of her brought her around to a scene of horror. Overhead, the sky had lightened into a blood-tinged dome in which floated a few stars like watching eyes.

In this horrid crimson glow she beheld a tableau: Ulgol, his head thrown back and teeth bared in a grin of pure ferocity, slowly grinding the wooden haft of his spear deeper into the base of Caribou's spine. If the spear had been a knife, it would have cut Caribou in half, and this seemed to be exactly what Ulgol was attempting to do.

Caribou, though bent backward in an unnatural bow shape, still battered at Ulgol's head with his own great fists, and he had done much damage. Ulgol's right eye was swollen shut, his nose was squashed flat so that every breath he took sent spatters of blood flying, and a long cut on his cheekbone flapped loose to expose white bone beneath. But the young giant, despite his terrible wounds, only laughed and redoubled his efforts.

Maya heard a creaking sound, and realized that Caribou's spine was slowly being torn apart. Even as she watched, her mate's struggles grew less forceful, his mighty blows going wild, his head flopping more loosely on his neck. His tongue lolled between his teeth as he fought for breath, and Maya knew that he would lose.

She looked about furiously for some way to help and spied Caribou's spear forgotten on the ground. If only—

She tugged frantically at her bonds, but Dag had retied them only moments before, and he had been far more careful than Ulgol. There was no give at all!

"Mmmph!" she grunted as she exerted all her strength, but to no avail. Caribou uttered a low, sighing moan and slowly dropped his arms. He tried to raise them again, but his attempted blow slid harmlessly off the muscled armor of Ulgol's shoulder. It would be over in a moment, Maya understood, over for both of them soon after. Unless—

She saw how to do it in a blinding flash of understanding. It was almost as if some message of explanation had been sent on the back of a thunderbolt, straight into her skull. She slipped her bound wrists down below her rear end, then sat down hard on the earth, wiggled, and pulled her legs through. Now her hands, still bound, *were in front of her*!

Ulgol concentrated furiously on his victim, bending him backward. Maya scrabbled forward until she reached Caribou's spear. Though her hands were tied, there was enough play for her to wrap her fingers around its haft. She cradled it in the crook of her arm, turned, and lunged forward with all the force she possessed.

The point entered beneath Ulgol's broken ribs, pierced his lung, angled up, and sliced his heart into two pieces. He arched his own back now, as if trying to somehow lift himself off the weapon that had destroyed him. His one eye bulged wide in the ruin of his face. Then, almost gently, he pitched forward. His weight impaled him farther on the point, which forced its way out his back with a sudden gush of blood.

Almost prayerfully he grasped the shaft with his hands as Caribou lurched away from him, but the blood-slick wood resisted his weakened grip, and after a moment he ceased his struggle and toppled forward like some vast tree falling.

Maya pushed her hair out of her face and stood panting over the huge corpse. Slowly the single eye closed. The smell of fresh shit and an acrid ammoniac odor filled the morning air.

A bird warbled sweetly into the growing dawn.

It was over.

4

At first she thought it had all been for nothing. She stepped over Ulgol's corpse as if it were nothing more than a boulder, her eyes on Caribou, who lay on the ground writhing. He had clasped both hands to the base of his spine, and in the fading pink of the rising sun she saw the long purple-black welt that disfigured the skin there.

For a moment she thought his back had broken, and nothing, of all the skills and mysteries she possessed, would cure that. But then, as her heart beat like a drum beneath her breasts, she saw that his slow, agonized movement betrayed none of the paralysis such an injury would cause. She knelt beside him and gently pried his hands away, then probed delicately with her fingers at the knobby lumps of his spine. He groaned at the treatment, and sucked his breath in noisily as she manipulated the heavy muscles, but she laughed shakily as her relief grew into a flood.

"It's all right," she said at last. "Bad bruises, but everything seems still stuck together." Then, without any warning at all, the tears began to flow down her cheeks, and she fell forward and wrapped her still-bound arms around his neck. "Oh, Caribou, Caribou."

She whispered his name over and over as if it were some kind of joyous incantation, and perhaps it was. After a time he said, "Woman, get off me. You're heavy." But the same kind of joy filled his own gruff voice, and she found herself suddenly laughing and sobbing at the same time. She slid to his side and he held her for several moments, until all her confused noises quieted.

"I love you," he told her then.

"I know," she replied. "I love you, too."

There seemed nothing more to say. They listened to the growing chorus of birds and watched the sky turn into a blue that echoed the color of Maya's eye. After a time, Caribou said, "I wonder if I can walk. That young bull damn near killed me." He stiffened. "Are you sure he's dead?"

She unwrapped herself and pushed up. She glanced over her shoulder. Ulgol had not moved. "He's dead," she assured him. Then she went rigid as a new thought struck her. "But the other one—"

Groaning with effort, Caribou levered himself to his feet. He reached down and pulled her up. His eyes darted about until he found what he sought—Ulgol's spear. He bent to grab it, but halted halfway and grabbed his back.

"Quick, pick it up, give it to me."

She did so, and Caribou turned slowly in a complete circle, but he saw nothing.

"Where is he?" he asked.

She had to stop and think a moment before she was able to reconstruct the jumbled bits of memory into something coherent. "He ran," she said at last. "That way." And she led Caribou to where she thought she'd last seen Dag and his mad scramble to escape.

Caribou moved slowly, and for the first time, Maya saw how much older he'd grown. It was like a veil lifted, and beneath, she suddenly saw all the years they'd shared, and the memories rushed over her like a flood. They overwhelmed her for a moment—little things and big. The feel of his hands in the warmth of their furs. His fury when he'd killed Spear that day. His tenderness as he'd slowly taught her his own language. His almost comic bravado when he led the hunters back, loaded down in triumph with fresh meat. The forlorn wail of his voice by the river, when he'd thought she would leave him. The joy on his face when he'd faced the steppe at the mouth of the Green Valley and asked her to follow the herds with him.

So much time, so *many* remembrances—and in that moment, Maya realized she had never loved him so much as now. It was an understanding that cleansed her of a confusion she hadn't even known she had. And it was an epiphany that freed her from another, darker riddle.

The Mother.

She'd always fought her own destiny, for even in moments of great victory, when the Mother channeled Her Force through Her vessel, a part of Maya had stood back and thought there was nothing good in her life. But there had been good, hadn't there? And the single greatest good lumbered past her, his still-sharp eyes scanning the brush for the signs of Dag's escape. If the Mother had given her great pain, She had also given her great joy.

There was a balance. She had simply not seen it before,

and sadness pierced her, for all the things the eyes of her heart had been blind to.

"Never again," she whispered to herself. "If I am a tool, then there is good in tools . . ."

"What?"

She shook her head. "See anything?"

Caribou pointed with the spear. "A lot of blood. He went off that way. I got him pretty good. He may be dying out there, if he's not dead already."

She eyed the brush doubtfully. Dag hadn't seemed on his last legs when he'd struggled his way free of their entanglement. "He may come back."

"He'll wish he hadn't."

She sighed. "We shouldn't tarry here, Caribou. I think they were close to wherever they were going. They seemed happy this morning, as if the journey was almost over."

He nodded, his features somber. "He won't be moving very fast, if he's moving at all. But there is something in what you say. He just *might* survive long enough to tell someone what happened here. So, the best answer is not to be here." He glanced at her. "Are you able to travel?"

She stared at him. In his condition, it was as close to a funny thing as he could have said. "Me? What about you? You look like you haven't slept in days."

He shrugged. "I haven't. But I'm still a hunter. I've got another day in me, if I need it. After that, I don't know. But I suggest we use what I've still got. We can be far away from here by sunset, and I think we should be."

"Yes. You're right. Tonight we sleep, though. And the next day and night after that, too." She grinned. "You're not as young as you used to be," she said.

His own grin answered her. "I'll show you tonight how young I still am."

That would be all right, too, she decided.

"Strip the big one of his pack," he told her. He lumbered toward the unconscious boy. "I'll finish up the rest of it."

She watched him, momentarily confused by his meaning. Then it became brutally clear. He reached the boy, shrugged, and raised his spear.

"No!"

He paused, half turned. "What?"

"You're going to kill him, aren't you?"

Caribou seemed puzzled at the question. "Well, of

course. What else am I going to do with him?" He glanced down, taking in the scrawny, battered body. "I don't think he saw anything, but—" He shrugged again. "Anyway, the shape he's in, it will be a mercy. Don't worry, he won't feel anything. I'll be careful."

And he would, she knew. For all his strength, he was a compassionate man, and she loved him for it. But she knew of another time he'd found a broken woman, and when he could have—probably should have—left her to die, he hadn't. Was there a similarity?

She wasn't sure. She thought so, though. And she remembered the boy's eyes, and knew she was right.

"Caribou, I don't want you to kill him."

Her voice hummed with the intensity of her certainty, and his eyes widened. "Maya—" He looked down, then up again. "Well, if you say so. He'll die here, though."

She shook her head. "No, he won't. He may die, but not here."

Pity was in his voice, and incomprehension. "Maya, surely you can see how sick he is."

"He won't die here," she said, "because we are taking him with us."

"What?"

"We have to," she said simply. "The Mother wants it."

"The Mother?"

"Yes. She does. We have no choice." And she told him about Serpent's eyes, and the tongue he spoke.

It took her a long time to convince him. He even knelt down and peeled back Serpent's eyelids to see for himself. Finally, after she'd repeated herself three times, he sighed heavily. "Did you Dream, Maya?"

"No."

"Then how do you know this is Her will?"

She couldn't explain. She knew she could have lied, but this was Caribou. So she simply shrugged and said, "I know. I can't tell you how, but I *know*."

"Why can't you tell me?"

"Because I don't know myself, Caribou," she said reasonably. "But we have to take him with us. I will try to save him, and if I do, we will bring him to the Green Valley."

"Why?"

"Because he is the reason I lay down my duty to the

People and left them on this journey. You knew there was a reason, didn't you?"

"I did, but I didn't know what it was." He came close to her, looked her in the eyes. "Are you absolutely sure about this, Maya? He will be a great burden. We'll have to carry him, and I don't know if I can."

This oblique admission of weakness, from a man who'd never admitted anything like it before, even to her, touched her deeply. But that nugget of certainty remained cold and hard inside her.

She stroked his cheek. "I'm sure, Caribou. We'll think of something."

"We'd better," he replied, and her shoulders sagged in relief at his agreement. "Well, you tend to him, if you can. Or we'll be carting a corpse." He glanced up at the sun. "And time may be growing short. Work quickly."

She went to Serpent's bed and knelt down. Her trained eyes quickly agreed with Caribou's assessment. It was a miracle that the boy had survived so long.

But then, it had been a day of miracles. No reason not to try for just one more. She couldn't know she would succeed beyond her wildest dreams—or Dreams.

5

The morning came full upon them. The sky overhead turned to soft, milky haze, while beneath, on the rolling lands beside the river, tendrils of mist slowly dissipated. She thought the day would turn hot later on—almost as hot as this boy's forehead, which seethed with dry fever.

At first she did nothing but look at him. It was her first chance to examine him up close, and her curiosity about this strange youth, who spoke in the secret tongue of Shamans and whose eyes matched her own, was boundless. But simple observation yielded up no clues to these riddles, though when she finally put her hands on him to continue her examination, she discovered yet another puzzle.

She had been trained by Old Magic, a great master of healing. As she ran her hands up and down Serpent's battered, emaciated body, she could almost hear the gruff old Shaman speaking into her ear as he showed her secrets and mysteries. He had already been ancient when he'd taken up her training, and his own lore had taken unexpected twists. Cynicism was one such twist, she thought fondly, recalling his exasperated answer to one of her questions.

"Maya," he'd told her, "you can call on the Spirits all you want, but I sometimes think the right herb, the correctly brewed tea, will do more good than all the chants or prayers in the World—particularly if your patient can't hear them. Make sure you learn about people and their bodies, Maya. If you do, you'll be a good Shaman."

And so he'd taught her to feel for lumps and twists of muscle, for bones cracked out of true, and taught her what he knew of remedies for such things. Spirits might capture human bodies and do great damage to them, but sometimes a simple brew—or an equally simple splint or bandage smeared with fragrant unguents—would be enough to defeat them.

This one can't hear me if I chant, she thought to herself—although she knew also that sometimes the chants worked, too. Perhaps the Spirits could hear the chants, even if the bodies couldn't.

His bones felt like the bones of a bird, small, fragile, light as tiny twigs beneath his skin. Quickly she discarded any thought for his other wounds—they were minor, and already healing over. But the laceration on his leg was deadly—the swelling, the long red blotches extending from the puncture told a frightening story. She bent down and squinted at the hole itself.

Gently she squeezed and wrinkled her nose as a foul-smelling pus, thick and yellow, oozed out. At this the boy moaned and tried to thrash, but in his weakened state he barely moved.

He wore only a clout around his scrawny shanks. There were places in the crotch that sometimes became swollen. If that happened, the evil Spirit was far advanced, and made treatment difficult. She ran one hand beneath the soft hide of the clout to feel there. Something bumped softly against the back of her hand.

Upon closer examination, she discovered that the front flap of the clout had been folded over the thong that held it around the boy's waist, to form a secret pouch. Her probing had told her nothing of possible swelling in the crotch, and so she began to unfold the clout to slide it off.

A stray shaft of morning sun pierced the haze, and in the sudden blinding glare she stared at the small object that had tumbled into her hand. She gasped. Her fingers opened nervelessly and spilled the thing onto the boy's belly, where it lay glinting warmly against the warm gold of his flesh.

The eye of the perfectly carved shape seemed to wink at her with jolly humor. But if it was a joke, it was a joke of the Gods Themselves.

How did it get here? she wondered, as the doors of memory slammed wide.

It lay nestled just above the curl of the boy's penis. Absently she noted another oddity. The boy seemed to have no balls. The sacs that held those nuts lay flat and flaccid against his skin. But this held her attention only a moment. She returned to the talisman he'd kept tied against his groin.

No balls. But his Mammoth Stone had balls. A penis, too. These adornments were right beneath the slight extension where his Stone had been broken off from its mate—how long ago? She couldn't guess—but she knew it was the mate to her own Stone, and now, through the unimaginable workings of Power, it had come to her hands beneath an empty summer sky. It could be no accident that this boy bore the marks of She who marked Her tools as She saw fit.

Till joined once again they bring the new day.

Now she knew what would be joined once again.

The boy grunted softly. The Mammoth Stone moved as his belly contracted.

"A tool indeed," she whispered. "Well, Mother, if this is Your tool, You'd better take notice. For without Your help, Your tool will soon be rotting into Your earth."

Carefully she wrapped the Stone in the boy's clout. Then she set to work, as she felt the ghostly fingers of her destiny draw tight around her once again.

"Caribou?"

"What?"

"If you can't carry him, we'll have to make a travois and drag him. And check the pouches of those pigs. Maybe they stole some of my medicines."

CHAPTER ELEVEN

1

The sun had clambered just past its noon perch when the Crone heard the women shouting thinly in the distance. She raised her old head and turned her wrinkles toward the commotion, her gums sliding across each other in half-remembered chewing motions—but her single eye snapped with alertness as she speared a glance across her shoulder at Gotha's tent and its gaudy Spirit markings.

She'd been feeling antsy all morning, her old bones itching with nameless anticipation. Something, she was certain, would happen soon, something important. She had not availed herself of her herbs or potions, but her faculties, honed by decades of practice, were often sharp without any chemical aids, and every instinct she possessed whispered of great doings. And soon. Perhaps, she surmised, as her faded gaze made out the small group lurching across the prairie toward her—perhaps it was now.

"Gotha," she called out. "Come out. Something's happened."

The flap over the door of the Spirit House slid aside and the Shaman's lithely muscled frame appeared. Gotha was nearly naked, only his privates covered by a soft clout of skin. He was coated with sweat and his eyes were slitted against the glaring light. He shaded his eyes and searched for the source of the call—"Crone? Is that you?"

"Over here, sonny," she cackled. "I don't think your mighty trackers found the brat. But it looks like they found something . . . or something found *them*."

Gotha turned and saw the hag perched like an ancient carrion bird on the half-rotted log that was her accustomed seat. He knew she could sit there for hours on end, hum-

ming to herself or chattering softly to invisible things—
they *might* have been Spirits, he supposed dubiously—
while the drool ran unnoticed from the corners of her lips,
and worse things leaked from her ravaged eye socket.

At the moment she seemed alert enough. He sighed. The
breeze felt cool on his slick hide, and he stretched hugely
to unkink his muscles from the awkward position he'd assumed inside the Spirit House. Casting spells was hard
work and, more often than not, to no avail.

It had been many days since the brat had disappeared,
and no sign of either him or his two pursuers since. It was
beginning to worry him mightily—so much so that he had
begun to use magic to see if he could help matters along.
He had also begun to consider the real possibility that the
boy was gone for good. The prospect had not cheered him.

"What are you howling about?" he asked the Crone as
he came up to her.

"Not me. Them." She pointed a shaking finger.

He shaded his eyes again. "The women? What's
that—oh."

The sun sent shimmering waves through the air so that
it danced above the earth like flowing water, and the stick
figures lurching toward the camp seemed to be floating on
a shifting silver lake. For a moment Gotha thought of
ghosts, and he shook his head.

"It looks like Dag has come back to us." He squinted.
"Alone," he added sourly.

"I think he's hurt," the Crone remarked. She seemed undisturbed by the prospect.

But Gotha was no longer listening. He strode forward to
meet the group of women who supported the bleeding
hunter, and all he could think of was Serpent: *Snake eat
him, I knew I should have cut off his feet!*

2

"Owwww!"

Gotha yanked hard on Dag's greasy black hair, jerking
the hunter's head back, arching him across his knees. The
wound in Dag's shoulder had scabbed over, but the sudden
movement set it to bleeding again.

"I ought to tear your worthless head off your shoulders," Gotha whispered, "and maybe I will yet. But first you have a story to tell me, *don't you, hunter?*"

He had carried Dag into the Spirit House himself, and lashed down the door flap behind him. What he had to do now would not bear witnessing, and he intended to be quick about it. He leaned closer, ignoring the stench from Dag, who had voided his sphincter in terror, and hissed into his ear, "Tell me now, hunter. Tell me your Snake-damned story."

So of course Dag told him everything. He held nothing back in the extremity of his terror, because every time he faltered even the tiniest bit, the Shaman, who crouched over him with his yellow teeth set in a grin that was more a grimace, took Dag's shoulder in his strong hands and twisted the edges of the wound farther apart. Once, when Dag could *feel* the flesh slowly tearing, he fainted, but when he woke, the nightmare was still there, watching with patient, implacable eyes. Those eyes frightened Dag more than anything else, because they were so calm. There was no anger in them, only a promise.

"Tell me more about the woman," Gotha said at one point, and after Dag quit screaming, he did so. Finally Gotha sighed and heaved the sweating, broken, blood-slick hunter aside.

"One blue eye and one green, eh?" He spat, and the glob of sputum landed directly between Dag's bulging eyes. Then he sighed. "I suppose I'll have to save your useless life, Dag." A horrid smile flickered on his lips. "How else will you be able to guide me to the place? But it will be painful, hunter. I'll save you, but I *promise* it will be painful."

It was. Dag fainted again, but by the next morning he was on his feet, and the hunting party had begun to retrace his trail.

Dag surveyed the spot blearily. Things had gotten more than a little hazy for him. The Shaman kept feeding him a bitter-tasting paste, but though it made him feel like he was floating sometimes, his shoulder, misshapen beneath a huge poultice, didn't hurt at all. "It was here," he said at last. "See, over there. Where it's all trampled down. I guess Ulgol didn't kill him."

And as he said that, Dag felt a pang of sadness as sharp as the spear that had shattered his shoulder. The alternative was simple enough. As he had scuttled away through the brush from this place, his last sight had been of two giants locked in mortal combat. If Ulgol had won, he would have already met them. But he hadn't. So he must be—

"Over here!"

Two hunters were dragging something from beneath a pile of dry branches. Dag looked over, then away. A single tear rolled down his cheek, though in his herb fog, the first wave of sorrow was oddly muted. He felt far away from himself, far away from this place. Far away from the massive body the two hunters dragged out into the light of day like a slaughtered bison.

"Oh, Ulgol," Dag whispered. "Oh, my friend."

"Spear wounds," the first hunter, a short, brawny man whose name was Rakaba, said, and shook his head.

"Keep looking," Gotha said sharply. "See if you can find the brat."

The second hunter, a tall, laconic man whose long black hair had coppery highlights, shrugged as he relinquished Ulgol's left foot. It fell to the ground with a flat, meaty sound that made Dag shiver. "Didn't see anything else."

"Well, look *closer*," Gotha said.

Agarth jumped at the words, as if somebody had prodded him with a knife point. He nodded, turned, and trotted off, his eyes scanning the clumps of brush that dotted the grassy plain.

"The boy is dead," Dag said. "He has to be."

"Then where is he?" the Shaman asked, his voice softly reasonable, but that wasn't the message Dag thought he heard. He thought he heard something like the cry of a striking hawk in that voice—the windy shriek that signaled torn eyeballs and shredded flesh.

Dag glanced up. For just one moment it seemed to him that the sky—which had turned the color of milk swirled in water—went completely black, and in that moment something *looked out* at him. Something so huge and remote his mind could not encompass it. So his mind didn't. He blinked, and realized that somehow he had fallen to the ground, and that the Shaman was standing over him, a sardonic expression on his face.

"They didn't find the brat, Dag," Gotha said. "But they

found a trail, and now you are going to find him for us. Aren't you?"

Dag nodded. He suspected he wouldn't live long enough to accomplish that task, but somehow, that didn't matter anymore. He would live as long as whatever it was that had looked out—not down, *out*—at him wanted him to live. "Yes," he whispered. "I will."

"Good," Gotha said. Then he turned away, his interest in the ruined hulk completely drained.

Dag lay on his back with his eyes closed so he wouldn't have to look at the sky. His lips moved slowly. The words he spoke were "Poor Ulgol." But what he really meant was *poor me.*

From somewhere far away, Dag thought he heard the Crone begin to laugh.

3

Gotha stood with his hands on his hips, eyeing the men who shuffled their feet and tried to avoid his gaze. After a long, disgusted moment he shook his head and returned his attention to the two hunters who lay almost side by side, one living, the other quite dead.

"All right," he said at last, "bury that one."

Dag's eyes clicked open.

No, not you, Gotha thought, *though it wouldn't be that bad an idea. I really don't need you anymore. You've shown me what you can.*

He stared at the wounded hunter speculatively, then shook his head. "We'll carry that one back to camp," he decided. Dag shuddered faintly and closed his eyes again. "He needs rest. It will be a while before we can take up the hunt again."

Rakaba pulled out his hatchet. "I'll cut some branches."

Gotha shrugged. He'd lost interest in Dag for the moment. Only now, when it was apparent that his prey was safely out of his clutches for the moment—if only for the moment—did his clever mind turn to the full import of what Dag had told him.

Introspection was not the Shaman's long suit—but he was capable of self-examination if the situation warranted,

and this seemed to be such a time. Head down, fingers rubbing his chin gently, he wandered away from the rest, his
feet already pointing toward the sound of the river and the
camp that awaited him. The camp, and the problems.

As he ambled along beneath a streaky-milk sky, Gotha
wondered what would happen to him now. Serpent had
been the symbol and the source of his Power, for it was
through Serpent that he discovered the will of the God.

The will of the God . . .

That was the heart of the matter, wasn't it? His mind began to drift as aimlessly as his feet. He stopped then, without realizing it, as the hugeness of the World smote him
without warning. Slowly he turned around. The horizon receded in every direction until it merged almost seamlessly
with the rushing sky. The deep thrum of the invisible river
filled the air with foreboding heaviness. The plains were an
endless carpet of springing green, dotted here and there
with darker stands of scrubby trees.

So big.

And man was so small.

Only the God could encompass all of it. If man, least of
the creatures who roamed these vast spaces, was to survive
at all, it could only be with the favors—no, the active
help—of the God who had created such helpless creatures.

Gotha licked his lips. The unimaginable silence made
the conversations at his rear seem insignificant, mere ripples in the greater fabric. And so they were, just as the
lives they represented were also infinitesimal against the
endlessness and ferocity of the World.

Why, he wondered, *did the God make us like this? So
tiny, so weak? Even the least of the great beasts kill us with
ease. Or the Spirits destroy us without warning, with wind,
with fire, with flood or starvation or the sudden bolt from
the sky. Only the God occasionally spares us, and even
then we can never be certain why.*

Perhaps it is a great joke.

But despite the wrenching, sometimes brutal things he
had done in his life, Gotha felt no regrets. It was a wrenching, brutal life his people led, and if somebody had to do
what was necessary to help them survive, so be it. He
would bear that weight, terrible burden though it was.

My mother killed my father for exactly those reasons.

The thought bubbled up from the nether regions of his

mind like a particularly bloated bubble of swamp gas, and in his ruminations it smelled as bad.

Unconsciously he wrinkled his nose. He hadn't thought of it for a long time, really *thought* about it. She had thrown it in his face only the other day, but she often did that. Usually he could ignore it, but now he wondered why she brought it up so often. Was it guilt? Was it some kind of decline with age that made her wallow in the past?

He came to a halt and stood silent, his brow furrowed in concentration. The memories filled him up like stagnant water, dreamlike in their awful vividness. Suddenly it seemed to him that he was there again, a boy not more than eleven summers old, facing his mother across a smoky fire . . .

Her eyes were usually soft and brown—he'd always loved her eyes—but on this day they were hard and clear as stones. The centers of them had shrunk to pinpoints, sharp as arrows, and now they seemed to pierce the very center of him. The Spirit House was full of smoke. His eyes watered. He felt sweat on his upper lip and licked the salt away as he listened to her voice, normally low and husky, a familiar warm sound, now tense and high, as if she might begin to scream at any moment.

"He is dying, Gotha, your father is dying."

"No," he whispered, though he knew it was true. He'd been too well trained to doubt her, though he wanted more than anything not to believe.

The heat inside the stuffy little structure was nearly unbearable. It made him feel dizzy, sent his thoughts whirling into a stew that grew more and more frightening, as if his world was spinning out of control. Perhaps it was.

He glanced over at the shapeless pile of furs that hid his father's unconscious, delirious form. Awful noises came from there, gobbling snorts, low moans, sudden gasps like punctuation to the snapping of the fire between them.

Oh, please, great Lord of Snakes, don't take him away, don't take him away from me! I'll be good, I'll learn everything You want me to, just like he says, I'll do Your will in the World—

And his mother, her eyes dilated from the drugs she'd taken to put her into the healing trance that hadn't helped at all, no, it hadn't, she must have somehow heard that endless shriek of words inside his skull—or had he spoken them?—and she reached forward and put her hands on either side of his head, caressed his temples, and he was surprised at how cool and dry and soothing her fingers were . . .

"Son, listen to me."

"Yes, Mama." He hadn't called her that for a long time, not since he was a little boy, but now, faced with the greatest mystery, he was a little boy again.

"I have to tell you something. And you must try to understand me."

He stared at her, his own eyes round pools of darkness. "What, Mama?"

She licked her lips, which had a bluish, shadowy cast in the flickering light. For a moment she looked like a Demon, a bad Spirit to him, and involuntarily he shrank back from her. She leaned out across the fire, so that the smoke that rose fitfully toward the hole in the ceiling wreathed her face, and now she seemed to float in the shifting cloud without a body, only a pair of eyes, and black lips moving across white, sharp teeth.

"I killed him, Gotha," she said. "It is my doing that he will die, and I do it for you."

"No."

He twisted out of her grasp. Something sharp and tearing clutched at the tight muscles of his belly, pummeled them, brought a sinking looseness to his bowels. "No, you lie," he said.

He didn't know *why* he said it, only that the words offered him some protection against unimaginable horror—he loved her. He loved his father. How could he make sense of what she said, when nothing about it made sense at all?

"Gotha!"

"No, no, no, *no!*" Now he was whipping his head back and forth, his long hair flying across his face, fire hotter than the coals before him rising to his cheeks.

Suddenly she sat back, and dropped her outstretched arms to her sides, and waited. "You have to listen to me," she said. "You have to understand."

He coughed, long, wracking heaves that threatened to burst his chest, tear his throat. When the paroxysm ended, it took him a moment to find his breath. He felt empty. He didn't understand why she would lie to him like this.

"You've chanted for him, mixed him potions, even Dreamed with the Mother, asking for Her help. It's an evil Spirit, you told me . . ."

She shook her head slowly, eyes now downcast, to Gotha's great relief. He couldn't look into her eyes any longer—those openings to the Spirit inside. Such calm, beautiful openings, to hide such a monster.

"I lied to you," she said. "I had to. But you have to know the truth, now."

"No!"

"Because you have to understand, my son. You will be Shaman soon. You have to understand why I have caused that to happen."

And still he couldn't believe her. He didn't *want* to believe her, because that would mean everything he had understood about his father, his mother, the World and all their places in it, was a lie as well.

In his own youthful mind he had already plotted out his role—on some distant day his father would lay down his robes and relinquish the Shamanhood to his son in the appropriate ceremony, and then Gotha would take up what was only the latest chapter in a family story that stretched back into the misty deeps of time . . .

But not like this, something torn and hurt inside him moaned. Not *her*—and now he stared across the fire with utter loathing on his face—*murdering* him.

But the part of him that made him what he was—a Shaman to be—knew she spoke the truth. She had the knowledge of herbs and powders to do this thing, and she had the trust of her husband.

"Why?" he said softly, and though the word was hardly discernible, she recoiled from the blunt force of it.

"The Mother . . ." she sighed at last. "She told me to do it."

The answer was not at all what he'd expected. Wise beyond his years, he'd imagined a tale of secret hate or, worse, a misguided and monstrous ambition to advance her son into the role of the husband. But this lame appeal to the Bitch Goddess?

He swallowed the bile that rose into his throat and threatened to choke him with disgust. "Her? Your weak

and womanly Spirit? *She* led you to . . . that?" As if in unconscious agreement, his father uttered a long, liquid groan
that finally bubbled into silence.

"Yes. She visited me in a Dream and told me what to
do." His mother's voice had grown stronger, more full of
certainty now, as if she understood his acceptance, and now
they were only discussing the justifications for an act already accomplished.

Which was exactly what they *were* doing, he realized
suddenly, as a strange mix of horror and humor seized him.
For it was wildly hilarious, this revelation of murder at the
behest of the weakest of the Gods, murder done by mate to
mate, with the fruit of the mating now forced to bear witness. Truly it *was* a joke, and black, bleak laughter clawed
through his voice box.

She shrank away from the sound. "Son . . . you must understand."

"Understand what? That you have poisoned my father
because your stupid, *treacherous* Spirit told you to? What
about me? What am I supposed to think?" Then the full
dread of this deed smoke him, and he wailed, *"What am I
supposed to do!"*

"Gotha, it is for the best."

He looked away. "I guess I should kill you, too. It would
be only fitting. We could burn the two of you together."

"Gotha!"

And now the hard, bitter outlines of the man to come
showed themselves on his face. "But it would defile his
memory, not to mention his flesh, to share the Sacred Fire
with the likes of you."

She stared at him, as if only now realizing the enormity
of what she had done.

Almost musingly, he continued. "Although perhaps if
that had been the usual way—if you had known you would
ride the smoke with him—maybe you would have thought
twice before you murdered him." He paused. "I don't suppose there is any way to undo what you did?"

She shook her head, staring at him as if he had suddenly
turned into a snake. As if the baby she had suckled at her
breasts, raised through his childhood, taught and trained,
even murdered for, had turned into something so completely ghastly that she could no longer recognize him.

And Gotha could read this thought on her face as plain

as winter trees stark against the snow, and he knew she was right. He *had* become something different. By confessing her awful crime she had made him her accomplice, and for that he would never, ever forgive her.

Nor, he knew, would he ever forgive the Bitch Goddess. In fact, for one single instant the two confused themselves in his mind's eye, and he seemed to see Her sitting across the fire, her evil face wreathed in triumph.

See who is stronger, she seemed to say. *See who really rules the World.*

But he couldn't accept that vision, that *Dream* (for that is what it was, his first true Dream, though he was too young to know it for what it was), and so he closed his eyes and shook his head, and when he opened his eyes again, She was gone, and only his mother—the murderer— remained.

He smiled at her and she shuddered. "No, I won't kill you," he said. "I have other plans for you." He sighed. "I don't think you will like them."

Suddenly he came back to himself, a lone man standing on the heart of the endless prairie, the sun ruffling his hair, a strangely soft smile playing on his lips.

He *had* taken his revenge, hadn't he? Oh, yes. And how surprised his mother had been when they'd stood together at his father's pyre, and he had turned to her and said, "An eye, Mother. The Lord of Fire demands an eye. He thinks you have seen too much."

And on that spot he had gouged out her eye with his own hand, plucked it from the socket like a rotten fruit, and cast it into the fire while she fell screaming to the ground.

No one had heard his whispered injunction as he had lifted her up again, blood streaming down her cheeks. "Mother, heal yourself," he had said. It was the last time he had called her that in his own mind. Ever after, to him, she was the Crone, and his only regret was that he had not taken both her eyes—although even that regret was tempered. Blinded, she could not have seen the horror she had become, mirrored in the horror on the faces of those who had to look upon her.

So he had learned his first lesson of the Gods, and it was

a teaching that had stayed with him until this day—*The Gods could not be trusted!*

Even in his own prayers he remembered that truth—and it had made him the worst kind of cynic, a man who tried to do good for his People even as he thought that good was probably impossible. A holy man of the strangest sort— one who wished *not* to believe in his God (who had allowed the treacherous murder of his own father), but was denied disbelief by the very strength of the Gods in the World.

And so he had taken his father's place, gifted with the weird powers his mother had already discerned, and swept up the threads of his life into his own hand. He had been a good leader, he thought, had kept his People as safe as he could keep them, despite the ferocious vagaries of the Power who supposedly guarded over them.

A game of tricks, he thought suddenly. *I trick the Snake, He tricks me.*

Then, eight summers ago, he had found the boy . . .

It had been well along in the moons of heat, and the People of Fire and Ice were enduring the first part of their destiny. The hunters had ranged far beyond the Home Camp, only to return with empty hands and emptier bellies. The children wandered the camp hollow-eyed, their guts swollen in spurious fullness. And Gotha had made his magics and sent his prayers and essayed his tricks to no avail.

His people looked to him, and he had no answer to them. It had reached a point where even the women made signs with their crossed fingers behind his back, and the Crone had begun to cackle openly of his impotence. The desperate times had emboldened her in her bitterness, for she took it as an omen of his doom. He had rejected the Mother, in her mind, and though she believed the Mother had instructed her to murder, she now thought that her great patron had turned away from all of them.

"You made your mistake, sonny. Now all of us have to pay for it."

He snarled at her. "What would you have me do? Worship your Bitch? *Pray* to Her? Or perhaps She has other ideas, eh? Maybe She's whispering in your ear even now, speaking of poison? As She spoke to you of my father?"

She cocked her head, her one good eye blinking quickly. "No, not that . . ."

"Eh? Not that, you say? But treachery is Her secret name, old woman."

"She is the Great Goddess," the Crone repeated stubbornly. "Not Lord Big Dick, who leaves us starving."

"Oh? And what has the Bitch done for us lately? Aside from causing you to murder my father? Where is *Her* bounty?"

"You reject Her, my son. And so She withholds Her mammoth and bison, Her sweet berries, all the things that are Hers and Hers alone."

Thus matters reached an impasse, for Gotha could not prove the Crone wrong through his own efforts to gain the help of the Lord of Snakes and Fire. For a time even his own faith wavered, and he wondered in his secret heart if perhaps his mother wasn't right after all.

And there was insidious attraction in such thoughts, for if the Great Mother *was* the stronger, then the murder of his father had been justified, and no guilt could be assigned to him for allowing his mother to live.

So he circled himself, a lame bull biting his own tail, and the people watched and waited and grew ever more hungry. Then one particularly hellish day, when the sun hung low over the World like an endless bed of coals and the grasses withered around the cracks in the stones, a hunter, Anu by name, came panting into the camp with news.

A group of travelers beyond the horizon, a small band but heavily laden with bags and pouches and heavier things they dragged on travois poles. No more than two hands of people, only four of them full-grown hunters.

"What do they look like?" Gotha asked.

"Their bellies are full. They laugh. They seem happy."

"Ah."

"And they move quickly," Anu told him.

"Yes. Then we must move quickly, too."

Gotha selected twelve of his best hunters for the task. They moved with practiced precision, despite their desperation, for they knew what would come. Travelers themselves, they had hunted their own kind all their lives, as their fathers and their fathers' fathers before them. The Lord of Snakes and Fire had fashioned them so. Who were they to gainsay them? And now the Lord brought them sustenance once again, in the traditional gift of unwary prey. They moved out at a fast trot, and if the muscles that wielded their spears were a bit wasted, it didn't matter. The sinews of the God were their strength, and that was enough.

"Who is stronger now, hag?" Gotha hissed as he led his band forth.

But she only cackled horribly and said, "Be sure you come back, my son. And when you do, thank Her for Her gift."

He spat on the ground at her feet, and then was gone in a swirl of afternoon dust. They caught up with the smaller band just before dusk, beneath a sky of fire and blood, and fell on them as a hawk takes the mice in the field.

The Shaman—if that's what he was—fought longest, and finally Gotha himself stepped forward after Anu took the warrior's spear in his gut.

"Ho, hunter, I will kill you now!"

The foreign Shaman only bared his teeth and thrust his bloody spear point at Gotha's face. Beyond the man Gotha saw the reason for such defiance—a boy crouched beside a torn, screaming woman, a boy with unearthly eyes.

The man must be his father, Gotha thought as he moved to the attack. It was over quickly, for the enemy Shaman was already weakened from a hand's worth of wounds. A feint, another, and Gotha plunged his weapon into his enemy's chest and brought forth a spray of hot blood.

As he stooped to wrest his spear from the ruin, something small, hard, and shrieking wrapped itself around his head and shoulders. Startled, Gotha sat down hard, and a moment later felt the squalling brat lifted away. He looked up to see the boy dangling from the fist of another hunter, whose ax was poised to bash those baby brains onto the father's corpse.

"No," Gotha said, and almost laughed at the comical way the boy squirmed, his face red with terror and rage. "Let him live. He's young, he'll forget soon enough and become one of us. Look how great his heart is! He will be a mighty hunter."

Perhaps it was the brat's green and blue eyes. Gotha never knew exactly what it was that stayed his hand, and he was to wonder over it mightily in the coming years. The eyes? Or the God? The one thing he was sure of, and even the Crone did not dispute him, was that She the Great Bitch had had nothing to do with it. Nothing.

Nothing at all.

They had stripped the men and left them to rot, raped the women, then loaded them up like pack animals with their own stolen goods for the trip back. It was a merry trek, for the small band had been well provisioned with dried meat and ground berries and fat mixed together, enough food to fill the bellies of the Tribe for at least a little time.

Truly a gift sent across the windy plains by the Snake as proof of His Power. Or so Gotha announced as the clouds built above their camp while the men argued over the spoils.

Gotha took the boy, who had lapsed into a stuporous vagueness that nothing seemed to penetrate. He left him nothing but his clout, after searching it and discovering only a small, yellowed carving of a mammoth. The carving was obviously valuable, but the boy had shown little interest in it, even when Gotha took it from him. So he wrapped it back up and returned the scrap of clothing to the brat, and thought no more of it.

Two days later, exasperated at his inability to get the boy to do anything other than wander blankly around the camp, where he frightened some of the women who suspected evil Spirits, he decided to try sterner measures.

"Carry that wood to the fire," he said gruffly.

The boy stared at him. A thin string of drool traced a silver line from the corner of his mouth. His mismatched green and blue eyes seemed empty as a sunny pond. For a moment Gotha wondered if the women were right, that some evil Spirit had stolen the boy's thoughts. He'd seen such things, and if this were the case, the only alternative would be to put the boy out of his misery. But there was a spark to the brat, and Gotha thought that perhaps it was only the shock of losing his family so violently that had rendered the boy mute and stumbling. He had seen things like this, too, and sometimes the only cure was time. But there were ways to help that along, too—and forcing the boy to take part in the daily routines of the camp was one of them.

"I said, carry those logs," he repeated, and put his face down close to the brat. "Do you understand me?"

The boy stared.

"Here." He grabbed the boy's thin arm and dragged him to the scatter of logs. "Pick these up. Carry them there."

All this with pointing and pushing.

The boy moved slowly, his features empty. Gotha finally got a single log into his grasp and sighed with exasperation as the brat stood immobile. Staring at him.

His temper got the best of him, a sudden flame, and almost without thought he backhanded the boy across the face. Shock treatment. Wake him up.

And the boy spoke. "Do not harm my Speaker," the boy said. He dropped the log. He raised his right hand and touched the reddened marks on his cheek. Slowly the arm fell to his side.

Gotha gasped. He had understood the boy's words clear as the sound of ice breaking in the winter. But the boy spoke in the secret language of the Spirits, the very tongue Gotha had learned from his own father, the only words through which a Shaman might communicate with He of Snakes and Fire.

Now he stared at the brat, who returned his gaze with limpid idiocy. Gotha shook his head. "All right," he said, and this time he spoke softly, in the same language the boy had used, "forget it. Go away. I want to think."

But the brat seemed to understand no more of this than he did of Gotha's everyday idiom. His unending vacant gaze abruptly unnerved Gotha, and once again his temper rose. He pushed the boy away. The boy stumbled bonelessly backward, tripped over his fallen log, and fell heavily, striking his head on a stone.

Gotha watched him. He writhed slowly, and the movement seemed almost snakelike to the Shaman. Then the boy looked up at him. His unsettling eyes had glazed over with pain. His lips moved.

"Shaman, you must take My People south to the rivers. I will fill your bellies and you will hunger no more."

Gotha's heart thudded. The voice filled him with horror. It was no childish piping, but rather something both deep and sibilant and somehow very distant, as if the speaker spoke across a vast gulf. In that moment he knew.

It was the God. Somehow, the God chose to Speak to

him through this brat. A fierce joy filled him then, for here was justification for all that had gone before. The Lord of Snakes and Fire had sent him an omen and a great well of Power. The Lord favored him and his People.

The Lord loved him, as He had loved his father.

And from that day forward, the People of Fire and Ice prospered.

Gotha blinked. Once again he awakened from his musings with a start, surprised to find himself alone on the prairie with his memories fading slowly into the wind.

All well and good, but now the brat was gone. Why had the Snake taken him away? It must be some sort of a test. Or a punishment, though Gotha couldn't understand why he and his People must be punished. He had followed all the God's instructions, every one.

The Gods cannot be trusted.

But sometimes they could be tricked. And everything about this—the strange woman whose eyes matched the brat's eyes, the escape of the boy, his rescue—all of it stank of the untrustworthiness of the God. The God played His tricks.

I will play mine, Gotha thought. *I will get him back. And then we will see. If only Dag had managed to bring them both back. How stupid of Dag. I will have to make sure he understands how stupid he was . . .*

The Shaman turned back and raised his voice. "Hurry up! We don't have all day."

By midmorning of the following day, the People of Fire and Ice were on the move again. The trail was not impossible—the twin marks of the travois poles they followed would hold in the dry earth for days.

More than enough time, Gotha thought as he jabbed Dag in the back with his walking stick. The tracker stumbled on, his face down, sunk in his private and public agony.

I'm coming, brat. Coming for you. And for her . . .

CHAPTER TWELVE

1

THE GREEN VALLEY

Rooting Hog, Wolf thought, much resembled his older brother, although somewhat compressed. He possessed huge, rounded shoulders, a wide midsection still corded with muscle, arms that dangled into big knobby fists, thighs like the trunks of small trees—but although he mimicked Caribou's proportions, he was much smaller than his elder brother. It was strange how little Rooting Hog and his graceful, lithe son resembled each other. Wolf knew nothing of genetics, didn't even understand that sex had anything to do with reproduction, but he did know that families more often than not resembled each other. There were other differences between the son and the father as well.

He pondered them as he faced Rooting Hog across the cold hearth inside the Chief's house. No children played here today, no women laughed, for he had sent them away for this private conversation. Rooting Hog seemed uncomfortable. He sat cross-legged and shifted from one bulky ham to the other as he waited for Wolf to say what was on his mind.

For his part, Wolf guessed that the man across from him already knew, or at least suspected, what Wolf would have to say. He had dressed himself in his best finery—a painfully new tunic of soft caribou hide scraped to exquisite thinness and cured to the consistency of butter. His hair had been dressed by one of his two women and was tied back from his broad forehead with a thong from which dangled wooden beads. He wore full trousers even in the heat, and because of this, he paid a price for his appearance. He sweated, and the stink of him filled the house with a pungent, bitter odor that even Wolf noticed above the usual smells of his dwelling.

Hot, or nervous? Wolf wondered. *Maybe a bit of both. And maybe I'm a little nervous myself. I'm about to give away my firstborn daughter, and the fact that she's the Keeper of the Stone is no help at all.*

Wolf cleared his throat, and Rooting Hog's interest perked up.

"Hot, isn't it?" Wolf said.

"Very hot, Chief. Very strange weather."

"Yes."

Silence . . .

"How is your son these days?" Wolf asked.

"Sharp Knife? He's fine. A little wild, like all the young men, but at least he's not useless, like his friend Long Snake."

Both men stared at each other, faint smiles flickering in the gloom. Long Snake's libidinous concerns were already a matter of campfire legend.

"Does that boy think about anything but his dick?" Wolf wondered.

Rooting Hog shrugged. "I doubt it. It's the only thing the Mother gave him worth the sweat off my balls."

At this, they both laughed, to cover up the pang of youth lost. "To be young again," Wolf murmured, but Rooting Hog said nothing, and the silence stretched again.

Wolf sighed. "I've heard that your son is sticking *his* dick in my daughter."

Rooting Hog's shoulders flinched at that, but he kept his chin high and stared straight at the Chief. "I have heard the same thing."

"From who? Has Sharp Knife kept you informed of his crimes?"

Rooting Hog raised his hand. "Crime is too strong a word, Chief. They are young, they get carried away—"

"Ordinarily I would agree with you. But she is the Keeper of the Stone."

Now it was Rooting Hog's turn to sigh. "I know. What are we going to do about it? What do *you* want to do about it?"

Wolf smiled faintly. "My first instinct was to remove the

offending organ from your son's body and feed it to him." He noted the way Rooting Hog's eyes narrowed at that, and forestalled him. "But I thought further, and decided that was not a good solution."

Rooting Hog's cheeks took on a pale shade of pink. He chewed at his lower lip. "So what did you decide was a good solution?" he asked, his voice suddenly ominous.

Wolf stared at him gravely. "That you and I should become Clansmen together."

Now Rooting Hog smiled at last. The relief on his face was so evident that Wolf clamped his teeth on his tongue to keep from laughing out loud.

"That is an excellent idea," Rooting Hog said.

"I thought so," Wolf replied. "But I need to know some things, my friend—and so do you. First, I've heard no rumors about you, but I want to hear it from your own mouth. Are you one of the Snake God's people?"

Rooting Hog's chin jutted out even farther. "I am not, nor is any member of my family." He paused, uncertain for a moment, as if his denial—and his admission, for that is what it was—needed further buttressing. "I was once, of course. But the Mother defeated the Lord of Snakes, and it was clear who was the more powerful of the two. And the Mother has kept my family warm, clothed, and well fed here in the Green Valley. That is good enough for me."

Wolf stared at him. "It is not, I hear, good enough for some of your people."

Rooting Hog blinked, his uneasiness plain. "I don't know—there are always a few outcasts, young fools. That's all they are. Nothing for you to worry about, Chief. I pledge you that." Another thought struck him, and his eyes widened. "You don't think Sharp Knife—?"

"No, no, I didn't say that. And if I did, we wouldn't be having this conversation. But plainly speaking now, Rooting Hog, Lord Big Dick has some new followers, doesn't he?"

"Yes. A few."

"The Shaman knows about it. I know about it."

"Too many people know about it," Rooting Hog said sourly. "And maybe don't know enough about it."

"What do you mean?"

Rooting Hog rolled his shoulders. The worst was over now. Wolf had given his permission for Sharp Knife to mate with White Moon, and had evidently decided to over-look Sharp Knife's crime of fucking White Moon without permission. The Chief seemed to have other issues on his mind, and Rooting Hog, though his squashed nose and heavy features gave the impression of stupidity, was any-thing but a stupid man.

He rubbed his nose by way of delay, while he tried to guess at what the Chief was really interested in. They'd al-ready discussed the most obvious connection between the two issues, and Rooting Hog's denial of any involvement on the part of Sharp Knife with the heretical worshipers of the Forbidden God had evidently reassured the Chief on that score.

"Do you want information?" Rooting Hog said at last. "The names of the blasphemers?"

Wolf leaned back and closed his eyes. "You misunder-stand me. I can find out such things for myself. What I want to make sure is that you understand what is involved here. I do not give my daughter to your son simply because they make a handsome pair." Now he leaned forward and regarded Rooting Hog keenly. "*You* know what Sharp Knife will become, if he mates with White Moon."

But Rooting Hog did not reply immediately. He rubbed his big hands together in a curiously touching gesture that betrayed his intense nervousness to Wolf, who was heart-ened by this display of uncertainty. It told him that Rooting Hog had not come with a flood of well-prepared words, as would any seasoned plotter.

For his part, Sharp Knife's father now understood Wolf's concerns. The Chief was, in effect, offering his support to Sharp Knife as his successor. With that unspoken admis-sion, the question now shifted to the price that the former People of the Bison would have to pay.

"I can't speak for all my tribesmen, Chief," Rooting Hog said slowly.

"I didn't say you could. But you speak for many, and the rest at least listen to you. You say you have been happy here, as part of the Two Tribes. But we must learn to live as a single Tribe, Rooting Hog. The old ways are gone. My sister is gone. Only the Stone, and the memories, remain. Do you understand what I am saying to you?"

Rooting Hog nodded, because he did understand. But he

spoke to show that he also understood exactly what the bargain entailed.

"You want to bring the Tribes together into a single Tribe, by mating the Keeper of the Stone with Sharp Knife, who will become the leader of the Bison Clan and, eventually with your support, the Chief of all the People. Very well. I agree. You know that Shaggy Elk, our current leader, is very old. What you may not know is that his words have been mine for several moons now."

But Wolf only smiled, and for an instant Rooting Hog wondered if the Chief didn't know far more than he had revealed. But if he did—well, they would speak of *that*, too, and perhaps he could lift the burden from Rooting Hog's shoulders.

"What do you want me to do?" Rooting Hog said.

"Do? I don't want you to do anything right now. Except this, Rooting Hog. Pledge to me that you share my goal of a single Tribe that unites all our People, and that you will do everything in your power to see that we succeed in reaching that goal. Will you swear that, in the name of the Mother who Keeps us all?"

"Yes, Wolf, I swear that in Her Name," Rooting Hog replied in a clear voice—and tried to ignore the sniggling little voice deep inside his skull that whispered of a yawning hole in the pledge itself.

Wolf glanced at him sharply, as if he had caught the barest echo of that same tiny voice, and for a moment it seemed he would speak. But then he simply nodded, smiled, and reached forward to clasp Rooting Hog's brawny shoulders in his own strong hands.

"Brother, we agree. I think we should bring the children together as soon as possible. To avoid any more . . . ah . . . meetings between them. Can you handle Sharp Knife?"

Rooting Hog laughed out loud. "He'll keep his Snake in his clout or I'll personally tie it in a knot he'll be a moon in undoing." And laughed again. "Seriously, he's a smart one. He'll understand. What about your daughter? I've heard his advances weren't exactly unwelcomed."

Wolf nodded grimly. "The Keeper of the Stone will keep to her house until the ceremony. Believe me on that."

Rooting Hog rocked forward on his haunches, then stood up. His head brushed the smoke-fouled roof and left a greasy streak of black on his forehead. He didn't notice. "And for the rest, we will speak of it again, my brother."

Wolf nodded. "Yes, we will. But now we will celebrate. Later, after they are mated, we will see to the rest. Two old men like us, we are still good for something."

"We're not old," Rooting Hog said. "Only the children think so. And what do they know? They're children!"

But as Wolf shepherded his would-be clansman out of the Chief's house, he thought of the Mammoth Stone and of his long-departed sister and wondered if all of them, from ancient to infant, weren't children.

"If she needs it," Maya had said. If this didn't work out, White Moon *would* need the Stone and the Power that lay hidden inside it. All the People of the Green Valley would need it.

Mammoth Clan hunters had found the body of one of their own only that morning, far out on the steppe, hideously mutilated. Wolf had never seen such marks, but Caribou had described them to him once. The Dark God, He of Snakes and Fire—they were His marks.

2

Old Berry and Muskrat waited for him in the Spirit House. When Wolf arrived the Shaman motioned him inside and, despite the unseasonable warmth of the day, carefully closed the flap behind him. Only a single shaft of light through the smoke-hole illuminated the interior of the structure, dimly reflecting off the mounds and stacks of paraphernalia the Shaman had gathered over the years.

Wolf wrinkled his nose at the concert of smells—dust and mold, sweat, smoke, herbs, the bitter odors of sickness and death, others both unknown or unnamable. Berry was already seated. She looked as if she were rooted in the earth, a great soft boulder. Muskrat squatted next to her, his eyes bright even in the gloom, and for a moment Wolf thought of a bird, not a small one, but one of the big ones that flew when the carrion began to rot. He'd known the Shaman all of Muskrat's life, and did not yet entirely trust him. Something weak there, he thought, flimsy and dangerous . . .

"Well?" Old Berry thumped her thigh and said it again. "Well?"

"The Keeper of the Stone will mate Sharp Knife, the son of Rooting Hog, at high sun on the day after tomorrow."

Muskrat cocked his head. "What did Rooting Hog say?"

"About what? He was happy."

"I'm sure he was," Berry said. "What about the . . . other things? Did he agree?"

Wolf considered. He had not yet entirely digested all the nuances of his encounter with the other man, and was still not certain that he had made the right choice. Something nagged at him, something *not right*. But what was it?

As he grasped for it, it receded from him as surely as a twig carried downriver. Then it was gone, leaving in its wake only the faintest whiff of apprehension, and then even that faded.

He had done the right thing—no, more than that—the *only* thing he could do, given the circumstances.

"He agreed. He swore to it."

"I don't know," Muskrat said. "It doesn't feel right. Once they were our enemies. And they still worship the Forbidden God. Did you tell him about that?"

"About this morning? No, I didn't. I think maybe he already knew, but we sort of agreed not to do anything about it until after the ceremony."

Muskrat spat onto the packed earth floor. "They're sacrificing people out there now. The hunter's name was Croaking Frog. He was a young one, but you knew him."

Wolf nodded. "Yes. How did it happen?"

The Shaman shrugged. "Who knows? Somebody cut him open and spilled his guts and took his heart and liver. The guts were still with him, more or less, but they didn't find the rest."

"Animals?"

"They hadn't eaten anything. He hadn't been there long."

"Where did they find him?"

"Half a day's trek away. Toward the northern camps, up by the Ice Wall. Still very cold there, of course."

"And you're certain it was the work of the Snake?"

Muskrat rubbed the side of his nose. In the wan light, lines Wolf hadn't noticed before stood out at the corners of his eyes, and curved from his nose down past the edge of his lips. "I'm not *sure* of anything. But Maya told me of Broken Fist's sacrifices, and Caribou told you. For Mother's sake, if Maya hadn't destroyed Broken Fist, you would have found out firsthand!"

"All right, all right. So let's say it *was* the work of the Snake—who of the Bison Clan were in the area?"

"Who knows? Half the Green Valley, Bison and Mammoth alike, are out on the steppe right now. It's coming on summer. Hunters' time."

Wolf chewed on it. "You're not saying that any People of the Mammoth Clan are involved?"

"I don't know what I'm saying, except that somebody is making human sacrifices to the Snake again, and it's only to be expected. We ignored it too long, Chief. Now it's gone too far."

"Maybe not," Wolf said. "Rooting Hog pledged to help me unite our two Peoples. He swore by the Mother—and I believed him."

But it was Berry who spoke the words of the tiny voice that Wolf had almost grasped. "Swore by the Mother, eh? Well, what if it's Lord Big Dick he listens to? What good is his oath then?"

Wolf stared at her. "I don't know," he said at last. "He told me he's already leading the Bison Clan, that Shaggy Elk is their leader in name only. If he has gone back to the old ways, then—" His voice trailed off and he shook his head helplessly.

"But I think he was telling the truth. I think he means to keep his oath."

"We are risking an awful lot on what you think," Muskrat muttered.

"Well, Shaman, do you have a better idea?"

Berry mumbled something.

"Eh, what? Speak up, Auntie."

"If only White Moon understood the Stone," she whispered.

"Well, she doesn't."

"If she needs it, you said Maya told you. Well, *we* need it."

Wolf spoke carefully. "We've been over this before. Whatever mistakes we have made, *if* we have made any, are long past now. We have to deal with today and tomorrow. I do wish one thing, though."

"What's that?"

Wolf smiled sadly. "That my sister hadn't left us. She would know what to do."

Berry's answering smile was almost bitter. She remembered Maya only too well. "Would she?" she asked. Then she lifted her huge, flabby breasts in a long sigh. "Well, it's too late for all of that." She glanced at Wolf, her face inscrutable as a weatherworn rock. "Will you tell the girl?"

"Yes. I'm her father."

She nodded. "I'll want to talk to her afterward."

3

I will help her if I can . . .

Old Berry recalled that promise she'd made to herself on the day White Moon had confessed her love for Sharp Knife as she now regarded the young woman who sat next to her on a well-worn log at the edge of the Jumble, with the sound of the springs liquid in her ears and the scent of onrushing summer in her nose.

White Moon was dressed in a simple robe of deerskin. She had pulled her dark hair away from her face and plaited it in a long braid that trailed down over her shoulder, accentuating her long, slender neck and high cheekbones. Her eyes glowed with the deep colors of emerald and sapphire, and all of a sudden Berry was struck by the unearthly resemblance between this girl and another, long ago. But that memory brought a pang of unease, for that joyous little girl she'd raised then had come to an unhappy life—trapped by a Power she'd not been able to understand until it was almost too late. Was a similar fate in store for this girl?

Not if I can help it, Berry thought. *I wish I weren't so old.*

"You seem very happy, White Moon," Berry said, and patted her on one knee.

"Oh, Auntie! Did you know all along? Why didn't you tell me?"

Berry smiled. "You mean about Sharp Knife? No, I didn't know. Your father only decided yesterday, after he and Rooting Hog discussed the matter." She aimed a mock-glare at the girl. "You were very bad, you know."

"Oh, I know I was, Berry. I couldn't help myself. You wouldn't understand, of course, how it was, but—" White Moon blinked. How could she explain to this old woman how Sharp Knife filled her every waking thought, made her hum to herself as she walked, brought a smile to her face at the strangest moments? *I love him,* she thought to herself, remembering the hot sensation of his tongue gliding silkily across the tips of her breasts ...

"I was young once, girl," Berry said tartly.

White Moon shot her a disbelieving glance, and for one moment Berry felt *really* old. But then she recollected her duty here, and resolutely continued.

"White Moon, you must pay attention now. I do understand—sometimes when a young man is very hand-some, the way Sharp Knife is, a young girl will forget what she should remember. That is why, when you are mated, such things are arranged by your elders. And you are lucky, for your father has decided that you are to have your wish and mate with the one you love. It might have turned out differently, and you are right to be happy. You are very lucky."

The fine muscles around White Moon's delicately rounded chin tightened then, and Berry was reminded of another stubborn young woman. "I don't care what Father decided. I would have run away with him if I had to."

"Yes, you could have done that—although I think Sharp Knife might have surprised you on that, my dear." She waved away the beginning of White Moon's objection. "But there is one thing you couldn't have run from, niece. And you know what it is."

At this White Moon turned away for a moment, as if Berry's words were something hanging in the air she didn't want to look at. But she turned back quickly enough, and Berry thought again of a kind of fearlessness she had witnessed long ago.

"You mean the Mammoth Stone?"

"Yes, niece, that is what I mean."

A silence grew between them, as White Moon marshaled her thoughts. Berry was content to let her do it, for she had just then realized they'd never really discussed what White Moon thought about her own destiny. Now she found her interest greatly piqued, for much hung on White Moon's own decisions. *And choices,* Berry thought. *If there are to be any choices.*

"I hate it!" White Moon said. "Auntie, why did Great Maya leave the nasty, awful thing with me? You were there, you must remember. Did she hate me? How could she? I was only a baby!"

All this came out in a single outraged wail, like the furious cries of a baby with a wet bottom. Berry leaned back from the force of it and blinked.

"White Moon, calm yourself! You are acting like a child."

"I don't care! That horrible old piece of bone, that's what it is, though all of you call it the Stone, and it's not a stone at all! What do you want me to do with it? I would have thrown it away long ago, but I was afraid to."

Thanks be to the Mother for that, Berry thought. But this was far worse than she'd expected. She'd imagined indifference and ignorance, but not active hate. Wiser heads, hers included, had mumbled to each other about rejection and choice, unknowing that the Keeper of the Stone had made her choice long ago. *How long?* Berry wondered suddenly. Then, *Go carefully.*

She reached out and took White Moon's fine, long fingers in her own swollen, creaking ones. "Listen to me, niece. I know you think it's unfair that you bear this burden—"

"I *won't* bear it, I *won't*!"

"Yes, yes, now be quiet a minute, dear. Let me finish. There. Are you calm now?"

White Moon sniffled once, then nodded, the color bright on her cheeks.

"Good. Now, as you say, I was there when Maya handed the Stone over to your father to keep for you. And I know what she told him then. At least I know *most* of it."

White Moon lifted her head slightly at this small admission of ignorance.

She smells a mystery, Berry thought. *Well, so do I.* "Anyway, I knew Maya, too. I knew her from the time she was born. And I can tell you this, niece. Your aunt didn't hate you. I don't think she hated *anybody.* But she did many things that you or I might not understand—maybe that even she didn't understand—because the Mother told her to do them." As she spoke, Berry wondered if the girl beside her was hearing the true message she was trying to get across.

Evidently not.

White Moon gave her head a stubborn shake. "Well, that was all to do with *her,* Auntie. It has nothing to do with me now, even if she did leave her rotten old stone, or bone, or *whatever* it is, with me. It just isn't fair to expect me to know anything about it, when none of *you* know anything. It's not fair, and I won't put up with it one minute longer."

And with that she reached into her dress and pulled out a small object wrapped in soft skin. Fingers clumsy with her anger, it took her a moment to get the thing unwrapped, while Old Berry felt her own heart begin to pound.

"Dear—Niece—*don't*!"

"Here, *you* take it, if it means so much to you!"

And Berry looked down in horror at the softly gleaming figure that tumbled onto her ample lap with a soft, thudding sound.

Plop.

She was mesmerized. Her ancient fingers moved slowly toward the gleaming thing. Only in the last instant did she manage to stop the involuntary creeping movement, and then it was the paralysis of terror that worked the trick.

"Oh, White Moon. Pick it up. *Pick it up, take it back!*"

White Moon stared at her, her eyes wide as her namesake. Some of Berry's panic must have communicated itself to her, for she retrieved the Mammoth Stone just before Berry's agitated movements would have tumbled it to the ground. Only when the Stone was safely back in the Keeper's hands did the frightening palpitations in Berry's chest begin to subside—but when she tried to speak, her chest was empty of breath, and nothing came out but a soft, deflated wheeze.

White Moon wrapped the Stone again, her lips puffing into a sullen pout. "It's nothing, Auntie. Just an old piece of bone. I don't see why you get so upset about it."

Berry felt a yawning emptiness grow in the pit of her stomach. This was worse, far worse, than she had guessed. Why, this petulant, spoiled girl was entirely capable of simply tossing the Stone into a lake. It meant *nothing* to her. They, the Elders, had turned many of their plans on

White Moon's role as Keeper of the Stone, but the Keeper herself kept nothing but a worthless trinket.

Choice? Hah! There was no choice to make, there never had been, evidently. And whose fault was that?

Mine, Berry thought. *Well, perhaps it isn't too late. She must learn the truth, understand it, accept it. I must teach her, and I don't have much time.*

Oh, Maya! Oh, Mother! Why me?

After what Old Magic and Maya and all the others had endured, it seemed to her the one true lament of the Stone.

4

Rooting Hog walked with his son along the path that meandered past Second Lake, late in the afternoon beneath a slowly purpling sky. They made an odd contrast, the father short, broad, stolid in his movements, and his son, a full head taller, slender, seeming almost to dance as he moved along.

"You have been an idiot," Rooting Hog remarked. "To think you could fuck that girl without anybody finding out. The Chief's daughter. Has a Spirit stolen your mind?"

Sharp Knife paused, stared out over the lake at a flock of ducks that floated like dark specks on the silver surface. The day smelled fine to him—the summer trees emitting the scent of pitch, the lake throwing up rich odors of clean rot and lapping water. But then, everything seemed fine today.

He felt as if he could run like the wind, leap to the top of the valley walls, even fly if he wanted to. He looked down at his father.

"I knew somebody—Wolf, probably—would find out eventually."

At this Rooting Hog blinked, then narrowed his eyes. His son's reply opened a sudden new vista for him, revealed aspects of Sharp Knife he'd never considered before. Could it be possible that the boy—? A slow grin transformed his ugly features.

"You knew? You *planned* it?"

Sharp Knife shrugged. "How else could I get the inside track? She wanted me, but I feared that Wolf would select a mate from his own Clan. It would be the normal thing to do. What do you suppose would have happened if I'd gone to him in the usual way, or had you do it, and asked for her?"

He put a hand on his father's shoulder. "You know what would have happened. He would have turned me down. But this way, he had to take me seriously. It was what she wanted, and since I was already fucking her, he only had a single choice to make. Either turn me down—and punish me for my crime—or say yes. If he'd punished me, he would have risked the wrath of our Clan, as well as the fury of his daughter."

He grinned. "I still didn't know how it would go, but I thought I had a very good chance of succeeding."

This confession dropped Rooting Hog's jaw almost to his chest. He felt an odd shock—half pleasure, half fear—a curious blend that slowly gave way to utter surprise. For a moment he stared at his son as if he'd never seen him before. "You . . . thought of this all by yourself? No one . . . helped you, told you what to do?"

Sharp Knife shook his head. His long dark hair, flowing free in the afternoon glow, shimmered softly. "No one, Father. None of my friends, none of the elders, not even you. It had to be a secret. It must remain a secret, too. I'm only telling you because now I will need your help."

Rooting Hog still couldn't believe his own ears. He'd worried that Wolf would think he'd been plotting somehow, when in fact the true plotter—and totally unsuspected—was his own son. It was an uncomfortable feeling, as if someone he'd nurtured and raised and trained and thought he knew as well as the lines on his own palm had suddenly turned into a complete stranger.

"Son—Sharp Knife—tell me everything. How did you conceive this plan? Do you understand what you are doing? What will you do now?"

The questions tumbled from his lips in a torrent, so quickly that Sharp Knife stepped back and laughed. "Slow down, Father. Let's go sit by the water. I can answer all your questions—at least I think I can. And I have questions for you, as well."

I'm sure you do, Rooting Hog thought, still stunned at this revelation. He shook his head slightly, as if to clear his vision, but he saw clear enough. And then, finally, he be-

gan to smile. He and the other Elders had worried that
Sharp Knife, who had seemed a likely enough boy, if not
particularly bright, would not prove a willing foil for their
own plans. But they'd worried for nothing, it seemed. The
boy was already far ahead of them.

Maybe too far, a small voice cautioned him. *Does the
boy understand what is at stake here? Really understand?*

He clapped Sharp Knife on the back. "Yes, we'll sit and
talk. It's about time, don't you think?" But if Sharp Knife
heard the note of remonstrance, he made no sign.

When they were seated comfortably, leaning against a
sun-warmed rock with the lake at their feet, Sharp Knife
said slowly, "I do love her, you know."

Rooting Hog glanced at him. "You are young."

"Am I? Father, someday I will be Chief of the Two
Tribes. I've known this since I was a little boy. I may be
young, but I've got an old head."

Once again, Rooting Hog stared at his son in wonder.
Where had the boy found such talents, and how had he
kept them hidden from even those closest to him? How
could he have known what the Elders had planned for him,
hoped for him? And how had he been able to perfect his
own plan, which seemed now about to reach undreamed-of
fruition?

"Son, it is good that you feel for the girl. It will make
life easier for you. But tell me something—would you have
sought to be her mate if you hadn't wanted her for herself?"

Sharp Knife shrugged. "But I do want her for herself.
It's just that she happens to be the Chief's daughter and the
Keeper of the Stone, too. It all worked out very well, don't
you think?"

Rooting Hog mulled that over. It sounded like an answer
to his question, but it really wasn't. This young man already spoke with a twisted tongue, a beautifully twisted
tongue, no doubt, but still the truth slid around it. And he
had entirely too much confidence.

"But if she'd been ugly, and had an evil temper?" he
pressed.

Sharp Knife smiled sunnily. "Yes, isn't it wonderful that
she is none of those things?"

His father sighed and left off that line of questioning.
There were other, more important things to discuss any-

way. For the first time, Rooting Hog found himself speaking to Sharp Knife as an equal. It was an odd experience, and left him feeling slightly breathless, for the boy now revealed a breadth and depth of understanding that shocked him in its thoroughness.

"Once I am mated, I hope we have a boy as quickly as possible. If the Mother blesses us, that will happen, and it will greatly smooth my path. Some of the Mammoth Clan will not approve of me, and some of the Bison will be wary of White Moon. But a boy child, with the blood of both Clans in his veins, will be acceptable to everybody. And so, because of my child, they will accept me."

Rooting Hog nodded slowly. What the boy said was true. His children would truly unite the Clans, and perhaps found a new line of Chiefs, as well. But there *was* one thing the boy had not mentioned . . .

"What about the Mammoth Stone?"

"What about it?"

"Legend says that only a woman may wield it. Your son will not be a woman. And the Stone is the Power of the Mammoth Clan. If you hope to take that Power, how will you do it?"

Sharp Knife chewed his lower lip a moment, as he sought the words. "I have spoken with White Moon of this. She says the Stone is without Power, that it is only a worthless bit of carven bone."

Rooting Hog shook his head. "She is a silly girl. She seems to know nothing of the Stone. Nor do you seem concerned either, my son, and that is a mistake. It could be a deadly mistake."

"Why is that?"

"Because the Mammoth Stone has true Power, Son. You don't know it. You were a squalling baby when it was last used, but I remember that day."

Sharp Knife's eyebrows rose a bit. "You saw? Tell me of it."

Rooting Hog shifted uncomfortably. "Well, I didn't actually see anything. There was a strange storm, a storm of Spirits that covered the camp with howling wind and driving rain, and blocked my sight."

"Ah," said Sharp Knife.

"What do you mean, 'ah'?"

"Well, you didn't actually *see* anything. Maybe the Stone had nothing to do with what happened."

"Oh, so Maya broke the bones of the Shaman Ghost and forced Broken Fist to lie on a bed of fire until he cooked? They were both men in the prime of their strength. If she did do it, it is as great a miracle as if the Power of the Stone did it."

A soft breeze stroked slow ripples across the darkening lake. Sharp Knife stared blankly at the water, and when he spoke at last he seemed to grope for the words, as if he wished to select exactly the right ones, but wasn't sure if he could.

"Father . . . it doesn't matter. It was a long time ago. Nobody remembers what actually happened now. You were there, and you saw nothing. Maya and Caribou are gone. Muskrat the Shaman might remember something, but if he does, he's never said so. I don't think the Chief knows any more than you do, and Old Berry wasn't there at all."

Rooting Hog nodded slowly. "That is so, but—"

"So if I mate with White Moon and she believes the Stone is powerless, then perhaps it is. Except as a symbol. A symbol of our mating, and of the rank of our children. Do you see now?"

Rooting Hog mulled it over. It was a new concept. Did the Stone have Power of its own, or only if someone who understood it made use of it? He had no idea. But there was another kind of power, which men who exercised it understood instinctively. He had a small portion of such understanding, and it had led him to a shadowy kind of leadership. The essence of such power was simple—what men believed to be true became the truth. Many members of the Two Tribes believed that the Stone was powerful, and therefore they feared it, though it had lain dormant for more than two hands of years. Others—a minority, it was true—believed that the Lord of Snakes had returned to them, and so they sacrificed in the old way even though it was forbidden.

He had asked three questions. How did Sharp Knife conceive his plan? Very early, it seemed, and by himself. Did he understand what he was doing? Better than Rooting Hog, who was his own father. What would he do now?

That remained to be seen, didn't it?

"What will you do now?"

"I will mate with White Moon and pray to the Mother for boy children. She will show the Stone as a mark of our strength. And . . ."

"Yes, and?"

"I will destroy those who would sacrifice to our old Lord, because they are a threat to me."

Rooting Hog blinked. "That could be very dangerous, son. Do you know who—what—you are talking about?"

Sharp Knife leaned back, crossed his legs at the ankles, and regarded the shore over the tops of his toes. "I know much, Father. And you will tell me the rest, you and the other Elders. I told you I would need your help, didn't I?"

Rooting Hog felt his thoughts begin to spin just a bit, so that the onrushing dusk seemed full of shadows where unseen things lurked just beyond the edge of his vision. When he replied, his own voice sounded flat and empty inside his ears.

"Yes. And it is true, you *will* need my help, the Chief's help, the Elders. Anybody. Because unless you surprise me even further, what you seek to destroy is far more powerful than you have possibly imagined."

Sharp Knife considered the several sources of his information, principally the unending gossip of Long Snake and the Women's House he frequented. But neither Long Snake nor the women knew everything there was to know. "Maybe," he said. "But I will do it anyway."

Rooting Hog clambered slowly to his feet, then offered his son a hand up. "I believe you might," he said. "But there are many things you must learn before you set out. The first thing is for you to meet with the Elders of the Clan, the sooner the better. Will you do that first, before anything else?"

"I will, Father."

"Good. I will speak to them tonight. What will you do?"

"I want to be by myself for a while, I think. I may walk down to the mouth of the valley and look at the steppe."

"Don't try to see White Moon!"

"No, Father, don't worry. I'm not stupid."

As he said this, the full wonder of what his son had become washed over Rooting Hog like a great soft wave, and he shook his head and said, "No, I don't think you are."

CHAPTER THIRTEEN

1

Maya felt as if she had sweated all the water from her body, leaving nothing but dried-out flesh and a ringing emptiness between her ears. When she looked up from the ground in front of her, the sun burned blinding circles into her eyes.

"I have to stop," she said.

Caribou halted immediately. He didn't like the note of apology in her voice, nor did he understand where she'd found the strength to shoulder the travois pole all the day before and half the day now. He was exhausted, his muscles tense and numb at the same time. What must she be feeling?

Letting down the travois pole was one of the most exquisitely pleasurable things he'd ever done. They stared at each other. He felt a sluggish kind of shock as he looked at her, really *looked* at her for the first time since she'd killed the big hunter.

She looked older. The streaks of white in her hair that he'd grown used to were larger now, blending into each other. Soon her hair would be all white, he thought.

The lines on her face, especially the pair that bisected her cheeks from her nose to the curve of her jaw, were deep shadowed grooves, dark as the puffy, bruiselike swellings beneath her eyes.

Yet despite all this, she still looked strong, as the determination that had always been inside her slowly made its way to the surface of her skin and transformed her. Strong and fearsome, like the way he sometimes imagined the Mother must look, perhaps *had* looked on the day She'd entered the World to crush the Lord of Snakes and his servants.

Yet she was tired. She stood before him swaying slightly, and it took a moment to realize she was right on the edge of collapsing. Then he stepped forward and took her shoulders in his hands and said, "Here, you have to sit down."

She smiled at him, tiredly, gratefully, and let him lower her gently to the earth. He joined her and for a moment they simply luxuriated together in the absence of effort. After a time she turned to the travois, where the boy had either tossed in fever or thrashed about, moaning, in rivers of sweat, the whole time they had dragged him along.

She armed her brow, leaving a greasy, dusty streak behind. "We're going to have to stop anyway, Caribou. I have to try to help him." She paused, glanced about uneasily. "Do you think anybody has followed us?"

They had headed north after Caribou had rolled Ulgol's heavy body under some bushes, cut poles for a travois, and salvaged what he could from the packs the two men had left strewn about. They had marched until shortly after dusk, whereupon Caribou had chewed a bit of dried meat—*dead man's meat*, he'd thought at the time—and then sunk like a rock into a black pool of sleep. Today had been more of the same mindless plodding, with the weight of the boy seeming to grow heavier by the minute.

Their path had more or less paralleled the river, but at a distance—there were mud flats and treacherous bogs if you ventured too close, so they stayed well away and forged on through the swath of dry, rolling grassland that divided the darker woods from the hidden water. Only the sound remained, a deep, bone-humming rush that filled the air with ominous, beautiful music.

He shaded his eyes and looked back down their path, which was easy enough to spot. Two thin lines bisected the grass, marking where the travois poles had furrowed the earth.

"I don't think so," he said finally. "Most likely, if they got on our trail quickly enough, they would have found us by now. But I don't think that one that got away was in any shape to be in a hurry. I think he's probably dead by now. He was bleeding like a speared pig."

Maya shivered. She could still remember the sound Caribou's spear had made when she'd rammed it into Ulgol, and worse, the liquid creaking noise when Caribou had twisted it out. She had seen no such violence since the Shaman Ghost's death and the battle before it when Caribou had killed Spear. So much now reminded her of the past— and few of those memories were happy ones.

The Mother loves blood, she thought suddenly. _She hungers for blood and She doesn't care how She gets it._

She shook her head. "I think we should go down by the river and make a camp. I'll need water, and I want to look for certain herbs."

He nodded. Then he glanced at the boy who at this point neither thrashed nor moaned, but lay as still as a dead man. "Why, Maya? Why do you care so much about one sick brat, and not even of our Tribe?"

She realized then that she hadn't told him of the new Stone she'd found, and even as she opened her mouth to speak, she closed it again. For some reason she didn't want to reveal the Stone's existence. Not yet. It wasn't time.

Is it You again, Mother? This is Your doing, isn't it? It's too bloody, too strange, for anything else. You are here with me now, aren't You? Why won't You Speak to me?

"His eyes are like mine," she said slowly. "I think I am meant to save him. That's why I was made to lay down my Shaman's robes and leave my People. To come to that place and find him and heal him."

Caribou watched her. "And bring him to the Green Valley?"

After a moment she nodded. "Yes, I think so."

He didn't say anything for quite a while. Then he sighed. "Well, we'd better go. If we hurry, you'll have time to find your herbs before dark. Will you want a fire?"

"Yes."

"Then over there, I think. Those trees are close to the water."

She followed his pointing finger. _Mother, I feel tired._ "Let's get going."

After they both climbed slowly to their feet, it took them several minutes to work the cramps from their calves and thighs and take up the poles again. The boy hardly stirred when they resumed the trek, but two bright red spots that smoldered on his pale cheeks proclaimed that he still lived. For a while, at least . . .

2

They found a likely spot where a long finger of forest petered out almost on the riverbank, which at that point was solid enough, though rocky. Caribou quickly discovered a game trail nearby, and decided that he would hunt the next day—but not today.

"Unless you want me to do something, I'm going to lie down right here and sleep until the sun comes up tomorrow."

She smiled and touched his seamed, haggard features. He looked ready to fall down. "Don't worry about me," she told him. "Get some rest." She glanced at the boy. "I don't know how long we'll be here. I don't know how long it will take."

He followed the direction of her glance. "Do you think you can do it? I've never seen anybody so bad off and still live. The Spirit that has taken him must be terribly hungry. It is eating the flesh right off his bones."

"I don't know. If I am meant to save him, then I will. If not—" She shrugged wearily. "Then he will die, and it will all have been for nothing."

"Are you sure you don't need me?"

"I need to find my herbs." She turned her head and eyed the trees. Shrubs grew beneath the canopy, and intermixed with the bushes, a profusion of smaller, bright-leafed plants. "This is a good spot, Caribou. I will do my best."

She sighed. "I wish I still had my Spirit Tent. I was only able to bring a few things, and much of that those hunters ruined."

Caribou remembered the reek of urine on their destroyed camp. Well, they had paid. "Maya, I hope this is right."

"I hope so, too. We'll just have to see."

He opened his mouth in a yawn so wide his jaws creaked. She laughed softly and patted his cheek. "Sleep now, my love. I'll keep watch."

It took her most of the afternoon to find what she wanted—a single green stalk thick with cheerful orange berries, some dusty gray leaves, a handful of roots that were purple on their rough exteriors, but creamy white on

the inside. She kindled a fire close to the comatose boy and
then sat for a while beside him, one hand resting lightly on
his neck, where her fingers listened to the beat of the Spirit
within. It was weak and thready, failing in its struggle
against the invading Spirit, and she wondered if it wasn't
already too late.

*Mother, You will have to help me if you want me to do
this thing,* she thought. She straightened her shoulders.
This would be the toughest battle she'd ever fought, wrestling with the Demon that was destroying this helpless
child.

She leaned back and massaged her own throbbing forehead. The sun was a furnace, but no hotter than the boy's
cheeks. He was a mess. For a moment she simply sat and
looked at him, her trained eyes ticking off the signs she understood. The old scars were plain enough—because of his
fever, they stood out in thin, pink patterns that covered almost all of his body. Much of it looked like whip marks to
her. He looked to have been beaten almost constantly his
entire life. Then there were the fresher wounds—bruises
fading to dull purple-yellow patches, scabby cuts and
slashes. His right leg, swollen to nearly twice the size of
his left, was the worst problem of all.

The suppurating ulcer on his thigh was where the Demon had entered him, and it still was there, festering deep
beneath the entrance wound. It was this she would have to
conquer, she and her herbs and experience and luck. *But
I've seen worse,* she thought. *Not often, and I didn't always
heal it. But sometimes . . . if She helped.*

It took her a while to make a fire. She'd decided her arm
wasn't broken, only badly bruised and stiff, but each effort
she put it to quickened the dull, throbbing ache that radi-
ated from the ugly black-and-blue knot on it.

Thank the Mother it's only my left arm, she thought
tiredly. After the fire had begun to crackle merrily, she
trudged to the river and filled the water bags. Heating water in bags was tricky, but it could be done. She waited until the stones she'd piled over the burning wood began to
smoke and snap in the heat. Then, carefully, she balanced
them out with two heavy sticks—the agonized protest from
her arm brought tears to her eyes—and dropped them hissing into the bag she'd propped open with another stick. She
took the bag by its neck and began to shake it gently, to

keep the hot rocks from resting against the wet leather and
burning through it. Finally steam began to puff from the
bag and, after a time, a fragrant, herbal smell. She dipped
one finger into the soupy tea and nodded to herself. It
tasted right. Now to get some into him.

She took a piece of soft hide and soaked it until it was
mushy with the hot liquid. She had to push his lips open to
get the makeshift twist into his mouth. His lips felt dry and
swollen, and the inside of his mouth was arid as a desert.
The moisture awakened some deep reflex in him, and
slowly he began to suck. Almost like a baby, she thought,
astonished at how melancholy that thought made her feel.
In fact, for one instant she felt almost completely un-
manned, and wondered why she should feel that way. Had
she not borne children, several of them? Yes, she had. But
they were gone now, left behind by the will of the Mother,
who cared nothing for children, families, or loss. *She* only
cared for Her own concerns.

A pent-up warmth flowed out of her then, compassion
for this ruined child, even love, though she tried to tell herself *that* was silly, she didn't even *know* him. Yet try as she
did to deny it, she couldn't banish the realization that she
did love him, as deeply as she had ever loved any of her
own sons and daughters.

"My son," she whispered, and knew it was true, even
though it was untrue in any sense she understood the words
to be.

He mewled softly, his lips pressing at the wet hide. A
thin string of drool glistened on his chin. At least he still
had that much juice left in him.

After a while she replenished the herbal tea-tit, and then
set to work on the heart of the matter—the bloated, oozing
wound on his thigh.

First she bent down and put her nose right to it and inhaled deeply. She smelled a dark, rotten odor, like decom-
posing meat—and that was exactly what it was, she
thought, that stink rising from the edges of the wound,
which had turned black and sickly shining. Deeper into the
center the pus leaked out, thick as honey, but with bits of
clear mucus floating in it. A Demon's soup, she thought.

*Get it out. It might kill him right here, but if I don't clean
it out, it will kill him later, and not much later at that.*

She got up, went over to Caribou, and bent down again.

Caribou had rolled himself into a tight bundle on the ground, but she could reach the pack beneath his head easily enough. It took a moment to find the knife, and he snorted softly in his sleep but didn't wake up.

She carried the knife back, examining it as she went. The chipped edges had gone dull—too dull for what she needed. She set the knife down and walked slowly to the rocky verge of the water, feeling the strong rushing power of it deep in her guts. Finally she found a likely piece of rock. It was shaped the right way, though she would have preferred her old wood tools, the ones Stone had first taught her to shape flint with, so long ago.

As she sat cross-legged with the knife point down, wedged against a flat stone and steadied gingerly with her left hand, she remembered as plain as day Stone's oft-repeated instructions, almost like a chant humming in her head.

It's the pressure, not the stone. Find the right spot and push just enough, and the rock will flake away. The edges are hidden inside the flint, Maya. You have to find them and let them come out.

And so she pushed the smooth, rounded stone she'd found against the edge of Caribou's knife, and after a time she *did* see the edge inside, and pressed a little harder, and with a soft, clicking sound a bit of flint fell away and the edge was there. She squeezed her lips together in concentration as she worked, and only relaxed when she had finished. She ran the meat of her thumb down the wavy edge and felt it *almost* cut her flesh, and knew it was sharp enough now.

She settled herself again and felt the boy's forehead. It was cooler now and slick with sweat. The tea had done its work. More often than not, it would drive out the Fire Spirit when it got to burning inside a person's body. That, she knew, would be a help.

Once again she simply stared at him, storing him up. It was as if she needed to get a picture of him, with his tiny birdlike bones almost poking through his tortured flesh, that somehow moved *inside* her skull—and that was a part of it, too. It might even become the hardest part. Doubly hard, because she didn't know if she still had it in her to do it.

Well, cross that stream when it came time.

If Caribou had awakened at that moment—and he didn't,

though if he had, certain things might have made sense to him later on—he would have seen a strange tableau. He would have seen Maya crouched over the boy, his head cradled on her lap, and a fierce, *intent* expression on her face, so that her features seemed shadowed and dark even in the high tide of the sunlight. And he would have thought once again how *strong* she looked, like some ancient, weary, *indestructible* old bird, and if he'd thought about it a moment longer, he might have felt a thrill of fear run cold fingernails up the slate of his spine, for even though it was Maya, it was also *something else* sitting there, its miscolored eyes burning with relentless compassion.

"*Papa,*" the boy muttered. She heard it clearly, again in the tongue of the Spirits, and wondered what dreams might be roaring behind his closed eyes. For a moment she almost decided to lift his eyelids with her fingertips, to see if anything peeked back out at her, but she didn't. For the moment it was better not to know. The need to *know* would come soon enough, and contemplating that coming time spread a blot of fear in the core of her, because of what that *knowing* would involve.

She hefted the knife blade in her right hand and thanked the Mother once again that her left arm was the one banged up. If it had been her right, the boy would be as good as dead. But it wasn't, and so she sighed and pushed her hair out of her face—*Look how gray it is!* (but it wasn't gray, it was white)—and bent to work.

She had prepared a hot paste of herbs and water that she let cool enough so that she could hold a wad of it clumsily in her left hand. She placed this on a leaf nearby, where she could get it when she needed it. She squinted against the sunlight, put her face down close to his leg, and probed with the point of the knife at the center of the wound. At first she poked gently, and when he didn't stir—the tea she had given him dulled pain as well as broke fevers—she clenched her lower lip in her teeth and quickly carved a cross deep into the swollen abscess.

The result was like hitting a bag of raw meat with an ax. Thick, stinking blood exploded into her face. A smell like a rabbit dead ten days, sweet and putrid, erupted from the fresh cuts, along with such a gush of yellow, rotting mucus that she wouldn't have believed it possible without seeing it with her own eyes.

The boy screamed.

At least, he tried to. What came out was a muted groan that barely carried the distance to her ears.

She ignored his protest, wiped the rancid bloody slime from her face, and took his thigh into both her hands. She gritted her teeth against her own pain as she kneaded the flesh like dough, grimacing as more of the demon juice spewed forth. Finally, clean bright blood began to flow. Quickly she packed the wound with the thick, purplish paste. When she finished, she took a length of deerskin and wrapped it tightly around his leg to hold the poultice in place.

Finally she rocked back, dizzy with weariness. But it wasn't over yet. The worst was yet to come.

"I got your juice, Spirit," she whispered. "Now for your soul."

She stood up, ignored the chorus of creaks and pops from her knees and various other joints, and set off for the river. The demon's brew of dark juices was in her hair, on her hands and arms, oozing slowly beneath the top of her coat and sliding like warm snot down between her breasts.

She wanted the feel of clean water on her skin desperately. Pinching her nostrils shut, she went down to the water and stripped off her clothes and swirled them in the eddying currents by the shore. Then, holding on to a man-sized boulder firmly embedded in the bank, she lowered herself into the chill water and stayed there until her teeth began to chatter uncontrollably. Only then did she step out into the lengthening shadows of the afternoon, retrieve her clothes, and plod back to lay them by the fire to dry.

She sat naked by the flames, hugging her knees, her head resting on her arms, utterly drained. The bone-weariness she felt was unlike anything she'd ever experienced. Every part of her ached, except her head, which felt both numb and without weight—as if it might float away from her body. She knew that all she had to do was relax her pose, stretch out by the inviting warmth of the fire—it was growing cooler now—and she would be asleep in an instant. And she probably wouldn't awaken until the sun returned the next morning. But that, of course, would be too late. Far too late. The boy would be dead then, for it wasn't enough to leach the demon juice from his body.

Something else remained, something dangerous, and not only for him.

Dangerous for her, too.

She pushed the thought away and began to make her preparations. The bright orange berries were so pretty, she thought, as she crushed them into a new kind of tea—not for the boy, this time, but for her.

The brew was bitter. She thought that was fitting. The brew of her life had *always* been bitter.

She stretched out next to him, so that their bodies touched. His skin felt cool and lifeless. His chest barely moved. He might as well have been dead, and he would be, she thought, if she couldn't do this thing. Her last thought, before the World slipped away, was simple.

Mother, if this is Your doing, then help me now!

3

The light came first, dim and shadowy, and she floated in it. Her mind seemed divided into two parts. The first, and smaller, part stood away from the rest of her and spoke in calm, cool tones. This part seemed concerned with observation only. It was like a tiny watcher, and she often had the feeling that this portion was like a new limb, only recently added to the rest of her. What remained, the far larger piece of her, melted into the Dream and sometimes wasn't able to hear the smaller part at all.

Yet it was this lesser, newer part that spoke first, in cool, serene, almost disinterested tones: *You have to bring him here.* The voice receded then, and she gave her greater self to the slowly swirling light.

Carefully she unfolded the mental picture of the boy she'd stored up earlier. At first it was a dim, murky thing, only a darker shape that floated before her in defiance of the currents of light.

She concentrated, willing detail to emerge: his eyes, the shape of his brow, his long black hair. It took an almost physical effort. She wanted to *reach out* to him and shape the formless blur into the simulacrum she sought, but she knew that wouldn't work. Only when she had summoned him fully into her Dream could she face him on her own terms.

Slowly, then, the curve of an eyebrow. Then an eye, blue. The other followed, an emerald catching the light. The beak of his nose, bent slightly from an ancient injury. Wings of dark hair, floating.

A face. His face, shining on a body of smoke.

It went faster then, as she added more and more detail.

Spindly arms, long delicate fingers, ribs as stark as winter trees. The slow pelvic curve, hollow beneath his stomach. Finally legs, knobby knees, feet.

She felt more than heard a soft clicking sound, like two small stones snapping together, and then he was there. In this light the wounds on his thigh pulsed redly, as if a fire had burned down to coals in his flesh.

He was there. And now, so was something else. She saw it immediately, for she had expected it, but even so, its appearance made her throat tighten and sent a chilly quaver through her muscles.

It began as a wisp of smoke rising lazily from the glowing wound on his thigh. The smoke was strange, glimmering, full of iridescent color, not really dark at all. It was transparent, but somehow it possessed a weird kind of solidity, and she knew it was quite real, at least in this place.

It ascended from the wound with sinuous grace, making her think of snakes, though she knew it wasn't a snake. No, this was a lesser Demon, a malevolent Spirit but not the Great Power she knew of old. One of His minions, perhaps.

The glittering fume spread slowly into a fanlike hood that hovered over the boy, and in it, glaring out at her, two red eyes. Furious eyes, bubbling pits of rage.

You don't like it, do you? she thought.

Almost as if in reply, a spot of darkness yawned beneath those eyes, and from it issued a howl of such savagery she thought her ears would break. Then came the breath of the thing—a thick, hot cloud whose stench sharply reminded her of a childhood memory.

It had been when Old Magic still lived, before her life had shattered into a hundred broken bloody pieces, back in the time when she still went to the Spirit House every morning. On that particular morning Old Magic was having one of his better days, and he emerged from his abode with an energetic light in his faded eyes and an unaccustomed spring in his step. They would, he announced, go for a walk.

She'd been a girl then, a special girl though she hadn't understood *that,* but what she had understood was that under no circumstances was she *ever* to leave Home Camp by herself, or even with her playmates. So while they ran wild and free through the nearby woods, discovering interesting rocks and bugs and blossoms, laughing and shouting in their untrammeled liberty, she had to stay behind, unless Berry or Old Magic wanted to go with her. Which they usually didn't, for they were too busy stuffing her girlish skull with the lore of generations—and while that knowledge was often interesting, it was sometimes dry as dust. So Magic's announcement was cause for joy.

"Oh, Uncle—" she called him that, though he really wasn't, just as she called Berry "Auntie," though she wasn't either—"can we go all the way to Second Lake? I want to see the ducks."

He had smiled and nodded in his old man's way, the wattles of flesh at his neck bobbing loosely, and said, "That is exactly where we are going, little Maya." Then he'd gone on about certain herbs that grew only near the lake, and how they would gather some and he would explain—but she heard no more. She skipped out ahead of him beneath a perfect morning sky, and thought about herbs not at all while he hobbled slowly behind her, grumbling good-naturedly and calling out to her to *slow down* and *wait for him.*

And they had indeed found the herbs he sought, a dark green patch of them growing almost out of the water, fat white bulbs at their base, but they had found something else, too. Rather, Maya's nose had found something.

At first she'd thought it was simply part of the lake smell, a rich and deep odor comprised of mud and the things that rotted in mud, but as they grew close, the odor took on a harsh brownish-yellow urgency. Magic didn't seem to smell it at all, but she understood that. He was old, and sometimes absentmindedly ate even spoiled meat without noticing.

He was mumbling something about the yellowish underside of a stalk of weed he was waving like a fan, but she wasn't listening. She *couldn't* pay attention. The stink was so strong it was like a loud noise drowning out the old Shaman's lesson for the day, and she knew that she would remember nothing until she discovered the source of that horrendous reek.

It wasn't hard. She simply followed her nose. And wished later that she hadn't.

"Ugh."

The old man had finally noticed that she was paying him no heed, and had hitched over to her in that old man way of his, where he seemed to *lift* first one leg and set it down carefully, then *lift* the other and do likewise. It took forever, or so it seemed to a girl who moved as quickly and gracefully as a doe in the springtime, but finally he reached her and began, "Maya, what's the matter with you, you silly girl? You have to listen to me, how do you ever expect to learn any—"

Mutely she pointed at the thing at her feet. He looked down.

"Ugh," he said.

"Ugh" seemed to be the only response anybody could make to the forlorn nest half-hidden in the dripping greenery at the edge of the water.

Something had killed the mother duck, perhaps a malign animal Spirit, for the corpse was undisturbed. Sometimes other animals wouldn't eat flesh that had died that way. She had been on her nest for a reason—one of her eggs had burst open beneath her, its filling hardening into a viscous greenish slime that glistened evilly in the sun.

The bugs marched in and out of her eye sockets in a long procession, their brown carapaces slick and shiny. Her feathers had gone dull, so that she looked dusty and gray. A few stuck up, left that way by the wind. One single webbed foot, also gray, but shrunken and twisted, poked out.

"Ugh," Magic said again. "Get a stick, Maya. Don't touch it, just push the nest into the water."

She found a likely branch, broke it off, returned. But her stomach was heaving queasily and she didn't want to look at the horrible thing, so as she poked at the nest her aim was off and the point of the stick struck the pitiful duck instead. Struck and *entered* the body, which seemed to be full of some hideous gelatin.

She gagged and pushed harder, and finally with a low,

ripping, *sickening* noise the whole glutinous mass tipped out and plopped into the water.

In pieces.

The stench that had arisen then was the awful memory this monstrous whiff of demon breath brought back to Maya now. She wanted to turn away, but that would be fatal, for the boy, perhaps even for her. In this half-world where Shamans and Spirits could meet, you never turned your back on a Demon.

Especially not one with great yellow dripping fangs, a tongue like a lump of swollen, sickly red meat lolling between those fangs, and spurlike claws as long as her fingers.

It towered over the boy, seemed to crouch on him as if she'd interrupted its feeding. Which was exactly what she had done.

If it's anything, it's a wolf, she thought as she stared at it with awe. She'd never seen a Demon Spirit so huge, so full of rage and hunger. *How did the boy survive this long?*

The coat of the beast was torn and matted, clumps of twisted, metallike hair springing out, bulging in unlikely places over misshapen clots of muscle and bone. The thing exuded an overwhelming aura of power, a black, exploding rage, an inexhaustible hunger, and now it turned its insane boiling eyes on her, as if it saw her for the first time.

Be careful now, that still, remote voice whispered in her ear, sounding thin and drawn, as if it had been stretched over some unimaginable distance.

Oh, yes, she thought. She willed herself toward the towering thing, and now it reared up, its grotesque paws clicking bunches of claws in and out, in and out, with a sound like bones being shaken in a bag. Smoke dribbled from its distended nostrils, and a rue of bloody fire began to leak out the sides of its jaws and trace a smoldering path through the rusty thatch of its muzzle.

Another wave of grotesque stenches smote her full in the face as she approached it. The boy at her feet seemed shrunken and far away, a tiny doll caught like a discarded plaything between the two of them. She spared him a single glance and saw that he still slept, pale and waxy as a corpse, two unhealthy bright spots burning on his cheeks.

Now she could hear the bellows thunder of the beast's lungs, and the gale of its reeking breath tugged at her hair, scorched the lashes around her eyes. Its claws, sharp as new-broken bones, clicked and clacked at each other.

Let him go! she shrieked suddenly. *He is mine now, not yours. Leave him! Get out of him!*

The awful howling that ensued nearly shattered her ears, and then, with preternatural suddenness, the beast sprang upon her, its mighty thighs pistoning as the talons there sought the soft meat of her belly while its snapping jaws bore down toward her throat.

She grasped it just behind its forepaws and pushed it back while it screamed in fury. Fire bloomed suddenly in its gullet, a new red tongue that blistered the skin on her face, but Maya wrestled on, pitting the strength of her years, of the Power she'd gathered over those years, against the Power she despised.

Down, beast! DOWN, *I say!*

But it fought her, even as her voice tore at it and wounded it terribly. The sound blasted one eye clean out of its skull, and ripped great chunks of smoking flesh from its heaving chest, yet it fought on, its frenzy unabated. If anything, its wounds galvanized it to greater strength, and it twisted against her grip while it barked and growled and rumbled its hate.

Yet Maya felt she was winning, felt the strength of the beast begin to ebb, and for a moment she allowed herself a small feeling of triumph.

You know your mistress, beast! she screamed at it as she forced it backward, away from the boy. The rope of smoke that connected it to the wound on the boy's leg stretched, thinned and she knew it was close to snapping, and she thought, *One more good shove,* and—

The walls of the Dream World cracked apart.

Power roared in from everywhere, fantastic jagged bolts of light that struck the beast again and again and filled it from snout to tail with a strength so terrible that Maya felt her own bones breaking beneath the weight of it.

Fangs like bloody spears closed around her, shook her as a bear shakes a rat, and flung her away. It was that quick, a single toss, and she felt herself falling, falling out of the Dream World.

Nooooo!

But it was over and she had lost, she knew, and a great

sadness filled her. Too old, too tired. She had failed. The boy would die now.

Papa?

The tiny cry cut through that raging well of Power with a force so absolute, so complete, that for an instant everything stopped.

And into the utter silence—

Papa, where are you? I'm so tired . . .

That plea, so lost, so lonely, tore at her heart. Somehow she gathered the rags of her strength and righted herself. The beast, oddly diminished, loomed over the tiny form, which had not moved at all as far as she could tell. Nevertheless, she had no doubt it was the boy himself who had spoken.

My son! she thought, and threw herself forward once again, heedless of the churning Power that enveloped the beast as it rose to meet her new attack.

This time their clash shook the very foundations of the Dream, and for an instant she saw the real World, saw two fingers stretched out next to each other as the dead would lie upon the ground, and then the vision vanished and she fought in the heart of the beast while it ravened all about her, continually renewed by the surging waves of force that battered in from every corner of the Dream World.

She vised her hands around its neck, and though it roared at her touch, it seemed unable to escape. Tighter and tighter she drew the noose of her fingers while its molten eyes bulged like bubbles filled with fire.

And then she felt it come, a very tornado of Power. Her hair stood out from her skull, spitting and snapping with tiny lightnings. The beast was renewed once again. Its mighty neck expanded with a single jerk and broke her hold.

Ah, Mother, He comes, Your ancient enemy is upon me now. Come to me, Mother! Come now!

But as a terrible, claw-studded paw raked across her belly, and she felt the awful warm-cold-empty sensation of her own bowels spilling out, she knew her prayer had not been answered.

I will die in this place . . .

It was a forlorn thought, but she knew it was true. It was the great danger of these things, and all Shamans feared it.

Anything was possible in the World of Dreams, even the death of the Dreamer itself.

She fell heavily against the boy's body, draped across it, her guts spilling out and soiling his alabaster skin. One hand flopped across his pelvis, thumped on something hard, rolled away.

It was all she could do to think, but somehow she managed it. *What?* His pouch. Even in the Dream he wore his pouch, and something hard was inside it. Her fingers scrabbled, reached inside, touched the bony little figurine—

No, the vast calm voice tolled, *it is mine.*

The light was dying from her eyes as she rolled off him and stared up into the slavering jaws of the beast. But even that dread creature must have heard *something,* for its vast muzzle withdrew. It cocked its head as if trying to hear something perhaps too high for any other ears, but then, as suddenly as it had withdrawn it snapped forward again.

And stopped.

For the boy stood between them, the boy and . . . *something else.*

She couldn't see anything but the boy's slim form, though she knew he did not stand alone. But he did stand, and his eyes were open, and in his hand was his Mammoth Stone, and it *glowed* with the light of a thousand stars.

He paid her no attention, did not so much as glance at her. His attention was for the beast. But he didn't wrestle with it. He merely stared at it for a long moment, and then, with a tiny shake of his head, said, "I am not yours. You may go now."

And with that he reached down and, almost gently, took the cord of smoke that bound the beast to him, and snapped it with a single motion.

"You are free now," he told it.

All around her she heard the ancient familiar sound of vast doors slamming, the sound of them shaking the foundations of all the Worlds at once.

Somehow the beast was gone. Only she and the boy remained.

He stood over her as she lay across his body *(What? How can that be?),* and now he was turning to look down on her and she would see his face. *Suddenly she was as afraid as she'd ever been, and then—*

"Maya! Wake up! Are you all right?"

Caribou's seamed face, full of concern, swam into her watery vision. She felt cold as ice, and no wonder. It was dark. A sky full of clean stars twinkled down at her. He had stoked up the fire, the light of which danced merrily on his features, and for a moment she wondered what had happened. Unbidden, her hands strayed to her belly, feeling for the awful wound that was there, but she felt only smooth skin.

"Come sleep with me," Caribou whispered. "I'll keep you warm. You were making awful noises." He paused, as if seeing something in her eyes, then continued. "Don't worry about the boy. I covered him up. He seems to be much better now, by the way. The swelling in his leg is gone, and he is sleeping easily."

He shook his head. "Will you come with me?"

She could only nod. He helped her up and half carried her to their bedroll. The weariness that had stalked her for days finally pounced, and she was asleep almost as soon as she'd gotten herself snuggled against his warm, hairy hide.

Only a single thought, one she didn't understand at all: *It wasn't the Mother. I don't know what it was, but it wasn't Her.*

CHAPTER FOURTEEN

1

Dag thought that death must be a lot like this. Death must be hot and dry and lonely and full of pain and endless effort. And no hope at all. Maybe this *was* death, this long, slow, stumbling march through the parched grass along the river, while his wounds rotted deeper into his body, and his fevers wrapped him in the veils of waking dream.

The People of Fire and Ice followed a single pair of tracks with dogged concentration; or, rather, they straggled along behind Dag, whom Gotha had placed at the van as he had promised earlier. In his dreamlike way Dag understood; it was his punishment to lead them until the moment of his death, and in some even stranger way he thought that was fitting. No matter that his world had shrunk to those two parallel trails, which meandered along the river like the imprint of some endless invisible snake. He had made his choice before the God long ago, or at least it seemed long ago, though it had only been a few days, and his choice had been to kill the woman. But he had failed, and so even though he might have made the right decision, he had not succeeded, and now the God was exacting His punishment.

In the World, he thought, the price of failure was always death. His would come soon enough. In the meantime, the tracks remained, and he followed them.

2

Gotha stared at the Crone and thought about the price of things as well. What price had *she* paid in the service of *her* Goddess? He could see the outward manifestations well enough, the shrunken body, the twisted limbs, the empty festered eye socket. And more and more she had begun to reveal a harder payment, for it seemed to him that her Bitch Goddess was slowly stealing her wits and leaving nothing but babbling emptiness in their place.

"What are you raving about?" he said in exasperation as a chain of drool caught the firelight in a glittering web on her chin.

"We are doomed," she muttered, her good eye flashing white in the shadows, but oddly canted, seeming not to see him at all. "Doom, doomed, all doomed." She paused, and then her ancient head came up, the tendons in her withered neck straining with effort. *"Turn back before it's too late!"*

Gotha, who had leaned closer in order to understand her mumblings, jerked back in disgust, and wiped frantically at the spray of spittle that befouled his face.

"You old witch!" He raised his fist—but dropped it again as she cowered away, her diseased gums glistening.

"Don't you hit me! I'm not your brat. I don't speak for you, but for Her!"

The revulsion he felt was so strong it was almost physical. For a moment he thought he saw worms, soft white squirming things, crawl from her eye socket, and his stomach clenched into a fist that belched up and gagged in his throat.

He blinked in horror. But then it was only a trick of the light, or the night, or his own overheated loathing of her, and after a moment he was able to force himself to relax.

"You're crazy," he said finally, when he was certain he could control his voice. "The Lord takes His vengeance on you."

His judgment seemed to summon her back from whatever dark fantasy had claimed her, and her good eye screwed its focus onto him.

"Does He? I don't think so. I'm paying for my crimes against Her, but I don't care. When I've paid enough, She will raise me up again. Raise me so high your filthy Snake, who slithers in the muck, even He will fear me."

She pronounced this heresy in such tones of level certainty, as if she were no more than describing the weather, that Gotha flinched. Was it a prophecy, or were her words only the ramblings of an old woman, the murderer of her own mate, now finally sinking into the bitter twilight before death?

He was surprised to discover that the question meant more to him that he would have guessed, for it touched on even greater questions: What had happened to his life, and why?

In short succession he'd lost the fount of his Powers, been compelled to question his own God more sharply than ever before, and then uprooted from his reasonably pleasant existence to begin a chase after an ominous woman who represented—what?

What did all this mean? Was he being punished in some way? If so, for what? And even more important, by whom?

The Gods cannot be trusted.

Suddenly it seemed that the Crone faded away. She disappeared beyond the mists of his sudden concentration, while the wind blew long and the stars lit the sky above. He hunched forward, and stared at the red-gold coals beneath the flames—and somehow those coals summoned him into a place of fire, a place he'd never visited before, but which he knew as surely as he knew the confines of his own house.

For this place was a house, too, a House of Fire, and in it lived its Lord, who was his Lord as well. But it was a strange place, and a part of him that stood away from the rest was aware of that strangeness, so like a Dream, until he realized with a start that it *was* a Dream.

"A Great Dream," he murmured, and the Crone's eye widened at that, but he didn't see, for his own eyes were closed, the eyelids flickering faintly in the movement common to all Dreams.

She knew the signs. She's seen them a hundred times before, but this time cold sweat covered her forehead and shivered down the gray saggy flesh of her arms. She hugged herself and began to rock forward and back and forward again, never turning her eye from his face.

In the dim light he seemed transformed into glowing

shadow, and darkness rode in the hollows above his cheekbones.

"My son," she whispered, and reached for him, but then
drew away as she realized he wasn't that anymore, either.
He was Gotha the Shaman now, and beyond his mother's
touch, no matter what she'd sacrificed for him.

He would never understand how much she had loved his
father, nor, for that matter, how much she loved *him*. And
yet for all of it she was only the half-blind Crone, no
longer mate nor mother, though the iron bonds of that love
still held her in a relentless grip.

No greater love . . .

She moaned softly before the vacant flicker of his eyelids. Too late for her, trapped long ago by *greater love,* but
what about him? *What about her son?*

"Gotha . . ." She wanted to say it wasn't too late, but the
words got lost somewhere in the toothless pink cave of her
mouth, because the words were lies, and it was too late.

She wondered where his Dream was taking him, and
would have given her remaining eye to know which of the
two awaited him at the end of his journey.

The oldest question: Snake or Mother? Bitch or Fire?
He or She?

Fire.

A great Cave of Fire, a field of Fire, a sky of Fire. All
around him, above and below, the flames breathed in utter
silence. He stood on the field beneath the sky and faced the
mouth of the cave, where something even brighter than the
flames slowly began to emerge.

His mind creaked, trying to encompass that emergence.
The best he could do was to think of how you could look
at a fire, even the hottest campfire, easily enough. You
could stare right into the heart of the flames without flinching. But you couldn't stare at the sun, because if you did
look deep into that great light, strangely enough your world
would go dark forever. This—(*great bellowing silent
breathing growing growing growing*)—was brighter than
the highest sun of high summer's high noon.

And worse. The space around him trembled, and he
sensed that this *thing,* whatever it was, was *bigger* than the
sun, which after all was only a light that hung in the sky,
no bigger than his palm. And this big thing, this *huge* thing

was trying to come through the mouth of the Cave of Fire from *somewhere else,* and It was having a hard time of it. That merely trying to fit Its vastness through the opening of the Cave might damage everything beyond, might make the World of Fire crack apart in a shower of sparks greater than any inferno he could imagine.

Could break the World, he thought, and as he thought it, he knew it was true.

Oh, my God, he whispered.

And that was true, too.

It had never been like this before. Not when he'd chewed the berries, not when he'd thrown the herbs dried into gray curlicues on the coals of the fire and breathed in the smoke, not even when the little dreams took him unawares, with no reason but their own happening. He'd spoken with a wolf, once, and danced with another, but most often his dreams were dark-shot swirling things, or hard bright jittery things full of vibrating lines and low, growling sounds. Sometimes he would wake with nothing but a fading shard of remembrance, a word or a picture, even a smell. Sometimes he brought back nothing.

He knew it would be different this time. This was a Great Dream, in which the God made Himself known to His servants. He'd never had one before, nor had his father. Not even the Crone had ever claimed to speak directly to her Bitch. But the lore of Shamans told of such things, though always with a warning.

Great Dreams were dangerous!

Not with the simple dangers of lesser dreams, either. A Shaman could lose his way, even his life in a struggle with an evil Spirit, but the legends spoke of even greater losses in Great Dreams, though about such losses the lore was vague.

And no wonder, Gotha thought. *I will never have the words to tell of this Light, this Fire. And even if I did, I wouldn't. No normal man could bear it, or the knowing of it. For this Thing is more terrible than I have ever thought. It is the Life of Worlds, and the Death of Worlds, and It cares not at all for me.*

Thus Gotha hung pinioned in the Light of his Lord, and the Light flayed his skin and blinded his eyes and ripped deep into the most secret heart of him, to a place Gotha had never known he possessed, and took the thing It found in that place, and made it His own.

Its final Word was simple.

Trust in Me.

He woke weak and trembling and covered with a thin film of perspiration, more frightened than he'd ever been before, and the worst thing was, he couldn't remember what was causing the terror.

"Light," he mumbled over and over again, and the Crone shuddered as she wiped his brow, because he shivered uncontrollably as he spoke.

But when he came fully to his senses, he pushed her away. "Ahg. Get *off* me, Hag."

For once in her life she welcomed the insult, because whatever had happened to her son, at least this part of him was unchanged. It allowed her to hope he'd survived his Great Dream with the rest of him intact.

Nevertheless, her voice trembled as she tried to hide her own fear. "Are you all right? What happened? What did you . . . see?"

He must have heard the tiniest lilt of hope in her final question, because he curled his lip as he pushed himself up on his elbows and glared at her.

"See? You mean did I see your slimy Bitch?"

She recoiled, and put one withered hand over her mouth, but didn't say anything.

"Yes, be horrified, Crone. You should be. I didn't see Her, though. I told you, She has no power over me, nor over the One who calls me His own, either. It was Him I saw, and . . ."

But now his voice faltered, and he shook his head, as if whatever he was about to say had been on the tip of his tongue, but now it was gone. "And He told me—"

"Yes?" she whispered.

But he couldn't finish, and so he only shook his head and snarled, "Leave me alone. I'm tired. I want to sleep."

He watched her for a moment, making sure she was withdrawing, that she wouldn't launch a new assault of questions, but she only returned his stare with one of her own one-eyed grimaces and then, her mouth suddenly loose and vulnerably open, she turned from him and sought her stinking bedroll.

He lay on his back, his face bathed in starlight, and tried to remember. Had he seen the God? He was certain of it, but when he tried to recall the details, a soundless white explosion went off in his brain. He put his hands over his eyes, but the light remained. Had the Crone looked at him then, she would have been even more frightened, for when he took his hands down, his eyes were screaming cups of agony. Finally the light faded. He stifled a groan and rolled over, fumbling for his sleeping fur.

Not that he thought he would be able to sleep, but to his surprise, he dropped off almost immediately. A fading thought: *It's inside me . . .*

And so It was.

3

Well before dawn, the women of the People of Fire and Ice began to stir about the campsite. Singly or in small groups they hauled wood to the smoldering coals of yesterday's fires and kindled new blazes. They trekked down to the river's edge—the waters hereabouts had widened and slowed to a muddy brown crawl—and poked in the muck with sharp sticks, seeing juicy waterborne roots, which they buried in the coals. They unwrapped bags of meat and hacked the larger joints apart with rude stone hand axes, then trimmed the remainder with sharper knife edges. They used the same knives to cut thin sticks and sharpen them into points, upon which they impaled the meat they'd already prepared, and balanced the primitive shish kebabs over the flames. By this time the stones in the fire were hot enough to use for cooking water, and soon the savory odors of soup mingled with the rich smell of hot fat spattering in the blazes.

The women had been hard at work for almost an hour when the eastern sky turned gray, then silver, then an unearthly rose-pink as the last stars of night slowly faded away.

The children were the next to wake, and the older ones were given a few bites to hold them until the men finally rolled out of their beds. Mothers pulled sucking infants to their breasts, to quiet their hungry whining. And then, at long last, as the sun rolled in blinding splendor above the horizon, the men emerged, belching, farting, scratching themselves as they sought the bushes for their morning shit, most of them naked, their morning erections displayed proudly as token of their masterly position in the only world they knew.

Gotha woke late, and was pleased to find himself clear of eye and mind. He stretched and yawned while the morning clamored around him, and for several moments only thought about how good the sun felt on his shoulders. He rubbed the sleep grains from his eyes while he took a long, satisfying piss, and then wandered slowly over to the main fire, where several women were already serving the men.

They ate with their hands and their teeth, rich juices running down their chins into their sparse beards, their almond-shaped eyes slanting and winking with pleasure. This was the best time of day, when everything seemed possible, when the blessings of the God were most evident.

Gotha knew how they felt about things. He felt that way himself, sometimes, when things were going well, when his magic worked and the hunters came back laden with game or, even better, empty-handed but full of the path to a slaughtered mammoth somewhere out on the plains. Then the whole Tribe would eat until they puked, their bellies swollen with the fat they hungered for so much they would eat it hot and raw right from the kill.

But today, Gotha thought as he gnawed on a gristly chunk of bison—getting old, that bison had been killed four days ago—*today they won't hunt bison or mammoth or caribou. Today they will follow a different kind of spoor, and maybe, if I'm very lucky (and I* will *be lucky, I know I will), I'll find the devil woman who has stolen my brat. And then . . .*

And then.

His teeth flashed in a white smile, almost as white as the light that had burned those new paths in his brain the night before, and everybody smiled back at him, pleased to see the Shaman in such a good mood.

Everbody except the Crone, who was seated in her usual place nearest the fire, gumming her own rag of meat. She saw that smile and turned to one of the pair of old biddies who attended her.

"Fetch me another fur," she said. "It's cold this morning."

It wasn't, but the old woman did as she was told. Everybody did what the Crone told them to do. Everybody except Gotha, who only hated her, but thought he didn't fear her at all.

"Not at all," he told himself as he stared at her. After her first glance, though, she ignored him, and after a moment he turned away. "Dag!" he bellowed. "Where are you, you useless pig?"

He strode off briskly, liking the way the blood pumped in his leg muscles, enjoying the way this new feeling sang in his veins. Liking the bit of fire that burned somewhere inside him, somewhere that had been almost empty before, but was now full.

Slowly he was beginning to understand what had been there, what the fire had taken, what holy barter he'd consummated in the night's burning dark.

He'd traded his Spirit for his destiny, and now he knew what that destiny would be.

It would be glorious.

"Dag!"

The bundle of furs looked somehow sad and shrunken, and he only kicked it once. As soon as his foot touched it, he knew.

Trust in Me.

The flies had crawled inside his furs to lay their eggs on the shiny crusted mass of his shoulder, and with Gotha's kick they buzzed out in a greenish-black swarm. He looked down with mingled disgust leavened only a bit by a sense of undefinable loss. Dag had once been almost a friend.

No matter. The tracks were plain enough, and Dag had failed his Lord.

Trust in Me.

The fire beat inside him like a little heart, secret and comforting. Now some of the hunters came up, and stood and shook their heads and clicked their tongues.

"What are you staring at?" Gotha barked. "Haven't you ever seen a dead man before?"

They cut him glances but turned away from his jolly features quickly, as if he were as frightening to look at as the corpse at his feet. None of them argued when he kicked the forlorn corpse one more time before he roared at them,

"Well? What are you waiting for? Get your lazy women to work breaking camp! We have a long way to go today!"

There would, it seemed, be no death ceremony for Dag.

And if some of them thought maybe that was for the best, that the Shaman Gotha seemed not to be himself anymore, and that if he *did* perform the ceremony, Dag's Spirit might end up in a worse place than it was right now, well—none of them said it out loud. Not until later, and by then, it was already too late.

4

Three weeks later the tracks disappeared.

Rabaka, the short, brawny, talkative hunter, approached Gotha with Agarth in tow. As usual, the taller hunter with the coppery hair was silent, but he nodded occasionally to confirm what Rakaba told the Shaman.

"The brat is walking now," Rakaba said. "Come over here and look."

Gotha followed the pair—he thought of them as a matched set, much as Dag and Ulgol had been—to the spot where Rakaba stood. The tracker waved his arms and spoke quickly, his eyes on the ground, as he ticked off what his lifelong knowledge of tracking told him.

"Those two long poles, see how they were cut? And the worn places on them, where the bark is rubbed away?" He glanced up at Gotha, his eyes sparking with excitement. "Travois poles, of course. They kept the cords and left the poles. And now"—he moved a few steps away—"the grass is dry here, and the wind has blown it around, but if you look close, you can see."

He gestured and Gotha squatted in imitation of the tracker. "Hold your head down, so the sunlight makes shadows."

Gotha, no tracker, peered uncertainly at the short, dry grass and the soft earth beneath. Only after considerable squinting was he able to make out the faintest marks, heightened by the angle of the sun. He nodded, but without conviction.

"Take my word," Rakaba assured him. "Those are *three* sets of tracks, a very big pair, a smaller pair, probably a woman, and the least of all. Those are the boy's footprints, and he's walking now. That's why they got rid of the travois."

He stood up, rubbed his chin, looked out along the top of the bluff they'd been following for several days. The land here was slowly rising toward the north, and the river, compressed between a pair of bluffs, moved faster and cut deeper. The sound of it was louder, less a dull, grumbling roar than an all-pervasive hiss. The smell of water was stronger, too.

"They'll move faster now." He paused. "And be harder to track. Dragging the boy has slowed them down, but not any longer."

Gotha still wasn't sure the amorphous marks he was looking at told any story at all, but the evidence of the discarded travois poles was plain enough. He sighed, stood up, and scratched the side of his nose. Actually, he'd been expecting something like this. Both Dag and Ulgol had expected the boy would die, from the condition of his wounds. But evidently the brat had either been very lucky, or one of the two with him had known the ways of healing. Most likely the woman, Gotha guessed, for Dag had told him she understood the speech of the Spirits, which was the mark of a Shaman.

Even so, at first he'd hoped to find the boy's body somewhere along the trail, discarded and half-eaten by scavengers. When this didn't happen, and the days of their journey along the river lengthened into weeks, he began to think the boy would survive. As time passed further, he started to feel certain of it. And not simply from the physical evidence. No, there was too much else involved—the boy's escape, the troubles Dag and Ulgol had when they tried to track him down, the mysterious appearance of the woman on the scene, and the final escape after Ulgol's death.

The timing. Too much coincidence. Gotha didn't much believe in coincidence, not when the Gods began to meddle. And after his Great Dream, he knew the Gods were meddling. He didn't know how, or why, and he doubted he would ever discover an answer to the second question. Gods did things because they were Gods, and that was reason enough why. As for how, the Shaman thought that de-

spite his inability to remember the details of his Great
Dream, he was beginning to understand.

This journey was meant to be. He was *intended* to follow that enigmatic trio and at some point, maybe tomorrow, maybe many moons from now, he *would* finally meet
the woman who spoke the tongue of Spirits.

"Well, what are you telling me? Can you track them, or
not?"

Agarth spoke for the first time. "Yes, Shaman, we can."
He glanced down at the tracks at his feet, then back at
Gotha, but said nothing more.

Gotha was convinced. Rakaba, who babbled like a
brook, might say anything that popped into his head, just to
keep his Shaman in a good mood. But dour Agarth only
spoke when he had something to say. Gotha trusted that.

He nodded curtly. "Good enough, then." He paused, then
shielded his eyes against the sun's glare and peered north
along the river bluff. "How far ahead are they, do you
think?"

Rakaba answered quickly. "A hand of days, Shaman.
They've been moving faster than we have all along, even
dragging the boy. We have a whole tribe to move, after all.
And now that the boy can walk, they'll go even faster." He
started to say something else, then stopped and glanced at
Agarth.

Agarth shrugged. "Unless they stop, we'll never catch
them."

But Gotha only nodded again, as if this was no more
than he'd expected, and said, "Don't worry. They'll stop."
He turned and stalked away, and the two hunters exchanged long looks. Finally Agarth shook his head. It
seemed crazy to continue, but if that was what Gotha
wanted, they would go along. Anyway, what choice did
they have? Shamans knew more than other people. Everybody knew that.

5

The trek resumed, still hugging the river bluff's top, because that was the easiest way to go. The river itself pre-
cluded travel much to the left of this trail, and thick woods

grew up from scraggly underbrush not far to the right. Out
in front of the main party a thin screen of trackers, Agarth
and Rakaba in the lead, pointed the way north, always
north.

Gotha ambled along near the center of the tribe, surrounded by hunters not needed for tracking, women loaded
down with packs and babies, small children scampering
and shouting at each other, and the few old people of the
Clan. He could hear the Crone not far behind him, grumbling about nothing in particular as she stumped along,
aided by a walking stick and another woman, both almost
as gnarled as she was.

The summer days were as hot as even the oldest remembered, and some were already muttering about omens. But
small game remained plentiful, even if the larger animals
seemed to have become scarce. Now, past the noontide, the
sky shimmered cloudless and flat above, its color remind-
ing Gotha of those strange lakes that flickered near distant
horizons, only to vanish when you got close to them. Everybody called those things Spirit Lakes, and sometimes
the young men tried to find them, but they never did.

A Spirit Sky? Gotha mused as he trudged along. But the
sky never disappeared, did it? It was always there, and the
sun—a blinding white hole in the canopy—was always
there, too.

So much of the World stayed just the way it always was.
Only men changed, and the animals—but rivers, rocks,
forests—these were always there. It seemed fitting, he supposed. The most powerful Spirits resided in these long-
lasting things, but the most powerful Spirits of all, the
Gods Themselves, Gotha suspected, might live even beyond the sun and the sky, which were the most permanent
things of all. The land changed, rivers grew and shrank, but
the sky—and the starry lights, the great white moon, and
the burning sun were always the same.

So where did the Gods live? Perhaps in those heavenly
lights, but Gotha thought not. He wasn't sure why he
thought that way. He didn't remember his Great Dream.
Nor did he know why the words *Trust in Me* had floated
into his mind as he'd stared down at Dag's pitiful corpse.

But he held the safety of his People in his hands, and the
only way he could assure that safety was by congress with
all manner of Spirits, Demons, and Gods. So he thought

about such things a great deal, even more so of late, and some of his thoughts were very disturbing.

The sun beat on him like a great silent hammer. Sweat ran down the knobby ridge of his spine and pooled in the crack of his ass. The air he breathed in was so dry it parched his lips. He could hear the flat hum of clouds of insects floating above the nearby scrub. He was aware of all this, but had stopped noticing it, so deep was he into his own cogitations. Even the Crone's querulous whinings faded away, so that he seemed to walk in a silent world of his own, lonely and yet somehow exalted, where his musings began to seem grander than those of other men.

I am the Chosen one, he thought. He blinked as he thought this, and a small tick began to jump just beneath his right eye, but he didn't notice. The thought was so seductive, so ... *right,* that a wave of pleasure as sweet as any orgasm swept along the rivers of his veins and crested in his groin, his chest, and his skull at the same time.

The thought and the reaction to it staggered him, and he put out his hands as a blind man would, to steady himself. *I love my life,* he thought. *Ahh, I love it all.*

And in that crystal moment, he did love it, the mountains, the trees, the sky and the waters beneath, the beasts that roamed the great World, the tiny things that slunk and crawled, the grasses that grew—but most of all he loved his People, so lost and lonely in the World, and yet possessing a spark of ... *something* that was greater than anything else.

It was this spark the God loved, he knew suddenly, and knew that the God was inside him now, for how else could he have understood this great truth?

I am the Chosen one.

He almost began to weep, but distant cries shook him from his glorious reverie. They echoed thinly across the rusty grasses, almost lost in the hissing avalanche of the river, and for a moment he thought they'd found the fugitives they were seeking, or at least the boy's body.

The headmost trackers, only capering stick sketches in the distance, leapt and waved their arms. He cupped one hand behind his ear and made out faint words.

"Salt! Salt! Come quickly, we've found salt!"

Like everybody else, then, he dropped all his thoughts and his doings, hitched up his clout, and ran.

6

More than anything else, this was the turning point; for Gotha, for the People of Fire and Ice, and for much else that was to happen. What the hunters in the van had discovered was far more precious than gold, which they cared nothing about, or food, or water, or any of the other necessities that anchored the slow turn of their daily lives.

For many thousands of years the descendants of these people would seek, fight, and die for the white treasure that the hunters discovered, just as their ancestors had done likewise for many more thousands of years.

Even the animals shared the craving, some so strongly that without the occasional natural salt lick to provide the magic elixir for them, they would die. Humans could go far longer than those simple beasts without salt, gaining some of it naturally from the foods they ate. But just as they used all manner of herbs to spice their food, the most precious of all the condiments was this crumbling white powder. It had myriad uses, some far beyond a simple flavoring.

It was as if the People of Fire and Ice had discovered a great fortune, a mountain of gold or jewels in a distant future age, the kind of thing they would weave into stories around campfires for the rest of their lives.

"Remember when we found the salt?" they would say, and roll their eyes and smack their lips and pound their crossed thighs in memory of their extraordinary good fortune.

By the time Gotha reached the foremost trackers, who were gathered around a spot in the earth, all of those men were down on their haunches, performing a curious ritual.

Carefully, almost reverently, one of them would lick a forefinger, then reach down and scrape it across one of several dull, flat plates that protruded like giant crystals from the crumbly, rocky earth near the edge of the bluff. Then the hunter would raise his finger, plunge it into his mouth, and make loud smacking sounds. He would nod, his lips would stretch into a wide grin, and he would say, "Ahh! Ahh!"

And then another man would do likewise.

For one absurd moment they reminded Gotha of a pack

of huge birds, squatting and pecking away. A crazed belch
of laughter logjammed in his throat, but when it burst
forth, nobody paid any attention to him. They were all
laughing too hard themselves, out of plain and simple joy.
Gotha couldn't help it. The craving thrummed in his belly,
too, and within moments he was down on his knees, savoring the treasure for himself.

That was the end of the trek for that day.

7

The hunters went out all that afternoon, while the women
kindled two huge hearths, for if the hunters were lucky,
there would be a great feast that evening. Throughout the
camp a new mood began to grow—where there had been
unease of late, because of the loss of the Speaker and the
Shaman's terrible moods, a slow kind of hope began to
percolate. As the afternoon wore on, while the women
lugged piles of deadwood from the nearby forest to the
edge of the hearth, even the children began to sense it, and
their joyous cries filled the bustling camp.

Gotha had ordered the Spirit House fully set up. He
knew their journey would stop for a day or two. No power
on earth would make his People leave this salt lick, at least
not until they had chipped out a great store of it, and replenished all their depleted supplies.

Agarth and Rakaba were the first to return, lugging the
carcass of a deer between them. In short order other bands
of hunters straggled out of the woods, bearing all manner
of small game, from rabbits to large, waddling ground
birds, to wild pigs, even another deer. It seemed the God
had decreed that the People would know his bounty to its
fullest, for none of the hunters returned empty-handed.
Soon a pair of spits supported the deer over the fires, while
smaller game dangled from sticks planted in the earth. The
women, chattering happily among themselves, ground up
chunks of salt into a fine powder and threw handfuls of it
over the roasting meat. A cloud of incredibly rich smells
soon floated over the camp, mixed with the sound of hungry bellies griping in impatience for the feast.

Near dusk clouds began to build along the horizon beyond the river, and from their perch high above the opposite bank, the people had a fine view of the sun as it set in a serpentine purple blaze over the roof of the forest beyond. Men slapped each other on the back for no reason. The boys wrestled with each other in gales of laughter, while the women hummed or sang cheerful nonsense songs.

As the quality of the light changed, became deeper purple, fading toward dark, a light breeze sprang up. It ruffled the leaves of the trees and sent clouds of birds flapping noisily against the sky, their passage more heard than seen. One of the hunters began a ribald chant, and soon others joined in. Even Gotha, dressed in a shirt and leggings and sitting cross-legged on the ground in front of the Spirit House, found himself humming along and tapping his finger in time with the beat.

By the time the sun was only a thin crimson line along the western horizon, the women began to utter high-pitched shouts as they hauled the meat off the fires.

"It's ready, come and get it, come eat!"

The chanting stopped as if cut off with a knife, and suddenly the only sounds were the hurried shuffle of many feet racing toward the fires. A single baby let out a squall, shockingly loud in the silence, but that was all.

Gotha rose in dignity and strode toward the nearest hearth, his hand upraised. The gesture halted the crowd, who stood waiting. They would not eat before he did, but that didn't stop them from gazing hungrily at the piles of charred, smoking flesh, as tongues slid wetly across quivering lips at the mouth-watering aroma that floated in everybody's nostrils.

When the Shaman reached the fire, he lowered his hand and began to speak. His voice was soft, but it carried easily to the farthest reaches of the camp.

"The Lord of Snakes and Fire sends His blessing to His People," he began, and several of the nearest hunters smiled at that for, practical men all, they knew how hard they worked to bring back that game. Yet they couldn't argue, for the Lord had made the animals they hunted, and many times past, He had hidden them from the best efforts they could make.

"We have followed His ways, and He loves us for it. Give thanks to Him who gives us our lives . . ." Gotha con-

tinued, perhaps drawing out his little speech as he sensed
the growing impatience of those same smiling hunters.
Then he raised both hands at once and called out loudly,
". . . *and eat of his endless bounty.*"

A moment later, not even the baby still squalled, its
mouth having been stuffed with a juicy morsel of hot fat.
The only sounds were of teeth tearing into the crusty meat,
and grunts and sighs of indescribable pleasure.

8

The Crone belched heavily and wiped a smear of grease off
her bony chin. She squinted at the eastern woods, where
the sun was just beginning to glitter through the green
crowns. A flock of crows circled lazily there, and she followed their movement with her single eye. Bad stomach
today, she thought. Too much of that fat.

She might have thought of some small bad Spirit in her
belly, but over a life of many years she'd come to notice
things—how a griping stomach often came after rich food,
and went away shortly, how her knees ached badly just before a rainstorm, but when things dried out the pain went
away. While she still dealt with the little Spirits, all of the
small things that concerned the daily lives of women, she
no longer worried about Demons in her bowels. In her own
way she was as cynical about the denizens of the Unseen
World as her son was, though like all dealers in the spiritual, she told her feelings to nobody. She'd come to trust in
the efficacy of belief more than the truth of reality, and did
nothing to disturb belief in those she served.

Which was a good thing, she reflected complacently as
she watched the camp slowly stir awake after the night's
orgy of consumption. She *did* believe in the reality of the
Goddess, and even of the God, though He held a place of
far lesser respect in her private pantheon of the Rulers of
the World.

She had sacrificed her mate to that belief and, she now
understood, had also sacrificed her son. Though Gotha still
lived, he was as distant from her, and her love, as was her
long-dead husband—and while she would never stop griev-
ing over this, she would have done the same thing again if

the Goddess ordered her to do so. There were greater things than even the bond between mother and son.

There was *the greater love,* and because of it, she sat in the honeyed beams of morning and considered how to thwart Gotha and the Snake he served so well.

She had never had a Great Dream, but she dreamed, and in those Dreams the Mother sent her messages in various ways. Of late, ever since she'd wounded the Speaker and—perhaps—driven the brat away, she'd been dreaming of much the same thing. It always began in the same way: Walking ...

Walking across a meadow so green it hurt her eyes to look at it.

The meadow spilled gently down toward a thicket of mighty trees. Beyond this emerald bay the land rose again, drifting in silver mists until it lost itself in the tangled feet of mountains higher than any she'd ever seen in the real World.

Here she was young again. She walked upon the meadow proudly, the long muscles of her thighs pumping with the heat of her blood, her head held high. She could feel the heavy weight of her breasts, shifting back and forth above her distended belly, and she knew she was pregnant. She could feel the tiny movement inside her, and when she looked around, her vision was as clear as the air through which she moved.

Yet this part of the dream always left her feeling queasy, for there was an odd aura to the place. She could never quite shake the conviction that the meadow, the trees, and all the land beyond were utterly empty, yet *waiting* for the imminent arrival of something or someone.

Was the child she carried the one this dream world waited for? She didn't know—the child (*Gotha?*) told her no tales. In her waking moments she thought it wasn't him this world awaited, but another. She also suspected that she would not want to walk through those gentle grasses if that thing or that one *did* arrive. She didn't think she could face that arrival, that it would break her as easily as a twig beneath a stone.

That part of the dream only lasted a moment, though. Then, with the eerie rapidity only dreams can offer, the scene would change. She would find herself somewhere else, doing something else.

Running . . .

But now she was old. Her bones, robbed of their shielding pads of fat, rubbed against each other like dry sticks. The sound of her lungs rasped harshly in her ears. She labored through flashes of light and dark—it seemed she was lumbering slowly, oh, so slowly, down a forest path, but she only caught horrifying glimpses of the dread woods, full of ancient gnarled black trees whose leaves rotted on misshapen branches that reached out for her like claws.

She saw this world through a single eye, flat, dead, gray. There was no sound, though she had the terrible idea that the world itself was full of noise, long, booming sounds and low, grinding whines that were unlike anything she'd ever heard—and she would think, *Oh, please, don't let me hear this!*

Her sagging, wrinkled belly slapped at the tops of her shriveled thighs as she dragged herself along the path—fleeing? pursuing?—and she knew she had only moments before she would fall, and she would finally hear the monstrous Spirits that roamed those woods as they came at last to claim her flesh, her bones, her—

She pushed the thought of that final price away, and stretched her arms out as if she could somehow pull herself through the turgid air, remembering even in the Dream how Gotha's face had looked when she'd told him the truth about his father's death, and then she tripped and fell, her few pitiful wisps of white hair clinging sodden to the sides of her old skull.

It grasped her in wrinkled talons as she fell, pulled her down into its soft, decaying embrace, and she stared into the vacant, maggot-swarming pits of its eyes, smelled its sweet, corrupt breath, and she screamed *"Noooooooo!"*

She always woke with rivers of sweat dripping down the cleft of her shrunken breasts, her one eye wild and bulging, her heart hammering as if it would burst right through the walls of her chest.

And she always knew that dead face, always recognized that dead embrace.

Gotha. *He will kill me at the end.*

The message, she thought as she sat placidly in the morning, chewing a bit of meat, was plain enough. The path was not hers, but his—and at its end lay death, not just for her, but for all.

This the Mother told her.

No greater love.

9

The Crone chewed on meat and Dreams and considered salt, and after a time, she conceived a plan. This trek after the poisoned brat and his demon rescuer was madness, doom.

She would stop it. Oh, yes she would.

She set about it.

CHAPTER FIFTEEN

1

THE GREEN VALLEY

Until the moment of his death, Sharp Knife would remember every tick of that day, as bright and clear as if it had just occurred, for it would always be the highest point of his life. Now, in the middle of that day, all he wanted was a little peace and quiet. He needed to think about what had already happened, and what would happen because of it.

He walked with his head down, a hundred thoughts swirling like blowflies between his ears. He paid no real attention to where he put his feet. They knew the path well enough.

His way took him away from Home Camp, through the teeming huts of New Camp and the pretty glitter of First Lake, along the edge of Second Lake where ducks paddled right up to the shore, their beady eyes observing his passage with bright, ducky interest, then on through the belching stinks of the mud flats that preceded the towering white streamers of Smoke Lake.

He nodded and smiled absently at those he passed on the trail, and they smiled back, because his youth and his beauty attracted everybody. But he didn't really notice them, and his mumbled greetings were only the reflexes of a naturally gifted politician.

The meeting with the Elders had lasted from just after the morning meal until almost noonday. He had surprised the six men who gathered with him and Rooting Hog in the nominal Leader House that belonged to Shaggy Elk, and they had surprised him.

He paused at the edge of Smoke Lake, his reverie interrupted by a sudden hissing. He lifted his head expectantly in the direction of the sound, which seemed to come from the center of the lake.

Ah. And there it came. A final belching sound, then a rill of bubbles, and suddenly a long white feather of water and steam began to rise from the surface. Slowly it built, its center a churning cloud, until it towered taller than the trees, bending slowly in the wind, glittering so white he narrowed his eyes at its splendor. After a minute or two, the sound lessened, and then, slowly, calmly, it began to subside. At the end only a spreading pattern of rings remained to show the geyser had ever existed. Sharp Knife stared at the mossy bank of the lake and watched the rings peter out right at his feet, and shook his head with a start, as if he'd just then awakened.

He stared around, surprised. Had he come so far? He couldn't remember a single detail of his walk. It was a good thing the geyser had shaken him from his musings; he might have wandered, all unseeing, all the way out of the Green Valley—which wasn't as harmless as it seemed. Beyond Smoke Lake were the Rock Falls that still housed a pride of cave lions, and his hands were empty. The knife tucked in his belt would have been of small use if one of those gigantic saber-tusked beasts had stumbled across his meandering passage.

He glanced about, and found himself alone. This far along the path it was relatively untraveled, used mostly by bands of hunters headed out to the steppes. The women did most of their weed hunting and tuber digging and fish catching and rodent trapping back along Second Lake. Nor did the fading musky stench of the bubbling mud flats bother him much. The odors were odd, but bearable, particularly with the light breeze that blew up from the mouth of the valley, bringing with it faint scents of pine and dry grass and dust to mingle with and leaven the heavier stinks of the mud.

The day had turned into one of those beautiful soft things that even a young man might remember after his bones had gone brittle and his heart weak, when he sat around a winter campfire and mused on the glories of his youth. Bees moved with erratic precision through a sand of bright red blossoms at his back. Birds called raucous insults at each other in the trees. A low, vast, rustling sound brought his head up, until he felt the wind that was its cause, as it moved each leaf and needle in the bowl of the Green Valley.

He searched around until he found a soft hummock right next to the warm waters of the lake, and a comfortably shaped rock, smoothed by the wind and warmed by the sun, for him to set his back against.

He settled down and closed his eyes a moment and sighed at the beauty of, well, the beauty of *everything*. Not just this perfect summer afternoon, but the meeting with the Elders, the face of White Moon—*everything*.

By the standards of his People he was still young, barely fledged—yet he was at that moment experiencing the kind of elation that some men would never know their whole lives long—the prospect of completely fulfilling all his hopes and dreams. Suddenly his muscles went loose in a spasm of relief, and this—*collapse* was as good a word as any—this *shudder* surprised him all the more because, until it loosened every fragment of cartilage in his spine, he'd had no idea just how worried about *everything* he'd become.

After a few moments the spasm passed and he grinned shakily, mildly ashamed of himself. Surely it wasn't manly to feel your bowels go weak and watery with nothing more fearsome in sight than a single blackbird cawing and flapping its slow way across Smoke Lake.

Still grinning, he let that bubbling elation fill him up until he felt as if his eyeballs would fizz right out of his head. He heard an odd, soft, rhythmic sound, and it took him a second of honest puzzlement before he realized he was chuckling aloud—and at this he burst into a full peal of laughter.

The blackbird, startled, veered sharply away from the strange creature on the lakeshore, and the even stranger sounds it was making.

Sharp Knife watched it go—heh, heh, heh—and wiped his eyes and thought of how much the bird's ungainly movements reminded him of Shaggy Elk, and once again the meeting with the Elders replayed itself in his mind . . .

"Let me do the talking. You don't need to say anything until they ask you questions. And they *will* ask questions,"

Rooting Hog said. Then he slapped his son on the shoulder and said, "Ready?"

Sharp Knife grinned, and thought that he should be the nervous one. Not his father, who, after all, was not the one who'd been fucking the daughter of the Chief—who also just happened to be the Keeper of the Stone. But Rooting Hog was as jittery as a man dancing barefoot on a mound of fire ants, and Sharp Knife wished he could think of something to say to calm him down. But he couldn't, so he merely nodded through his grin and said, "Will you go in first, or should I?"

They stood a few feet away from a low, bark-covered structure built beneath a pair of ancient oaks, whose green canopy made the Long House of the Bison Clan seem more a cave than a structure built of time-hardened saplings bent to shape, chinked with mud to keep out the arctic winds of winter.

Sharp Knife knew it would be hot as a flat rock beneath a noonday sun in there, but the Long House was the most private place the Bison Clan possessed. Though the Clan had been a part of the Two Tribes for at least ten turns of the seasons, no Mammoth Clansman had ever set foot inside it. The Elders still met here, to decide on matters of marriage, of Clan politics, as well as certain spiritual concerns they preferred to keep from the Shaman Muskrat.

Today they would meet once again, to consider the issue of Sharp Knife and his ambitious penis, which had presented them with both the greatest opportunity and the most ominous threat they had debated since their defeat at the hands of Maya and the Mammoth Stone all those long summers ago.

Rooting Hog considered. "I will go in first," he said. "I am one of them. You are here on sufferance only, or at least some will say that. When they learn the truth of matters that will change, of course, but at first, I will take the lead."

He stopped and stared at his son, as if he were trying to think of something else to say, but there was nothing, and finally he turned, squared his shoulders, and marched resolutely toward the open flap of the door. Sharp Knife followed, steeling himself for the oven within, and as he watched his father give his heavy ceremonial robe a final shake before ducking through the doorway, he was glad he

was only a supplicant. He wore a fancy clout, two patches
of soft hide held around his narrow waist by a thin cord,
decorated with a dense pattern of colors and markings, and
he rightly suspected he would be the most comfortably
garbed male in that oven today.

Not that it matters, he thought as he bent down to avoid
bashing his head on the top of the door frame. *When we
are done, they won't think of me as a child anymore. I
hope . . .*

He stared out over the lake and wriggled his toes. All
fear was gone, all hesitation past. The Elders, indeed, no
longer thought of him as a child. *If anything,* he thought,
*they are a little bit afraid of me. I'll have to do something
about that, reassure them. For the time, at least, I need
their help . . .*

Then, because he was alone and no one could see, he let
his features harden into an expression no other man had
ever looked upon—for that expression, as cold, as obdurate, as *irresistible* as the great Ice Wall to the north, mirrored his innermost thoughts:

*Someday I won't need any of them, for they will fear me.
And they will have good reason . . .*

2

HOME CAMP

White Moon tapped one foot unconsciously as she balanced a squalling infant on her lap while she tried to corral
a yowling three-year-old boy with her remaining free hand.
It was driving her crazy. All she could think of was how to
escape. Escape and find Sharp Knife, and leave all this
madness behind. She didn't care about *politics,* or what
was *proper,* or even the *wedding ceremony. I just want to
fuck him,* she thought distractedly.

The inside of the Chief's house was in its usual state of
bedlam. Both of Wolf's wives, three of his daughters, and
most of their collective children were jammed into the stifling interior. None of them seemed very happy. Every
once in a while the eldest of the women, Soft Doe, would
glance over at her first daughter and shake her head.

White Moon ignored her mother's disapproving looks. The fierce, pouting expression on her face plainly announced she had other things on her mind. "Little Lion, *stop* that!" The three-year-old boy, naked, sweating, and slick as a fish in water, twisted triumphantly out of her grip and took off across the jumbled floor of the house bellowing happily, one of White Moon's ceremonial necklaces made of polished nuts and pearlescent shells trailing from his upraised hands like a banner.

"Mother, *grab* him," White Moon wailed.

Soft Doe raised her head from the piece of hide she was sewing into White Moon's wedding robe and said, "He's not going anywhere, Daughter. And neither are you."

White Moon finished wiping the baby's bottom, patted his tiny butt briskly, and set him down on a fur at her side. "Mother, can't I just step out for a *minute*? It's so hot in here, I think I'm going to faint."

Soft Doe eyed her without sympathy. "We're all hot, dear."

White Moon heard the unspoken words easily enough. *We're all hot, dear, and if you hadn't been such a foolish girl we could all be outside, but you were and now we have to sit in here and swelter while we watch to make sure you don't make a fool of yourself all over again.*

"Just for a little breath of air?" White Moon pleaded.

Soft Doe sighed and put down her work. "Your father said you can't leave this house until the ceremony, Daughter. And you will not. Here."

She tossed the patch of hide over to the girl. "Work on this. It will give your hands more to do, and your mouth less."

"Oh, *Mother!*"

But Soft Doe only shook her head, plainly rejecting any further protests. White Moon clicked her teeth together. It was all so *unfair!*

This should have been the happiest time of her life. All her wishes were coming true, but now it seemed that everybody she knew was angry with her. She should have been in the Girls' House, chattering happily with all her friends as she worked on her robe, but instead she was a prisoner in her father's house.

Oh, how she longed for just a moment with Sharp Knife! *He* would know what to say to cheer her up. In fact, she thought as her eyes grew dreamy, he wouldn't have to say anything. Just hold her in his strong arms until the unpleasant world faded away.

It was a sweet little dream, but that's all it was. The truth was right before her, all around her in the dour, sideways glances from her mother and the rest, in the air of disappointment that had wreathed her father like a bad smell when he'd told her she would have to stay in the Chief's house until she was mated, in Old Berry's unending grumbles and admonitions.

A faint smile flickered on her lips. Old Berry. At least White Moon could see through *her* easily enough. The old woman might be annoyed with her, but underlying her plain-as-bark outspokenness, White Moon was certain she still heard the cadences of love. She wondered what Berry had been like as a girl, though she had trouble imagining such a thing. Berry was *old*, had been *old* all White Moon's life. Nevertheless, she must have been young *once* . . . had she been a bad girl then? Somehow, White Moon suspected that she had been, and that she would understand the unfairness of her present predicament better than anybody, maybe even better than Sharp Knife himself.

She peeked across at her mother, but that woman was resolutely ignoring her. If only Berry would come to visit, maybe she could be persuaded to—

A new thought struck her. What did Sharp Knife think about all this? Was he pining for her as much as she was for him? *Poor thing.* Suddenly she was certain of it, certain that if she could only get out of this wretched house for just one instant, Sharp Knife would find her. A picture of him lurking behind nearby trees, crouching down in the Jumble with water dripping from his hair, hoping somehow to catch a glimpse of his beloved, flashed up sharp and clear as a spring morning behind her eyes. She could just see him, his face mournful, full of love and worry for his beloved's plight.

It was, to be truthful, a funny little picture, and she almost giggled at it, but then the essential sadness of this hypothetical scene—no, not hypothetical, her overheated imagination suddenly announced—rose up and filled her eyes with tears.

She sniffed.

"What's the matter with you, girl?"

Soft Doe, not really a hard woman, but fearing her husband's wrath far more than her daughter's unhappiness—even if the girl *was* the Keeper of the Stone, though for the life of her, Soft Doe couldn't see any effects, good, bad, or otherwise, from *that* on her daughter—she saw no choice other than to follow Wolf's instructions exactly.

But the poor girl looked ready to burst into tears. It was not a pleasing prospect. The house was already tense, and if White Moon decided to go into hysterics (Soft Doe had seen young girls indulge themselves in far worse just prior to their marriages), the Chief's house just might become unbearable.

For her part, Soft Doe's query was enough to banish the heartrending picture of Sharp Knife she'd so carefully constructed, but her mother's question immediately set off another train of thought.

The matter? Did her mother think she was sick? Well, she was, sick at heart, at least, but that didn't—

Now, *sick,* though, that was another matter entirely. Wasn't it? If you were sick—well, not really sick, but just a little sick, you didn't need to have that awful bald Shaman, Muskrat, burn his smelly leaves and berries and set up an awful wailing for the Spirits. But you might need the help of the old Root Woman, who knew all the right things to fix up a sore belly, or break a fever, or relieve the pain of those cramps all women got sometimes. The old Root Woman whose name was Berry.

White Moon uttered another sniff, this time louder, richer, wetter, and, to punctuate her performance, shifted on her seat as if she were in great pain and rubbed her belly briskly.

"Mother, I feel sick."

This came out as a half groan, half moan, so full of histrionics that for a moment Soft Doe stared at her doubtfully.

"How do you feel sick?"

"My stomach . . . my head hurts. I feel hot . . ."

But for some reason, this announcement had exactly the opposite effect that White Moon hoped for. Instead of smiling gently and saying, "Do you want me to call Old Berry?" Soft Doe said with evident alarm, "Hot? Your stomach? *White Moon, have you been having your woman's bleeding?*"

Utterly at a loss, for a moment White Moon only stared at her mother as confusion tugged her chin down and her mouth open.

"Huh? Bleeding?" Of course she had, for almost a year now, as regular as the moon that rose and waxed fat and white seven or eight days after the bleeding would start. It had been just a hand's worth of days ago, in fact . . .

She explained this to her mother, whose sigh of relief was as audible as it was mysterious. "Oh, thank the Mother!" Soft Doe said finally, while White Moon stared at her as if she'd gone mad.

"Mother, what are you talking about? What does my bleeding have to do with getting sick?"

A little plan had sprung full-blown into White Moon's thoughts, but now she wondered if she had blundered somehow. Her mother's reaction was way out of proportion—it was almost as if White Moon had described the symptoms of some horrible demonic possession. Which would certainly call for the Shaman Muskrat's ministrations, and that was the last thing White Moon wanted.

Nevertheless, she pressed on. "I just feel sick to my stomach a little, Mother. Can't you call Old Berry? She has a potion she makes, I've had it before, remember last summer? I'm sure it's nothing—" And now she paused, heaved a mournful sigh, and rubbed her belly again. "It *hurts,* Mother."

Soft Doe hoisted herself to her feet with a speed that surprised her daughter, and would have surprised her more greatly if she'd known what "sickness" her mother *truly* feared. If her daughter had been marked with a baby *before* the mating ceremony, it would have been strong evidence of the Mother's displeasure, and would have forever tainted the union. It might, in fact, have been enough to prevent it entirely.

But a stomachache? Old Berry could deal with that, and gladly. "I'll be right back," Soft Doe said. At the door, she stopped and turned. "You stay right here, you understand?"

"Yes, Mother," White Moon replied docilely. She folded her hands in her lap and waited. If everything went *just* right . . .

3

"Uh *huh* ... uh, huh ... huh *huh*!"

The odd, cold expression disappeared from Sharp Knife's face as if it had never existed, to be replaced with raised eyebrows and a questing, alarmed stare.

What was that noise?

Slowly, he stood up, being careful not to make a sound, as his right hand sought the knife in his belt.

"Huh! Ah, *ah* ... ahhhhhh ..."

It sounded like something dying. A trail of frozen ants marched invisibly down Sharp Knife's arms, leaving a patch of goose bumps in their wake. The noise seemed to be coming from farther down the path, just beyond where it bent to follow the shoreline. There was a stand of maples there, overshading the trail and creating a bower next to a rocky outcropping. Sharp Knife knew that place. A slow grin spread across his features. He dropped his hand from the knife.

Come to think of it, he recognized those sounds, too.

Now his eyes began to dance. He crouched down and began to make his way along the trail, until he was almost around the turn.

The sounds rose to a crescendo.

"Uh ... eeeee!"

This last, an almost whistling gasp, was Sharp Knife's signal. He cupped both hands around his mouth and bellowed as loud as he could as he leapt around the turn into the lakeside lair he'd known so well as a child.

"Aaawallffff!"

And collapsed to the ground holding his belly and laughing uncontrollably at the sight that greeted his eyes.

He'd caught Long Snake, stark naked, in full pursuit of his favorite hobby, that is, at the exact peak of his ejaculation. The member from which Snake derived his name lay across his belly, engorged and red, still spitting its load of white juice while Snake's eyes, now bulging like duck eggs, tried to jump out of his bone-white face.

Sharp Knife crouched next to him, brought his own head down right to Snake's nose, and whispered a single word.

"Boo."

Long Snake stared up at him. "You pig," he said at last. They both burst into laughter.

Sharp Knife settled down next to his friend. "Your latest way of making snake spit, I suppose? The one you were telling me about?"

Snake absently wiped the sticky white goo from his belly and retied his clout. "No, something new. You want to see?"

Chuckling, Sharp Knife shook his head. "I'm surprised you have the energy."

"I always have the energy. I am a fountain of male juice," Snake replied stoutly. "It's my only talent, you know that." He paused. "What were you doing in the Long House this morning?" He eyed his friend doubtfully. "You don't look like you got your butt whipped much."

"How did you know about that? It was supposed to be a secret."

Long Snake snorted. "Secret? When all the Elders go traipsing through the camps in their best finery, and Rooting Hog puts on the hide of a bison on the hottest day of the year? I think more than half the Clan saw you trailing along behind him, trying to look properly respectful."

Sharp Knife hadn't thought of that. Normally he didn't miss such things, but in the excitement of the meeting ... He shook his head. "That obvious, huh?"

Long Snake nodded. "What did you expect? The whole valley is buzzing about you and White Moon. In the Girls' House, it's all they've been talking about for days." He dug in his right nostril, found a small green wad, and flicked it away. "So, what happened? *Did* they kick your butt for putting your snake in the wrong hole?"

His eyes danced with such gleeful expectation—Snake was always getting in trouble with *his* cock—that Sharp Knife burst out laughing all over again.

"No," he said, shaking his head and wiping his eyes, "they didn't kick my butt. They weren't pleased—at least they acted like they weren't—but what were they supposed to do? One of their own is going to mate with the Keeper of the Stone. What *can* they do? Punish me for finally giving them a bit of real power again?"

But these last words brought a thoughtful cast to Long Snake's features, where thought was such a rare guest, and in so doing, Long Snake unwittingly taught his friend a lesson. The lesson was made even clearer by his next words, spoken slowly, as if he'd just then considered them for the first time.

"Power?" he said slowly. "I never thought . . . But yes, sure, you're going to marry the Keeper of the Stone. Aren't you?" Snake paused, slightly confused. "I mean, if they didn't punish you, then they're going along with it." He brightened. "Well, of course, what else could they do? The Chief's already given his permission, is that it?"

Then a new idea struck him, and his mouth opened in surprise. "You'll be the next Chief, won't you?" He scratched the side of his nose. "Chief of the Two Tribes . . ." There was soft wonder in the way he whispered the words. He looked at Sharp Knife then, and Sharp Knife felt a sudden pang of sorrow, for that appraising glance marked a change in their friendship. He saw the change and understood it—but it still made him sad for what he had lost, what he might lose in the future. He had dreamed that the Elders would see him in a new light, but he'd forgotten that others must see him that way, too. Even his oldest friend.

He put his hands on Long Snake's shoulders. "Yes, that is what it most likely means, my friend. But it doesn't mean that anything changes between us. We will still be friends, just like we always have." He had intended this to come out forcefully, reassuringly, but instead, there was an almost plaintive note to his final words, and as Sharp Knife stared into Long Snake's features, he saw that the other young man had heard it, too.

"Oh . . . yes. Of course. Just like we always have . . ." Sharp Knife said, but that *look* stayed in his eyes, and Sharp Knife understood that nothing *would* be the same now. From his earliest years, when his plans were little more than boyish daydreams, he'd wanted with all his heart to be *grown up,* to be taken *seriously,* and now that it was finally happening, he was surprised to find out that even his dreams had their painful parts.

Like now. And worst of all, there was nothing he could do about it. Now even his closest friends would have to figure in his calculations of power and glory. He felt his world recede just a bit further, and tasted for the first time the curse of leaders, the curse even the best of them must learn to bear.

Loneliness.

I can bear this, he told himself. *I must bear it.* But it was a price he hadn't measured before, and it made him doubly sad because of that. It was even worse because this sense of loss intruded on what was otherwise a perfect day, and if he'd thought further, he might have discovered one of the greatest secrets of the Gods—that no gift is given unencumbered. Some price must always be paid.

His price would be greater than most, but he didn't know that yet. And so he clapped Long Snake on his shoulder and said as heartily as he could, "I want you to show me that new way of making your snake spit. You promised. Unless you're too tired now?"

The challenge was perfectly aimed. It drove that odd look right off Long Snake's face. "Tired? Are you crazy? Here, just lay down. First, you have to raise this leg up to *here . . .*"

And for a time, Sharp Knife was able to pretend that he was a boy again, playing a boy's games. It was a sweet moment, and he would remember it later, when the World grew dark around him, and sweetness was locked in the unreachable past.

4

"What's the matter with you, girl?" Old Berry said tartly.

Her bulk seemed to fill up the Chief's house as she stood over White Moon, her fists planted stolidly on her vast hips, her round face set in a stony frown.

White Moon did her best to cower beneath that forbidding gaze, but it was all she could do to keep from laughing, for she thought she detected a twinkle in those black eyes. Everybody else, of course, gave the old woman as wide a berth as possible, given the constricted confines of the house, but Old Berry ignored them all, even Soft Doe, who had brought her here.

"My stomach . . ." White Moon said mournfully, and rubbed her belly as if Old Berry might need tangible evidence of the offending region.

Old Berry snorted. "Nerves," she announced grumpily.

"Girls always get them in times like these. All you need is . . ."

White Moon saw her escape hatch slipping away and made a last, desperate bid to preserve her plan.

"I don't—I think it has something to do with—" And she motioned to the pouch that swung at her side.

Old Berry's gaze sharpened instantly. She knew well enough what was hidden inside that pouch. Her thoughts turned on it almost constantly now, as she worried about what it might portend for White Moon's future, for *all* of their futures.

"What makes you—" Then she stopped, for she had no intention of discussing *anything* about the Mammoth Stone in front of half a dozen gawping mouths, a full dozen straining ears.

She turned toward Soft Doe. "I'll take her back to my house," she told the older woman. "It's probably nothing serious, but I need my things to be sure."

Soft Doe felt a shiver of apprehension. Wolf's instructions had been both forceful and explicit. "But her father . . ." she protested weakly.

"Oh, pah! I'll speak to her father. Don't worry, Soft Doe. I'll keep my eye on her." Unspoken in this was Berry's obvious belief that even though Soft Doe was the girl's mother, Old Berry's eye was to better trusted than that of the woman who hadn't even been able to spot her own daughter's willing—no, *eager*—complicity in her own seduction.

"You will? I suppose it's all right, then . . ."

But Berry ignored all this as she bustled the girl to her feet. "Right to my house, girl, you understand me? And not a word to anybody, or back here you come."

"Yes, Auntie," White Moon said, her eyes downcast to hide the triumph that glowed there. So that wretched Stone was good for something after all. The idea opened new possibilities, and she intended to explore those possibilities just as soon as she made good her escape from the Chief's jail house.

What White Moon, in all her innocent plotting, did not understand was that in using the Stone as she did, she was indeed discovering something important about it. And about herself as well, though she wouldn't put this all together for a time yet.

Instead, keeping her head bowed, she merely said, "I'll be back soon, Mother," and followed old Berry's broad back out of the Chief's house into the light of the blazing afternoon.

She kept her word, looking neither left nor right, nor speaking a single word to anybody she passed, though all eyes followed the small procession she and the Root Woman made. A soft buzz of conversation, like bees in an especially blooming patch, accompanied her passage, and she pretended to ignore this, too, though the obvious fascination with her mere presence excited her in some obscure way. It was her first brush with fame, and with the awe fame brings, but she didn't associate that with the Stone, either. Not then.

What she really thought about as she marched forward was Sharp Knife, and though she kept her face resolutely turned toward the front, her eyes sought him everywhere. She shivered. Her belly felt hot, dry, parched. She thirsted for the sight of him—but found him not.

The Chief's house of the Two Tribes sat near the center of Home Camp, the settlement the Mammoth People had built in those first days after White Moon's grandfather, Skin, had crested the North Rise and first laid eyes on what they would come to call the Green Valley.

Home Camp was now small and crowded compared to the much larger New Camp across the stream along the shores of First Lake, but it remained the center of the valley, for here, besides the house of the Chief, were the Men's Mystery House and the Spirit House where the Shaman Muskrat held forth. Also here were the oldest families of the Mammoth Clan—those of Stone, and Skin, and all the rest, and last, but most certainly not least, the small and smoky house next to the Girls' House where Old Berry still lived.

At the time of White Moon's birth, this teeming quarter had been almost deserted; nine of every ten who had lived here had fallen to the terrible plague that had nearly destroyed the Mammoth People in the dread winter so well remembered by those who survived. That it now bustled again was also because of the Stone White Moon carried so unconcernedly in her pack, but she had never thought of that, either. She was a young woman with no sense of history, because what she knew of history came of half-whispered rumor or garbled legend, most of which she thought had nothing to do with her at all.

It was not her fault, of course. The true history was known to only a few, and even to these, imperfectly. Wolf, Old Berry, Muskrat, some of the Elders of the Bison People, but no more. Even those not of this group who had seen the fall of the Shamans did not understand what had happened, and few of *them* had actually witnessed the Shaman Ghost shake himself apart, or the Shaman Broken Fist immolate himself on the fire he'd intended for Maya.

And so sixty seasons of human error had piled up to account for the present state of White Moon's ignorance. She had not wanted to know anything, and those who could have told her were afraid, for reasons of their own, to do so. She kept the Stone without knowing why she should, and understood nothing about it at all—except that perhaps she could use it in some small way to extort her desire from the old woman in front of her, who seemed to fear it so much.

In this manner do small things beget larger things, toward ends no one, not even the wisest, may know or even guess. They are left for the Gods Themselves, whose work they are. Therefore tools go in ignorance, for the Gods may also be merciful, knowing that for tools, knowledge is painful. Thus the Gods spare their tools as much as They can, for knowledge has always been the wealth of the Gods, and its possession by tools only the beginning of the great fall.

Yet tools have always sought knowledge. It is in their nature to do so, and since the Gods created Their tools, They also assured Themselves of an existence free of two curses: predictability and boredom. Even the Gods enjoy an occasional roll of dice whose spin They don't absolutely control.

White Moon spun toward her wedding, while Sharp Knife spun his elaborate plans, and the Shaman Gotha spun his revenge against a murder and a murderess he could never comprehend, and Maya spun her dream of peace and rest and a laying down of burdens, while Serpent spun— what? Who knew what the broken boy spun as he moved closer to the center of things?

Only the tool users, the First Makers, and They were not

telling—for it might be argued that even They did not know.

"Get inside, and be quick about it," Old Berry said. She held aside her door flap and made shooing motions until White Moon was safely inside. The girl entered reluctantly; things weren't going quite as she had hoped. For all her keen-eyed searching, she'd seen no sign of Sharp Knife, either lurking or pining. Her beautiful vision had lost a bit of its luster, and truth to tell, she felt more than a bit of exasperation with her errant lover. Where *was* he, if not pining somewhere close by, waiting for a glimpse of his beloved?

It was an unsettling question, for it raised other unsettling questions, questions White Moon did not want to consider on the very eve of her wedding. But it was growing harder for her not to think about these things; recent adversity had taught her some new lessons.

She seated herself inside the dark, stuffy house, which smelled of bitter herbs and fermenting berries and strange, spicy scents that were at once dry and heavy. It was at least as hot here as it had been inside the Chief's house, and it appeared that Old Berry would not even allow the luxury of an open door flap. Wheezing with the effort of stooping over, the old woman laboriously began to tie the rag of skin tight against the door frame.

"Oh, Auntie. Can't you leave it open? Better yet, why can't we sit outside and feel the breeze a little?"

Old Berry ignored these protests as if she hadn't heard them. When she was done, she turned and, with much huffing and puffing and a sudden crack of knee bones, lowered herself to her well-worn log seat.

"Sit outside? I thought you were sick, girl."

"Well, maybe a bit a fresh air would help."

Old Berry grunted. "And maybe a bit of straight talking would help, too. What's this about the Stone? Or was that all just a lie, too?"

"I'm *not* lying, Auntie. I *do* feel bad."

"That's not the same as feeling sick, White Moon," Berry said gently. "And you really aren't sick, are you?" She paused, listened to the telltale silence, then added more sharply, "Answer me, girl! And don't tell any more lies, either."

"No, Auntie, I'm not sick."

"Mmph. I didn't think so. Your mother is a bird-in-the-head, girl. Did you know that?"

White Moon loved her mother, but her private regard for that good woman was much the same as Berry's. She stifled a giggle and made no reply.

"She believed your silly story, but she was afraid of something I'm sure you never thought of. She feared you were going to have a baby."

White Moon blinked. "What? You mean right there? But don't I have to get fat first? And . . . and, I don't know, pray to the Mother. See the Shaman?" Another thought intruded on the whirl. "I have to be mated to Sharp Knife first, don't I?"

She listened to silence.

Finally Berry spoke. The sound of her voice puzzled the girl. It almost sounded as if she were laughing. "Well, not exactly," Old Berry said. "What has your mother told you, White Moon? About babies, and such?"

White Moon didn't even have to think. She could summarize her mother's entire body of information in a few short sentences. "The Mother puts babies inside a woman's belly. A baby is a gift from Her. They are Her mystery, and our mystery, too."

Berry nodded. As far as it went, this was entirely true. But Soft Doe was not terribly bright, and this only confirmed it. Yes, the Mother put the baby inside a woman's belly, but keeping it there, and bringing it out alive into the World—she shook her head and clucked softly.

"There is a little more to it than that," she said, and proceeded to enlighten White Moon on the mysteries of a woman's moon-time blood, and the meaning of its stoppage, and sundry other bits of knowledge necessary to a new bride.

When she finished, she felt more strongly than ever that this upcoming marriage was a mistake. Sharp Knife might be ready—in fact, a quiet voice told her he was entirely *too* ready—but this headstrong girl was still a child. Oh, she could learn. She would *have* to learn. But she had been raised like one of those curious insects that spins webs into thick balls around themselves, and though they might burst through these self-woven walls as butterflies in the springtime, Berry doubted that any such delightful fate lay in store for the Keeper of the Stone.

And that was the consideration that kept getting lost in all the political maneuverings and tribal struggles that were bound up in this mating ritual. Berry doubted that Sharp Knife had any idea what the Stone actually embodied, and White Moon had already betrayed her almost total ignorance on the subject.

What would happen when such a potent thing became the plaything of two children? What might it mean for them? For the Tribes? For *everything*?

She considered this, and she made up her mind. She had the rest of this day, the night, and the following morning. She knew her own power well enough. She could keep the girl here, if she so desired. Wolf wouldn't care whether White Moon stayed with her, or in the Chief's house, as long as there were no more breaches of propriety. *Well,* she thought grimly, *I can prevent that, at least. And Wolf is like all men. The less women cluttering up his house, the better he'll like it.*

Maybe it will be enough time. At least she won't go to Sharp Knife completely ignorant. I can tell her much of what she needs to know. Perhaps not everything—even I don't know everything. But I know more than most, more even than Maya. What would Maya want me to do?

And in her secret heart, she knew the answer to that. She would want the same thing done for her niece that Old Berry had once done for her.

Then, Berry had taken years to do it. Now she had only a few hours. It wouldn't be enough, not nearly, but it was all she had. It would have to do.

"Help me up, girl." And when, with much creaking and wheezing, that was done, she instructed White Moon in her most fearsome voice. "I will speak to your father. You will stay with me until your wedding. Do not leave my house while I am gone." She glanced sharply at White Moon's face. "Not even for your husband-to-be. Do you understand me, White Moon? Not even if he comes begging at my door, you are not to see him or even speak to him. Will you promise me?"

White Moon stared at the old woman a long time. She had never lied to her before today. And she understood that Old Berry thought something terrible was at stake here. But she knew herself, too. It was a promise she couldn't keep.

"I promise, Auntie."

Amazingly, Old Berry, with all her experience, believed her. It wasn't the first mistake she had made in her long life, nor would it be her last. But it would be one of the worst.

"I'll be right back. It won't take a minute. Sit down and wait for me."

"Yes, Auntie," White Moon said.

Old Berry didn't tie the door flap behind her. She hadn't been gone more than a minute before White Moon slipped out behind her, ran light-footed down the path, and disappeared into the broad reaches of the New Camp and the forest beyond.

5

Sharp Knife and Long Snake, still friends, still laughing with their dark heads together, but with a new distance between them, walked slowly back toward the Shield Wall that overlooked the two camps and First Lake. Dusk was beginning to tint the western sky above the left-hand cliff wall, and Sharp Knife glanced up, momentarily entranced by the beauty of the sky there. He had no idea his uncle, the great Black Caribou, had once peered over that very same wall and counted the multitude of houses below with something like awe, for the Mammoth Tribe had been great before the plague that had struck them down. Even today, long years later, the People of the Mammoth had not quite regained their former numbers, though because of the Bison Clan, many more people lived in the Green Valley than ever before.

But Sharp Knife had not even been born when Caribou had led that little expedition, and he, like White Moon, suffered from an ignorance of history. In fact, with very few exceptions, all the people of *both* Tribes labored under this historical myopia, for those who should have—would have—taught them were either dead or long gone. Only Old Berry had much of the knowledge needed to piece together the unbroken string—and even she was not conversant with what had died with the Shaman Broken Fist, who had worshiped the Forbidden God.

Sharp Knife nudged Long Snake in his skinny ribs and said, "Pretty, isn't it? It will be a soft night tonight. And soon—"

Snake understood the wistfulness in his friend's voice easily enough. "Yes, soon enough you will be able to send your snake wherever you want, and nobody will be able to say anything at all."

Sharp Knife laughed. Long Snake always put things in such . . . blunt terms. But there was truth in what he said. The plans were laid as well as he could lay them, and while those plans were the first thing in his mind, another portion, less obdurate, was glad that White Moon would be a part of those plans. Oh, yes, he would have fucked her and married her, even if she'd been as ugly and old as Old Berry herself. But she wasn't, and he looked forward to her soft flesh, her trusting eyes, the warmth of her embraces.

For one instant, as pink spread itself in slow layers across the rim of the cliff, he wished he held her right now—but the thought passed quickly. She was confined to her father's house until the wedding, and that hard, planning part of his mind was glad of it. When he had sought and won her, she was a prize to be taken, in token of what he thought of as a greater prize. After the marriage, she would be a different kind of trophy. But right now, she would only be a complication, and he was glad that events had placed him beyond her reach for the time being.

No, tonight he would go with Long Snake and meet with his other friends and drink fermented berry juice and laugh and tell stories and dance. He had already had a taste of the changes to come, in the way Long Snake had looked at him. But for the moment, that was forgotten. Tonight was for a celebration, and he meant to have it. It would be, he knew, the last time they would ever be boys together, and in his own strange way, he mourned that knowledge.

"Dark soon," he said. "We'd best hurry. They'll have a roaring fire by now."

Long Snake nodded and clapped him on the back. "If you are very funny, I will tell you a secret tonight."

"Oh? And what's that?"

"I know the absolute perfect way to make a woman scream with pleasure."

"Oh, ho! You do, do you? Well, then, I promise you I will be *extremely* funny."

They laughed at each other. But who could tell? It was Long Snake. He might actually know such a secret.

6

White Moon hid in the forest until it began to grow dark. She had figured out a makeshift plan. Of course it was impossible that anybody should see her and Sharp Knife together. She understood that much, and it had never been her intention to create a scandal. In some nebulous way she understood that such a thing might threaten her marriage, and she had no intention of allowing any such thing to happen.

As for the rest, her father, Soft Doe, Old Berry—well, they would scold her, no doubt, but if she admitted nothing, then there was nothing they could do . . . or so she reasoned.

Just a few moments with Sharp Knife. That was all she wanted, and what was so bad about that? She knew he pined for her as much as she did for him. No doubt he was moping around his house, his beautiful Spirit leaden and gray, as he waited for the ceremony to finally make them both free.

What a surprise she would make him! Just a kiss or two, a few whispered words, and then she could go back to Old Berry's house and take her medicine.

She wrinkled her nose at that. Old Berry. Medicine. Somehow it sounded funny that way, but she wasn't exactly sure why.

Sharp Knife occasionally stayed with his parents, but White Moon was fairly sure he wouldn't be there tonight. His usual place was in the Young Men's House, a raucous, whooping enclosure of youths who had not yet found mates. It was a wild place, certainly not fit for a young girl, but she had no intention of visiting the house itself. Indeed, she intended to wait until she saw her beloved, and then, she was certain, she would find a way to attract his attention.

She settled behind a low stand of prickly shrubs, well concealed, and watched the pounded earth and the great hearth before the long, low structure. Preparations were being made there. The fire had been kindled by midafternoon, and now a fine deer hung stripped and roasting over the banked coals. Several hide water skins were also there, and from the smell, she didn't think they held only water.

Two drummers had begun to hammer out a seductive rhythm on a great hollow log, and she began to snap her fingers unconsciously. More and more young men drifted up, and even a few grizzled hunters from the Bison Clan. Everything seemed very festive. It would be a party, she decided, and she could guess easily enough who would be the guest of honor.

So where was he?

7

Old Berry was seething. It showed pain enough on her wide, sagging face. People took one look at the thunderclouds there and stepped quickly out of her way.

She stumped along, trying to distribute her weight between the two walking sticks she carried. She could have summoned her old crows to help her along—but that might have been dangerous. Not that things could get much worse.

Drat the girl!

Still, it was better than no one knew what she was doing, even though without help she had to lumber along very slowly. Her journey, though confined to the boundaries of the two camps, had been as labored as anything she'd ever done.

It had begun the moment she'd returned from the Men's Mystery House, where she had informed the Chief that she would take charge of his daughter until the ceremony.

And thank the Mother I told him that, she thought, as she paused on the Main Path and fanned her sweating cheeks with one hand. *Now all I have to do is find the miserable girl and bring her back as if nothing had happened.*

"Hello, Old Berry."

"Hello, Muddy Crow." Berry planted her staffs and stared at the other, who was a middle-aged woman with deep lines in her face and a heavy scar on her right cheek.

Berry recalled the scar; she had treated it on the day her mate had given it to her in a rage.

"You are walking well, I see. That is good."

Berry nodded. She had a question she wanted very much to ask, but she couldn't figure out how to ask it without causing even more trouble. Then Muddy Crow solved the problem for her.

"I saw White Moon a while ago. I heard she was with you."

"Yes. I . . . sent her to get some things for me." Old Berry was uncomfortable with the lie, but it was the best she could do on such short notice. And half the camp must have seen her march the girl into her house.

"Oh? Well, she left Main Path and went into the woods beyond New Camp. That way." Muddy Crow gestured vaguely off toward Berry's right, and in that moment Berry knew where her quarry had gone.

"I'm sure she'll be along any moment. After all, she has to get ready for the ceremony tomorrow."

Muddy Crow aimed a flat gaze at her. "I heard you were supposed to watch her."

"Well, I *am* watching her, woman. Now get out of my way!"

With this, Berry made to stump ahead, and after a final sharp glance, Muddy Crow stepped aside. Grunting softly, the Root Woman moved on down the path, and finally turned off herself on a smaller way, but one still much traveled.

The end of this particular path was the Young Men's House of the Bison Clan. She could hear the pounding of drums and an occasional shriek of addled laughter. Grimly she lumbered ahead, wondering what sort of disaster awaited her there.

8

Sharp Knife and Long Snake arrived at the Young Men's House without further incident. Sharp Knife raised his hands in reply to the boisterous chorus of shouts that greeted him.

"Hey, Knife. You got Snake along to teach you what you need to know?"

Sharp Knife laughed and rubbed his crotch. That got a big laugh in reply. Somebody handed him a hollowed-out gourd full of a familiar, evil-smelling liquid. He took a deep draught, swallowed, and made a face.

They all cheered again.

Then the party really began to perk up.

White Moon had watched her mate-to-be's arrival with growing trepidation. From her perch back in the scrub, where she crouched on numb, aching thighs, a cloud of midges buzzing in her ears, she could see no way of attracting his attention without attracting attention to herself as well.

Worse still, as she watched from her dark hiding place, she saw that if Sharp Knife was pining away from her absence, he was doing a wonderful job of keeping it hidden. Just now, for instance, in the flaring light of the fire, he was capering stark naked around the circle of the hearth as he tried to pour some of that nasty-smelling stuff they were all drinking into his mouth and missing badly. It didn't seem to bother him, for he choked, then burst out laughing, and sprayed the fermented juice all over Long Snake's equally naked back.

His face was red as the berry juice, and shone as brightly in the firelight. For a man pining away, he seemed to be having a very good time.

Suddenly she realized how tired she was. She'd been crouched behind these rotten bushes for what seemed like hours now, and every muscle in her body was sending an individual protest to her brain. Moreover, she hadn't eaten all day, and now her belly was adding its own occasional *goinggg* to the choir. On top of that, she was beginning to believe she might have made a terrible mistake in running away from Old Berry's house. What was the old woman doing now? Had she gone to Wolf and reported his daughter's escape? What would he do?

She wasn't certain, but she didn't think it would be pleasant. Abruptly a slow red wave of resentment rolled over her. *Why is Sharp Knife having such a good time, while I'm huddled miserably in the dark?*

Somehow he should *know* she was here. Why didn't he

know? And so she shivered in the darkness while her resentment turned to fury, and quivered more as fury melted into rage.

Somewhere in the process anything resembling rational thought got completely lost. And so, at least to her, when she rose from the shrubs like some avenging Demoness, her hair a ragged fright, her eyes mostly white and staring, though scratchy-red with tears of frustration, it seemed the most normal, *plausible* thing in the world to do.

The drummers saw her first and stopped their pounding. In the silence, the shuffle of the dancers' feet was loud for a moment, and then this, too, went silent.

Long Snake tapped Sharp Knife on the shoulder. "Over there," he whispered. He sounded badly frightened.

Sharp Knife turned, froze, stared. The hair on his forearms prickled up. For a moment he thought she was a ghost, with her eyes burning holes in her pale face, with her hands dangling at her sides, fingers curled into claws. His heart thudded in his chest. He opened his mouth, closed it, opened it again.

"White Moon?" he breathed at last.

All around him, he sensed naked shapes melting swiftly away from the fire, and his stomach heaved at the disaster he saw occurring right before his eyes.

What the Snake is she doing here, of all places?

For the first time in his young life, Sharp Knife was completely at a loss. All he could do was stand there, feeling this mad *doom* begin to swirl in the night air all around him, his jaw hanging as loose as a sick pig's shit, while she walked toward him with a methodical gait that reminded him, for some horrific reason, of the slow, twitching advance of a wounded cave lion.

She stopped just beyond the circle of light from the fire and threw back her head. He knew what she would do next. She would scream.

And as she inhaled deeply to do just that, he saw in one crystalline moment that all his dreams were in danger of crashing to the ground on this very spot. All because of one girl so terribly spoiled that she thought she could go anywhere, do anything, simply because of who she was.

"Go away," he said. "*Just . . . go* AWAY!"

She closed her mouth. Her swollen features crumpled.

Sharp Knife waited no longer. He did the only thing he could do. He turned and ran.

She raised her hand toward his retreating back, but the gesture was never completed.

"Oh, there you are, you dratted girl. I told you to be careful what path you took. But you wouldn't listen to me, and now we have to find our way back in the dark!"

Old Berry stumped into the clearing. She spared one scornful glance for the drunks sprawled here and there, and then plodded through them to the girl and took her hand in her own.

"Well, come on. We can't stay here. The place is full of drunken fools, and you've got those herbs I wanted. You didn't lose them, stumbling around in the dark, did you? Well? I said, *come on!*"

She gave White Moon's arm a shake, and this seemed to break the girl's trance. Berry nodded to herself. Lucky she hadn't had to slap her. It would make the story less believable. But this way, she just might pull it off.

"Lead the way, girl. My eyes aren't as good as they used to be—but mind you, when I say turn, you turn the way I say this time. Yes? Yes? Well, then, let's get back. We have things to do."

And, still prattling, she half pushed, half led the fire-shocked bride-to-be from the clearing.

It was one of the greatest performances of her life. The only greater one came just a bit after, when she pushed the girl through her door flap and followed her inside.

Somehow, she managed to restrain herself from strangling the Keeper of the Stone.

9

While Sharp Knife would always think of that *day* as the best of his life, that *night* would also hold an equally memorable place. It was when, he decided later, everything began to come unraveled.

Somehow the juxtaposition of the two would seem entirely fitting. But that was later, though not much later.

CHAPTER SIXTEEN

1

NORTH OF GREEN VALLEY

Raging Bison scented the kill. He *wanted* the kill.

He looked like his namesake as he bulled through the party of hunters beneath the overhang of the Ice Wall. He was a head taller than any of the others, covered with an explosion of black hair, his butt pumping atop thighs like tree trunks.

He snorted as he raced forward, his spear balanced on his shoulder as easily as a twig, his eyes glowing like cinders in anticipation of the kill.

He grinned a slaughterer's grin as he skidded to a halt beyond the tumult of the bull mammoth's counterattack. The animal trumpeted wildly, trunk thrashing between a pair of tusks as long as Raging Bison was tall, but the hunter held his ground.

He knew the truth; the bull was weakening. The end was near.

Raging Bison planted his feet and lowered his spear—an oak staff twice his own length—and waited for the right moment. As he set himself, grasping the spear with both hands, he ticked off the signs. One spear, broken off near its point, dangled from the bull's forequarters. Another spear was buried in the underbelly of the beast, and with every movement, more slick, spit-shiny intestines squirted from the wound. He spotted three other patches of red in the bull's sides.

It was a miracle, he thought, that the thing could still stand, let alone fight. But fight it did, and now its nearsighted eyes confirmed what its nostrils already told it: one of the darting things was close enough to trample.

The bull trumpeted again, rocking back on its hindquarters as it raised one foreleg. Then it slammed its tonnage down. The earth shook beneath its charge, but Raging Bison dodged beneath its tusks at the last moment and planted the butt of his spear into the earth.

The weight of the mammoth did the rest, as the immense creature impaled itself upon the weapon. The wood bent, but held. Raging Bison leapt away. He missed being splattered by a final reflexive stomp, but the bull was already dying.

He heard a *whumpf*! as the mammoth toppled, a moment of silence, and then the cheers of his three companions. By the time he turned, all had gathered around the carcass, and Black Otter was clambering onto the body with his spear upraised in triumph.

"Get off there!"

Black Otter turned and looked at Raging Bison's face. He paled and leapt down.

Raging Bison nodded. "First," he said, "we make a sacrifice to the Lord who gives us this bounty."

The rest nodded, as the fury of the hunt drained out of them. Black Otter looked down at the ground, his cheeks crimson.

Raging Bison threw back his head and, teeth flashing though his black beard, roared, *"All thanks to the Lord of Snakes and Fire!"*

He strode forward and tugged a hand ax from his pack. It took him several minutes of hacking, but finally he reached into a well of mangled flesh and yanked the mammoth's steaming heart into the sunlight. This he raised over his head, while blood streamed onto his face.

"Death to the Bitch and Her People, by the strength He gives us!"

They began to cheer again. A booming sound seemed to echo Raging Bison's cry, and they glanced north toward the wall of ice, which glittered beneath the sun as it rose into the empty sky.

Their Lord lived there. They were sure of it, as sure as they were that soon He would have as much Special Meat as He wanted. They would see to it. Raging Bison had made them that promise, and though he wasn't a Shaman, he was something better.

He was a hero.

Now, as had their fathers, they served the Lord of Snakes and Fire, whose time was coming round again at last.

How had they ever doubted?

2

Raging Bison had not always been a hero. He could, in fact, remember exactly when he had *become* a hero, and that was a long time after he discovered he was different, which was not at all the same thing as being a hero.

Like much that had happened, and would happen in the future, Raging Bison's discovery that he was different from other boys—he was still a boy, then, only seven years old—occurred during the time when the Gods reached down and touched many other members of the Two Tribes. But nobody really noticed the divine finger that marked him, almost in passing, during the tumult of those doom-filled days. He noticed, though—or at least later he did. At the time, he didn't realize that anything at all was out of the ordinary.

He had been playing with a bunch of other boys, a mixed bag of all ages and sizes, upriver from the main part of the Bison Clan's river camp, but still well within sight of the three captured hunters from the enemy Tribe who were bound to poles set into the ground. The captives had been there for some days. One, a huge man, dangled unconscious and bleeding, as did a second, smaller man. Only the Shaman Broken Fist, the Chief Black Caribou, and a few blood-hungry women still hung about the third prisoner, the youngest, whose torture was just about to begin.

Raging Bison wanted to get closer, but every time he tried, one of the women would shoo him away. It irritated him, though he felt no fear, not of the women, nor of the prisoners, either. But he stayed back and pitched stones at unwary birds with his two friends, Black Otter and Otter's younger brother, Raccoon.

His first hint that something was wrong was the scream

that trailed off into a low, choking gurgle. It brought his head around. It took him a moment to scan the camp. Finally, down by the prisoners, he saw a woman with an odd, sticklike thing protruding from her neck. As he watched, she fell slowly to her knees. She was covered with *blood.*

He began to run in that direction, but a wicked *whooshth-chunk*! halted him abruptly one step away from the heavy spear quivering point-first in the earth before him.

He stared at the weapon that as far as he could imagine had appeared by magic. His mouth dropped open as wide as his eyes. Slowly he reached out and touched the haft, which still vibrated.

A little voice inside him whispered, *That thing just missed punching a hole right through your back.* A vivid picture of *that* clicked through his thoughts, and he shivered—but not from fear. A wild, rumbling excitement shrieked up his spine, coursed through his shoulders, and raced down his arms. Without one further thought, he grabbed the spear shaft with both his small hands and began to twist it. A moment later, with a dry, rasping sound, the formidable stone head came loose.

Bison struggled to balance the heavy weapon, his muscles all quivering wires and hot dangling ropes, clumsy as only a boy can be, yet still somehow graceful as he wrestled with the unwieldy thing.

"Bisonnnnn!"

It was Black Otter's voice, but squeezed through a shrieking filter of unblemished terror. Raging Bison turned and saw the painted Demons erupt over the low bluff behind them, screeching and howling and waving their spears. For a moment Bison froze, but only for a moment. Then that small voice began to talk to him again, calm and collected, cold as ice inside his skull.

Look, they don't see you, they're running down the bluff toward the camp.

Nodding faintly, Raging Bison followed the invaders with his eyes. Yes, it was true—whoever they were, they didn't seem interested in one small boy, even though the boy now held a man-sized spear pointed at them as they rushed past, roaring their unintelligible war cries at the top of their lungs.

"Bison! My brother, O Lord of Snakes, look at Raccoon!"

Otter was a bit farther up the hill, capering back and forth from one leg to the other, his hair wild, his eyes bugged and staring as he pointed frantically at a spot past Bison's right shoulder. Not understanding at first, and not wanting to take his eyes off the raiders who were veering to the right as they thundered on toward the center of the camp, it took him a moment to understand Otter's panic. Then he saw Raccoon, so scared that brown streaks dribbled down the inside of his skinny shanks, running wildly across the rocky ground, his eyes closed, his arms waving aimlessly.

Directly toward the onrushing pack of attackers.

A sort of white haze filmed across Raging Bison's vision, and he became aware of a dull, roaring sound pounding in his ears. It was either his own blood, or the passage of air across his eardrums, for he was running then, running without hesitation or thought, his path cutting directly through the now-scattering pack of enemy hunters, bouncing and dodging—

Grabbed Raccoon around his skinny waist and heaved.

Rolled.

Safe under a bush. Feet pounded past, but now the invaders had other things to worry about, as the men of the Bison Tribe launched their counterattack.

"There, it's all right now," he whispered into Raccoon's ear as he held the trembling, stinking boy. After a while Otter slid under the leaves and joined them, his eyes frantic with excitement and terror.

"That's the bravest thing I ever saw anybody do, even Caribou," he breathed, awe shining on his white, drawn features. "Weren't you scared?"

Raging Bison shook his head. "No," he said. "Were you?"

Wordlessly, Otter nodded. "Come on, really—you *were* scared, weren't you?" It was as if the boy sought some sort of absolution, a shared terror in which each excused the other's weakness, but Bison only shook his head again. He stared at his friend thoughtfully.

Could it be that being scared was the normal way of things? But how could that be true?

He'd never been frightened in his whole life, not once.

Not of anything, or by anything.

Up until that very moment, he'd thought everybody else was the same way. But now he began to understand the truth.

He lacked something essential. He was different.

It began to drive him mad.

3

Several years were to pass before Raging Bison became a hero, and by that time, he had endured enough to gain a measure of wisdom, sufficient, at least, to understand the difference between what he was and what he did.

His utter fearlessness was a part of what he was—but his heroism was because of what he did. Bison was not much given to deep thoughts—he was a boy, and then a man, of action—but in the long, sighing emptiness of the relentless steppe nights he came to some truths about himself—and in those truths he began to perceive the dim and shadowy shape of his own future.

The first thing he figured out was that, because he was unable to feel fear, he was incapable of what other men thought of as bravery. It seemed to him that being brave involved more than simply facing danger. True bravery was the act of conquering your own fear of danger. But he couldn't do that, because he had no fear, and therefore he couldn't be brave, either.

The small, hardly noticed compartment in the dark part of the back of his mind that encompassed these vaguely unsettling calculations was inventive enough to come up with another deduction, though.

Because of the thing he lacked, he could do things other men could not do. He could face down a cave lion with only a club. He could be one of the youngest men in the Two Tribes to single-handedly kill a mammoth. He could walk up to the largest man in the Green Valley (though few were bigger than him), and that man would step out of his way. The lack of fear inside Raging Bison leaked off him in a continuous cloud; in the way he walked, in the way he carried his head, in the way his eyes examined you, calm and empty as the eyes of a wolf contemplating a rabbit.

But Raging Bison couldn't come to any final conclusions about heroism. It *seemed* an expression of bravery, which he privately considered himself incapable of. In fact, he had almost decided that heroism was a function of other people's belief, that if people thought you a hero, then you *were* a hero. But to be a hero to yourself? If you couldn't know fear, then it was impossible to be brave, and without bravery, where was heroism? The unalterable fact was he was different; he had never known fear, not even one time, and he had slowly come to hate that difference.

He hated it for a simple reason. More than anything in the World, Raging Bison wanted to be a hero. To *himself*. But his most heartfelt desire was doomed—for he didn't know how to be afraid. The conflict *couldn't* be resolved. And though he drove himself to ever-greater feats, madness beckoned ...

Then, two summers ago, out on the high steppe beneath the Ice Wall, something happened.

He couldn't solve the problem by himself. He lacked some essential part. But he discovered that another could solve it. It changed Raging Bison's life forever. Or at least Raging Bison thought it did, which amounted to the same thing.

Now, as he chewed the dripping flesh of his latest heroic kill, Raging Bison remembered, as he always did at such times, the moment that his life had changed ...

4

"Ho, Bison!"

Raging Bison turned to face his friend Otter, who lagged several paces behind him with the rest of the small party of hunters—five altogether. They had been making their way along the verge of the Ice Wall for several days now, angling from west to east, following a long trail of watering places they knew from past expeditions along this route.

Bison shielded his eyes against the sun, which glittered off the wall of ice in numberless sparkling shards, so that the air seemed to dance with light. All along the face of the wall the ice groaned and rumbled constantly, and occasionally cracked wide open, spilling an avalanche of huge white chunks with sounds like bolts of lightning. Even in high summer it was cool here, a breath of damp chill blowing out from the ice, and all of them wore heavy furs against the dank wind.

"What?"

"Over there, toward the east!" Otter replied.

Bison followed Otter's gesture and saw the first of the blue-gray puffballs just beginning to surge above the horizon. *Storm,* he thought, and wrinkled his forehead as he wondered how much time they had left. He squinted again. The boiling clouds were rising noticeably. They expanded as he watched. A lot of wind, then—such things weren't unknown in the uncertain weather along the boundaries of the ice. And even as he thought this, the first breezes, deceptively gentle, began to tickle the nape of his neck.

He grunted and wrinkled his nose. The breeze smelled dry and hot. This was the time of year for crazy storms, things full of lightning and wind, but sometimes no rain at all. And that was a danger he well understood. The threat from such a storm wasn't the rain, but the lightning.

He turned back toward the trail he'd been following. Just ahead, a steaming pile of brown dung, already covered with a twitching army of blue-backed beetles, signaled mammoth nearby.

They'd been following the small herd—a mother and two yearlings, from the tracks—for three days. Now, just when they were drawing into striking range, the storm appeared. Bad luck, no doubt about it. The tumult of the wind and the lightning might cause the great beasts to panic and stampede in any direction. It could take days to find them again. Worse, if the storm was full of rain, the trail might be washed out completely, and their days of patient tracking would go for nothing.

He checked the horizon again and made a quick calculation; if the wind held without rising much, and the small herd in front didn't get spooked, they just might be able to pull it off before the full fury of the storm arrived.

"Come here." He motioned toward Otter and the others. "What do you think?" He pointed at the huge pile of shit.

Otter got down on his knees and sniffed. A faint aura of warmth touched his cheek, and he nodded. "Not far." He knew what Bison was considering, and glanced up at him.

"We might be able to do it," he said. "But we'll have to hurry."

"That's what I thought. Well"—Bison shrugged—"we know how to do that, I guess."

They loped off, running before the storm. Their loping pace was tireless—they could keep it up all day, if they had to. But they didn't—not more than an hour passed before Bison, whose eyes were the best of all of them, raised his hand and brought them to a halt.

"There," he whispered.

It took them a moment. Finally Otter made out the dun-colored mounds trampling slowly through the waist-high grass about half a mile ahead of them—one large and two smaller, just as the spoor had indicated.

Otter and Bison exchanged glances. With the actual sighting of their prey, the real hunt began—if it began at all. Bison checked their quarry. They weren't moving much. He suspected the storm was upsetting them, and at first, their instinct would be to stop and huddle together. Only if the lightning spooked them would they break up that protective formation, and if that happened, the hunt would most likely end in failure.

But there were other problems. Under normal circumstances, five hunters facing three mammoths would pursue a kind of hunt so old it was nearly reflex to them. They would approach the group, being careful to keep off-wind from them, and watch them carefully for a day or two, until they were as familiar with the habits of each mammoth as they were with the smell of their own turds. Only then would they try to separate the herd and drive the weakest of the three toward their waiting spears. It was slow, but it was also as safe as they could make it.

Now they were contemplating something much faster, and much more dangerous—a simple, stealthy approach as close as they could get to the huddling group, and then a sudden, all-out attack on whichever mammoth looked the smallest, slowest, or weakest.

This method had several disadvantages. The first was, of course, that they would really have no idea which of the three might be the easiest prey, though they could guess the mother of the group would probably not be the one. Moreover, without time to study the herd, they could not really plan an attack. Instead, they would have to rely on their spears to bring one of the beasts down, always a chancy proposition. Even more chancy if the mother took it into her head to attack them while they did it. Add in the further uncertainty of the weather, and the whole thing might turn into a deadly fiasco. Each of them knew of more than one hunter who had made a fatal misstep under similar circumstances.

Otter considered all these things and grudgingly admitted they might do better to break off for the time being, wait for the storm to pass, and hope the herd didn't stampede out of their reach entirely. Then, with a little luck, they might pick up the trail and continue where they had left off.

He knew it was fear that whispered these thoughts into his ear, and that didn't bother him much, for a wise man knew when to listen to his fears. He was just about to recommend the prudent course when Bison shook his head.

"I think we can do it," Bison said. "The one to the right, the smallest one, has been lagging to the rear. We should go for that one."

One of the other three hunters, a lanky man of the Mammoth Clan called Twisted Elbow, spoke up then. "I wish the Shaman were with us," he muttered. "He could ask the Mother for magic to help us."

A strange expression passed across Bison's face at that. Twisted Elbow was the only Mammoth Clansman with them, and he only because he didn't get along well with his own People. Nominally, in fact, Twisted Elbow as nearly a hermit, keeping his tent far down the Green Valley, away from Home Camp and New Camp. But even so antisocial a man as Twisted Elbow couldn't hunt entirely by himself, not if he sought the great beasts, and so, for reasons nobody really understood, he chose to hunt with those who weren't of his own Clan.

Nobody liked him very much, and that seemed to suit him just fine. He rarely spoke, but he was a good hunter, and so, when he'd asked Raging Bison if he could hunt with him this summer, the big man had agreed easily. Twisted Elbow might not be much for companionship, but he was competent enough on the trail.

Now Raging Bison felt a flicker of regret. He knew what the rest were thinking—and feeling. They were afraid. He wasn't, of course, and because no fear clouded his own calculations, he saw that if they were quick and lucky, they could bring down at least one of the mammoths before the storm arrived. They'd been trailing this small herd for three days, and he was loath to abandon the hunt just when success might be at hand. But if he allowed the fears of these men to take hold of them, then they might as well give up and seek shelter from the storm.

Twisted Elbow's remark was exactly what he didn't want to hear, for it offered an escape. In his study of fear in others—and he had studied it much, for he had to understand it intellectually rather than simply feel it—he had learned how pervasive, and how tricky, an emotion it was.

For instance, fear could feed on itself, spreading from one to many with wildfire speed. Also, he had noticed, fear possessed the power to make otherwise stupid ideas seem reasonable. It was not reasonable to expect a Shaman out here on the steppe, traveling with them, ready to beseech the Mother on a moment's notice. Yet because of the fear in the others, they might easily accept Twisted Elbow's remark as an excuse to give in to their own fear.

As he stared at Twisted Elbow, whose dark eyes held his only for a moment, then flinched and turned away, Raging Bison made up his mind. He had no fear of his own to conquer, so he might as well conquer theirs. Later they would thank him for it.

All of this—distaste, frustration, determination—was somehow expressed on his face, and Twisted Elbow turned away from it, perhaps because Raging Bison's fearlessness was already well known, and Twisted Elbow understood that his own cowardice lay at the bottom of his desire for divine help.

"I say we try to do it," Raging Bison said. "The grass is deep enough here. We can get close if we stay off-wind from them. See, the wind is in our faces."

Black Otter shrugged. "Me and Twisted Elbow take the point?"

Bison nodded. Those two were quick as Otter's namesake, and brave enough if they had to be. They would get in the first strike, and though neither of them was strong enough to land a killing blow, they might wound their quarry enough to weaken it for Raging Bison as they drove it toward him.

"We'd better hurry. Just go straight for them. One of you throw your spear, if you have to."

They nodded and set off, while Bison and the remaining two hunters crouched down in the grass and began to make their way quickly forward. Above them, the sky whirled slowly, a dome of ghostly gray-white thunderheads boiling over the dark purple shadows of the steppe beneath. Thin, jagged sticks of yellow-white light sizzled within the gloomy space between sky and earth.

The wind began to rise.

For a moon or so each summer, the temperature grew hot even close to the Ice Wall, and this summer had been no different. The dank breeze off the gigantic frozen cliff might keep the hunters in their heavy furs, but the sun shone down uninterrupted to scorch the arid plains below.

All along the verge of the glaciers the steppe baked; grass that had exploded after the last snowmelt of spring, gay with flowers, now rustled dryly in the fiery breath of highest summer, a waist-high blanket of straw, prime fodder for the roving herds.

Raging Bison and the other two hunters moved forward in a low crouch, raising their heads to eye level above the golden grassland only to check their position. Otter and Twisted Elbow had angled off in a wide circle designed to bring them up on the herd with the wind at their back on their final approach. If everything went well, their sudden spear-waving charge, accompanied by the stink of their sweat in the mammoths' nostrils, would panic the creatures toward Bison's waiting spear.

It was in moments like these that Raging Bison felt truly himself. If he couldn't feel fear, he could still face death with grace and honor. No one really understood him. He knew that. They knew he acted fearlessly, and they called it bravery. They simply couldn't imagine that it wasn't what they thought, for they couldn't conceive of a man without fear. If they could, no doubt they would call him a Demon, for by their standards, he would not be human.

Madness.

Am I human? he wondered as he used a hand gesture to bring the others to a halt. They were fairly close to the three mammoths now, close enough to hear the grunts and chewing sounds and snorting wheezes of the big animals as they ate their way through the banquet that waved gently all about them.

It was an interesting question, and it worried him sometimes. He was pretty sure he would never be able to answer the question, even to his own satisfaction—nor could he think of any reason why he had either been blessed or, depending on the viewpoint, cursed by his curious lack. In the end, it all boiled down to one thing.

I'm different. That's all, I'm different.

He glossed the thought lightly, and resolutely turned his attention from the vast black well of pain over which it floated. He was not afraid of that well, but it made him wary, for he thought that if he fell into it, he would go mad. But he considered none of this on a conscious level. It was only a huge darkness somewhere inside of him, invisibly pressing up, but he was able to keep the heavy stone of his rational mind pressing down with equal strength.

It was an utterly terrifying balancing act, and it couldn't go on forever, but he wasn't afraid. No, not at all.

Only . . . different.

(*I'm crazy.*)

"Hi! Hiya . . . hi! Hi! Hi!"

Carefully, Bison peered over the top of the grass. The three mammoths had all turned toward the east, where the storm was, and stood frozen with their trunks raised. Then the mammoth mother trumpeted, turned on her hindquarters, and began to lumber slowly toward the spot where Bison and his two companions lay waiting.

"They're coming!" Bison hissed. "Get ready."

He carried two spears, one very different from the other, each designed for a special task. The first, short and light, was designed for use with what Bison called a "throwing stick." This was simply a shorter stick with a loop of thong tied to the end, in which the butt of the throwing spear rested. It didn't seem like much, but it imparted great force to the throw, much more than a man could by himself. The Mammoth People had used the thing, and when the Bison People had seen what it could do, they had taken it up themselves. It was why Bison had suggested that Otter throw his spear—with the throwing stick, he wouldn't be able to actually bring down a mammoth, but his cast might do some real damage, weakening the victim for the other weapon Bison now unlimbered.

This spear was a good twelve feet long, its shaft as thick as his wrist, the sharpened stone head as long as his forearm. It was a terrible weapon, designed to allow the hunter to close with the mammoth, but still remain—or so it was hoped—beyond the slashing range of the tusks. But even with this spear, it was no easy task to kill a mammoth. It took nerves of stone, great strength, the ability to stand before the onrushing pile of maddened meat that was a mammoth in full charge. It was the most terrifying thing a hunter could do on purpose.

Raging Bison was the best man at it in the Two Tribes. He hefted the spear, feeling its length flex slightly, and was satisfied. He could plant the butt of the spear in the earth and stand unmoving, until the mammoth buried that sharp stone head deep inside itself with the weight of its own charge. He could do that without flinching, and when he was done, his forehead would be dry as bone.

He could feel the others' eyes on him as he set himself. The wind was still blowing toward them, and in the lowering murk of the storm overhead, the mammoths, whose eyesight was poor under the best of circumstances, would probably not be able to see them until it was too late. Especially if Black Otter and Twisted Elbow did their jobs right. Which, Bison thought as he cocked his head to listen better, it seemed they were doing.

"Yip yip yaaa! Yaah! Yaah! Hihihihihi!"

They were yelling at the top of their lungs, but the sound came to him thin across the distance, barely able to slide between the deeper registers of the wind . . .

The wind!

He looked up at the sky then, really *looked* at it.

Blue-black . . . witch-fingered lightning bolts . . . boiling dark clouds piling, piling . . . long, booming, rumbling wind rising, tearing at his hair, scratching gritty fingers across his naked eyes, slapping his cheeks . . .

The heavy belly of the storm broke open and spewed great clawing fingers of light.

A bolt cleaved the air not a hundred paces away. Almost instantly, the thunderclap brought their hands to their ears. Bison dropped his spear. An electric sizzling filled the air.

He stared at the back of his hand. Faint blue sparks danced
off the curly black hair.

Something round, glowing, spitting sparks *wehooshed*!
by on their left, leaving a black, smoking trail through the
yellow straw grass.

But no rain. Just wind and light and noise—

And then fire.

Bison stared at the tossing prairie grass and his mouth
dropped open.

Why hadn't he thought of this? And a part of his mind
replied, *Because if you had, you wouldn't have gone on
with the hunt. You would have run as fast as you could for
the Ice Wall, for the safety of a frozen hole three men high
above the grass!*

He stared at the tinder-parched grass that curled and
smoked, as the Demons of the air hurled bolt after bolt into
a God's campfire.

One of the men with him moaned, and Bison smelled
shit as the man's bowels let go. He turned and saw the
other man—a short hunter named Smooth Egg because
most of his hair had never grown out right, not a smart
man, no, not smart at all—raise his long spear upright as
he struggled for balance in the howling wind.

"No!" Bison screamed. *"Drop your spear. It calls the
demon bolts—"*

Too late.

The stroke hammered out of the storm, down the spear,
and set Smooth Egg dancing in blue flame. Raging Bison
watched him burn. His eyes went first, bubbling into a
thick, red-dark sludge in his sockets, and Bison felt a stab
of memory. He had been close to the sacrificial fire the day
Broken Fist had died.

Fist's eyes had looked like that as they'd cooked in his
skull.

Now the flesh on Smooth Egg's chest began to char. Odd
wisps of smoke burst from bloody fissures and then *chunks*
of scorched meat began to fall from Egg's upper arms and
belly.

More fat there. It just drops right off, Bison thought, a
wild hilarity churning inside his skull. Somebody was
screaming in the distance, and Bison slowly turned in the
direction of the sound and saw a wall of wind-ripped fire
advancing toward him. Just ahead of it ran the three mam-

moths, their trunks thrashing, their heads tossing, the sounds they made blending into one long, high-pitched shriek of terror.

Something—now he saw it was a man—ran right next to the herd, but neither paid any attention to the other. The maddened animals swerved this way and that, and one—the youngest—suddenly pounded off at a tangent, right into the snapping jaws of the fire.

The beast's long hair burst into flames as it ran, and that was the last Bison saw of it, a huge, four-legged torch roaring in agony as it disappeared into the greasy black smoke.

The world smelled hot and savage. He spun, his mind coldly clicking off options. He couldn't go *that* way, there was fire. And fire behind, now.

Lightning crackled overhead, a continuous fusillade, setting new fires. Smoke roiled up, gradually blending with the low-lying clouds.

A little rain would help, Bison thought, but it seemed this was one of those weird storms. Maybe it would rain later. After they all were dead.

Black Otter, arms pinwheeling, slammed into him and knocked him over. He tried to untangle himself, but Otter wouldn't let go. He clung like some kind of demented spider, all arms and legs, his eyes blind and bulging, spit spraying from his mouth, shit from his ass, and—

Raging Bison felt a quiver of fear. As he struggled with Otter, he almost didn't notice it. Not at first. But then it grew. It started in his belly, a weakening of the muscles there, and then it spread to his chest, where all of a sudden his lungs seemed to lock tight.

It became very quiet. He was aware that his throat was clogged with *something,* and that *something else* had begun to hammer in his ears.

I'm afraid, he thought, with slow bemusement. His thoughts whirled and he felt weak and dizzy as he stared up at the maelstrom sky. *I'm afraid ... so THIS is fear ...*

And it seemed to him that as he stared at that sky, that it opened for him, and something peered out *into* the world, and that something was pleased with what It saw, for It spoke to him.

"TAKE FEAR AS MY GIFT, FOR IT IS MINE ALONE TO GIVE."

Just that, and then, like a trick of the eye, the clouds

rolled shut, and Bison could barely remember the opening, for one instant, had looked like—

Nothing. Nothing at all. Like fear. Fear looked like nothing at all. Thus was Raging Bison redeemed by fear, and set free on the endless plain.

Bison clouted Otter in the jaw and knocked him out, then hoisted him to his shoulder and set off athwart the advancing fireline, jogging toward the Ice Wall. He understood what he'd seen and heard. And felt.

Not Her, with Her sweet rolling greenery and Her squalling babies, but Him. He whose Snakes were fire, whose flames rose from the groin as they descended from the sky.

Whose secret name was Fear.

After the epiphany of Fire, he felt perfectly sane from that day forward. Fire and Fear, the balance he'd sought so long.

Fire and Fear.

Bow down. Worship.

Sacrifice.

CHAPTER SEVENTEEN

1

Ever since she had fought Serpent's Demon in the world of Dreams, Maya had felt a growing urgency. The little rhyme spoke its monotonous prophecy inside her skull whenever her attention wandered.

One she would keep, the other send away
Till joined once again, they bring the new day.

Maya was certain she knew what the jingle was about. There were *two* Stones, and it was her destiny to see them joined. Why else had the Mother torn her from her comfortable existence and set her wandering in the empty lands? Why else had She brought this broken boy to her, if not to heal him? And why else did She fill Maya's sleep with vague, menacing dreams of pursuit and danger?

"They're still following us. I know they are," she said to Caribou, some days after Serpent had recovered enough for them to abandon the travois.

Caribou shrugged. "They could be, I suppose. It won't be easy for them now. We're moving pretty fast."

In his own mind, Caribou allowed himself the luxury of discounting Maya's fears. They had killed one of the hunters, and wounded the other badly enough that Caribou thought it possible *he* hadn't escaped either. But he trusted Maya's Dreams or, to be more precise, he trusted Maya, and so he led them on without complaint, though Maya pushed them at a pace he privately thought was unnecessarily strenuous.

He glanced over his shoulder at the boy who followed them as pale and silent as a ghost. The boy gave him the willies. Maya could sometimes coax him into a monosyllabic "conversation," speaking the Spirit Tongue, but otherwise Serpent—for that was his name, he'd admitted that much—kept as quiet as a stone.

It wasn't natural, Caribou thought, but then nothing about this trek was natural. They were retracing a way he'd nearly forgotten, although the route was easy enough to discern. Basically, they simply followed the river north and east. Eventually they would reach the Green Valley. Simple as that.

It had taken their wandering Tribe many hands of seasons to reach the place where Maya had been cast out, and now Maya proposed to travel that entire distance before the winter snows began to fly.

It wasn't as crazy as it sounded. In modern terms, they had a trek of about seven hundred miles, more or less the distance between Pittsburgh and Cairo, Illinois. At ten miles a day, a brisk pace but easily attainable by three unencumbered people, the journey would take two and a half months. They were actually making more than ten miles each day.

Now they walked along the top of the riverbank, with the water on their left, perhaps twenty feet below them. The river was wide and smooth here, and because it had eroded its bed to such a width, it was also shallow. They could see rocks sticking out of the slow current almost to the midpoint, where birds had roosted so long the gray stone was streaked white with avian manure. The smell of the water was such a constant thing they hardly noticed it anymore. On their right the forest brooded, a tangle of green darkness, full of the cries of birds.

What few things they still possessed they carried in packs. Even Serpent shouldered his weight, Caribou had to admit. They had rigged him a makeshift bag in which he carried some relatively fresh meat and Caribou's spare knife, as well as his firemaking equipment.

He also carried something else in the bag, but Maya wouldn't tell Caribou what it was. It was important, though. Caribou suspected that whatever it was, it had a great deal to do with Maya's constant urgings for speed.

Maya's arm had finally healed. She still carried it a bit strangely, favoring it, but he'd been afraid it was broken, and it wasn't. In fact, both she and the boy looked much better, despite their rapid pace. Caribou suspected that simply putting distance between whatever horror had filled the boy's previous life was doing him as much good as regular meals and Maya's careful ministrations.

He didn't like to look at the boy, though, and not just because of his pallid silence. The boy's flesh was a map of old agonies. The scars glittered like twisting white worms against the golden background of his skin, and Caribou, who could remember how such scars could come to be— *Broken Fist, I haven't thought of Broken Fist for a long time, have I? Not about that, at least*—shuddered every time he looked at those reminders of what man was capable of doing to other men. Or children. Some of those petrified wounds were *old*.

Caribou knew torture when he saw it. He just didn't like the queasy feelings of guilt that accompanied the evidence. He had been a part of such things once, and if he thanked Maya and the Mother for anything at all, he thanked them for rescuing him from that.

He glanced up at the sky, where the sun had begun its fall toward the western horizon. It was hot, but not uncomfortable. They would get another four hours in, at least, before dark.

"We're making good time," he said.

Maya nodded.

He knew she realized it. She'd seemed more relaxed lately, ever since Serpent had begun to walk.

"We're running low on meat. Maybe we could rest tomorrow, and you could hunt."

He slid his gaze toward her. It was a touchy subject. The last time he'd left her to hunt, she'd almost been killed. So had he. "Are you sure?" he said.

She turned and looked at the boy. Serpent was trudging along, his head down, his hair hanging over his face. Silent, as always.

"I think it'll be all right. If you stay close—within shouting distance."

The nearby woods were full of deadfalls, tangled thickets, outcropping of half-buried rock. Dangerous, perhaps, but full of small game. He still had his bow and a few arrows. They couldn't carry an entire deer, anyway. A brace of rabbits or a fat turkey would do nicely.

"I could do that," he said. "You and the boy keep my spear."

"We'll do that, then. A day won't hurt, I don't think."

Again he felt the urgency in her voice. "How is the boy?" he whispered.

"Better." She sighed. "I think he's beginning to trust me. I hope so. I need to know about him, before we get to the valley."

Caribou stopped. He was vaguely aware of Serpent also coming to a halt and staring at the two of them, but he ignored the boy for the moment.

"What are we trying to do, Maya? Is it to bring him to the Green Valley? Or just for you to get there? What do you think you will find?"

There was a frightening intensity to her gaze he didn't like at all. Though her arm had healed, she was still too thin. If only for that, to get some real food inside her, he was more than willing to stop for a while. Two or even three days, if he could talk her into it. But something was driving her, something beyond her Dreams, he suspected.

He watched the translucent blue flesh beneath her eyes as she visibly searched for the words she thought he would understand. He wanted to take her by her shoulders and shake her gently, until she really knew how it was with him. He didn't need explanations. He had never fully understood the forces that motivated her anyway. All he wanted was for her to tell him it was all right, that even if he didn't understand what was happening, she did. If he knew that, then he could let his mind rest easy. But he couldn't escape the nagging feeling that he was leading her into danger, and that she was well aware of it.

That she had *chosen* to go into that danger.

"Maya, will we be all right?"

A thin dribble of moisture filled her tired eyes. She touched his cheek. "I don't know. Does it make a difference?"

He heard the words, but words lied. The true question lay beneath the words, and it was simple: *Do you love me? Do you trust me?*

"If I was responsible for letting you come to harm—"

Now she placed one finger softly on his lips. "I have no choice, husband."

He sighed. The truth was as bleak as he feared. Nor did she say "we have no choice." She had left him a way out.

Did she know that way was forever barred to him, that he himself had locked that way?

"Maya, we could turn around. The World is great. There is a place in it for us . . . even the three of us, if that's what you want."

"Oh, Caribou, I *want* that more than anything." Her shoulders heaved, but she caught herself, even though her voice was husky when she continued. "But it's gone beyond that, beyond what I want. And I don't know what *he* wants. That's what I need to find out." Her eyes searched his, and for a moment the memory of her beauty was in them, and it stunned him.

He let his breath out. "We'll stop tonight, and tomorrow I'll hunt. And then we'll go on. I . . . I love you, Maya."

She nodded, and he felt more helpless than he'd ever felt before, even when he'd helped to sacrifice his own little sister on the Snake God's abominable fire.

"There's nothing I can do?" he asked.

She shook her head. "You can hunt well tomorrow, husband. I crave some fresh meat."

He nodded. "Then I will do that."

They went on.

2

Serpent watched the MAN take up his bow and walk off toward the forest, while the WOMAN busied herself with the remnants of the morning meal they had all just shared.

They had eaten the last of the rabbits he'd been carrying in his pack, and he guessed the MAN was going off to hunt. The WOMAN looked up from where she crouched by the fire and smiled at him. He stared back at her blankly, and after a time her smile flickered, then disappeared.

Serpent felt a pang at that. He liked the WOMAN'S smile. He just couldn't think of her smile as having anything to do with him. In fact, he found it hard to understand where the MAN and the WOMAN had come from in the first place.

The last thing he remembered was dragging his wounded leg into the woods that night he'd escaped from the Shaman whose name was Gotha. Oh, there were foggy wisps about two hunters, Dag and Ulgol, but he thought that must have been a dream. All he really knew was that the Crone had wounded him badly and somehow he'd gotten away. The next thing he knew was when he awakened, feeling curiously rested, with the sky rocking over his face.

At first he panicked, especially when he found he couldn't move his arms or legs. He'd struggled to free himself, but kept absolutely silent. He'd known he had to keep quiet, or THEY would find him, though he wasn't sure who THEY were. He was still clawing desperately at the thongs that bound him to the travois when things went blurry again, and he saw a hole full of darkness, and fell down it.

The second time he woke it was night. He lay on his back, his face turned up toward the stars, and the most delicious smell filled his nose. *Meat, some kind of roasting meat . . .*

His mouth flooded with saliva, but he tried to force himself not to think about the meat, because it wouldn't do any good, there would be no hot juicy meat for him. The Crone and the Shaman only fed him rotten scraps, if he was lucky enough to get meat at all.

Still, the rich, tempting aroma wouldn't leave him alone, and as he stared up at the stars, his nose began to operate on its own. It expanded with a long, wet snuffle and though he tried to keep quiet, he suddenly sensed movement nearby.

Once again he tried to escape his bindings, but to no avail. Then something soft and warm covered his forehead and a voice whispered, "There, there . . ." in soothing tones.

He couldn't understand the words, and soothing or not, they frightened him badly. He knew he couldn't get away from ropes around his chest, arms, and legs—and wasn't *that* an old familiar feeling?—but though he tried to lie absolutely still, his body betrayed him again and he began to shiver so badly that his teeth rattled in his jaws like stones skittering across a dry creek bed.

Again a soft rustle of movement. The hand—it was a

hand, wasn't it?—left his slickly cold brow, and then he felt fingers adjusting the skin blanket that covered him.

"Caribou, help me move him closer to the fire. He's freezing!"

Again he couldn't understand the words, but the voice was somehow familiar. More than that, it was soft, reassuring—he had to struggle with the next concept, but finally he dredged it up from deepest memory—the voice was kind.

A kind voice, he thought through a kind of pink, wonderful haze, and then he drifted off again.

The third time he woke, he stayed awake for a good length of time and discovered he had truly escaped the Shaman and his Witch Woman, the Crone. He thought he might still be a prisoner, but at least this MAN and this WOMAN didn't seem about to start torturing him again. He was still a terribly wounded little boy, but for the first time in his life, he possessed that most precious of secret treasures.

Hope.

His leg was much better, and when they untied him, he discovered he could walk, though in a limping, ungainly fashion. That night, still pulsing with this strange, new-found *hope,* he decided to wait and see what the MAN, and more particularly the WOMAN, intended to do with him. *Or to him.* He shivered when he thought of that, but he managed to quell the fear, at least long enough for him to get a grip on it again.

After that, his days become more regular, and at night, his sleep was deeper and more refreshing than it had been. He mended quickly, at least his body did. His mind was a different story. That would take a while, maybe a very long while. He didn't know how he knew that, but he did.

By then he was walking, trailing along a few paces behind them, keeping a watchful eye but gradually growing more and more accustomed to this strange new life where nobody wanted to hurt him. On the second day, the WOMAN left the MAN'S side and dropped back to where he walked. He watched her warily, but otherwise did nothing, not even when she reached out and ruffled his hair.

"What's your name?" she said, but he didn't understand and so made no reply.

She stared at him thoughtfully. Then, her voice deeper, more guttural, she spoke again. "What's your name, boy?"

That was when Serpent *really* went crazy.

3

From Serpent's point of view, it was as if a very loud, very *scared* voice started yelling as hard as it could into his ear, *"Get away, get away, get away NOW, she's GOING TO HURT YOU!"*

And for an instant it did seem that her face began to change, to melt almost, nose sliding to the side, teeth falling out, one eye bulging red and horrible, the other ... leaking. He knew that face, oh, yes he did. The Crone was coming for him, coming now, with her sticks and sharp stones and her long, yellow fingernails—

He ran.

Or at least he tried to. What he really did was essay a crabbed, stumbling hop, his right leg dragging behind him, his face screwed into a silent, shut-eyed shriek, and then he fell and she was on him.

"Listen to me!" she shouted, her face close to him. He understood her, oh, Snake yes he understood her, he'd heard that terrible tongue all his life, and all his life it had meant only blood and torn flesh and agony—

"I'm not going to hurt you!"

He shook his head back and forth violently, his eyes squeezed into two pink lines of denial, saliva drooling from the corners of his mouth.

She grasped his head between her hands and held it still. It cost her. The effort made the muscles of her neck stand out in hard, ropy lines. She brought her lips down to his ear and began to whisper, over and over, "I'm not going to hurt you. My name is Maya. I'm not going to hurt you. Not going to hurt you ..."

But she *was* hurting him, her fingers like cables of steel, squeezing his skull till he couldn't think, couldn't move, and the hot rusty *rage* boiled out of his lungs in a single gasping heave: *"Let me go!"*

She did.

He opened his eyes. Her own stared down at him, so

weird, the sapphire, the emerald, somehow he knew those
were the right colors, her eyes. A tentative smile crept
across her lips. "I'm not going to hurt you, little boy. Really I'm not."

He gazed up at her, caught by the sound of her voice as
much as by the words. Her face hadn't changed at all. It
must have been a dream, a bad dream. It really hadn't
changed.

The Crone had never smiled at him like that.

"I'm not going to hurt you, ever. I want you to believe
me. Do you believe me?"

So soft, her voice. He hiccuped. Then, slowly, he moved
his head a fraction up, then a fraction down. He did it
again.

She bent over and hugged him. "Oh, good. Oh, very
good," she said. "I promise. Never hurt you. Never, never."

Then she said, as she squeezed him tighter still, "Go
ahead and cry, little boy, it's all right. Go ahead and cry."

4

After that it *was* all right. She would speak to him occasionally in the Spirit Tongue, the one he thought of as the
Snake Tongue, and she must have understood his terror of
it, for she spoke only a few words at a time. After a while
he began to get used to it and wouldn't automatically sweat
and shiver when he heard it. Most of the time she talked to
the MAN, and he to her, and both would ignore him as he
slogged along behind them.

He knew their names. She had told him in the only
tongue they both understood, and maybe that was why he
still had trouble holding them in his head. Anything he
heard in the Snake Tongue had a disconcerting *slipperi-
ness,* as if it wanted to run right out his ears, leaving nothing but a feeling of slime behind. Nevertheless—*Maya.*
And *Caribou.* If he worked at it, he could remember them,
and while it was still easier to think of them as the
WOMAN and the MAN, he had finally begun to use their
real names when he spoke aloud.

"My name is Serpent," he said to no one in particular.
Her eyes widened, and once again he thought how pretty

they were. He'd never seen eyes like that before (*Oh, yes I have*), and they fascinated him.

He saw her interest, but realized he must have spoken in the tongue of the Snake, for she only said, "How are you today, Serpent?"

Though they had shared morning meal together, these were the first words they'd spoken to each other since he'd awakened.

He nodded and shrugged. It was still hard for him to talk at all, let alone speak in the Spirit Tongue, which raised ghosts that terrified him on a level so buried he might never be able to soothe it completely.

He could sense her waiting, though, and so he said, "Fine." The guttural rasp of the language hurt his throat. He suspected it always would.

"That's good. Would you like to help me with this?"

She was scraping the last bits of flesh from the bones of their morning meal onto a scrap of hide. Vaguely he supposed it involved cooking of some sort.

"Uh," he said noncommittally, stood up, and walked over to where he could observe more closely.

"I'm making trail meat," she said, still scraping away with the stone knife. He watched from above her, noted the streaks of white in her hair, observed the way the muscles in her upper back bunched and relaxed, bunched and relaxed.

An unfamiliar stirring began in his groin, but after a second or two it went away, leaving only a faint lick of disquiet behind.

The thing that had been bothering him for days now bubbled up in his skull, as strong as ever, and before he could stop it, the word popped out. "Maya?"

There. Not the WOMAN. Maya. Inside him, something breathed a sigh of relief, lay down, and quietly died.

She stopped what she was doing and looked up at him. Her smile was as wide, as *happy*, as he'd ever seen it. "Yes, Serpent?"

"What . . . what happened?"

"What do you mean?"

It was difficult to form the words. They rolled across his tongue like hard little nuts, and he almost had to spit to get them out.

"When you found me. Tell me."

"Oh." She spared a glance for what she'd been doing, then patted the earth at her side. "Sit down here. This will take a while, I guess."

Slowly he hunkered, then sank all the way down, crossing his legs gingerly. The pink web of scar tissue of his right thigh was stiff and painful. He put his hands on his knees and leaned forward.

She marveled at the beauty of his eyes. She had never seen her own clearly, only their cloudly reflection in a pond or puddle. Did hers look like that? She hoped so, and yet, at the thought, a twinge of regret made her squint in sorrow. So pretty, those eyes, but hers had been feared and hated. His, too? From the looks of him, far more than hers ever had been.

Like all Her gifts, a curse as well, she thought, and wondered what the future held for both of them. She sighed heavily and rocked back. "Well, the first I saw of you was when you came running out of the woods . . ."

5

When Maya finished her tale, the two of them sat for a moment, staring at each other. A thin film of sweat sparkled on the boy's forehead and slicked his cheekbones above the dark hollows that carved the space along his jaw.

"You . . . killed Ulgol? You did yourself?"

She sighed. "Yes."

"That was very brave."

She stared at him, trying to read the new note in his childlike voice. Was it fear? No, not exactly. She'd heard it before, she was certain—yes.

In the days before she'd left the Green Valley, in the days of her triumph. It was awe, and just a hint, perhaps, of amazement. Those who saw that triumph didn't really want to believe their own eyes. So a part of them found something else to see. Magic, perhaps, or Demons, or anything but a woman who had defeated two Shamans with nothing but the Power of a Stone.

His glassy stare made her suddenly feel uncomfortable. She glanced away. But he wouldn't let it go. She decided to ride with it, despite her discomfort. It was the first time he'd shown any real interest in anything, and she needed a key. Something to unlock him with. She was willing to pay a far higher price than a little uneasiness for *that*.

"Tell me again. What it felt like. The spear. Did he scream?"

The queasiness grew even stronger. His questions throbbed with a hot, eager savagery. It frightened her. But what choice did she have?

Slowly, the flesh along the top of her forearms crawling as she spoke, she recounted what she'd seen and heard. The hideous sucking crunch of the spear's entry. Ulgol's gasping cry. The way the blood had splashed, hot and sticky, on her face.

His eyes glowed as she spoke, and she had the eerie feeling that he was *seeing* with her, *feeling* and *smelling* and *hearing* it all; worse, she sensed no disgust or distaste at what she had done that day.

And why would he feel any such thing? Look at him, you stupid woman. Those scars didn't get there by accident. How many did Dag put there? Ulgol? And him only a tiny child. How many times must he have prayed for what I've just told him?

So she ignored the way he licked his lips, the way his eyes glittered, the way his bony shoulders tensed with eagerness as she described the horror she had committed.

But he doesn't think it's horrible, oh, no he doesn't.

He slumped when she finished. "That's ... all?"

"Yes. We loaded you on a travois and dragged you away as fast as we could. We were afraid, you know."

"Afraid?"

"Well, we didn't know if Dag and Ulgol had friends. Or if somebody else would try to follow us. Try to find you, I mean." She paused. She didn't want to upset him, but it was a question she had to ask.

"Will they?"

He stared at her. "Will they follow, you mean?"

"Yes."

He cocked his head. Finally he nodded. "Yes, I think Gotha will."

"Who is Gotha?"

His eyes widened in surprise. "Why, he's the Shaman of Snakes and Fire." He thought about it, then added slowly, "And I am his Speaker. He says he's my father, but that's a lie." (*How do I know that? I don't know. I just do. And I didn't know it until just now.*) "Gotha will come. If he can."

Maya shifted uneasily. The comfortably warm breeze that had sprung up, full of woodsy forest smells, now felt hot on her shoulders, hot and dank, like the breathing of some great, carrion-eating predator. Something lurking below the horizon, panting with dreadful eagerness to *catch up, catch them*!

Catch her!

She glanced at the boy. He was smiling faintly, his eyes dreamy. The expression was shocking, it was so unexpected for the news he'd given her.

"Caribou thinks anybody following us must be far behind."

The dreamy expression—like a little boy just discovering a new fruit to eat—never wavered. "Oh, yes, he is. But he is coming."

"Aren't you frightened?"

"Nooooo."

She gasped. That sound should not have come from his narrow, shrunken chest, from his thin boyish windpipe. It was deep and old and greasy, the voice of something akin to those she didn't *want* to remember.

"Serpent? Serpent!"

His expression changed, lingered, was gone. A boy stared back at her, puzzled now, as if he'd just awakened. She felt a deep chill in the lower regions of her belly, as if she'd eaten a big chunk of ice. She knew that look. The boy was a Dreamer.

Of course he is, she thought. *Why else would he carry a Stone? Does he know? I wonder.*

But those were questions for another time. Serpent looked very tired all of a sudden, and seemed half-dazed.

He mumbled.

"What?"

"I . . . what did you say, Maya?"

She patted his cheek. "You look tired, Serpent. You're not quite well yet, you know. Maybe you should rest for a while. We'll talk later in the afternoon, when it's cooler."

There were many things she wanted to know, but they would have to wait. She was thoroughly scared now, of

what she might have triggered in him, of what her own
course of action up to now had been.

Had she made a mistake?

She didn't know. But she had to find out.

She watched him limp back to his bedroll, stretch out
with his hands beneath his head, and almost immediately
fall asleep. It was true, he had a long way to go before he
was fully healed.

The question now was, did she want that to happen?
Should she *allow* it to happen? What would she unleash if
she *did* make him whole again?

But there was only One who might answer truthfully,
and of course She was silent. As usual.

Maya understood why Her enemies called Her the Bitch
Goddess—She was.

6

*The trouble with you, Maya my girl, is you can't make up
your mind about anything without somebody dragging you
over to it and rubbing your nose in it.*

Not true, she thought mildly. Why, I left the tribe—

*No, you were kicked out. If you'd tried to stay after los-
ing your Dream contest they would have dragged you out
into the forest and left you there. How much of a decision
did you make then?*

This was not going the way she wanted at all. Well, then,
what about when I made my choice before Her? Before the
Mother?

*Huh. Some choice. She dragged you kicking and scream-
ing to it, and still you fought for all the years of your life.
You even gave the Stone to that monster, the Shaman
Ghost, knowing full well he'd get it as far away from you
as he could. And when he did that, it took the Mother years
to get it back into your hands. Even then, you had to
choose between the Stone and Her on the one hand, and
the death of your own brother, along with the rest of your
People, and your own death, on the other hand. As I said,
some choice!*

That's not fair!

Who said anything about fair? It's true, and you know it.

You never make any decision unless you're absolutely forced into it, and even then, the choice has to be stacked so heavily one way or the other really isn't a choice at all.

Well, there might be something to all that, but what does it have to do with right now? What am I supposed to do about this ruin of a boy who bears Her marks and Her stone? I chose to save him, after all.

Oh, really? After you found the Stone, what choice did you have? Besides, did you really save him? Or did he do it himself? You looked like you were having some very bad problems in your Dream with him.

Fine. That *still* doesn't help me now, does it? There's something frightening about him, about his Dreams, about that *voice* he spoke in. And what is a Speaker, by the way? Does it have something to do with his Stone? As far as that goes, what does the *Stone* have to do with everything? Am I supposed to take him to the Green Valley? Or just *it*? Or neither one?

Ah, now you're beginning to understand. See, a choice at last, a real choice. Nobody holding a knife to your throat right now. You're a Witch Woman. Old Berry taught you everything she knew. It wouldn't take you half a day to find the right verbs. He could go to sleep after a nice meal and just never wake up. That would be one choice, wouldn't it?

Yes, I suppose it would.

Uh huh. But he's getting better, stronger now. In a few days you'll be able to pick up the pace even more. With a little luck, you could be in the Green Valley before the leaves turn color. Maybe even find out what that wretched rhyme means. Join everything together and see what happens.

That's a choice, too, I guess.

He says he Speaks for the Shaman of Snakes and Fire. That's interesting, isn't it? So who does he belong to? Her, or Him? Say, this is a lot of fun, isn't it?

But you can't ever guess what She wants. If you're a tool, you're a tool.

That's an excuse and you know it. Just because you've used it all your life doesn't mean it's anything more than an excuse.

I don't know.

You have to decide.

I don't know.
Decide!
I don't know.

7

As they hiked northward, the land and the forest began to
change. The hills grew higher, rockier, more forbidding,
and in the woods, there began to be less of maple, oak, and
hickory, and more of the tall green pine trees whose thick
needles stayed on through the snows of winter. Maya remembered this change from before, and knew that the farther north along the river they traveled, the more rock and
pine they would see. Finally even the vast dark evergreen
forests would dwindle, and give way to the slow roll of the
steppe, with its endless grasses and few clumps of stunted,
wind-twisted shrubbery. Only in the Green Valley itself
would she find a mixture of pine and oak and all the rest.
She had no idea why this should be, except that it was like
all things a gift of the Mother.

That was the legend, wasn't it, as Old Magic himself had
taught it to her? The Green Valley was a gift to the Mammoth People, a signal that their age-old journey had come
to an end.

Something about this snagged her memory. It had been
a long time since she'd thought about the legend, and much
of it had grown hazy and indistinct in her recollection.

"We're more than halfway home," she remarked to Caribou, who strode along beside her as if the pack of dressed-
out deer meat—he'd been extremely lucky in his
hunting—weighed no more than a sack full of leaves.

He glanced over at her, his eyes widening slightly. He
couldn't remember how long it had been since she'd referred to the Green Valley as home. Many full turns of the
seasons, at least.

The air of urgency about her was even greater now, and
it had begun to worry him, because he had decided there
was more to it than simply getting to the Green Valley as
soon as possible.

His wife had something else on her mind as well. She
wrestled with it at night, when she sighed and moaned in

her sleep, and sometimes even spoke, though *that* was in Shaman talk and he couldn't understand it.

Maybe the boy could, though. More than once he'd been awakened by her mumblings, and stared across the fire to see a pair of eyes glowing in the reflection of the coals. To be truthful, the whole thing had begun to unnerve him; he was only a hunter, though still a good one, he liked to think. But that was all he'd ever been (*Not quite true, but forget about that*), and he sensed that her problems were far beyond any help he could give.

He couldn't help her with whatever it was she struggled with in the shadows of sleep, nor lessen the tight line of her lips as they moved faster and faster into the northlands. As for the boy, he didn't understand him at all and, in fact, was beginning to get a little frightened of *him*, too.

His resolve at the beginning of the trek had been a simple one: to stay with Maya, and see that she reached the Green Valley safely. He hadn't really thought beyond that goal, but now he was beginning to question the whole enterprise. The boy was certainly not anything he'd bargained for. And he was worried about something else, too. He didn't think that even if somebody was trailing them, they could catch up before his party reached their destination. But their trail would be easy enough to track, and if pursuers kept at it long enough, they would eventually come to the Green Valley as well.

He didn't feel very comfortable with *that* idea at all. He had his own memories of a time before Maya, when his own People had not been above a little manhunting. What if those who followed—who the boy said were following—were of similar stripe? Certainly from looking at how they'd treated the boy, they weren't a people Caribou would want to met without several strong hunters of his own to back him up.

He was no longer a Chief, but he still thought like one, and his thoughts were troubled by all this. Still, he trusted Maya to make the right choices for all of them. He'd done so for most of his life, and he supposed he would continue for whatever time he still had left.

But it was worrisome, no doubt about it, and the idea he might be leading some latter-day version of Broken Fist right to a valley full of rabbits waiting to be trapped was the most worrisome of all.

He could even think of one possible option, but he hadn't brought it up to her yet, because to carry it out would slow them down. He could make their trail very hard to follow, but it would take time and effort, and with each day, Maya's face—her cheeks flaming with two small, hot, red spots that also had begun to worry him—pointed more eagerly than ever toward the north.

Still, he thought he might bring up the idea pretty soon. All she could do was say no, and he guessed he could live with that, too.

It would be a great relief, though, if she would make up her mind about whatever it was that was nipping at her so hard. If she could do that, he would trust her answer about his own suggestion a lot more easily.

"Yes," he told her, "another moon or so, and we'll be there." Then, "Maya, whatever's bothering you, can't you tell me about it? Maybe I could help. I mean, I'm not a Shaman." (*Thank the Gods, I'm not.*) "But I know other things."

She smiled at him. "No, husband, this is a problem of my own making." (*Well, of* Her *making, which comes to the same thing.*) "I'm sure something will come to me." (*Not likely. She* hasn't said anything to me for years. Ever since I left the Stone, in fact. Hmmm . . .*)

"I've been thinking about that Shaman, that Gotha the boy told you about. If he's following us . . ." Caribou went on to outline his own fears about that, but to his dismay, when he was finished, Maya looked even more distressed.

"Oh, dear. I hadn't even thought about that."

"Well, I could make it a lot harder for him to follow. It would slow us down, though."

She paused, her features still and thoughtful. Finally she sighed. She looked so confused, so depressed, that his own heart ached for her. Was there nothing he could do to help her?

"Caribou, I don't know. What you say is most likely true. And I am afraid of this Shaman. When I think of him, I remember Broken Fist and the Shaman Ghost, as well. I don't want to bring *that* to the Green Valley. But something inside me tells me to hurry, that we must get to the valley before . . ."

"Before what?"

"Before something terrible happens."

He stared at her. "What is going to happen?"

Her reply was as much wail as speech. "I don't *know*!"

And so the matter rested. They made camp that evening in silence, each shrouded in the gloom of his or her thoughts. They lay nested together by the dying fire, enjoying the warmth, but neither had much to say. Finally, thinking uncomfortably of a new Broken Fist, Caribou dropped off. The last thing he remembered was Maya still tossing restlessly beside him.

8

Maya heard Caribou begin to snore gently, and an almost absurd sense of relief washed over her. Only at night, it seemed, when both the boy and her husband were safely asleep, was she able to think clearly. When both of them were awake, she felt as if she were the focus of their hopes, their fears, their very lives—and yet neither of them had said or done anything to make her think that way.

But she did. A part of it, she supposed, was simply the burden of being a Shaman, though she was no longer even that. But she had been, and she guessed that Shaman part of her was so deeply ingrained by now it would never let her go. They had looked to her, for healing, for hunter's magic, for good luck—all those things the Tribe could not get for themselves, but only obtain through her intercession with the ghosts, the Spirits, the Gods.

She was used to being needed. Was it only her fevered imagination that made her think she might be needed even more, now that she was not a shaman?

Decide.

I don't know . . .

But I do, she thought suddenly. *It's been there all along, I just haven't noticed what it really means.* All of a sudden the rhyme was tolling itself out in her brain.

The secrete, she decided later, was in thinking *about* it, rather than merely trying to decipher what it might mean. Her mind had split into that weird duo, and once again she began to talk to herself, her lips moving silently in the darkness.

When did I first start hearing it?

*About a moon before your Dream contest with Buffalo
Daughter, wasn't it?*

Yes, that seems right.

And you never heard it before?

No. Old Magic never spoke it. I'm sure I would remember. It wasn't a part of the Prophecy of the Stone. He
would have told me of that, I'm sure.

So where did it come from?

From Her. It came from the Mother.

How can you be sure?

Where else would it come from?

The boy, perhaps? His master, the Lord of Snakes?

But it began *before* I found him.

*Then it must be Her—but what about the Healing
Dream? That Power that rushed to him, when you called
on Her for help? It wasn't Her, was it? But if it wasn't Her,
then* where did the Power come from?

I don't know.

Decide.

I don't know . . .

She closed her eyes. A moment later she slept. But she
already had the answer. It would just take a little more time
for her to recognize it.

9

Maya floated in darkness so absolute it comes only in
Dreams. She knew it was a Dream, and she wondered what
it portended. The darkness felt odd, almost as if it were *expecting* something. If she had been able to make the connection, she would have thought of it as a *pregnant*
darkness. Instead, she merely floated in it—well, that
wasn't exactly right, either. You couldn't float in nothing.
You could only be a part of nothing, and she felt like that,
as if she were a mote of darkness in the larger, waiting
dark.

Waiting for what?

She had no sense that she'd ever been any place but
here, in the empty dark, but with that curious dreamlike
overlay, she was dimly aware that she *had* been elsewhere,
though now it seemed that the other place was the Dream,

and that she'd left this darkness only for a time, and now had come back to it.

The dark was familiar. But it was empty.

She waited.

It came floating from nowhere, from everywhere. At first it was only the tiniest spark of green light, so small she wasn't sure if it was really there or not. Slowly it flickered, brightened, began to grow.

But it wasn't something coming from far away. The light hung in the center of the dark, she knew somehow it *was* the center, and it expanded bit by incremental bit. Once again, without understanding, she knew that the dark was expanding as well, to make room for that seed of emerald light.

She hung in silence for a long time. Finally, the light began to resolve into shapes, and the brighter it became, the faster it grew, so that when she finally saw its splendor, she saw it all at once.

Saw, but didn't understand.

The turtle floated easily, its horny flippers swimming slowly in the endless night. On the back of the turtle stood a great Mother Mammoth, Her mighty tusks upraised, and Maya knew Her for what She was.

But that wasn't all.

From the vagina of the Mammoth issued a huge, iridescent Snake, whose eyes glittered like rubies. The Snake twined around the body of the Mammoth like a vine around a tree, so that the two figures seemed a single gigantic totality. The head of the Snake rested gently in the Mammoth's mouth.

The Mother Mammoth trumpeted then, and in reply the Great Snake opened is red jaws. A tongue of pure flame belched forth, and on the flame tossed something like a small stone. It was a very small stone, and Maya thought it should have burned to ash in an instant, but it didn't. It hung, spinning slowly, flashing its twin colors of green and blue, a tiny, indestructible jewel.

This incredible tableau held her for only a moment, though, for now the turtle on whose back the mighty figures were but an insignificant swelling, something like a pimple that had only recently burst, now the turtle began to slow its paddling.

The shell of the turtle was of dusty green and gray,

plates whose stonelike solidity hinted at age so old nothing human could ever comprehend or number it. The head of the turtle began to turn. She felt a feeling of strain, as if this movement was stretching things it was dangerous to put too much pressure on. Yet the slow, creaking motion continued, and now she saw one scaly eye, thick as the hide of the largest bison, begin to wrinkle.

A slit appeared between the flesh, a slit of jade light that made her think of spring, of morning, of every good beginning she'd ever made in her life. The light frightened her, and made her feel joy at the same time. It was the dawn light, the refracted flash just before the rising of the sun—and it was the starlight that filled the night after the sun was gone.

It was the most beautiful thing she'd ever seen, surpassing even the Place of Dreams, yes, even the face of the Mother Herself—and she had a feeling that was only right, that all of these beautiful things, and everything else besides, were encompassed *within* that light, *within* the light of the turtle's eye.

Now the darkness, the emptiness, had passed, the expectation was fulfilled by the light that filled darkness to its farthest space, and Maya floated in the light, became a part of the light, knew she had always been so, and would always be so.

Of the Light.

Then, slowly, the eye of the turtle began to close. The light lessened, vanished. In the dark, the turtle's flippers began to move again, and then, with the majestic grandeur of morning and dusk, the turtle and its strange burden moved on, shrank, disappeared.

Maya floated in darkness.

But she remembered the Light.

10

She woke to the call of birds, the smell of a freshly stoked fire, the sound of slow-flowing water. She felt fine, refreshed, as if in her sleep all her wounds, even the incurable wounds of age, had been soothed.

She sat up and stretched. "I am *hungry*," she remarked to no one in particular.

She stared at Caribou across the fire. In her renewed vision, he looked younger, more handsome. Next to him the boy, Serpent, sat with his ribs stacked beneath his armpits, but she could see what he would look like with flesh on his bones and all his scars healed.

A beautiful boy, a beautiful man, she thought, and wondered at the ring of prophecy in the words.

"A pleasant morning, isn't it?" Caribou said, grinning. He poked at the fire, pushing a fine sizzling hunk of deer meat to one side. "It's about ready," he told her.

She ate like a wolf. When she was done, she touched his shoulder. "I decided," she said, and smiled.

His eyes flickered, but he grinned in return. "Well?"

"We go north. As fast as we can," she said.

When they reached the place by the river, high summer was ending, and a horned moon rode the soft fall sky.

"Here is where I found the Mammoth Stone," Caribou said, the veils of memory brushing softly across his eyes. "Here is where it all began."

Not really, Maya thought. *It began a long time before that. But it is ending now.*

She took Serpent's arm and pointed him toward the rocky bluff. "Beyond there is the Green Valley," she said.

"We—all of us—are home."

CHAPTER EIGHTEEN

1

THE GREEN VALLEY

Muddy Crow saw them first. The way she told it later, she'd thought they were dusty Demons risen from the steppe itself. But that was after it was all over, and it seemed good to her to make the story better than it really was.

Muddy Crow had spent a good deal of her life trying to make things better than they were. She had not had much luck at it. When she had met Old Berry on the path the day before, she hadn't wanted to speak to her, but a kind of sick envy made her stop and confirm that something was wrong with this sudden wedding between White Moon and Sharp Knife, something beyond just the strangeness that Wolf would marry the Keeper of the Stone to a youth of the Bison Tribe.

Muddy Crow had heard the rumors. Rumors were the only things in her drab existence that still had a vibrant, lively power over her. In fact, she collected rumors as a jackbird collects bright, shiny objects—blindly, avidly, without making any effort at distinction or discernment.

Muddy Crow didn't care whether the rumors she gathered were true or false. All she desired was to *know*. It was the knowledge she craved, not the truth. A false rumor was just as good as one that turned out to be true, because even the lies had their own kernels of knowing—in how they were told, in who told them, in what the rumors indicated about how the emotional wind was blowing.

Muddy Crow could not have explained all this to anybody, not even to herself. But she wasn't much interested in explanation, in *reasons*. She just wanted the rumors, for through the rumors she could live, if not a better life, at least a *different* one, and that meant everything to her. Old Berry, to her dour delight, had given her another juicy one to chew on.

As Muddy Crow gabbled to Red Hair the following morning, "That girl was over by the Young Men's House of the Bison Clan. You can *imagine* what was going on." She licked her lips and rolled her eyes.

Red Hair, one of Old Berry's wizened "companions"— *crutches,* she often thought—nodded with bleak wisdom.

"She wouldn't take me when she went out. I thought it was strange, especially since it was coming on dark, and Berry's eyes aren't so good anymore. Mother knows, if she tripped and fell in the dark, she'd never be able to get up again, not without help."

"I saw her march the girl onto the Main Path, not a hundred heartbeats after I spoke to her," Muddy Crow said. She left out that she had hung about on purpose, hoping to see just such a thing. Mentioning that wouldn't make the story any better at all. In fact, it might make Muddy Crow sound like she was *looking* for the troubles of others, and that wouldn't do.

"White Moon looked just *awful,*" she whispered, the tone of her voice leaving no doubt in Red Hair's mind of the probable reasons for the girl's disarray. After all, what you would expect of a girl—unmarried, for Mother's Sake!—who would visit the Young Men's House in the midst of a drunken revel? No doubt, Muddy Crow's expression said, White Moon got exactly what she bargained for.

"There is something wrong with this whole thing," Muddy Crow continued. "It smells like a fish belly left out in the sun too long."

Red Hair, who knew Old Berry a little better than Muddy Crow did, forbore to offer her own judgment, since she had a fair idea of how many ears the Root Woman could put to the ground if she wanted to. But she more than half agreed with the Muddy Crow's breathless air of shock. White Moon's behavior *was* beginning to stink of scandal. After all, she was supposed to be married this very evening! Moreover, Red Hair knew for a fact that White Moon's father, Wolf, had banished her to the Chief's house until the ceremony. So what was she doing traipsing through the woods in the dark of night?

There was something funny about her mating that Bison youth, Sharp Knife, wasn't there? Especially when there were a hand of Mammoth boys perfectly suitable?

But Red Hair wasn't about to say any such thing to a flap-lip like Muddy Crow, who would most likely braid anything she said into something Red Hair certainly wouldn't want to hear about later. She also knew how rough Old Berry's tongue could get, and had no urge to feel its sandy lash.

"Well," she said, "most likely it'll turn out for the best. She's a strange girl, but she's the Keeper of the Stone."

Muddy Crow nodded grimly. It was a fact. The previous Keeper of the Stone had been pretty strange herself. Maya—she hadn't thought of her in years. *I wonder what happened to her?*

This same thought was floating gently in the back of her mind, just waiting to bob to the surface again, when Muddy Crow looked up from her root gathering not far from the spot on Smoke Lake where Sharp Knife and Long Snake had tarried the day before.

A jingle of fear rang chimes up her spinal chord, for she didn't recognize the three figures making their way up the Main Path. The mists around the lake were heavier than usual, and the westering sun kindled bits of floating jewel-fire in the air around them. For a moment she *did* almost think they might be ghosts—they had such a dusty, insubstantial look to them.

They hadn't seen her yet. She was off the path, squatting on her hams, and they were looking north, toward Home Camp. As they grew closer she heard the faint *shush-shush* of their feet, and that mundane sound did more than anything else to reassure her about these strangers. Ghosts moved without sound, she knew that much at least.

But they still were strangers, and now they were very close. Muddy Crow's eyes were just fine, despite her other failings—one of which had led to the long scar on her cheek, but that was a different story—and though there was a tantalizing familiarity about the two adults in front, she still didn't recognize them.

As they passed her on the path the man slowed, as if he heard something or perhaps smelled something. He raised his hand and the woman and the boy stopped. Slowly he turned, left, then right—and looked straight at her.

"Ho, woman!" he boomed.

Muddy Crow jumped and uttered a terrified little squeak.

The strange woman said, in the tongue of the Mammoth People, "Caribou! You've frightened her." She stepped off the path and hunkered down next to Muddy Crow, who raised one cowering arm.

"Don't be frightened, old woman," Maya said, keeping her voice soft, soothing.

Muddy Crow bridled a bit at that. She recognized the tone. It was the same one she used when looking after other women's children. But she wasn't a child! Who was this woman, to speak to her so? And "Old Woman"? Why, this stranger, with her streaked white hair and lined face, with her faded eyes—

Caribou? Eyes of green, eyes of blue?

Caribou?

Muddy Crow's teeth began to chatter. Waves of goose-flesh marched up and down her ribs, her arms. "Mm ... Maya? Are you Great Maya?" Her voice came out as a very low, controlled shriek.

Inside, her mind babbled to her, *You insulted her niece, you insulted the Keeper of the Stone, and now Great Maya has returned to boil your eyes inside your addled skull, to tear your tongue from your gibbering mouth, oh—*

Maya shook her. Muddy Crow collapsed in a boneless heap on the bank, shivering and moaning. "I didn't—I'm sorry—*don't kill me, O Mother, please don't let her kill me!*"

Maya raised her eyebrows as she stared at this amazing display. She was mildly surprised that a woman she didn't recognize had identified her so quickly, and then remembered her eyes. No matter how old she got, how much she changed, her eyes would still be the mark of who she was.

The reaction to them had not, as far as she could tell, improved with time. Oh, she supposed that utter terror was better than homicidal rage, but either way, she abruptly wondered if she'd made the right decision in hurrying back to the Green Valley.

Much might have changed over the years of her absence. She badly wanted to take this ugly, sniveling woman by the shoulders and shake her until her hysterics stopped, but from the looks of things, that wouldn't help matters much. So she rocked back on her heels, sighed, and brushed the hair out of her face.

"Caribou, why don't you take Serpent down the path a bit and wait for me? This could take a while."

Caribou nodded and motioned toward the boy, who had been watching the scene with wide-eyed interest. He still only understood a few words of Mammoth talk, but this woman didn't seem overjoyed to see Maya. He wondered what kind of greeting awaited the three of them from the other inhabitants of this strange valley.

"Come on, boy," Caribou muttered, the inflections of his words conveying his message clearly enough. The two of them moved a few paces down the trail, then stepped off and found a place where they could sit and watch the lake. Caribou thought he would have something to show the boy any minute now.

Maya remained hunched down, close to Muddy Crow but not touching her, for fear of setting off a new round of hysterics. Gradually the scared woman began to quiet down, until finally she trailed off in a fit of hiccups.

When Maya judged that there was little more danger of another explosion, she said softly, "Why are you so upset? Are you afraid of me?"

"You ... are Great Maya!" Muddy Crow replied, as if that explained everything.

Great Maya? What in Mother's name did *that* mean? "My name is Maya, yes. But I've never been called Great Maya. Why do you say such things?"

Muddy Crow gradually opened her eyes. All she saw was Maya's calm, mildly concerned features. She plumbed her memory, trying to remember the woman who had left so long ago. Yes, it could be this one—and the more she stared, the more certain she became.

Unfortunately, the certainty brought a renewed wave of fear. "You heard me speak ill of the Keeper, and you came back to punish me," she quavered.

Now Maya's mouth opened a bit. "I what? What are you talking about, woman? What's your name?"

In an odd way, Muddy Crow found herself beginning to enjoy this. Though she was certain the moment of her death was at hand, Great Maya didn't seem to be disposed to killing her immediately. No doubt she would later, but

evidently she first desired to play tricky Spirit games. All
the Great Spirits like to play games, Muddy Crow thought.

*Very well, if it's games she wants, I'll play along. Who
knows? If I please her, she may spare me.*

"But, Great Maya," Muddy Crow said, "how do you not
know my name? If you could hear my voice from your
Spirit Land, you must know something as easy as my
name."

Now Maya openly gawped at the woman. "I don't live
in a Spirit Land . . . and I've never heard your voice in my
life." She paused. *This woman is old enough to have been
a part of the Tribe before my departure,* she thought. *She
recognized my eyes. She knows who I am, but I don't remember her.*

"Won't you tell me your name?"

Muddy Crow eyed her slyly. Games. Finally, she nodded. "My name is Muddy Crow." She spoke as if she
expected something terrible to happen as soon as the words
were out of her mouth. But all Great Maya did was nod.

"I don't know you, do I?" she said.

Muddy Crow's head was beginning to throb, right behind the temples. Another wad of hysteria was lodged just
beneath her voice box, and the lump seemed to be slowly
expanding. She could only gurgle a bit by way of reply.

Maya watched Muddy Crow carefully, as she might
watch a cave lion cub—seemingly harmless, but capable of
sudden explosions.

"Muddy Crow, you have nothing to fear from me. I
mean you no harm. I haven't come to kill you, or anything
else. I don't even know who you are. As for the rest, I
don't have the slightest idea what you are talking about!"

That knot in Muddy Crow's throat began to shrink. Veteran gossip that she was, she had developed over the years
a sharp facility at separating truth from lie when she heard
the spoken word. Every shred of experience told her Great
Maya was speaking truth. Though Spirits, particularly
Great Spirits, were capable of many things that normal
people couldn't do. And Spirits all were notable liars. Any
Shaman would tell you that.

Nevertheless, the years of trust in her own talents settled
her a bit, enough at least for more questions. "Are you a
Great Spirit?"

"Mother, no! Whatever gave you an idea like that?"

Now Muddy Crow gawked. Maya's shock seemed entirely genuine. But if Great Maya weren't a Spirit, how had she known what Muddy Crow had said, and returned to punish her within a few hours of the speaking of them? Unless . . . there was another possibility?

Muddy Crow licked her lips, which felt hot and dry, almost as dry as her eyeballs. "If you didn't come for me, Great Maya—"

"I wish you'd stop calling me that!"

"—whatever you say, Great . . . uh, Maya—anyway, why did you come? To honor the Keeper of the Stone at her wedding today?"

"The Keeper of the Stone's wedding?" Now Maya's head began to whirl. She felt as if she were hearing things in a Dream, where nonsense was expected. Surreptitiously she pinched the soft flesh of her inner arm. It hurt! No, this wasn't a Dream. It just sounded like one.

"Muddy Crow, I think you and I need to sit down here, just like sisters, and have a good long chat . . ."

It took even longer than Maya had hoped, but in the end, appalling though it was, she had some grasp on how her return might be heralded throughout the Green Valley.

The welcome, it seemed, would be far from what she'd expected. She'd left as a self-imposed exile, a Shaman, something, perhaps, of a heroine. Now she returned as a divine being, a Spirit. It would cause problems, she thought, but she could think of a few advantages, as well.

Anyway, the Mother had never said her life would be simple. Even so, she couldn't quite put out of her mind that the Mother, wherever She was, was chuckling over the plight of Her tool.

She helped Muddy Crow to her feet. The old woman had almost completely relaxed, and seemed willing to unburden herself of every tidbit of gossip she'd heard since Maya's departure.

Maya led her down the path to Caribou's perch by the lake. The boy was leaning up against his brawny arm, his eyes closed. Maya smiled at the picture they made.

She was just about to introduce Muddy Crow to the rest of her little family when something in the center of the lake *uurrupped*! a huge belch, and steaming water vomited into the sky.

Serpent let out a yowl and leapt to his feet, with Caribou

only half a jump behind him. In all the excitement, nobody noticed when Muddy Crow scuttled sideways, turned, and ran down the path as fast as she could go.

2

Serpent quivered beneath Maya's hand like a startled rabbit while she explained about the Spirits that lived in Smoke Lake. Eventually the boy quieted, accepting her assurances that those Spirits, while surprising and a little frightening, were harmless. By the time she had him soothed, Muddy Crow was long gone.

"Mother, where did that stupid woman go?" She glanced around, then sighed. "Off to babble her news to anyone who will listen." She looked over at Caribou. "And from what she says, *everybody* will listen."

Caribou cocked a questioning eye at her. He thought he knew Muddy Crow's type. "A flap mouth, is she?"

"Mm hum," Maya said. "But it's not only that, husband. It looks like the Mother has brought us home at a particularly interesting time." The tone of her voice left no doubt of her exasperation with the Mother's sense of timing. Undoubtedly, the Gods had a low sense of humor.

Maya led them back onto the path, and as they walked along, she explained about the wedding intended for her niece that very evening.

"You can guess what a stir *our* return will cause. While we were gone, they seem to have made me into a powerful Spirit of some kind. Great Maya!" she snorted.

Caribou chuckled softly, though in his private thoughts, more than once over the many years, he had regarded his wife in much the same way. But he said nothing of this, merely shook his head and replied, "That ought to create a little excitement for the ceremony."

Maya cast a walleyed glance of irritation in his direction. "Excitement is exactly what I'd hoped to avoid. But the timing of this—how will I explain I knew nothing about White Moon's wedding? The Two Tribes are already buzzing enough, without my throwing a dead fish into the kettle."

Muddy Crow had told her more than she'd either understood or intended. Maya's sagacity regarding the nuances of tribal society was as sturdy as ever, and the possibilities inherent in what the old woman had told her grew more dismaying with every moment she thought about them.

"Well," she said at last, "there's nothing I can do, I guess. I'm here, and now it's too late to turn around and go back." She gritted her teeth. "If we'd only managed to arrive tomorrow, after it was all over. It would have made a lot of things easier."

Caribou trudged stolidly along, idly scanning the woods along the path. He didn't understand Maya's concern, to be truthful about it, but he was quite used to not understanding Maya. Sometimes it was best to say nothing, simply aim a friendly ear in her general direction and let her talk it out. So he merely said, "Easier, how?" and continued with his ambling progress.

Maya rubbed her temples softly. The immediate answer to Caribou's question was simple enough. From what Muddy Crow had told her, there was a sizable part of the Two Tribes—mostly of the Mammoth Clam—that would seize upon her return as a sign that the wedding should not take place. A minority, though, would take it as a felicitous blessing upon the union. As for whatever deeper politics might be involved—and she was certain those more hidden concerns existed—she would have to wait until she could speak to Wolf.

A smile spread across her face at the thought. Wolf! Though she hadn't admitted it to herself, she was immensely relieved. She'd been gone for a long time. Infants had grown to marriageable adulthood in her absence. New names and faces might dominate the Two Tribes. Anything could have happened to her brother. He might even have died. But Muddy Crow's gossipy concerns had reassured her. Much had not changed. Wolf was still Chief, his daughter still kept the Stone, and even Old Berry still lived!

Now that *was* a miracle. The Root Woman had been ancient even in Maya's childhood. That she was still up and about, more or less, was more welcome news than she had hoped for. Even Muskrat, the callow boy she'd tried to teach a Shaman's lore, still lived in the Spirit House where once Old Magic (*and the Shaman Ghost, don't forget* him) had held forth.

In many ways, it seemed to her that the Mother had preserved Her People against Maya's return, almost as if it had been Maya she wished to change, rather than the Mammoth Clan. Yet Maya was equally certain this was not entirely the case. She had only the bare bones of recent history, and that colored through the memories of a bitter, gossipy old woman. Much had no doubt changed, and more than just Muskrat's loss of his hair. Muddy Crow had referred to *him* more than once as the "bald fool." Muskrat, it seemed, had not absorbed well the lessons Maya had tried to teach him about the more worldly, practical aspects of Shamanhood and what would later be called "public relations."

Oh, well. I didn't have much time to teach him. I wonder if he'll be glad to see me. Somehow she doubted it.

They had progressed past the mud flats—Serpent wrinkled his nose at the mélange of stinks bubbling from the steaming bogs there—and now approached the edge of Second Lake. Maya found her worries suddenly fading as she looked out once again over the sapphire waters where ducks bobbed placidly and the wind pushed silver ripples into ever-changing patterns of liquid silence.

How easy it is to remember only the good things, she thought sadly. A host of memories flocked to her then; the sound of the ducks as they took wing at dusk, the querulous voices of Old Berry and, before her, Old Magic as they lectured her on the secrets of leaves and roots and berries, the feel of hot flint against her palm while Stone taught her about the heart buried deep inside those dark red shapes, how gently those hearts must be coaxed to give up the blades locked within.

Other recollections, darker and bloodier, batted like savage moths against this cloudy pane of time, but she managed to ignore them as she looked once again at a part of her childhood, one that had brought her—and still did, she now realized with a kind of cool wonder—more pleasure than she would ever know again.

Life is hard, she thought. *But life goes on.* And if that seemed a simple sort of summation for all that had occurred in her lifetime, well, then, so let it be. Life *was* simple, for all that man and Gods might do to complicate the thing.

She was musing on that little homily when Caribou

touched her shoulder lightly and said, "We've got company."

She looked up, then around. Serpent, whose terror-honed sensitivities were sharper than any she'd ever known (except the Shaman Ghost's, of course . . .), had moved in closer to her and Caribou, and walked carefully, his head sweeping slowly back and forth, his nostrils wide and fluttering.

Like an animal . . . But she could feel it, and when Caribou took her arm and squeezed it to turn her slightly, she saw them, as well: furtive little flicks of movement in the forest shadows, a flash of smooth skin, even what might have been eyes, glittering from the gloom.

She felt a chilly breeze slide softly across the fine hairs on the back of her neck, though the leaves were dead and still. "What—" she began, but Caribou only squeezed a little harder and whispered, "Shhh."

It was eerie. The sun overhead was dropping noticeably, as afternoon slid on toward dusk, and the light around Second Lake had taken on a clear, almost fluid quality. Her senses felt painfully alert. She could *hear* them now, the hushed intake of breath, the rustle of skin against hide, the hidden footfalls.

It was like being ushered along by a crowd of ghosts. But they were real people, she knew, even if no one had yet found the courage to show themselves.

She wondered if any of them remembered her from before, and doubted it. For a moment a vision of Old Berry, creeping along through the bushes, painted a hilarious picture in her mind. Then practicality reasserted itself. From what Muddy Crow said, Old Berry could hardly walk, let alone sneak through the brambles like some timorous forest creature.

She fought the nearly uncontrollable urge to shout, "Come out, come out, wherever you are!" and instead whispered in reply, "I see them. Just keep walking. Somebody will meet us soon, I think."

Yet it took much longer than she thought it would. They continued on past Second Lake and were almost at the point where the Main Path divided, when she saw the group of figures gathered ahead.

She had already marveled at the size of New Camp on her left, although the much-trampled earth between the many houses was empty and eerily still. Cookfires smoldered untended. She could imagine children cowering inside those houses, restrained by their mothers from venturing outside to watch "Great Maya" return.

I'll do something about that Great Maya *situation the very first thing,* she thought. *I'm no Spirit, nor do I want to be.*

The welcoming committee stood in silence at the fork of the path, their hands formally outstretched in greeting. As she grew closer, she could make out their features, and a sudden gladness tugged at her heart. They were all there, some nearly as she remembered, others changed almost beyond recognition.

She wouldn't have recognized Muskrat as the skinny boy she'd trained so many years ago. Now, aside from his baldness, there was a dour, forbidding look to his lined features, his sunken eyes. He stood near the center of the group, next to Wolf, who looked a little older, a lot more tired, and very glad to see her, if his grin—still the grin of a boy, she thought—was any indication. On Wolf's other side was an older man, stocky, whose face was familiar. She struggled a moment, then remembered Rooting Hog, Caribou's younger brother. There was still a lot of resemblance between the two, but as for the young man who stood on Rooting Hog's left hand, she had no idea. The youth was very handsome, though.

There came a stir and a large, dark-wrapped figure pushed to the fore, and now Maya broke into a smile so wide she felt her jaws creak. Old Berry! And trailing along next to the Root Woman, a girl of breathtaking beauty, whose glinting emerald-and-sapphire gaze made it plain that Maya's niece had grown into spectacular adulthood.

Maya had tried to maintain a slow, dignified pace, but when Old Berry broke into a smile as wide as Maya's own and extended her arms for a hug, Maya forgot all dignity and broke into a run. A moment later she was enfolded in the almost forgotten—but oh, how sweetly remembered now—warmth of the ancient Root Woman's embrace.

"Welcome home, Maya," Old Berry whispered, her voice rusty and choked and—were those *tears*?

Yes, Maya thought, they were tears, and then she realized that she was weeping as well.

Now they all crowded around, murmuring, touching, and

finally Old Berry released her, and Wolf stepped up in her place.

His hug was stronger, but just as welcoming. She buried her face in the crook between his neck and shoulder, and smelled his musky male odor. "Oh, Wolf. I've missed you so."

He nodded as he squeezed, and whispered in her ear, "As soon as this is over, we have to talk. Anyway, welcome home, Maya. I've missed you, too."

One by one she received an embrace from the rest of the greeting party. The handsome young man was named Sharp Knife and, surprisingly enough, was Rooting Hog's son. Muskrat was the only one who didn't touch her. He bowed stiffly from the waist, his eyes shadowed, and said, "The Spirits praise your return to your People, Great Maya."

"I'm not—" she hesitated. She thought to herself, *Oh, let him have his mumbo jumbo. I'll fix it later.* "It's good to see you in fine health, Shaman Muskrat," she replied, equally formal. He bowed once again, then stepped back, his satisfaction evident that the Spirits had been properly acknowledged.

The girl came forward last, and she moved slowly, as if overcome by shyness—or by fear. Her dark hair tumbled about her pale features like an ebony waterfall. Maya stretched out her hands to her. "Come, White Moon, let me see your face. My, aren't you a beautiful girl."

White Moon's cheeks bloomed a sudden pair of red roses, and her fantastic eyes turned down in embarrassment.

Doesn't she know how pretty she is? Maya wondered. She hugged her deeply, then held her at arm's length as she looked into her eyes. They were red and puffy around the edges, as if she'd been crying recently.

Tears? On the day of your wedding? That *bears some looking into,* Maya thought. So did the tension evident in the girl's body as she breathed, in a voice so low and tremulous as to be nearly inaudible, "Aunt . . . Great Maya, it is an honor to meet you at last."

This has gone far enough, Maya thought. "Dear," she said briskly, "I am your Aunt Maya, and I'm not a great anything, no matter what you've heard from other people. You may call me Auntie, for I'm *much* older than you."

She hugged her niece one last time, and did not miss the sharp glance her little speech had drawn from the Shaman Muskrat.

That one, she thought, *has made a life of his own, and he doesn't think my return is helping it at all. Well, it was only to be expected. I'll have to soothe his worries first thing. Mother knows, I've had enough trouble with Shamans in my time.*

A rising murmur brought her head up, and she nearly gasped, for the wide crossroads, and the environs of New Camp beyond, had suddenly become a sea of wide-eyed people.

"Great Spirits," she said to Wolf, "so *many* of them?"

He chuckled. "That's not all of them. Many hunters are out on the steppes with their families."

"Goodness! Well, the Mother has been good to our People, then."

Something shadowed in Wolf's gaze forewarned against further talk. "Perhaps," he said, "but enough greetings, sister. Shall we go back to my house? I'm sure you must be tired." He glanced at the sun. "And hot," he added. "And I would like to meet your son, as well."

"My what?" She turned, wondering what in the world Wolf was talking about. Then she understood.

"Oh, you mean *Serpent*." She laughed. "Here, boy, come meet my brother." She took Serpent's thin arm and tugged him gently forward. "He's not my son," she added, "but I'll tell you that story later."

Wolf's eyes widened. Plainly he wanted to say more—Maya could see him looking first at the boy's eyes, then at Maya's own identical ones, but he kept his counsel and merely hugged the boy briefly and said, "Welcome to the Green Valley, Serpent."

Serpent, though his vocabulary was limited, understood the gist of Wolf's greeting and replied carefully, "Thank you, strong Chief."

Caribou's done some coaching, I see, Maya thought. She let Serpent retreat back to the shelter of Caribou's side, and said, "Let's go on to Home Camp." Now her eyes began to shine. "I want to see *everything*."

"And so you shall," Wolf replied. "But I still want to talk to you. And quickly."

3

Wolf stared at the woman who sat next to the open door of his house. They were alone. He had shooed out the women and children. Dusk was yet two hours away, but already the drums were beating.

"Maya," he said at last, his voice thoughtful.

She smiled at him. "How are you, brother?"

He watched her and thought of the little girl he'd once known, and the terrible things that had shaped the woman she had later become. Now she was changed again. She looked smaller, frailer, and somehow softer, as if her years away from the Green Valley had rubbed away the jagged edges of her earlier life.

"I'm fine, Maya. I'm healthy, my children are strong, my wives happy. The Two Tribes have prospered in your absence. The hunters range far and return with heavy loads for the winter, and the valley gives us roots and plants and fish for the catching. Even ducks, with the aid of your gift of bows and arrows."

Maya smiled gently. "I'm glad to hear that, brother."

"But what of you, Maya? What happened to those who left?"

She sensed he was dodging the question he really wanted to ask, and since she wasn't at all sure how she would answer *that,* she told him of her tale of the missing years, and of her final confrontation with Buffalo Daughter.

He nodded pensively when she finished. He had listened with only half a mind, for the rest of his attention was on the unasked questions. To Maya, his concerns were so obvious she felt herself relent. Maybe he could even be of some help.

"You want to know why I came back here, don't you?"

He sighed heavily. "You know your niece is to be married to Sharp Knife of the Bison Clan tonight?"

She nodded, remembering Muddy Crow's flood of bitter gossip. "I wish her every happiness," she said.

"So do I . . . Maya?"

"Yes?"

"Why *did* you come back? Did you know the Keeper was to be married?"

She smiled softly, thinking of the beautiful girl. What had her life been like? Evidently easier than her own had been, but for all that, she thought she detected some deep sadness in her niece, so deep that perhaps even the girl herself wasn't aware of it.

What are you going to tell him, Great Maya? He thinks you have all the answers, but you don't have any answers, do you? Tools never have answers, they only do what they must do.

But that was dodging the issue, wasn't it? She had been Shaman here for a time, and this was her home, her People. She had chosen for them, and though that choice had been terrible, she had no regrets. But what was she to do now? If the Mother had sent her here, She had not vouchsafed any further instructions.

One she will keep, the other send away
Till joined once again, they bring the new day . . .

Was *that* the answer? If it was, she would have to be very sure of it—and she had no time. *No time at all!*

"Wolf, tell me about White Moon and this wedding. Tell me everything. There's more to it than just a marriage, isn't there? Sharp Knife is my nephew by marriage, but he is of the Bison People. What does it mean?"

He rocked forward and grasped his knees in his arms. The crowded paths of Home Camp were bustling now, as laughing families arrived from the farthest reaches of the valley for the festivities. Laughter floated in the air, and the sweet smell of wood smoke and roasting meat. Several feasts were in progress at once, and through it all, the drums pounded out their insistent, rhythmic songs.

Wolf listened to the sound of the drums for several moments, and then he told Maya everything.

When he finished, Maya looked even smaller and more tired, her thin form outlined in the light from the door. "Oh, dear," she said. "I've just made things worse, haven't I?"

He shrugged. "I don't know, sister. Have you? I was hoping you would have the answers. You still haven't answered my first question, you know. How *did* you happen to come back at exactly this time? Did you know about the marriage somehow?"

How much to tell him? How much do I know?

She raised her shoulders and let them fall in a gesture that was as much exhaustion as anything else. "No, I didn't know about the wedding, Wolf. But I think the Mother did." She paused. "I don't think She wants the wedding to take place."

Wolf drew back, his face tight with shock.

Maya plowed on grimly. "You see, my brother, She sent me. And She sent White Moon's mate *with* me. His name is Serpent. *He* is to be the husband of the Keeper of the Stone."

4

"Wolf is frantic now, of course," Maya said in the cool dimness of Old Berry's house.

"I can imagine," Berry said. "It's always upsetting when the Goddess meddles in the affairs of Her People." Berry breathed a rusty exhalation, sounding so tired that Maya wondered how much longer the old woman had in this World. *How did she hold on so long? Was she waiting for my return?*

"And She meddles so *much*," Berry continued. "Maya, are you certain this is what She wants? You know what an uproar—no, worse than that—calling off the wedding will mean."

Maya rubbed her forehead slowly. It had been a long day, and it wasn't over yet. She wished she could give the answer the Root Woman wanted to hear—a resounding *yes*, full of conviction of inner knowledge, of the Word of the Goddess revealed. But she couldn't, for the Mother had told her nothing, only narrowed the choices until no choice was left. Why else had She put Serpent, with his eyes and his Stone, in her path? With the Gods, Maya believed, there was no such thing as coincidence, not for Their tools. But there was no certainty either.

"I have said what I believe to be true," she replied, picking her words carefully. "It is all I can do. I would have rather not had to make the choice so quickly, but—" She spread her hands and shrugged. "My preferences are of little moment. As usual."

"So much at stake," Berry whispered. "So little time to decide." She paused, fanning herself with one meaty hand, breathing heavily. "It will tear the Green Valley apart."

"Don't you think I *know* that?" An unattractive buzz of self-pity filled Maya's words. She heard it, and was ashamed. She had never asked for these burdens, but she had been born to them, and she had learned to *bear* them, for the sake of her People, for the sake of her Goddess. Now was no time to go soft and weak—the choices were stern, but they must be made.

Thinking this strengthened her, and she sat up a little straighter. "The decision is made," she said. "Whether I made it, or the Mother made it for me, doesn't matter now."

She leaned forward. "Berry, unless I'm wrong, you still have a lot of influence—at least with those who matter."

Berry nodded her head a fraction, the motion a curious blend of wariness and complacency. "There are those who still listen to an old Root Woman," she replied.

"Yes, I'm sure there are. So they will listen when you tell them that the wedding must not take place. You needn't mention Serpent—not yet, that would be too much for people to accept all at once. Simply say that Great Maya— Mother, how I hate that!—has returned, and in respect of that, the wedding must be ... *postponed* for a while. I think people will understand. Obviously, my return has upset some people, and maybe made others happy. But I don't believe in coincidence, Berry. And neither, I think, do you."

"There are no coincidences," Berry said, and while Maya didn't entirely agree with this, it suited her purpose to nod and continue.

"A delay, at first. Just a delay, while Great Maya determines how best to honor the Keeper of the Stone."

At this, however, Old Berry's eyes widened a bit. "The Keeper? But you are back now, Maya. Surely you will take up the Stone again? The Keeper is a silly girl and, worse, a willful brat. She had Kept the Stone, but now its rightful owner must reclaim it."

Berry stopped, then stared keenly at Maya. "You must have the Stone, Maya. Otherwise, I won't help you to get what you want."

"Not what I want, what She wants!" *Couldn't the old*

woman see? What a horrible bargain. I hadn't thought of that at all . . .

"The Mother wants you to bear the Stone, Maya," Berry said adamantly. "Can't *you* see *that?*"

And, of course, that was the other meaning of the coincidences, the defeats, the treks, the meetings, everything—*You won't let me leave it, will You?*

Maya's shoulders slumped in submission. "All right," she said. "Perhaps you are even right."

"It's your gift," Berry said. "You can't escape it. Not now, not ever." Maya heard the compassion in her voice, but she heard the stoniness of doom, as well.

"Not as long as I live," Maya said. She slapped her knees. "Well, then, I suppose we'd better get started. Wolf is waiting for me to finish with you. Then he will speak to Rooting Hog. I suppose I'd better talk to White Moon. Will she be a problem, do you think? She seemed a sweet girl."

Old Berry chuckled sourly. "White Moon a problem? Oh, I think she'll be more than that. Much more."

5

"I won't do it," White Moon said.

The two women sat in the silence of the Chief's house. The drums had fallen quiet. The whole valley was quiet except for whispered murmurs as the new rumors, borne by women like Muddy Crow, swept across the gathered crowds. Maya had seen them standing in small knots of people, their faces intent, but when she passed through them, most looked away from her.

Maya stared speculatively at her niece. The girl faced her, shoulders rigid, her beautiful eyes flaring like campfires on the winter steppe. White Moon's face was set, and on it Maya red the signs. Terror, and rage. Both focused on her aunt, who was Great Maya, and who was ruining her life.

Or so she thinks, Maya thought. *But she is so young. I wonder if she can understand the bargain I have made. Mother, how I wish she could understand! But she can't, for her life has been easy, and the Stone has never squeezed her in its adamantine grip.*

"Only for a time, dear," Maya said softly. "I have just returned. You will have your marriage, don't you worry." *Mother forgive me for that lie—a marriage awaits you, girl, but not the one you expect.*

The Stone does have you in its grip, Maya realized suddenly. *And you are just now beginning to feel the terrible strength of it. Ah, the fate of tools!*

"No," White Moon said, and shook her head once. "I will marry Sharp Knife this night, as planned. Nothing will stop that. Do you understand? *Nothing!*"

But there was a quaver in her voice, and tears were starting at the corners of her eyes. *She knows,* Maya thought. *This is nothing but a tantrum. She knows . . .*

She reached over and patted the girl on her knee. "Dear, this is for the best. You must trust me." Then she played her highest card. "The Goddess knows what is best. For you, for the Stone, for Her People."

"I hate it!" White Moon balled her fingers into small, hard fists. The pot of her rage boiled over, tinting her cheeks red, turning her eyes into blazing coals. *"I hate Her, I hate the Stone, I hate YOU!"*

When she finished this outburst she sat glaring, her face bloated and ugly, panting like a pig in the sun. Maya had recoiled, wiping her cheeks—the girl had splattered saliva all over her face—and a part of her longed to simply slap some sense into the brat. Brat? What a deceiving name. Little monster was more like it.

But the greater part of her sympathized deeply with her niece. After all, what was this frenzied outburst but evidence of emotions Maya herself had known all her life? Yet she couldn't allow that sympathy to color what she must do now. When she had tried to reject the burden of the Stone, that rejection had meant near disaster for everybody. She couldn't allow White Moon to make a similar mistake. Greater things were at risk than one girl's happiness.

And I'm offering to take the burden from you, you stupid girl! Maya thought. *If you only knew what a gift that is.*

"I'm sorry, White Moon, but I have already made the decision. There will be no wedding tonight."

You are young. It seems like the end of the world now, but you'll survive. You'll get over it.

White Moon uttered a single, despairing shriek, turned,

threw herself down, and began to pound the earth floor of the Chief's house with her fists.

Maya watched for a moment, then stood, and silently made her exit. Outside, Wolf stood, his eyes anxious.

"Leave her be for a while," Maya said. "She's upset now, but she'll be better soon."

Wolf nodded slowly. "I'll send her mother later."

"Yes, that's good." Maya turned. "I'm so *tired,*" she said. "Where is Caribou?"

"He's at Rooting Hog's house. With the boy." Plainly, Wolf would have liked to discuss *the boy* further, but a fusillade of wails from the inside of his house interrupted him. "I'll get her mother," he said quickly.

Somebody should have spanked the little beast when it would have done some good, Maya thought. *But it's too late for that now. She'll just have to grow up.*

"Take the Stone from her and bring it to me," Maya said. "I'll be with Caribou."

"Yes, Maya," Wolf replied.

Something in his tone made Maya pause. *Oh, dear. Here I am, not back even a day yet, and already I'm ordering the Chief of the Two Tribes around like a boy. What a mess. Am I ever going to get anything* right?

"I'm sorry, Wolf, I didn't mean—"

He grinned his old familiar grin at her. "Don't worry. I understand. It's hard, isn't it? I've always been glad it wasn't my burden to bear. But it will get better, now that you're back. I'm sure of it."

Of course, he couldn't have been more wrong.

Chapter Nineteen

1

If Gotha wondered whether he was leading the People of Fire and Ice on a fool's errand, he didn't show it. Things had gone too far for that.

It was the Crone's fault, of course. *She* had almost managed to put an end to the whole thing, and in defeating her plots, he had committed all of them to this chase forever. Or at least until he found the boy. He had locked in his options, he might have said. Or been locked in, he might also have said. Whichever, he'd been forced to choose, and because of the miserable old bag who was his mother, it had really been no choice at all.

He wiped sweat from his brow with one dust-caked hand and squinted at the scenery up ahead. Actually, scenery was too descriptive a word for the rolling, lion-colored swell of the steppe. It was all dry grass now, and endless, blank blue sky. They had left the woodlands far behind as they toiled north along the river.

She almost beat me, didn't she? Gotha spat heavily at the thought, his mouth full of bitterness. *I should have strangled her years ago, but I didn't. I still haven't, and I hope that isn't my worst mistake. But I think I will need her, I don't know how exactly, but her time is not done yet.*

It was a curious thought in one who had been so sorely tried. It was coming on noon now, the hottest part of an already hot day, and his breath burned in his lungs as he tramped along, remembering . . .

2

It began simply enough, and that was the beauty of the deception. Though it was a lie, the evidence all around seemed to make it look like the truth. And all lies, Gotha knew, all *great* lies, needed that element of truth to make them work.

It was the bounty that did it. Gotha woke the morning after the first feast with his belly still heavy and distended. A slow, hot lethargy filled his limbs. He glanced out the door of his Spirit House with surprise, noting how high the sun rode the morning sky. He had slept far longer than was his usual habit, and even now felt like nothing more than rolling over in his furs for another nap.

It was the food, he guessed. He hadn't eaten so much fresh meat in at least a moon, certainly not since the tribe had begun this trek north.

Gently he rubbed his distended belly. He *would* have gone back to sleep, but there was no denying a bladder full to bursting. Groaning softly, he staggered out of the Spirit House and relieved himself on the ground in a long, intensely satisfying yellow stream.

While he idly flapped his penis dry, he looked out over the makeshift camp. Evidently he wasn't the only late sleeper. The few tents set up still mostly had their flaps tied shut, and dotted here and there were the shapeless furry lumps of sleeping rolls. Only a few lethargic children walked listlessly about, their brown tummies bulging.

Gotha stretched. He felt a little better with an empty bladder, but the call of his furs was still appealing. He yawned. Yes, a nap would be a fine thing, and he would awaken refreshed, he told himself, ready to finish harvesting the salt so they could resume the trek on the following day. Today, he decided, he would let them rest.

"Ah, sonny, up and about already, are you?"

He turned slowly at the cracked voice and saw the Crone hobbling toward him, her awful grin showing like the slimy pink belly of a worm in freshly turned mud.

"A little sleeping after all the feasting?" she continued, her voice an awful parody of greasy good cheer.

"Don't talk to me," he grunted, and turned away. "I'm going to sleep some more."

"Oh, yes, get your sleep, sonny. After all, there's no reason for hurry *now*, is there?"

He paused in his move to duck back inside the house and cocked an eye at her. She stood a few feet away, her gnarled claws clutched together, rubbing dryly at each other, and positively *beamed* at him.

"What are you talking about?"

"Oh, nothing, don't you worry, just get started on that nap of yours. I'll wake you before noon, unless you want to sleep longer. After all, what's a mother for?"

For a moment the absolute horror of *that* thought startled him—a mother is for *murder* was the first thing that popped into his mind. The second thing was more practical. *What's she so happy about?*

The days when Gotha's mother being happy meant happiness for Gotha were long gone. He turned and stared at her full on, his eyes squinted warily. "What have you done, you old hag?"

She returned his stare steadily, her one good eye a mockery of innocence. "I haven't done anything, son. You did. When you set out after that little monster. You blasphemed against Her, and She sent you gifts instead. Gifts for all of us. Not your filthy Lord Big Dick, mighty Shaman. *Her! Her gifts!*"

A horrible suspicion began to creep into his skull. He turned away from her and raced through the camp. Each furry lump he came to, he kicked as hard as he could. He left a trail of grunts, mutters, and groans in his wake, as men and women sat up and rubbed bruised heads and aching ribs.

Their eyes followed him. The Shaman, it seemed, had not awakened in a good mood. Maybe it was something he ate. Some of them looked at it a bit differently. Maybe he would eat *them*.

There had been things like that, off and on. Not since the Speaker had come to them, but now the Speaker was gone. Maybe the old ways would return. But the Crone had told some of them that it need not be so. Those were the ones who followed Gotha's enraged passage with narrow, considering eyes. And the Crone had chosen well. Those who considered were capable of carrying out their own conclusions.

Gotha roared on. By the time he learned of his mistake, it was almost too late.

3

After Gotha had kicked his way through the camp, most of his rage had dissipated, leaving a queasy cold lump of fear in his belly. The Lord only knew what kind of demonic mischief his cursed mother, in the name of her Bitch Goddess, might have worked while his guard was down.

I have to watch the foul bitch every moment! Take my eyes off her for a second and she's at me again. Ought to KILL HER KILL HER KILL HER—

He was grinning madly when he approached the salt out-cropping and found his worst fears confirmed. That lunatic smile *stretched* into something horribly hilarious, a murderous laughing grimace that left his jaws aching the rest of the day.

Kill her, yes, KILL KILL KILL!

"Get hold of yourself," he whispered aloud, while his blood pulsed like a drum in his ears and a red haze obscured his vision. The world tilted, swayed, and he thought for a moment he was going to vomit up all that rich greasy meat onto his naked toes, but he managed to hold everything down.

At first glance it didn't look like much. The plates of salt were nearly unchanged. He could spot a few places where the outcropping had been worked, chipped away, because in those parts the scars were pure, eye-squinching white. That wasn't the problem. The *problem* was that there were the sticks wrapped with hanks of dark hair and topped with tiny verminous skulls—rats, chucks, rabbits—planted all about the salt lick he had openly proclaimed a gift from the Lord of Snakes less than half a day before!

Her totems! The marks of the murderous Bitch Herself!

He grabbed his hair and twisted it until the pain brought tears to his eyes. With the agony came a curious calm, as if a soft blanket of soothing, cool snow overlaid his rage and banked it. After a while he relaxed.

"Thank you, Lord," he muttered. It would, after all, most likely make matters worse if he just went back to the camp and ripped her face off with his naked fingernails. Now he felt composed enough to avoid that mistake, at least for the time being.

Think, O mighty Shaman. What has she done, she and her Bitch? Something treacherous, no doubt. She's staked out the salt lick with Her icons. What has she said to those who would listen to her?

(*And who might they be? I wonder. I would be very interested in finding out* their *names.*) That awful, lopsided growling grin had crept back on his face, but he didn't notice.

KILL HER!

But he would have to go slow, yes, it would take a while to repair the damage. If he went about it the wrong way, one of those whom she'd convinced just might find a way to slip a knife into his back and settle the issue permanently. He didn't want that to happen . . .

BURN HER ALIVE! SCOOP HER ROTTEN EYE OUT WITH HIS OWN HANDS!

It would have made both the Crone and her Bitch Goddess too happy.

"Oh, Lord, guide me now," he whispered, and glanced up at the sky, which showed no sign. Nothing, not a bird, not a cloud, nothing.

"Typical," he muttered, and turned around and walked slowly back to the now-awakened camp. By the time he reached the first bedroll, which now clumped at the feet of a hunter named Skregath, his features were relaxed and his gaze was clear.

"Good morning to you, Skregath," he said politely.

The hunter eyed him uneasily. "Good morning, Shaman," he replied.

Were you one of them? Gotha wondered. He walked on.

"Mother?" It cost him more than he could ever say to call her that—and in front of the People, no less! "Could you join me in the Spirit House a moment? It seems we have something to discuss."

4

She had barely stuck her wizened head through his door flap when he grabbed a hank of her ratty white hair and jerked her the rest of the way through, then *heaved* her across the dirt floor where she thunked like a side of meat against one of the stakes driven into the ground.

"Uh *hoo!*" The air punched out of her in an awful gurgling belch and she lay still, her one eye staring at him blindly, her ruined eye leaking something runny and yellow.

"Well, Mother, what have you gotten up to now?" He smiled at her, then stomped down hard on her exposed belly. A great gassy fart exploded from her rear end and he made a face.

"You stink, you rotten old woman. Why haven't you died yet? Are you a curse of some kind?"

She shook her head dazedly, and tried to get one shrunken arm underneath herself. It was like watching an ancient rat try to scrabble out of a hole. After a time she rolled over and lay on her back, her chest heaving. Gotha thought about putting his foot right through that flimsy rib cage—oh, *listen* to those bones crack like dried sticks—but he had promised himself. Oh, yes, a promise is a promise is a—

Stop that!

Yes, anger is a good thing, but everything has its place, and right now putting his mother out of the misery he'd already put her *in* wouldn't be the smartest thing he could do. In fact, knocking her around like this probably wasn't that good an idea, either. His luck hadn't been all that wonderful lately. All he needed now was for her to die on him before he could straighten out whatever plots she'd spun while he'd let his guard down.

So he hunkered down on his hams, propped his elbows on his knees, cupped his hands beneath his chin, and peered at her curiously. "What did you do, *Mother?*" His voice was as flat as his gaze.

She winced, then groaned, more to herself than with any hope that her pain might have an effect on him. "You hurt me, sonny. I think a rib's sprung loose. I'm getting old, I guess."

He stared at her while he gnawed furiously on his lower lip. Blood trickled from the corner of his mouth, but he didn't notice. "I'm going to hurt you a lot more if you don't *tell me what you did!*"

A moment of silence froze between the two of them,

punctuated by his steaming glare, by her chill cyclopean gaze. Then she hiccuped and the spell broke.

"I talked to people," she rasped. She rubbed her throat. "That's all, I just talked to them, told them the truth."

"The truth isn't in you, bitch. What lies did you tell them?"

For a moment she made no reply, only rubbed her throat softly, carefully, as if something was damaged inside there. It was possible, he supposed. He hadn't been careful, or gentle, in the beginning moments of their conversation.

KILL HER Kill Her kill her . . .

"Oh, be quiet," he murmured, feeling suddenly exhausted. "No, not you. Tell me what you said."

She had hitched herself into a crooked sitting position, and there she squatted, rubbing her elbow. "I told them the truth," she said softly, "just like I tried to tell you. The salt came from the earth—it is Her gift, not the bounty of Lord Big Dick. And I have Dreamed about it, about the salt—our Mother gave it to us, even though you don't believe in Her, because She wanted our people to have a sign."

The Crone's voice had grown steadier throughout this little speech, and by the time she paused, there was a ringing quality to her words that frightened him.

"You didn't Dream!" he snarled.

"Oh, but I did, Gotha my son. I Dreamed, and She told me about your madness, about this insane chase. The salt was from Her, as a sign for us to stop." Suddenly her single eye seemed to swell with certainty. "Gotha, please, you must give this up. Here is a good place for us, next to the river, next to the forest. We can hunt, fish. She made the hunting good for us, and She will again. You *saw* how much game the hunters brought back!"

Gotha took in a deep breath. If he hadn't known her words were lies, he could almost have believed them himself. But they were lies, nevertheless.

"You said this to others? And put your infernal totems all about the salt lick?"

She nodded. Crushed though she was, there was the stink of sickly triumph wafting from her. "It's too late, my son. Not everybody, but enough, believe me. Believe *Her*." Now she looked away.

"You are my son, Gotha, but if you try to take the people away from the salt, away from this place, you will die."

Gotha rocked back, stood up, towered over her. His eyes were bloodshot holes in his head, but his voice was as calm as he could make it, which was very calm indeed. "Will I die like my father, do you think? Or will it be quicker, you murdering bitch? A knife in the night, a rock bashed through my skull when my back is turned?"

He spat contemptuously on the ground. "I know none of them will face me head on, for your Bitch is the Goddess of Treachery. But we shall see, *Mother*!"

The load of venom in his final word was so great that the Crone actually grunted, as if he had kicked her in the head. But he hadn't done that. He had kicked her in the heart instead.

He turned and stalked out of the tent.

5

Gotha walked to the edge of the camp, away from the river and the salt lick. As he walked through the camp he felt the stares—some curious, but more resentful, even angry. And he understood the source of that hostility—he knew his people as a Shaman knew them, their dark secrets, their fears, their simple hopes. He loved them all, but they were so *stupid*.

And that cowlike stupidity just might kill him. They left the Spirits to him, and that was fine, but the bargain had changed him without changing them. They trusted in simple things, and left him to wrestle with the complexities of the Spirit World. So he grew cynical, and they grew malleable, and in the normal course of things that was just the way he liked it. But now he faced the conundrum of all Shamans, priests, ministers—the malleable flock could be as easily worked by one as another. And the Crone, in her cackling treachery, had understood this, and made use of it.

The Mother had always been the minor God, but now the Crone took advantage of the People's dissatisfaction with Gotha to try to turn the People away from the God whom Gotha served.

He rubbed his chin and watched the way they moved slowly about the camp, the way the children seemed to sense the tension and grow quarrelsome, the way the women huddled together, the way the men cast their glances in his direction. Oh, they knew he was angry—and that was a bad sign. Never before had he seen such sullenness, such a slow, plodding resistance to his anger. They had stepped out of his way when he walked, lowered their heads to avoid looking at him, turned their backs on his anger.

It meant that they feared something else more than they feared him, and that was a great turning point.

God destroy the salt!

It boiled down to a question of belief. Who would they believe? Him, and his Lord, or the Crone, and her Goddess? He chuckled bitterly.

Shafted on my own spear, he thought, the image sickeningly vivid, all the more so because of the likelihood that such a thing might actually happen. The People were stupid and trusting, but they could only be pushed so far. And *because* they were stupid, they hated indecision, hated *not knowing.* They had trusted him to *know* for them, and now they were uncertain.

Life was uncertain enough without the Gods brawling between themselves. There was an easy way to end the quarrel. All they had to do was end the life of one God's servant, and the disagreement would end with it.

And I guess it will be easy enough to figure out who they choose. Not Gotha, who has sent two of their hunters to their deaths, who has led them from the places they hunted for years, and how proposes to drag them away from good water, good hunting, and salt to continue what must seem like a wild goose chase into the barrens of the north.

For what? To recover a boy they all hated and feared anyway. He grinned sourly. *Put it that way, and I might go along, too.*

Except for one thing—the Lord of Snakes and Fire. In order to let them stop here, in order to give up the holy chase, he would have to renounce that Lord's power—and his mother would win at last.

He couldn't do it.

He didn't know if he could do what he would have to do otherwise, but he couldn't do *that.* He would die first.

Which might be exactly what would happen, but he no longer cared about *that,* either. He made his decision in that moment, and as he did so, a mighty peacefulness crept into his thoughts and soothed them.

He walked back into the camp and found Rakaba. "You and the others," he told the scowling hunter. "Go cut wood and bring it back. Build a great hearth. I want fire . . . a *big* fire."

6

There would be a delay. Gotha planned on three days. It couldn't be helped, three days were better than ending the pursuit, better than disobeying the Lord of Fire.

As he sat in his Spirit House later that day, he was astonished at the thoroughness of the Crone's treachery. She had whispered her lies to *everybody,* and those lies had taken root in places he would never have imagined possible. The soil must have been much more fertile than he'd ever suspected.

Rakaba, for instance. He had always believed Rakaba and his dour friend Agarth were two of the staunchest, most unquestioning believers in his fiery Lord. But today there was a shadow on Rakaba's normally rattling tongue, and the copper-haired hunter only nodded and made no move to follow Gotha's instructions.

The Shaman folded his arms across his chest. "Well," he said. "Did you hear me, Rakaba?"

"I heard you, Shaman."

"So? Then get going. I want the hearth built and burning by nightfall."

Rakaba lowered his eyes. Hesitation made his features tighten. "Shaman?"

"Yes, what is it, Rakaba?" *Has she convinced him, too? Dag or Ulgol would have jumped—but they are dead, aren't they?* Gotha felt his stomach clench into a hot, uneasy lump. *Are they all against me, then?*

"Why do we have to find the brat?"

Now Gotha's stomach spasmed as he sought to control the rage that surged up inside him like bubbles of burning gas, the sour digestion caused by the swallowing of his own pride. But he had to be careful. The Bitch had done

Her work, and he was no longer free to pound Rakaba into compliant mush. Rakaba might fight back, this time.

So I have to explain myself to this babbling clod, Gotha thought. *Well, why not? Everything else is turning to shit. Why not this, too?*

"Rakaba," he said, pouring as much sweet reasonableness into his tone as he could, though he almost sickened on the honey in the words, "our Lord has told me what we must do. He had given us the bounty of salt and game to speed us on our way. I don't question Him, and you shouldn't, either. But He has His great enemy, and She is great indeed. Still, fear not Her whispered lies—for that is all they are. And I will show not only you, but all our people, who is the stronger of the two, the lying Bitch or our mighty Lord. In three days' time, all will be made plain. Until then, trust me as you always have. Will you do that? I promise you, our Lord will remember His own, when all this is behind us."

Rakaba brightened visibly at this little speech, and Gotha thought, not for the first time, how easily the People could be swayed by fine words and an air of conviction. *Poor lost things, they are only tools . . .*

"A hearth, Shaman?" An undercurrent of excitement sparkled in the question.

Gotha smiled. "Yes, Rakaba, a great hearth. In three days there will be a Test, and we shall see who is the stronger. But first"—and now he slapped Rakaba heartily on his brawny shoulder—"bring me wood and bring me stone."

"For the *Test.*" This not a question, but a breathless statement.

"Yes, hunter, the Test. The Test of Fire."

7

The Crone slept out in the open, wrapped in a raggedy bed-roll, a piece of hide so old and stinking it was a wonder it protected her at all. She carried it, wrapped around her few remaining possessions—mostly the herbs and berries of her witch-work—on her back, supporting herself with a stout stick she'd cut herself many years before. No one ever offered to help her, not for as many years as she'd owned her stick, and she could remember the day she'd cut *that* as easily as she could remember her own name.

Her name was Gayatha. Her lips moved as she mumbled it to herself, *Gayatha Gayatha Gayatha* . . . A tuneless little chant that sometimes she found soothing. Nobody else called her Gayatha anymore, had not done so since the day her own son had ripped one of her eyeballs from her skull and burned it before her single remaining eye.

Ah, Mother, the things I have suffered for you!

Nobody called her Gayatha anymore. *Crone,* and *Hag,* and *Bitch* were the kindest names she could hope for now, and these from her own blood. Yet he had let her live, and because of it, the rest of the Clan of Fire and Ice left her alone, even feared her a little.

And I can be useful, oh, yes I can. She knew the secrets hidden in roots, in the berries and the juice of berries, in the herbs she found and dried. She could heal, and she was particularly skilled in the complaints common to all women, the cramps, the pains, the blood.

She had midwifed every child of the Tribe. Such womanly concerns were for the most part beneath the interest of the mighty Shaman, but it was the niche within which she had survived and, eventually, even prospered.

After the feast she had first spoken to the women and, later, the men. Not all the women, nor certainly all the men, but enough. The women listened better, and that was good, for they would plant the seeds in their own men, given enough time. And when she had spoken to as many as she could, she had taken three of them and gone to the salt lick and put down the sticks with their furry, bony loads and marked the place for Her who watched over womanly things.

She Who Gave Birth To All.

Now, as the Crone who had once been called Gayatha watched her son stride from his house, upon which floor she sprawled in numb agony, she knew that if she were to survive at all, she would have to win.

Gotha might have to die for that to happen.

She thought about this as she forced her spavined legs beneath herself and groaningly wobbled upright. Gotha and his brat. The Shaman and the Speaker.

That was a story, one she had tried to end a hundred times before, but Gotha had always stopped her. She had persevered, though, and although she hadn't managed to kill the brat, she had at least managed to drive him away.

Let him stay that way. Poison! Doom!

The Crone didn't understand exactly *why* she hated the brat so much, except that as long as the Speaker Spoke for the God, the Goddess remained only a small thing in the life of Her People. A minor Spirit, good only for women's concerns, though Gotha knew full well the Mother's Power, having tasted its fury before.

He had never forgiven her for it. Or forgiven the Goddess, either. Sometimes the Crone got the two confused, especially when she'd been Dreaming. Now she understood the difference fully, for her Mother had finally made good on the promises offered so long before, the promises that had led the Crone to work murder on her own mate.

The Crone stumped to Gotha's door, ducked slowly, and climbed outside in time to see him storm out of the camp. To her, his rage was plainly visible, almost baking off his skin, but he was able to hide it from the rest. A small throb of pride began to beat in her breast, though she fought to extinguish it—he had become a great Shaman, greater even than his father.

But she had spun her webs well. Agarth's wife had listened to her, and Skregath's two grown daughters and their husbands, and others besides. The Crone understood that the People were upset, almost mutinously so, by the deaths of Dag and Ulgol and now this forced march into unfamiliar territory. No one had liked the Speaker, and few cared much for the Shaman's crusade to capture him.

The discovery of the salt was the final straw, that and the plenitude of game hereabouts. It was, in fact, more than that—it would be the *excuse* that allowed them to defy their Shaman, for even a Shaman might be destroyed if it could be shown that his relations with the Spirits had been poisoned.

The People depended so utterly on Gotha's intercession with the World beyond the World that if he failed them, then they would destroy him. Before he could destroy them.

For a moment she felt a tug of pity, just as she'd felt it years before as she mixed poison for her mate. But only a tug, and only for a moment. The ways of the Goddess were hard, and the Crone had grown old, but she still had some strength left.

It would be enough. She was certain of it.

The Mother had told her so.

8

Gotha supervised the laying of the hearth all that day, and personally struck the sparks that ignited the deadwood piled within the stones. Once the blaze had begun to crackle, he ordered more wood—this fresh cut, still green, huge logs of it. Several of the hunters, along with their women, had hacked at living trees for hours to supply this smoky fuel. Gotha knew that it would take the whole night for everything to burn down to an even bed of coals, and then, on the next day, he would pile on more wood, and so on the day after that, until the coals burned white and pure in a layer as deep as his knees.

Three days to prepare the fire. Three days to prepare himself. On that first night, as he bent all his concentration on making the hearth ready, he didn't think about the Crone at all. Nor did she trouble him with her presence. He was vaguely aware of her clumping about the camp, but always on the edges, pausing here and there to hold whispered conversation. He supposed those murmured cabals had to do with his decision, but as long as she stayed away from him, he let her be.

She had made a deadly mistake, and soon enough she would learn just *how* deadly it was. In the meantime, let her prattle and plot. Only in the back of his mind did he note with whom she spoke. He was Shaman, after all, and for him all knowledge was potentially valuable.

Lord, show me my enemies, for they are Yours.

So far, the Snake was being obliging. And as the fire popped and roared into the darkness, sending up whirling clouds of sparks, he felt a Power flow from it. Greedily he sucked it up. Three days hence, he would need that Power, for without the mastery of Fire, he would die.

Bitch, prepare yourself, his mind roared along with the flames. A fierce exultation seized him and he raised his arms. *Soon I will come for you.*

It seemed to him he could see the face of his father in the flames, and he bowed toward it. Then it was gone, but it had smiled.

He was certain of it. The Snake had shown him so.

9

The Crone watched the hearth grow higher, the coals deeper, and as it grew, her dread grew with it.

The Test of Fire!

She hadn't counted on *that*. She hadn't even *thought* about that. But now she had to think about it, because she had to decide yet again. It had all seemed so simple before. Now nothing was simple. In one more day the hearth would be ready, and *nothing at all would be simple!*

She stood on the far edge of the smoking pit, her face scorched by the heat radiating from the white-hot coals, and thought about how the circle always came round, how the circle had begun, and *how it had come round at last.*

Mother, must I do this?

But no answer came to her, for she faced a great fire, and the Mother did not cloak Herself in flames. The Crone stared into an inferno, and though her skin shriveled in the heat, her innards felt cold as ice.

The People of Fire and Ice. The People of Two Names. The People of Two Gods.

A long time ago, that had been. The circle had been drawn, a change had been made, and now the circle had come round again.

Circles of fire, circles of ice. The People had survived both, in a journey so long and so long ago they had nearly forgotten even the fact of it, let alone the details. But *something* had been handed down, something perhaps branded in their very cells, a *duality* that lived on, and that bound them still in the strands of its making.

The Two. Always the Two.

The Crone's husband had killed her mother. She had killed her husband. Now her son would kill . . . her?

The circle unbroken. The circle of fire.

The *Test* of Fire.

"Oh, Mother, give me strength."

But the night was silent and the forest empty, and the water only hissed in its banks, and there was no answer. The Crone shivered and wrapped her filthy skins about her and stared up at the frozen stars.

Finally she sighed and turned away from the pit. Morning would come soon enough.

"The circle . . ." she mumbled, but nobody heard.

10

Gotha was not aware of all the facts concerning his family history, particularly those relating to his maternal grandmother and the role his own father had played in her death, but even if he'd known, it wouldn't have swayed him in the slightest. He might even have appreciated such resonance among the various generations of his Shamanic forebears.

As night fell on that first day of the fire, he sat crosslegged in his Spirit House, naked, and stared into the tiny bed of coals glowing on the earth in front of him. Minuscule licks of blue flame chased themselves across the glowing crust; his sharp features, highlighted from below, were shadowed and spectral. He had not eaten that whole day, had not touched food nor water since the feast the night before.

Now he lifted a small pouch and took out some dried roots, selected a ragged fragment, slipped it into his mouth, and began to chew. He had tied shut the smoke-hole of the Spirit House, but had only closed, not tied, the door flap. When the root began to do its work, he would need to be able to get out quickly—or risk filling the small enclosure with the stench of his own feces. The root was a powerful purgative.

He chewed for a long time and swallowed with grim difficulty. He knew from experience the root would try to come back up.

Next, he found another pouch, and from it took three shrunken, dried-out, brownish lumps that had once been fat, white mushrooms. He placed these into a carved wooden bowl and began to grind them to powder with a painstakingly shaped piece of stone. As he did this, he spat into the bowl, so that eventually he finished with a thick, gluey paste. He set the bowl aside, rummaged around, and found yet another small pouch, and from this he took several pinches of a fine gray dust and scattered them across the coals. The dust ignited in bursts of multicolored sparks, releasing a thick, pungent aroma that filled the Spirit House immediately.

He inhaled deeply. Then he found the bowl of paste, dipped in a finger, and brought it to his mouth. The paste had a sharp, bitter taste, and he grimaced as he licked his finger clean. Almost immediately he felt a rush of warmth. Sweat bloomed on his forehead and across his chest.

The sensation faded after a moment, but he was relieved. The dried mushrooms had been old. He'd been worried they might have lost their power, but they hadn't.

He folded his hands across his genitals and settled back to await the onset of purification. Several minutes later he leapt up and ran from the Spirit House, in the first of many such trips. By the next morning there would be nothing left inside him but enough psychoactive alkaloids to derange a hundred Shamans.

By the time of the Testing he would be as crazy as a shit-eating rat—and far more dangerous.

11

Dusk.

The first stars winked open like distant, watching eyes above the forest. In the gathering gloom, the trees seemed to curl closer round the circle of fire, their shadow like a vast, slow cat seeking heat. The river made its presence felt with fog, which oozed from the sluggish black water and drifted in ghostly veils about the camp.

The circle was like a half-healed wound—a cracking scab of dark, glowing ash over the deeper meat of coals so incandescent they glowed almost blue. Tongues of yellow spat up from fissures in the crust, wavered delicately, and fell back again.

Two drummers hammered on hollow logs. Around them, half a dozen hunters chanted hoarsely, the sound frightening the few blackbirds that flapped over the camp and then veered sharply away.

The whole tribe was there, but no one stood closer to the pit than the length of a tall man. Any nearer and the heat broiling off the coals would blister unprotected skin. Some stood alone, others in small groups, but all of them swayed slowly, like shadow stick trees tossing in a hot, invisible wind. A kind of longing, feverish as the pit itself, baked off them. Even the children, avidly sucking their thumbs, glowed with that fervor. Something, their bulging eyes seemed to say. Something happening.

The sun slipped over the edge of the world with deliberate grace, a colossal crimson eye slowly closing. The drummers picked up their rhythms, and every now and then one of the chanting hunters would throw back his head and let go a shriek that punctured the dark like a crystal spike. In the gathered flock arms flashed jerkily, mouths dropped open, teeth gleamed, fingers twitched and snapped.

Fueled by the pounding of the drums the madness spread, uniting one and all into a single sweating, rolling mass, overheated and trembling on the brink of communal orgasm—

The words came soft and low, a fervid murmuring, then swelled into a crashing tide of sound, a welcome, a curse, a prayer:

"gotha Gotha GOTHA GOTHA GOTHA SHAMAN!"
The drum beat.
He came.

12

He walked in a straight line from the Spirit House to the circle of fire, his head up, his eyes staring from his skull, the pupils of those eyes as swollen and round as polished ebony beads. He wore a ceremonial robe made from the hide of an albino deer. Around his neck whispered hundreds of burnished shells strung into necklaces that caught the glow of the fire and reflected it in shimmering waves of pearlescent light.

His long, undressed hair flowed down his back, across

his shoulders, over his chest. In his right hand he bore a long knife. He grasped with his left hand a staff with carved snakes twining about it. The eyes of those snakes were embedded chips of red quartz that glared with lifelike fury.

He listened to the sound of his bare feet as he approached the wall of heat.

Sh-shhh, sh-shhh.

Dust puffed up between his toes. He didn't notice. The tribesmen bayed at the night, howled at the fire, waved their arms at him. The drummers battered a frenzied crescendo in which all rhythm disappeared, a roar of mindless screaming thunder.

The Shaman Gotha saw none of this, heard none of this, not really. Hallucinations had been ripping and tearing at his brain, savaging his eyesight, for a full day now.

He *saw* a mighty faceless thing, a blob with arms and flickering teeth, a ravenous beast whose golden skin was covered with mouths like a thousand pustulant eruptions.

He *heard* inchoate noise from those mouths, a desperate keening that rose and fell like the winds of a storm.

He *smelled* blood, the hot stench of it choking his nostrils, filling his lungs, so that it seemed he might drown in it, but instead, he inhaled and exhaled blood, and that seemed good and warm and natural to him.

He *felt* strength bubble through him, crackle in his bones, bulge and stretch in his muscles, electrify his nerves. His hands felt slow and mighty, as if he could reach out to them, rend, tear, crush them with contemptuous ease.

Where was the bitch?

Ah. There. Waiting . . .

Good.

"Come with me, bitch, to the fire that awaits us all," he said, and smiled at the sound of his own voice rumbling like an avalanche in the cave of his skull.

13

Gotha raised his arms and silence descended as abruptly as a spear plunged into a heart.

He began to chant. His voice sounded like the whine of

a huge insect, rising and falling. He spoke in the tongue of
the Spirits, and no one understood him—except the Crone.

He put out his hand. She took it, and faced him, and replied in the same tongue, and again, no one there understood what they spoke of that night.

It might have been murder. It might have been treachery.
It might have been promises kept, or broken.

It might have been the weight of their Gods, or it might
not have been. It might have been the destiny of tools.

It might have been madness.

Hands linked, the two of them stepped up onto the bed
of coals and began to walk. Smoke billowed up around
them, so that the vision of the People was obscured, and
that might have been a good thing, too. The doings of the
Gods were not for the eyes of mortal men.

What was remembered were the screams that came out
of the smoke, gobbling, gasping things that began low and
grew, and didn't end until the Shaman Gotha carried a limp
form from the clouds to the edge of the fire and stepped
down, his feet unmarked by any stain or blister.

After twenty days the Crone was finally able to limp
along, her ruined feet bound in rags of skin. She couldn't
move with any grace or agility; four of her toes were
burned stumps.

There was no more talk of the Mother, or salt. The turning point passed. The chase resumed.

14

Six weeks later Agarth escorted the small band of alien
hunters to the Shaman's Spirit House, in the middle of the
camp the Tribe had built on a rocky place by the river.

"What is your name?" Gotha asked the big hunter who
seemed in charge of the group.

Though the language used was unfamiliar to the hunter,
there was something hauntingly familiar about the rhythm
of it. Anyway, the questioning tone made the meaning
plain enough.

"My name is Raging Bison," the hunter replied.

Gotha slapped his own chest. "I am the Shaman Gotha."
They smiled at each other.

BOOK THREE

THE GODS THEMSELVES

Do we, holding that the gods exist,
deceive ourselves with unsubstantial dreams
and lies, while random careless chance and change
alone control the world?

—Euripides

The skirts of the gods
Drag in our mud. We feel the touch.

—Christopher Fry

There's a divinity that shapes our ends.

—Shakespeare

Our destiny rules over us, even when we are not yet aware
of it; it is the future that makes laws for our today.

—Nietzsche

CHAPTER TWENTY

1

THE GREEN VALLEY

Caribou stretched his arm out a little farther and grasped Rooting Hog around one thick wrist and yanked. "There," Caribou said, "I can still hold my own with you, little brother."

Rooting Hog, who had, with Caribou's help, managed to heave himself over the final ridge at the top of the cliff wall, grinned as he pounded clouds of dry, red dust out of his furs. "Want to wrestle over it, big brother?"

Caribou laughed and shook his head. "I'm an old man, brother. I have to be careful. You might hurt me."

Now it was Rooting Hog's turn to bellow in delight as he delivered a buffet to Caribou's shoulders that would have felled a young mammoth, though Caribou only swayed a bit and then stepped away from the canyon rim, shading his eyes against the afternoon sun.

Caribou could not have described what he felt as he slowly pivoted, his dark eyes taking in the stupendous scene above, below, and around him. Awe, perhaps, at the endless blue arch of sky, with its slow-ghosting freight of cloudy ships and the fading carpet of tawny gold, stretching like a dream into the north where the Ice Wall lay shrouded in permanent misty curtains. Maybe even an odd sort of comfortable loneliness, a feeling of being both *outside* and *above* as the ceaseless wind whipped his hair back from his face while he stared out over the Green Valley and its toy houses and insect-sized people.

Whatever he felt frightened him more than a little, because the dark power of it reminded him more than he wished just how insignificant he was in the face of the unrelenting grandeur of the World.

It was the same feeling he got whenever he spied the vast herds just over a golden horizon raising a cloud that darkened half the sky. *Does Maya ever feel this? I wonder.*

"You know what? It was right here—over by those black rocks, there—that I first saw Home Camp. You remember?"

"Mm. That was when you and Rat and the others brought Maya back?"

Caribou nodded slowly. "Uh huh. Scared the shit out of me, I can tell you. Never saw so many people in one place in my *life.* I was terrified they'd see me up here."

"Yes, Rat told me about it, too. Said the worst thing was when you killed that god-awful huge cave lion and didn't even let them take a trophy." He paused. "No, that's a lie. Rat said the *worst* thing was when you made them wait while you counted everybody in the whole damned Mammoth Tribe. Speaking of shit, Rat said he had to clean his own furs later, in the asshole area."

Both men chuckled.

"I was in a hurry that night," Caribou said, still grinning slightly. "Besides, that was when I found Maya."

Rooting Hog stumped over to him and draped one arm across his shoulder. The two men stood silent a moment, gazing down on the valley. "What's she like, brother?" Rooting Hog said finally.

"Maya?"

"Mm hmm . . ."

"She's . . . not what you think, brother. I can't explain it, really. Oh, I know you see her now as some kind of mighty Spirit. But you remember when she lived with our People, before she killed Broken Fist? You liked her, didn't you?"

"Yes. She used to sneak me choice bits of fat when nobody was looking."

Caribou chuckled. "Well, she's still that way. Softhearted. Oh, there's stone and bone in her—she's tougher than I'll ever be. But that's not how I think of her."

Rooting Hog nodded slowly. He didn't quite understand, but if she had made him happy—and Rooting Hog had a fair understanding of his brother and the restless things that had tormented him all his life—then that was all a man could ask for.

"Do you still love her?"

Caribou turned and looked at him, and Rooting Hog marveled at the softness that spread across the face of that great, grizzled hulk. "Oh, yes."

After that, the two men were silent for a time, simply enjoying the fine day and their companionship in it. Eventually, Rooting Hog remembered the real reason he'd dragged his brother away from the valley. Privacy. What he needed to say he didn't want anybody overhearing.

"Caribou?"

"What?"

"Tell me about the boy."

"What boy?"

"That strange one. Serpent."

"What about him?"

Now Rooting Hog paused. He sensed he was treading on fragile ground, but it was imperative he discover what he wanted to know. He took a deep breath.

"Is he your son? He has Maya's eyes—and the Keeper's."

You mean the Mother's eyes, Caribou thought, suddenly wary. *What are you* really *after, little brother?*

But he supposed the question deserved the best answer he could give, because the matter was much more complicated than it might seem on the surface. Also, he suspected he could guess Rooting Hog's concern. He hadn't been back in the valley long, but it had been long enough for him to learn certain things himself. Still, he picked his words carefully.

"He isn't my son . . . but Maya thinks perhaps he is her son."

Rooting Hog stared at him. "What is that supposed to mean?"

So Caribou told him what little he knew of Serpent's history, and all he knew of how they had come together. "Maya thinks the Mother sent him to her—or her to him, she's not certain which. Though I don't think it matters much. They're together now."

"Ah. Um. Well, do you take him for your son *now,* I guess I mean to ask?"

Caribou understood perfectly well what Rooting Hog meant to ask. Caribou had left his own blood children—and the family responsibilities that went with them—

moons and miles away. But Rooting Hog's firstborn son was right here below, somewhere between those two mighty walls, and Caribou could guess all was not well with the boy.

His return, almost as much as Maya's, had upset the accepted order of things. Once, he had been Chief of these Two Tribes, and before that Chief of the Bison Clan. All that had been nearly forgotten, but by coming back, he had forced them to remember again.

Maybe now was a good time to begin to set things to rest. "I don't want to be Chief again," he said softly. "Why do you think I built my house so far away from the rest of you?"

Rooting Hog nodded. "I had guessed as much. I told the others so. But it isn't you I'm concerned about. What about the boy? Do you claim birthright for him?"

Caribou raised his eyebrows. It was an interesting question, and he wasn't sure how to answer, for he wasn't sure what the answer was—nor was he sure that even if he did know, whether now was the time, and Rooting Hog the person, to whom he should give such a reply.

Be careful . . .

The final and most complicated element of his hesitation about Serpent was also by far the hardest to articulate, even to himself, but he thought it might also be the most crucial. He thought Maya was probably right—there had been too much coincidence involving the boy. No . . . that wasn't quite right, either. There had been too much coincidence involving *all* of them. The boy might be the center of it, but Caribou was rapidly coming to sense a great web being spun, and the idea of what sort of spinner it would take to spin *that* kind of web made him feel both helpless and queasy at the same time.

Still, he didn't want to lie to Rooting Hog, who was his closest blood relative in the Green Valley and who, because Sharp Knife was his son, had both reason and right to be concerned. What, however, was the truth?

Caribou didn't know—not for certain, and that *was* the truth.

"I may adopt him for my own," he said finally. "As to whether I claim blood right, I don't know."

A shadow of irritation crossed Rooting Hog's blocky features. "That's not much of an answer."

Caribou shrugged. "I'm sorry, brother. It's the only answer I have right now."

Rooting Hog threw up his arms and walked a few paces away. After a moment he dropped his arms to his sides and turned. "My boy should have wed White Moon. But Maya stopped it. I don't know why. But now I hear rumors that she wants the girl to marry that boy of yours. So I want you to tell me, brother—is it true?".

And Caribou stared at him in open surprise. Then, suddenly, he began to roar with laughter. "Serpent? Marry White Moon? But that's impossible! He isn't a man." He took Rooting Hog by the shoulders and shook him to emphasize each word. "You mean you didn't know? Of course you don't—how could you?"

"What in seven evil Spirits are you talking about?"

"I'm talking about his balls, brother. Or actually, about his lack of them. Serpent doesn't have any balls. Only empty *sacks*. He can't marry *anybody*."

Rooting Hog's mouth dropped open. "Is he a Spirit?"

Caribou shook his head. "I have no idea. But he isn't a *man*, brother, and he never will be!"

Neither man noticed the thin silver line of smoke rising out of the west, an almost invisible line scrawled against the afternoon sky. And if either one *had* seen it, he wouldn't have thought much about it—obviously, it was only a campfire.

But if they'd stopped to think about it, it was very late in the season for distant fires. All the hunting parties should have returned by now.

All those that were *going* to return, that is.

2

Sharp Knife sat hunkered down with his chin on his knees, his arms wrapped around his shins, his eyes turned blankly on a huge flock of geese honking and squabbling across the surface of Second Lake. He had draped his long caribou robe across his shoulders, and so resembled a shaggy boulder perched at the edge of the water, somber and unmoving.

Even in midafternoon he could see his breath floating

before him in faint smoky puffs. As he stared at nothing, his lips moved silently, though the words echoed loudly enough inside his skull: *Destroyed. Everything gone. I might as well leave the valley forever.*

The drama of this litany, overblown though it might be, was painfully real to him. Sharp Knife suffered as only a man who has succeeded in everything can suffer when he first knows failure. His confidence was shaken because his first failure hadn't been a minor one—it had been the destruction of every plan he'd ever conceived, right at the moment of triumph.

Marriage—called off.

The Mammoth Stone—snatched from his grasp forever.

The Chiefdom of the Two Tribes—now impossible.

Even his minor dreams of power within the Bison Clan were uncertain, for Caribou was young enough to father sons, or, failing that, might designate someone else as the next Clan leader.

Caribou! Rooting Hog and Shaggy Elk might still pretend to authority—Shaggy Elk was still the Clan leader, officially—but everybody knew who *really* was in charge now.

I can't believe it!

Though he had watched it all happen, there was much truth in the anguished thought, for who expects a musty legend to return and reclaim his ancient place? But Caribou *had* come back, and with him Great Maya, and a strange-eyed boy who might, or might not, be their blood son, and with their return all Sharp Knife's plans and hopes and dreams lay about him in forlorn tatters.

He sat up straight and pounded his right fist onto his knee so hard he grunted at the pain. His eyes lost that dreamy, dazed look. He shook himself, and looked around as if surprised to find himself in this place. It was the old, familiar bower of his childhood, and scary though it was, he couldn't remember coming here.

That's bad, he thought. *Spirits stealing my mind.* The thought made him shiver.

As one, the flock of geese suddenly took wing, the sound of their beating pinions muted thunder. He watched them drift into huge, sky-filling vees and felt a pang of sadness as the great formations dipped and veered, then slowly disappeared into the south.

Winter coming.

Not that he needed the geese to tell him. The days grew shorter, the night colder, his prospects ever dimmer.

Winter coming for me, too. In his misery, he wondered if it was even worth it, to survive the imminent dark time. If he'd be *allowed* to survive it.

"Mistake, mistake, *mistake*," he muttered aloud. He had explained too much of his intentions to the Elders of the Bison Clan on that wonderful day when he'd thought all his dreams would come true. It hadn't seemed to matter then. Within a day of that meeting he should have been wed to the Keeper of the Stone, the daughter of the Chief, and his position secure. There might have been a few rumors, but rumors couldn't have harmed him, not with the power of his new station firmly in hand.

Fool!

He didn't speak this aloud, but he thought it, and it made him feel sick and shriveled inside.

How could I have been so stupid?

It was almost as if—and now he began to grope for the concepts—they felt strange, but somehow *right*—almost as if some Spirit, perhaps even a God, had decided to pull his dreams apart merely to show him that nothing in the world was certain, that the Gods should never be tempted. Then a new thought crashed into his sour reverie.

Did I try hard enough to please Her? Was that it? I didn't give the Mother enough, and so She struck me down?

His shoulders had tensed, but now they slumped again. It was an interesting light in which to view his downfall, wasn't it? For who *had* been the agent of his destruction?

Great Maya, of course, the handmaiden of the Goddess. It was *her* return that had ended the wedding plans—and they *were* ended, despite Wolf's weaseling talk of "a short delay, in honor of Maya's return."

Wolf might prattle such pap, even find some stupid enough to believe it, but Sharp Knife knew better. His father had been given the news personally, and Rooting Hog had told his son the truth: "The Chief's eyes shifted away. He wouldn't look me straight in the face when he talked of putting the ceremony off. He was lying."

Sharp Knife clenched his fists when he thought about

that, though some dim part of him agreed that it was only fitting. He had lied to others about his true intentions, and now the Chief had lied in return. A circle, neatly joined.

A single throb of agony spiked through his skull, and he grabbed his head in both hands and squeezed, hard. Just as quickly the bolt vanished, leaving a curtain of tiny white dots dancing across his vision.

So what do I do now? he wondered. *Eventually one of the Elders will babble the truth to his wife, and she will blurt it to one of her friends, and soon enough the Chief will know what I'd intended. Maybe he knows already, and is only staying his hand because—*

Because why?

Great Maya is back. Perhaps she *has something in store for me.* The old tales burped up then, and paraded themselves across the eye of his mind.

The Shaman Ghost. The Shaman Fist.

How they died at her hands.

"I have to leave," he said to the empty lake. He nodded to himself, as if the words pleased him, though he found them bitter indeed. But, as medicine is often bitter, once he had spoken, it felt as if a weight had flown from his shoulders as surely as the geese had flown from the lake.

He realized he'd made his decision. Now, all he had to figure out was how best to implement it. Without the weight of misery fogging his thoughts, he began to see a few possibilities.

Yes, he thought. *More than a few possibilities.*

3

Berry said to Red hair, "Have you noticed something strange about the returning hunters?"

The two women were pounding a fresh load of creamy white roots into a thick paste, which they would later use as a thickener for the stew bubbling in a leather bag suspended over the small hearth at their elbow.

Red Hair extended her lower lip and blew a lock of her coppery mop out of her face. She shrugged. "No, I don't think so. The hunting has been especially good this year, is all. A lot of meat for drying and making meat-and-berry paste." She puffed again and grinned in Berry's direction. "You'll not have to worry about going hungry this winter."

Thick pads of loose flab jiggled beneath Berry's massive arms as she pushed at the bowl full of roots. She knew Red Hair thought it funny how different they were—Red Hair skinny as a spear, Berry fat as a pig in a pile of acorns.

"Not about what the hunting parties bring *back*," Berry said. "About the parties themselves."

It was an odd question. Red Hair thought about it, but couldn't quite grasp what the old woman was talking about. She had the idea it would be plain as the nose on her face, when Berry explained it to her, and sighed. Berry loved to make her feel stupid.

Nevertheless, she gave in and asked, "What do you mean?"

"I mean, who *hasn't* come back. And how *many* of them."

"Ah." And now that Red Hair thought about it, she saw exactly what Berry meant. She wrinkled her eyelids as she ticked off the count. "Raging Bison and his family. Black Otter and *his* family. Uh ... Shaggy Elk's cousin, Sweet Water." She shook her head. "More, come to think on it. A lot more ..." She glanced over at Berry. "The Spirits have been unkind to the hunters."

Old Berry shook her head. "Too unkind, I think. So many? Raging Bison—such a mighty hunter—and *all* his family? All the *other* families?" She paused in her work. "A few hunters, perhaps. But not so many, and with all their relatives, as well."

Red Hair's eyes widened slowly. "So, what do you think *has* happened to them?"

"I don't know. But I don't like it. I don't like it one bit."

4

Maya felt as if the world had turned into a bowl of worms, and she was charged with pulling exactly the *right* worm out of the squirming, tangled mess. It made her head ache just thinking about it.

"Oh, dear," she said mildly.

"So you *do* see the problems?" Wolf said.

They seemed so companionable in their discussion that they might have been chatting about the softly glowing autumn leaves overhead, or the distant honks of the geese, as they ambled slowly down Main Path past Second Lake. Second Camp was behind them now, though the afternoon air was still heavy with the smells coming from the hearths there. Hunting parties, gone all summer, continued to straggle up the path, their pace impatient as they came to the end of their moon-long wanderings. Occasionally one such would pass them by, though only a few nodded greetings, and even fewer spoke. Many had no idea who the slender, gray-haired woman walking with their Chief might be. Those who suspected the truth said nothing, though their eyes grew big as baskets; these moved even more quickly to reach the camps and the great news that surely awaited them there.

"The biggest problem is that your niece is not prepared to take up the Stone," Wolf continued. "That is why you must bear that burden again. You must teach her. Berry and I have failed."

She glanced up at him. He had always been taller than she, and for some reason she found that comforting. "I wish that were the *only* problem," she muttered.

"What?"

"Perhaps the best thing would have been if I hadn't come back at all," she continued. "Mating White Moon and Sharp Knife would have been a good thing, even if the boy was, perhaps, more ambitious than he looks. He would have been a good Chief after you, I think, and the marriage *would* have united the Two Tribes."

Wolf brightened. "Do you really think so?"

"Yes, for what it's worth. Unfortunately, brother, I *did* come back."

"Yes." It was not in Wolf, though, to mourn the past. He was a cheerful man at heart, and he preferred to look to the future. It was a quality that had in the past served both him and the Two Tribes well. Anyway, he'd loved his sister before, and he still did, clearly and without complication.

And Maya understood. She had often wished for his sunny nature, his essential trustingness that things would turn out well. Of course, Wolf didn't have to deal with the Spirits, or, worse, with the Gods. He had his Shaman, and now his sister, for that.

Hope he doesn't learn to regret his trust, she thought, and turned her concentration to making sure he didn't. It would be hard, though—she still hadn't told him about Serpent and the Second Stone. There was a good reason for *that*: she had no idea what to say, for she still didn't understand Serpent or the role he might play, either. The Mother, as usual, kept Her enigmatic counsel on the matter.

Leave it to the tool to make the hard *choices,* Maya thought. *It must be nice to be a Goddess.*

Yet the overall pattern seemed obvious enough. If it hadn't, she would not have put a halt to the wedding. But what else could Serpent and his Stone, and the rhyme that had filled her thoughts for moons now, mean? Plainly it was intended for the Two Stones to be rejoined, just as the marks of the Goddess in both White Moon's and Serpent's eyes indicated *how* that rejoining was to be accomplished.

But what will it mean for the People? For both *Peoples?*

Wolf sighed. "At least with you wielding the Mammoth Stone, it will mean an end to this secret worship of the Lord of Snakes."

They had already spoken of this, though Maya was nowhere near as sanguine as her brother about his belief in that particular solution. "You say there have been human sacrifices? Someone is eating the Special Meat again?"

He nodded somberly. "Out on the steppe. A missing hunter here, a lost child there. Never so many as to arouse suspicion and, frankly, that is all I do have. Just rumors and suspicions. But I think they are true. It was one of the things that decided me about Sharp Knife and White Moon's wedding. That offered a hope of undercutting the religious resurgence by further uniting the Two Tribes."

He moved his hands in a helpless gesture.

"It would have gone a long way to putting an end to it. You see, I think it comes from the same spring as Sharp Knife's ambition. The Two Tribes have not been equal, and some of the young men of the Bison Clan seek power against the Mammoth because of that. It's natural they might return to the old ways, in hopes of regaining the power they have lost." He shrugged.

"Besides, they are young. They know little of what happened when you broke the Power of their God."

Maya shivered, though it was not particularly chilly this fine sunny afternoon.

"Nobody knows that. Not really," she said.

Wolf glanced down at her. "I suppose that's true, isn't it?" Then, "Maya? What *was* it like?"

But he was to be disappointed, for his sister only moved her shoulders slightly and said, "Unless you experience it for yourself, brother, you can never know—and if I have any wish in this life, it is that you *never* have such an experience."

"As bad as that?"

"Yes," she said shortly, and then smiled. "But it is past now, Wolf, long past. Forget about it. We have other problems. And I think the time has come to tell you the biggest dilemma of all. You see, I am going to need every bit of help you can give me."

He stopped, and took her by the shoulders, and looked down into her eyes. "You know I will give it, if I can. But what is this great riddle, Maya? Have you kept something from me?"

She nodded slowly. "I'm afraid I have. His name is Serpent."

"Serpent? The boy that came with you? The boy who bears Her mark—the eyes of the Mother?"

"It's not all he bears," she said.

5

Serpent had wanted it to be over as long as he could remember, but the smoke was the thing that convinced him the horror had ended. It really wasn't Maya. She had taught him her tongue, and now that fall was wearing on toward winter, he was able to talk with her about many things. But though in her own way she had tried to reassure him that he was safe now—it was the smoke that actually made him believe it was finally over.

The smoke, and what *didn't* happen as those sweet-smelling fumes began to fill the days and nights of the Green Valley.

He sat before the house Caribou had built, his skinny legs crossed beneath him, leaning against one of the sturdy struts the three of them had planted deep in the ground to hold the straw-and-clay-chinked branches that were the walls of his new home, and lifted his face toward the watery sun. The smoke, rich with the smells of meat in all stages of roasting, boiling, and drying, filled his nose and made his belly rumble. But that was all the smoke meant now. It was no longer a signal that he would be tied to a pole like an animal and tortured until he Spoke for the evil God as part of the countless feasts and ceremonies that marked the end of the summer hunting season.

Fall and spring had always been the worst times for him, the seasons of pain, and the first time he'd smelled those terrible, seductive aromas here in the Green Valley, the nightmares had begun anew.

Serpent picked up a handy stone and chunked it across the small clearing at the stump of a tree. Several other stones dotted the ground there. He thought about getting up and retrieving the rocks—some of them were quite pretty, smooth and polished by the fast-moving water in the stream—but decided it felt too good just to sit here in the sun and smell the smoke and know that he didn't have to fear the torture stake, or the Crone, or the Shaman Gotha.

Or the God.

A dull twinge from the puckered scar made him wince and rub his fingers gently across the gnarled flesh there, as if to remind himself the nightmares were over. Even the terrible dreams he'd suffered when the smoke had begun in the valley were fading, just as the scar on his thigh was fading. Somehow, he suspected, neither would ever disappear entirely, but he could live with a twinge now and then.

He sighed, scratched his belly, then looked idly about the clearing. So much was new. It was hard sometimes for him to sort out the kaleidoscopic sensations that thronged his skull and made his thoughts seem a fragile welter of sights, sounds, feelings. But the tension that had made taut strings of his muscles for so long that he didn't even know it was there until finally, bit by bit, it began to drain out of him was no longer evident in his face, or in the way he held his shoulders (as if expecting the blow always a moment away), or in the way he could actually look people in the face without flinching.

No one had threatened him here. If anything, the people seemed disposed to leave him entirely alone, and given his terrible past, he was well content to have it that way. He was a boy for whom solitude was a blessing, and though some quiet, deep part of him suspected that might one day change, for now he was more than content to simply sit in the sun, throw a rock every now and then, and have the pleasure of his thoughts for himself alone.

As far as being lonely, he had no concept of the meaning of the word. To fully understand loneliness, the pain caused by the lack of friends, one must first have had friends and known the loss of them. Alone and lonely are not the same words. He understood alone—it meant peace, a lack of pain, safety. Loneliness? Ask a deaf man to understand sound.

There was a lot to think about—and though much of it was puzzling, he thought he was beginning to understand some of it. A little, at least. Take, for instance, the location of the house in which he now lived . . .

He squirmed around, feeling the soft rasp on his skin of the bright new fur pants and the sleeveless tunic Maya had sewed for him, and looked at the strut against which he slouched. The wood that had once been so white (he had stripped the thin, copper-green bark from it himself) was turning dark as it dried out. Hardened droplets of sap dotted it in places. He grinned faintly. There were dark patches on the palms of his hands that were fading blisters, from also stripping the branches woven between the struts, like the woof in a giant basket (which, upside down, was exactly what the house was, a giant basket), and he saw once again the look on Caribou's face as he'd explained how to lay those branches just *so*. Caribou had shown him carefully how to do it, just as, later, he'd helped him apply the chinking of clay-mud mixed with moss so that the house would be proof against the winter winds to come.

Just looking at the house brought an unaccustomed glow to Serpent's chest, because *he* had helped to build it, *he* lived in it, and that made it *his* house, and he'd never had such a thing before. He'd never had anything that was *his*—well, with one unimportant exception—and so he would often find himself staring at the house, the expression on his face exactly that of a boy lost in a pleasant dream.

But the location of the house was worth a less dreamlike thought or two. He had walked through Home Camp, marveled at the number of houses, huts, tents, and people jammed up against the warmth of the shield wall at the utmost head of the valley, and also learned the myriad paths of the much larger New Camp, beyond the rock Jumble, the springs, and the stream that fronted Home Camp. As far as he knew, all those who lived within the valley cliffs lived in one of these two encampments—all except himself, Maya, and Caribou.

Instead, they had built their house off to one side of the Main Path, opposite Smoke Lake, far from any other habitations.

He asked Maya why they had done this, and she had brushed her hair out of her face and said, "This place has old memories for me." He had smiled a faint, sad smile as she said this, and something told Serpent not to pursue his question any further, though he had resolved to investigate the fallen tree and patch of brambles her gaze had flicked toward as she spoke the word *memories*. When he finally got round to doing it, though, he found nothing out of the ordinary, and wondered what it was about the spot that brought the sadness in Maya he'd sensed that day.

She was a woman of secrets. He knew that and wasn't frightened by it, even though he also felt that some of her secrets had to do with him.

"You mustn't show your mammoth carving to anybody, anybody at all," she had said one bright morning while they sweated with muddy hands and mossy straw in their hair, sealing up the sides of the house. Caribou had gone off somewhere with the bulky man who looked a lot like him, whose name was Rooting Hog—Serpent thought the name hilarious—and who, it turned out, was Caribou's brother.

Maya's warning had surprised him. He hardly ever thought about the carving, as long as it was safely in his pouch.

"Why?"

"Just . . . because. I can't explain it, Serpent, but I want you to do it anyway. Will you?"

At that point—for Caribou had explained to him what Maya had done, how she had saved his life once, and twice, and then three times—Serpent would have cheerfully cut off his finger bones and presented them to her for a necklace had she expressed any desire for such a thing. So he had nodded enthusiastically and said no more about it, though it was an interesting request. He hadn't known she was even aware of the carving's existence. Her warning intrigued him.

It intrigued him still as he tossed his pebbles beneath the sun. He thought it might have something to do with certain other things he'd noticed in the past moon or so, as his knowledge of the languages used in the Green Valley grew more facile. It had startled him at first to discover there were two languages in common usage—apart from what he thought of as the Speaking Tongue, which he and Maya alone were able to use.

Maya and Caribou had lived here before. It had taken him only a few days of close observation to understand that the great Chief of these people deferred to Maya in many things. Wolf was the Chief's name, and Serpent didn't think his respect came solely because he and Maya were brother and sister.

He asked Maya about Wolf, and again she smiled somewhat sadly and replied, "Oh, my brother and I were very close when I lived here before."

Anything about *before* seemed to make Maya smile sadly. He wondered what had really happened to her here. But whatever it might have been, it seemed to have no ill effects on her status now. Serpent had spent many days following her about the two camps, and had not missed the way people pointed at him. It took him a while before he realized it was his eyes that were the source of curiosity—and some other reaction that wasn't quite fear, but was close to it.

That bothered him. He felt his own position was precarious, for these were not his people. The People of Fire and Ice had not been his people either, though the Shaman Gotha had sworn otherwise. But the Shaman Gotha lied, and Serpent knew it—if not consciously, then on a deeper, more permanent level. His dreams might have told him the answer, if he had been able to remember them.

Nevertheless, he was powerfully sensitive to anything that might even remotely threaten him, and this odd relationship between Maya, his protector, and what were obviously her People both frightened and confused him.

There was much here that didn't make sense, and until he understood it to his satisfaction, he would be wary of it.

As for Caribou, undercurrents surrounded him as well. It took a while before Serpent was able to figure out that Caribou was not of Maya's People, and that the Two Tribes had not always lived together as one. In fact, it was Caribou and Maya who had, in some unspecified way, linked the Two Tribes in the first place.

All these things he learned with his ears and with his gift for melting into the background of things, for he had made no friends, and no one spoke to him. He was perfectly comfortable with that, however, for speaking and pain were still inextricably associated in his mind, and though he was slowly coming to realize this need not always be so, he was content to wait for any changes.

In any event, his nightmares lessened as his knowledge increased, and the days of fall dripped past him without any obvious incidents to shatter his slowly growing, though still shaky, self-confidence.

"Hello?"

His head jerked up, and for a moment his eyes rolled wildly—but then he recognized the voice, and settled back. He felt a curious feeling in his lower belly as he waited for her to show herself. She had never spoken to him, beyond a few polite greetings, but she shared his eyes, and this alone was enough to make him intensely curious. She frightened him though, and also caused another reaction he wasn't even close to understanding. Her name was White Moon. He knew that much.

The bushes rustled, and she stepped into the clearing, shading her eyes with one hand and looking around till her gaze settled on him with a surprised start.

"Oh," White Moon said. "You."

He smiled, but made no reply. Truthfully, at that moment he was so nervous he could barely remember the proper words in her language.

She put her hands on her hips and stared at him. "Where's my aunt?"

He shrugged, still smiling goofily. He *felt* goofy, as if that ridiculous smile might float right off his face.

"What's the matter? Baby lion got your tongue?"

"Uh . . ."

She shook her head. Today she wore a tawny golden tunic cinched at the waist with a thin cord, and hide "boots" that were merely pieces of skin tied around her feet and calves. Serpent thought she was the most beautiful thing he'd ever seen in his life.

"Where's Maya?"

All he could do was shrug, and feel the heat burning in his cheeks, and wish she could go away, because that peculiar feeling in his gut was getting a *lot* worse. And it wasn't exactly his gut. It was lower down than that.

Now White Moon tossed her own shoulders, walked over to him, and squatted down almost within touching distance. "I'll wait for her," she said.

Serpent nodded slowly, and hoped that his tongue would start to work soon. If not, his only other hope was that the earth would open and swallow him up.

White Moon eyed him curiously. A strange boy. And those eyes! Did her own eyes look like that? She hoped so. His were *beautiful.*

"What's your name again? Serpent?"

His cheeks burning crimson, he managed a stuttered *"Yuh . . . yes,"* then inhaled sharply as that *weird* sensation at the bottom of his belly started up again. He had no way of knowing that the feeling was his right testicle, leaving its place in his lower abdomen at last to start its journey to his empty scrotum, only thirteen years late.

When it finally arrived at its destination, followed shortly after by its left-hand mate, Serpent's life would change more than he could possibly imagine. The sharp knot of pain in his belly suddenly grew into a silvery dagger of pure agony. That pain, coupled with his embarrassment at the presence of White Moon, was suddenly *too much to take,* and—to his vast and utter amazement—he simply burst into tears.

White Moon, who thought she had some idea of Serpent's history, did the only thing she could think of for a scrawny, weeping boy.

"Oh, you poor thing," she said, leaned forward, and took him into her arms. This was how, in a lonely clearing, the first of many joinings occurred, though neither of those involved knew it for what it was.

Nonetheless, the Gods knew.

6

White Moon pursed her lips as she ran her fingertips carefully across the ridge of scar tissue on Serpent's upper right thigh. It was an ugly wound, or had been. Now the ridges were fading, though the skin was as hard as her fingernails and made a rasping sound when she scraped it lightly.

"Does it hurt?" she asked.

Serpent shook his head. His weeping jag had passed as quickly and inexplicably as it had come. His shame at the outburst had not passed so easily, but White Moon—used to dealing with children—had ignored his furious blushes and gone on as if nothing had happened.

She was fascinated by him. It was the first time she'd had a chance to talk with him without Maya or Caribou in attendance, and she intended to make the most of it. There were so *many* rumors, after all . . .

But now, as he sat next to her, the feel of his warm flesh still tingling in the tip of her finger, she realized he had changed somehow—or *she* had changed. Whatever, he was no longer the strange boy who had come with Great Maya and Caribou. He was *Serpent,* a boy whose body was covered with scar tissue, who burst into tears for no reason she could understand, who smiled at her with her own eyes, who was, in short, a *real person.*

She began to feel a little guilty . . . but not guilty enough to forget her initial purpose. He seemed a sweet enough boy, if a little jumpy, and he still wasn't proficient in the tongue of the Mammoth People, but White Moon had no trouble understanding him. All it took was a little thought, a little attention. And he seemed to thrive on it. It was as if nobody had ever *listened* to him before.

"It hurt a lot at first—well, the first I remember. Maya says I slept through the worst part. I don't know, maybe I did. It's all sort of foggy . . ." Twin lines had appeared above the bridge of his nose, but now they vanished as he grinned up at her. "Anyway, it's all healed up now."

Something about the way he said this tore at her heart. There was an ease, a certainty to his tone, as if he'd had so much experience with wounds healing on his body that one more miracle of cellular reconstruction meant nothing to him. White Moon, who had never known a hand raised in anger toward her, found it almost impossible to connect the webbing of pink ridges that marked much of Serpent's body with anything she could understand.

Surely nobody actually hurt *him like that?* (Oh, yes they did.) *But that would mean—*

She wasn't sure what it would mean. Or, rather, she didn't *want* to be sure, because that would mean the world wasn't the warm and comforting place she'd always thought, that horrors far worse than the displeasure of her father or a lecture from Old Berry might be waiting for her. Maybe even something worse than the way her whole life had been *ruined* by Aunt Maya's *horrid* meddling in her wedding, but of course that couldn't be true. *Nothing* could be worse than that!

(Oh, yes it could.)

"Do you like my eyes?" she asked.

Obligingly, he stared into them. "They're . . . very pretty."

"Of course they are. Yours are just like them."

It startled him. "Mine?"

"Your eyes, silly. You have the same color eyes as mine." And forgetting the legacy that went with her eyes, she said, "They're the mark of the Mother. It means you're special, like me."

Plainly, the boy had never thought much about his eyes. Maybe because he had to spend his time thinking about keeping his *skin* in one piece, one small part of her muttered caustically, but she brushed the thought away. She'd already decided she didn't want to think about that, and White Moon was very good at *not* thinking about things she wished to ignore.

"I don't understand," he said slowly. She had to strain to figure out the word *understand.* His accent was guttural, almost chokingly so.

"The Mother, the *Goddess,*" she elaborated, a little impatiently, irritated at having to explain what was, to her, the obvious thing.

Serpent shook his head. "Who is the Mother? What do you mean, Her marks?"

"Your eyes. If you have one eye green and the other blue, it's because the Mother gave you Her eyes. Hers are the same color." Then, suddenly conscious that she might be explaining things a little *too* blithely, White Moon back-tracked. But it hadn't occurred to her at all that Serpent might not have the faintest idea who the Mother was. She was vaguely aware that the Bison Clan had once prayed to a different God, but that was long ago and had nothing to do with her. That one hadn't really been a God, anyway—just some sort of evil Spirit that her aunt had vanquished with the Stone—

—the same Stone hidden in her belt pouch right now.

The thought had a chill, shivery feel to it, like the belly of a fish rising from dark water, flashing once, then sinking slowly down again.

The Stone was another thing she didn't want to think about. Until Maya's return, she had thought it the source of every one of her troubles, and even the return of the woman who'd once been called "She Who We Have Waited For" was nothing more than a part of the Stone's terrible history. Still, it shocked her to think of a world in which the Mother didn't automatically assume Her rightful place.

"Your . . . People worshiped the Mother, didn't they?"

"I don't think so," Serpent said seriously. "The Crone didn't pray to the Lord of Snakes, but everybody else did." Serpent spoke matter-of-factly, as if any other state of affairs was inconceivable. It was that tone of voice, more than anything else, that led White Moon to do what she did next.

"Well, I don't know anything about your Lord of Snakes," (*Lord of Fire, Lord of Breath,* oh, yes you *do*) "but this is Her talisman. It's the most powerful thing in the World, and it's *mine!*"

Her cheeks flushed a little as she fumbled with her pouch and the fur-wrapped object inside. Both Berry and Wolf had asked her for it, but something had warned her that it was a trick of some kind, and a well-practiced tantrum had taken care of *that* quick enough. She had already decided that she wouldn't give it up unless Sharp Knife said it was all right. She hadn't been able to speak to him yet—it almost seemed as if he was avoiding her, though surely that was impossible—but she knew he thought the Mammoth Stone was valuable in some way she didn't understand. And so, though she didn't value it, once her possession of it was threatened, she fought to keep it.

Wretched old piece of bone, she thought as she finally got it unwrapped. "Here." She thrust it forward. He reached for it and she took it back, suddenly recalling the musty old curse it supposedly carried.

"No, you can't touch it or it will lose all its Power," she said. "But you can look."

"Bu-buh-but—"

You mustn't show your mammoth carving to anybody, anybody at all.

It wasn't a memory. Somehow, Serpent *heard* Maya whisper the words into his ear right then, as he sat there looking at a carving colored amber with age, a carving *exactly* like the one in his own pouch. But—

You mustn't.

You mustn't show.

He shook his head.

"What's the matter?" White Moon said. The boy's face had turned a feeble green color, and his eyes had taken on a vacant, staring look that made her feel uneasy.

"Huh?" *Not exactly alike. Different, somehow . . .*

"Are you okay, Serpent?"

He blinked. "Uh? Oh, yes, I'm all right. I'm fine." But he was scrambling up from his cross-legged position, drawing back from her. "I've . . . uh . . . I have to go now. You can wait here for Maya, she went somewhere with the Chief, but—"

And then he was gone, disappearing into the dark rim of forest around the clearing, just a muted crashing noise, then nothing.

White Moon stared openmouthed and wide-eyed at the spot where he'd disappeared.

Now, what's the matter with him? she wondered as she wrapped up the Mammoth Stone and put it away.

Eventually her surprise faded, and finally disappeared entirely. She glanced up at the sky, and noted that afternoon would soon fade into evening. For one moment the clearing felt too silent, too empty, too *alone,* and she wished Serpent hadn't run off so quickly.

He acted like the Stone scared him to death. But that was impossible, wasn't it? How could he know anything about the Stone? He'd never even seen it before. Perhaps Maya had spoken of it to him, but—

Of course, Maya knew the Stone better than anybody,

even Old Berry or the Shaman Muskrat. The Stone had once *belonged* to her, but she had given it away.

"They want it back. *She* wants it back." The idea smote her with stunning force. So *that* was why Wolf and Old Berry had tried to take it from her. She had resisted, because in her rage and disappointment at the cancellation of her wedding, she would have refused them anything. But what would *they* do with the Stone? She was the Keeper. The Stone had been given to her—by the only person who could actually *do* anything with it.

As always, her calculations turned to Sharp Knife, and to the fulfillment of her desperate need. She would give *anything* for just a hundred heartbeats alone with him.

Hmm. I wonder if she'd be willing to trade me for it . . .

7

Maya glanced at Wolf, who stood at the edge of the clearing, his back to them, his hands clasped behind his back, well content to stay clear of the ugly little scene taking place.

A big help you are, Maya thought. She returned her attention to White Moon.

"*Trade* me the Mammoth Stone? Have Spirits stolen all your thoughts, you silly girl?"

White Moon's face had turned a dull brick-red. Her eyes were narrowed into flashing slits. At that moment she didn't look pretty at all.

"*If I can't have Sharp Knife, you'll never have the Mammoth Stone again. Never, never, NEVER!*" She was so enraged she actually *hopped* an inch or so into the air with each word. Hop, hop, hop. The effect was so comical that under other circumstances, Maya would have been hard put to keep from laughing out loud. But there was nothing funny about this nasty performance, and the only urge Maya felt right then was to give her niece a couple of brisk swats where they would do the most good.

"White Moon, I don't *want* the Stone."

White Moon whirled on her, her chest pumping, a trail of spit leaking from one side of her mouth, snot dripping from her nose.

"*What?*"

Serpent, who sat next to the doorway of his house, wrapped his arms more tightly around his knees, ducked his head, and tried to tuck himself into a smaller ball—but his eyes sparked, and missed nothing.

Maya put out her hands. "Niece, you are the Keeper of the Stone. I left it in your hands many years ago—and I did so without any intention of ever taking it up again." She dropped her hands and turned away. "I certainly don't intend to trade you *anything* for it. Whatever gave you the idea that I would?"

Wolf turned his head, his dark eyes alarmed. "Maya, I don't think—"

She cut him off with a quick jerk of her head. "Niece, go home with your father. And take the Stone with you. There will be no trades tonight—or any other night. It's time you learned some responsibility, young woman. The Stone is yours. I have borne it long enough, and though you've had it all these years, you've felt none of its burden. It's time you learned its weight, I think."

"*I hate you!*"

"Yes, dear. You've told me that already. Several times, I think." Maya flapped vaguely in her general direction. "Go, now. I'm tired of all this shouting. Go back to your house."

White Moon's features went pale. Two red dots flowered thinly on her cheeks. Then, for one short moment, her face actually seemed to *swell*, and Maya wondered if her niece would simply burst right in front of her.

But no such thing happened. White Moon stamped her feet one more time, whirled, and ran from the clearing. Maya wiped her forehead and let out a long breath.

"Sister? I told you I wanted *you* to have the Mammoth Stone. Surely you can see why—"

"Oh, be quiet, Wolf. Surely *you* can see how she is. But don't worry. Now she thinks I won't take it, so she'll find a way to make *sure* she gives it to me."

He slid a puzzled glance at her. "Are you sure?"

"She's a child, brother. Leave it to me. Obviously, you've no idea how such things work."

He shook his head. "Obviously, I don't. So I'll take your word for it."

"Yes," she said, "you might as well do that." She

paused, and realized she really did feel exhausted. Surprising how a little hysterical screaming really took it out of you. *Mother, I'm getting old.*

"Go find her, Wolf. But say nothing about all this. Especially say nothing about the Stone, even if she asks, though I don't think she will. Most especially, don't tell her she has to give the Stone to me. Tomorrow, I'll come see her."

"Are you sure?"

"I'm sure. Now, go. I really am tired."

"Maya, are you sure you aren't making a mistake?"

"I hope not, brother. I surely hope not."

CHAPTER TWENTY-ONE

1

THE STEPPE

Gotha looked from Raging Bison's engorged face to the Crone's wizened features, then over their shoulders at the others ranged beyond them. All he could see were their eyes, fastened on him in silent hunger, and he felt the old familiar chills begin to chase themselves up his forearms. He looked down and saw goose bumps erupting in ridges on the brown flesh there; wild, shrieking laughter began to build inside his skull.

It felt so good!

On the western horizon, smudgy clouds parted for a moment, showing the last of the setting sun, smeared into a crimson line. The baleful glow echoed the light of the great hearth where Gotha stood, his hands upraised. Next to the fire was a stake driven into the ground, and tied to the stake was a boy, no more than seven summers old. The boy, whose name was Shivering Wolf, mewed in terror.

Raging Bison had killed the brat's father and mother the day before, capturing their small party as it made its way toward the Green Valley after the season of hunting. They had refused the choice. Gotha hadn't expected them to do otherwise. They were of the Mammoth Clan, and worshiped the Bitch, and so Raging Bison slew them without compunction. He saved the boy, however. Gotha had told him what was *required*.

Gotha lowered his arms and looked expectantly at the Crone who, properly cowed, limped heavily to his side. She held a long knife, which she placed in the Shaman's right hand. Her ancient face was stony. She didn't raise her eyes to him.

Ah, Mother, Gotha thought. *Who is more powerful? Who do you serve now, whether you want to or not?*

Once again that savage mirth threatened to overwhelm him, but he throttled it down. "Get back, Crone," he hissed. Obediently, she retreated to her place and stood, face lowered, silent.

About sixty people—hunters, their wives and children—waited around the sacrificial pit. Most were of the People of Fire, but several were from Raging Bison's Tribe. Gotha could feel a hot, raging expectation burning off of them, spilling from their loosely opened mouths, glaring from their vacant, gaping eyes. He savored their hunger for a long moment, then took a measured pace forward and lifted his knife to the boy's chest.

Shivering Wolf gobbled in terror. As the blade's point touched his chest, his bladder let loose and spattered the earth at his feet with hot urine.

Gotha smiled as the stench filled his nostrils. His hand flashed in a single stroke across the boy's throat. Hot blood gushed; it painted the boy's naked chest, his belly, then dripped slowly from his pathetic little penis onto the ground. The *pat-pat-pat* sound was soft in the utter silence beneath the gory sky.

The boy slumped forward. Strange gasping sounds issued from the bloody mouth beneath his chin. Gotha grasped the boy's hair and yanked his head backward, exposing the gaping wound. He bent forward and placed his lips over the still-pulsing cavity and drank deep. The salty, coppery taste of hot blood filled his mouth, his nose. He raised his head, and those gathered saw his features as a shining crimson mask.

Gotha opened his mouth and *bayed* at the sky; after a moment scattered howls began to answer him. The sound swelled until the Crone could bear it no longer. She risked a surreptitious glance around. Nobody was watching her. She put her hands over her ears, turned, and walked away.

The feeding began.

2

Raging Bison wiped still-warm blood from his lips. He'd never felt stronger in his life, and he was certain it was because of this Shaman with the wild eyes. This Shaman Gotha, who knew Raging Bison's Lord, who worshiped Him, who sacrificed to Him in the old way.

Raging Bison laughed softly. He was no longer alone. The Lord had sent a mighty Shaman to him, a sign that He would cast down the Bitch at last. *The Lord of Fire smiles upon me,* he thought as fever rushed into his cheeks and thunder pounded joyfully in his chest.

The Special Meat tasted wonderful, rich with fat and salt. His only regret was that this sacrifice was so pitiful. A boy, a child! He would have much rather eaten the flesh of a mighty warrior, and so taken that strength, by the grace of the God, into himself. Somebody like the Chief of the Two Tribes, for instance. He wondered what Wolf's flesh would taste like. Saltier, perhaps. Stronger.

Someday I will find out, he promised himself.

3

THE GREEN VALLEY

Sharp Knife shifted on his perch atop the Jumble, from which he had a fine view of the Main Path as it debouched onto the green meadow at the edge of the stream that gurgled and glittered beneath the high shelf of Home Camp.

The evening breeze was brisk; occasionally he slapped his arms against his chest, hoping to pound some warmth into his torpid muscles. His breath smoked before him, sketching colored halos around the glimmering fires of New Camp. Shadowy figures came and went on the path below. He heard soft laughter, an occasional cheerful shout. Oaky fumes from the cookfires eddied about him whenever the breeze lessened, filling the darkness with the smoky smell of broiling meat.

He saw, heard, smelled them, the People of the Green

Valley in all their heedless numbers, but they couldn't see him, hidden in the bubbling silence of the water-laced rocks. It was an odd, disquieting feeling, as if he were invisible. A *powerful* feeling ... how he imagined a hawk must feel, circling high above its prey, waiting for the perfect moment to strike.

I'll miss them ...

So bittersweet, almost haunting, that thought. He hoped he would remember it, in the coming days of his exile. In some dim way he knew exactly what he was doing here. He was saying good-bye.

She came stumbling up the path, not paying any attention to where she was going. She flung her head from side to side. Her hair stuck out from her skull as if she'd been running frantic fingers through it or tearing at it. She stumbled to a halt at the worn rocks that made a rude crossing over the stream and stared wildly about.

He stood up and began to make his way down. "White Moon," he called softly. "Wait for me! I'm coming ..."

She looked up and recognized him leaping surefooted from rock to rock; even in the dark he could see her eyes begin to glow. He smiled a secret smile. He would leave the Green Valley, but not alone. And someday he would return.

"Oh, Sharp Knife," she called to him as he came close. "I hate them. I hate them all!"

"Shh, yes. I know, White Moon." He took her in his arms and squeezed her close. She felt warm, vibrant, almost feverish. He smiled again and nuzzled her neck.

"Did they take the Mammoth Stone from you?" he whispered in her ear.

She shook her head violently and made to push him away. "I'll throw it in the lake!" she hissed.

"No ... no," he soothed. He didn't understand why she was so angry, but it didn't matter. "Do you have it with you?"

She fumbled in the pouch at her side, finally managed to fumble out the hated talisman. "Here, if you want it, *take* it. *She* doesn't want it."

"Ah. Maya? It doesn't matter, sweet of my life. Keep the Stone. Put it back, you are its Keeper."

"But I don't *want* it!"

"Shhh." He held her for a time, until she relaxed against him. "White Moon?"

"Mmm?"

"Will you go away with me?"

"Oh, *yes!*"

She smiled. Only one small worry niggled at her. What if he changed his mind about taking her? But she thought she knew how to seal his decision so he could never forget. She glided closer to him, took his hand, then gently led him toward a hidden place near the stream.

White Moon was suddenly full of an eerie calm. *This* was what she'd waited for, hungered for. All the fears of the past several days dropped away as a great glittering tidal wave of lust rose inside her skull. Her eyes flashed in the dark. Everything became preternaturally sharp—the sound of insects buzzing in the weeds, the distant hoot of an owl, the sensation of Sharp Knife's hard jawline grinding into the soft place at the base of her neck.

Her skin felt painfully sensitive. She felt his hands slide down her back, fall to her buttocks, dig into the firm flesh there. He thrust his prick against her and she felt herself respond, felt the surge of heat in her belly as she pushed the mound of her cunt against his groin.

He grunted harshly. She wrapped her arms around his chest and crushed him until she felt his ribs creak. A low moan bubbled in her throat. His hands moved quickly, jerkily, tearing at her robe until, with a soft, ripping sound, the finely cured hide parted. She felt the fur trimming of the garment caress her as it dropped in a puddle at her feet, but barely noticed her nakedness as she pulled and yanked at his own clout until she had his prick free. Hungrily she grasped his length, rubbed the slick head of it against her belly.

"Ah," she whispered. "I want it, want your prick, want *it now*."

It jerked in her hand. She opened her eyes, saw that his head was tilted back on straining neck muscles, his teeth bared in a rictus of passion. She scraped her nipples across his sweaty chest, moaning again at the fire that leapt up in her. She could feel every delineation of corded sinew in his belly as he rocked against her, and then she pulled him down.

"Mine," she panted. "All mine."

So she took him as a hunter takes her prey, and rode a dark hot wave of night and honey into an ancient endless ocean. By the power of her own hand and cunt she sealed her fate. Perhaps the Gods laughed—but perhaps not. For against the limitless tides of lust, even the Gods might content in vain.

Thus did the Stone of the Mammoth People, the Motherstone, leave the Green Valley for the last time.

4

THE STEPPE

White Moon said, "Wait. I want to stop for a minute."

Sharp Knife, walking heavily beneath a pack half his size, let go of her hand. "Do you have to? I want to get as far as we can tonight, before they discover we have left."

She turned. "Oh, they don't care *where* I go. They have their *Great Maya* now. They don't need *me* anymore." Bitter self-pity dripped from her words. Sharp Knife sighed.

"Very well. But only a moment, mind. What is it?"

"I just want to look. It's so . . . pretty."

He saw what she meant, even as he understood what she *really* meant. He'd said his good-byes earlier, in the hidden dark above the Jumble. She would say hers now, with the long wind of the steppe sighing in her ears.

A fat creamy moon rode the sky, and in the dim pearl of its light, she was transformed into a luminous shadow with streaming hair. He smelled her musky scent, and in that moment, *for* that moment, he did love her.

"Take your time," he murmured. "It will have to last awhile."

"Last forever," she replied absently. "I'll never come back here."

They had turned east, toward the moon and the invisible valley. Countless streams of smoke mingled, drifted up, wavered, then blew away, shimmering in the moonglow.

They stood in silence for many heartbeats. After a time he took her hand. "We have to go on," he said.

"Where are we going?" she asked.

That blind trust decided him. She had left the Green Valley and all her life behind, without once asking that simple question. And since there was no turning back, he told her.

When he finished, she moved close and looked into his eyes. "As long as you are with me, it doesn't matter."

"I will be with you always," he replied. In his own way, he even meant it.

5

THE CAMP OF THE PEOPLE OF FIRE

Black Otter turned uneasily on his seat as he heard the heavy footsteps approaching.

Raging Bison rather enjoyed winter, and as autumn wore on and the grass on the steppe shaded gradually from warm gold to a chill, silvery gray, his spirits began to grow positively buoyant. "Ho, Otter," he roared, and clouted the smaller man square in the middle of his shoulder blades.

Otter pitched forward, both he and the chunk of cold meat he'd been gnawing knocked sprawling. Bison burst out laughing.

"That's pretty funny, little man!" he roared, outrageously pleased with himself.

Otter scrabbled feebly about in the dirt for his fallen snack, found it, and gingerly began to pick himself up. "Very funny," he muttered, then grimaced and tried to reach around and rub the spot where a red welt was already beginning to turn blue around the edges.

"I think you broke my back," he said as he settled himself back on the log he'd been so rudely separated from.

"Hahahahahah!"

Otter regarded him sourly as he tried to wipe grit off his meal. Nothing like inflicting a little agony to put the big pounder in a good mood, he thought. *If he'd really crushed my spine, he probably wouldn't stop laughing for a moon or so.*

"Hahahah . . ."

"Oh, shut up," Otter said. He looked at the hunk of meat, spat, and tossed it away. "There. You can have it if you want!"

"Hahahahahahah!"

And if that's a sense of humor, I'm sure glad he's not mad about anything ... But Otter was used to it. Raging Bison was his best friend, and Otter was perfectly content to keep it that way. Consider the alternatives. You *didn't* want Raging Bison as an enemy, that was certain. Raging Bison's enemies had a frightening tendency to die younger than they should.

Take young Sharp Knife, for example, Otter mused, as he glanced over at the slender young man who was pounding in the last stakes for the tent he'd packed on his shoulders. *That* must have been an enjoyable little trek; the Green Valley was two days away even under the best of conditions, and on the night Sharp Knife and the girl had floundered into camp, light snow had been swirling about, sharp as wind-whipped sand.

The arrival had caused quite a stir. Even that crazed Shaman, Gotha, had bestirred himself from his Spirit House to greet the newcomers, though he hadn't spoken long before scurrying back to the warmth of his house. He'd come out the next morning, though, and hauled Raging Bison into the Spirit House for a chat, and Otter figured he could guess pretty well what those two had discussed for such a long time.

Sharp Knife's reputation had, you could say, preceded him. Not to mention the extra added attraction he'd brought along—the Keeper of the Stone.

Did she bring the Mammoth Stone with her? he wondered. Now that would make things *really* interesting. Although things had been getting interesting even before the two latest arrivals.

Raging Bison seemed to have lost his fascination with Otter's spinal cord, for he wandered away, still chuckling to himself. *Probably looking for a mammoth to choke,* Otter told himself. *I wonder what would happen if he took a clout at that boy over there* ... *now* that *might be the most interesting thing of all.*

Raging Bison seemed oblivious to Sharp Knife, but Otter thought that wasn't the case at all—in fact, Bison ignored the boy so thoroughly it had the opposite effect. These Fire Clansmen might not know it, but Sharp Knife, merely by his presence, created a problem for the hunters of the Bison Clan who'd attached themselves to this Shaman of the Forbidden God.

It was simple enough. Raging Bison had been the natural leader of the Bison hunters, if only by virtue of his strength and his reputation for utter fearlessness. Bison was a hero. But Sharp Knife might be something more.

His lineage, for instance. The boy was the brother-son of the legendary Caribou, and thus, in this camp, the closest thing to high blood they had. Moreover, his ancestor wasn't his only claim to fame. Those who hunted with him said his only equal was Wolf, the Chief of the Two Tribes—and even before Otter had left the Green Valley at the beginning of summer, there were rumors circulating about the boy and the Keeper of the Stone. Otter had discounted those rumors at the time—after all, surely Wolf would marry off the girl to someone from his own Clan— but now it seemed the rumors had been true.

She'd come with him. *And if the Stone had come with her?*

My. What an interesting winter camp it looked to be. Black Otter rubbed his hands together and chuckled softly. *Interesting. No doubt about it, interesting.*

6

Gotha peered around the edge of his door at the camp outside. He pulled back inside quickly enough. A wind full of wintry knives was roaring along out there. *Lord, it's cold in these wretched northern wastelands!*

The boy had finished setting up his tent. Gotha hadn't been able to see him *or* the far more interesting woman he'd brought with him. A telltale trickle of smoke rising from their tent told a plain enough story. No doubt they were inside, maybe even—

No. Don't think about *that*. (She's the most beautiful—) No.

Gotha sighed and refastened the flap over his doorway. The hide made a sharp flapping noise as he finished tying it down. Just for a moment, Gotha regretted having led his People so far from the warmer climes they'd known for generations. True, they were the People of Fire and *Ice*, but the ice part had been so long ago it was a matter of fading legend more than any reality these tribesmen had ever encountered.

He was proud of them, though. The legends might be fading, but evidently something still remained, for everybody was adjusting far more easily than he'd expected. He'd even made plans to quell another mutiny, if, as he thought quite possible, such a thing occurred. But he'd been wrong, for nothing of the sort happened. Even the Crone said almost nothing, and things remained quiet.

It's a good thing I let her live, he thought, not for the first time. *She makes a wonderful object lesson, hobbling around like that.*

He stoked up his small fire. The inside of his house was reasonably warm—at least his breath no longer hung around his head in chilly white clouds—and while he didn't look forward to the deeps of winter with the same enthusiasm as that huge lunatic from the Bison Clan, he thought he would make do better than he'd hoped.

In truth, almost everything had gone more smoothly than he'd hoped. The only thing he wasn't sure about right now was the arrival of the two newcomers. He'd spoken at some length with Bison about them, but he hadn't yet conferred with Sharp Knife or the—what did they call her? Keeper of the Stone?—anyway, the woman, White Moon.

He sighed, wrapped his shaggy blanket—once it had ridden the bones of a huge buffalo—closer around his shoulders, and closed his eyes. *White Moon,* he thought.

Behind the darkness of his closed eyelids, Gotha began to pick and sort through the bits of knowledge he'd gathered so far about the young woman.

Daughter of the Chief. The Shaman allowed himself a small smile. He wasn't exactly sure what that nugget meant—except that even in the highest reaches of the Green Valley, there was dissension strong enough to tear families asunder. But beyond that, what else? Could the girl be used as a hostage? Raging Bison had suggested such a thing, but Gotha had already detected the whiff of Bison's own festering hate and fanatic blood lust. He thought of the big hunter more as a weapon than an ally, for Bison didn't understand what he believed in so ferociously.

The Gods cannot be trusted, Gotha reminded himself. Raging Bison doesn't understand that. And so Bison di-

vided all things into two parts along a simple chasm—
those who worshiped the Lord of Snakes, and those who
didn't. His plans for the second group were as unsophisticated as his belief. Kill them.

But Gotha couldn't afford anything so unquestioning for
himself. He had the welfare of all his People to consider,
as well as the ever-growing contingent of newcomers,
whose reasons, he guessed, for defecting from the Green
Valley were as varied as Raging Bison's were singular.

*Belief isn't enough. The Gods must also be considered,
and Their Power.*

Which turned his thoughts back to White Moon, and the
second thing about her he had to keep in mind. She was,
according to Bison, the Keeper of the Stone. Gotha wasn't
entirely clear on just what the Mammoth Stone might be;
he imagined it was some sort of talisman imbued by myth
with special powers. Bison had told him it was so, but had
elaborated with a garbled, childish tale of powerful Shamans destroyed and Tribes defeated many seasons ago.

Gotha had discounted much of this as the foggy recollections of a child who hadn't understood what he'd seen,
much as a child might not have fully understood what had
happened the day he'd contested the Crone atop the pit of
fire.

It came down to belief, but belief of a far different nature than the mindless, almost uncomprehending variety
displayed by Raging Bison. When Gotha had climbed up
on the mound of white-hot cinders, he had done so without
qualm, for after three days of fasting, praying, and drug-
induced dreaming, he'd been absolutely certain the fire
could not harm him. The God could not be trusted, but in
the matter of ritual, if the correct preparations were under-
taken, and the faith of the Shaman was strong, then divine
blessings were usually bestowed.

The fire walk had been a test of *certainty*, and the
Crone's convictions had been less potent than his own.
That was what the Test of Fire had come down to, and he'd
never doubted the outcome for an instant.

The Crone's ruined feet were testimony of her lack of
faith, no doubt because her Bitch Goddess was not able to
impart a sufficiency when opposed by Her master, the Lord
of Fire.

Nevertheless, Gotha had enormous respect for the lesser

degrees of belief, even those engendered by the Great
Bitch. Which made White Moon and her talisman all that
more interesting. He suspected that while Raging Bison in
his unsophisticated passion might discount the Keeper of
the Stone, others would not be so rash, and so he could not
afford to, either.

Gotha decided that he wanted to see this mysterious
Stone with his own eyes, and determined to question its
Keeper about any Powers it might hold as soon as possible.

And then there was the thorny question of Sharp
Knife—a riddle Gotha thought was of far more urgency
than anything involving a musty charm and its youthful
Keeper.

He had met the young man for only a few moments, but
as their hands had clasped and he'd stared deep into the
boy's dark, flashing eyes, he'd felt a curious charge of energy shiver between them, a sensation eerie in its familiarity. It had taken him a night's worth of thought before he'd
been able to identify the source of that likeness—and the
knowledge had both surprised and unsettled him.

Sharp Knife reminded him of himself. He sensed the
same restless longings, though less focused than his own,
but that was understandable. The boy was young yet.

Still, the force, the *magnetism,* was in him. As a Shaman, Gotha understood such gifts should not be taken
lightly. Men with ambitions and the strength of will to realize them could be dangerous—unless they were har-
nessed and their talents directed into more desirable
channels.

Desirable to me, Gotha thought.

Raging Bison had told him of the boy's lineage—
brother-son to another of the Green Valley legends, a great
hunter and Chief named Caribou. Mix the blood-power
with Sharp Knife's own physical prowess (which Bison,
secure in his own strength, had been quite open about), and
Gotha found himself considering a man who could either
be of tremendous help to him, or just as easily, if mishan-
dled, of equal danger.

It was a touchy question, and it needed to be handled
right away. He couldn't afford to let it lie, lest undercurrents inimical to Gotha's own goals begin to form.

"Yes," Gotha said aloud. "Him first. *Then* her."

Which was, of course, *his* mistake.

7

Sharp Knife pulled White Moon's sleeping form closer to
him in the snug pile of blankets, and luxuriated in the freedom he felt. It had been the right choice to leave the Green
Valley, even though what he'd found beyond its walls was
not what he'd expected.

His plan, if anything so inchoate as the vague course of
action based on the jumble of hints, rumors, and guesswork
that had led him to depart could be called a *plan,* had certainly not included the Shaman Gotha and his People of
Fire and Ice.

What he *had* expected to find was Raging Bison and
many of the supposedly "missing" Bison Clansmen. It had
been common knowledge—at least among the Bison
Elders—that Raging Bison had returned to the old Forbidden God. He'd even taken his hunting party out much
earlier in the season than normal, as if he could no longer
bear to live within the Green Valley where the Mother held
sway.

So Sharp Knife had set off with the idea of following the
great circle along which the hunters moved, expecting to
find a small camp somewhere along the way, with Raging
Bison as its Chief. The only fly in that bit of honey was
one he'd not mentioned to White Moon—that Bison and
his cohorts might have simply left the area entirely, moving
on as a separate Tribe. But he'd observed the fearless
hunter for many years, and had smelled the stink of bloody
fanaticism all over him. Raging Bison, he'd guessed,
would not be content with simple retreat. He was a hero. It
wasn't in him to run away. No, if he was out on the steppe
at all, he was plotting a return to the Green Valley, most
likely bearing the scourge of his ancient Lord in fiery judgment.

Well, he thought as he shifted comfortably against White
Moon's soft, yielding flesh, *I was partly right, at least.*

Partly right in this case, though, was just about the same
as being completely wrong. This Shaman Gotha put a dras-
tically new twist on things.

For one, Sharp Knife had planned on gradually usurping
whatever leadership role Raging Bison might have been

playing at. He hadn't thought it would be difficult—Bison was known for his bravery, not for his brains. And while Sharp Knife also planned to return to the Green Valley, his intention was not to burn it, but to rule it. He thought the combination of his brains with Bison's brawn might, over a period of time, be sufficient to accomplish that goal.

He hadn't expected to find a mind equal to his own out here on the steppe, nor a sizable tribe whose traditions did not include a brother-son of Caribou as a potential Chief.

It gave him pause. It gave him *considerable* pause.

Thoughtfully, his gaze dropped to the woman sleeping so sweetly at his side.

Would you love her if she wasn't *the Keeper of the Stone? The daughter of the Chief?*

Well, maybe . . .

8

The Crone crawled painfully from her bedroll and hobbled off to take her morning shit. The cold had seeped into her bones so deeply that each movement made her think of knives plunging deep into her flesh. As she huffed and grunted along, she thought that even if she survived this winter, it would be her last. She could never take another. The thought was bittersweet. The laying down of her long burden seemed welcome, but the failure she had shown her Goddess made her wonder just how welcome she would be in the Spirit World to come.

It was not a happy thought, but then, few of her thoughts had been happy lately. Her final downfall had been, of course, the Test of Fire. She had prayed to the Mother for strength, and had fasted and chewed her roots and berries just as Gotha had done, but when she'd walked to the edge of the pit, she'd felt none of his certainty. In fact, she'd felt very much like what she was—a shrunken, half-blind old woman whose power had leaked away long years ago.

So the conclusion had not surprised her, except for the fact she'd survived at all. Some deep part of her, as she had taken Gotha's hand, was busily preparing her for death, and even now she couldn't be certain that would not have been the more pleasing outcome.

She finished her business and began the slow, painful march back to her sleeping roll. The sun was up, but not far, and even though the wind had died for the moment, the morning air was so cold it burned in her lungs. As she hobbled along, she squeezed her fingers into fists, hoping to pump a bit of warmth to them, though she knew it was probably impossible. It seemed she'd been freezing ever since the Test. Her feet, mercifully, were numb—but then, they had been since the coals had seared off flesh and even bone.

He looked down at me, his face as red as the fire itself, dark madness in his eyes, and whispered through my screams, "I will lift you now, bitch, for my Lord is not merciful, and you must suffer for your sins."

"So I have," she muttered, and shook her old head at the thought that bubbled up unbidden: *Perhaps He is more powerful than She.*

"Hello."

The Crone looked up into the face of White Moon, who smiled, reached down, and took the ancient woman beneath her arm to help her along. The Crone didn't understand the word, but the intention was easy enough, and so she smiled, flapped her toothless gums by way of gratitude, and let this strange girl lead her back to her bed. But when White Moon reached the Crone's pitiful scrap of shelter—a fetid pile of scrappy hides next to a tattered pack surely too big for the old woman to carry—a look of dismay crossed her features.

"No fire?" she asked, but the Crone only stared up at her blankly, and so White Moon tugged the old woman gently toward her own tent, where a fresh hearth was just beginning to throw off a circle of welcome heat.

White Moon settled the old woman close to the blaze, and wrapped one of her own blankets around her shoulders. Then she squatted, stoked up the fire a bit more, and regarded the Crone with bright-eyed friendliness.

The Crone returned the look with equal interest. She'd heard all the rumors. This girl was called the Keeper of the Stone by those strange new hunters who had joined with the Tribe. It seemed the new people also worshiped the Lord of Fire, though some of them called him the Lord of Breath, as well. But Gotha remained triumphant—whatever

His name, the dread Lord seemed to be the same, and Gotha's power was only swelled by the new arrivals.

All except for this girl, evidently. The Crone hadn't heard much, but what she did know indicated that White Moon worshiped a different God—and that she bore a talisman of Her Power.

They called it the Mammoth Stone.

The Crone waited to see this thing, but she didn't know how to ask. That could be fixed, though. It would only take time, and the Crone had enough of *that*. She hoped.

She pointed to the cheery morning blaze, smacked her lips, and said, "Fire."

White Moon stared at her.

"Fire," the Crone repeated.

After the third time, a look of comprehension suddenly brought a smile to her lips. "Ah," she said, and nodded vigorously. "Fire."

It was a beginning.

9

White Moon felt absurdly grateful for the hideous old woman's company that morning. She'd only been in the camp a day now, but what she'd seen so far didn't look all that promising.

She'd been very surprised at the number of refugees from the Green Valley—surprised and vaguely unsettled. Most of them had regarded her stonily—and she thought she knew why. They were all of the Bison Clan, and if any of the rumors she'd heard from the other young women were true, they were Clansmen who had returned to the unspeakable worship of the Forbidden God.

Did Sharp Knife know? she wondered.

The big one, Raging Bison, made her most uneasy, for he had stared at her the hardest, and there had been nothing friendly about his gaze. No, in fact, she associated his expression with that frightening blend of hunger and rage most often exhibited by the wolves that occasionally came right up to the edges of the new camp to snarl over the garbage middens scattered beyond the outermost houses.

The others that she recognized either ignored her or

openly turned away from her, as if they didn't even want to look at her—or were afraid to do so. It was not what she'd expected, not at all, and the situation awakened a cold feeling in the pit of her belly that Sharp Knife's renewed affection—*And isn't that worth a thought or two, also?*—only partially assuaged.

So this ugly old woman's apparent offering of friendship came as a blessed relief. She was of this new Tribe, about whom White Moon knew nothing, and when the Crone began, slowly and patiently, to teach her the language of the People of Fire, White Moon was delighted.

Deep into her lesson, she thought nothing of the hard little shape in the pouch at her side. It had nothing to do with her anymore.

"Fire," she repeated carefully. "Fire."

CHAPTER TWENTY-TWO

1

THE GREEN VALLEY

Maya stared at Wolf in disbelief. "Gone? What do you mean, she's gone?"

Wolf shrugged. "White Moon is gone. No one has seen her since last night. She didn't sleep in my house. I thought she was with Old Berry, but when I went there this morning, Berry hadn't seen her either."

Maya glanced up at the sky. Fat clouds scudded by, white on top, dark and heavy-bellied beneath. The wind danced at her feet, raising petals of dust.

"The weather is changing," she murmured. "Storm coming." She turned to Wolf. "There's no place for her to go. Where could she run to? Did you seek through New Camp? What about—" she paused, then nodded. "What about Sharp Knife? Has he seen her?"

"No one has seen Sharp Knife."

They looked at each other. "And the Mammoth Stone?" Maya said slowly.

"Nowhere to be found."

"Oh, Mother . . ."

2

Serpent jumped at the tone of her voice.

"Did you get it?" Maya asked anxiously. Serpent looked up at her, edgy at the tension in her voice. Something to do with that girl, he supposed. Ever since White Moon had

run off with Sharp Knife, Maya had been acting strange.
Ever sensitive to the fluctuations of his emotional environ-
ment, Serpent was starting to worry about her. He wasn't
positive, but he thought her face looked different, as if
there were more lines in it. Older, anyway. And she jumped
at every unexpected noise. On top of it, her temper had
grown uncertain—Serpent was never sure what might set
her off, either into anger or a sullen kind of
concentration—both of which were usually directed at him.

"I got it," he said, and showed her the empty bag he'd
been told to bring. He tried a smile on her. The expression
still felt odd on his face.

She ignored the overture. "Good. Today we look for a
particular kind of berry. They used to grow around
here . . ."

They were beyond Second Lake, approaching the mud
bogs that led into Smoke Lake. It was cold in the valley,
and getting colder each night. Fall was coming to an end.
The days were growing as short as Maya's temper. The
steam that issued from the bog and the lake settled along
the Main Path in dense patches of fog that smelled of rotten eggs. Serpent wrinkled his nose.

"Why are you teaching me all these things?" he ventured.

She whirled. *"Because you need to know them!"*
"Why?"

It was a reasonable question, he thought.

But she only pursed her lips, wrinkled her brow, and
shook her head.

That Stone the girl showed me, Serpent thought. *That's
why.*

3

Caribou finished tying a spare bow to the back of his pack.
Rooting Hog helped him hoist it up and get it settled comfortably on his broad shoulders. The two men's breath
frosted the space between them.

"Do you know where you're going?" Rooting Hog
asked.

"Not really. From what you've told me, they must be out

there somewhere. I'll trek along the hunting routes until I find something. I doubt they're hiding. With all this new snow, they won't expect anybody to come out of the valley until spring."

Rooting Hog clasped his brother's forearms in his own big hands and said, "He's my son. He's your brother-son."

Caribou looked into Rooting Hog's eyes. "I don't plan to hurt him," he said softly. "He's a boy, despite all you told me. He may have planned like a man, but running away with White Moon—and the Mammoth Stone—that was a boy's prank. A frustrated, frightened boy."

Rooting Hog sighed. "I hope you're right, brother. But two moons have passed us by. If it were what you say, surely he would have returned by now. As cold as it is here, it's twice as bad out on the steppe. Even if he found the others who didn't come back."

"Raging Bison," Caribou grunted. "I remember a boy of that name."

"The same. A strange one then, stranger now. And more dangerous. You want to watch yourself if you meet up with him, Caribou."

Caribou snorted softly. "He may not even be *out* there, brother. Many didn't come back from the summer hunting, but there might have been other reasons."

Rooting Hog looked at him. "Do you believe that?"

Caribou held the stare for several seconds, then shook his head. "No. He's out there. Somewhere."

"There's something else."

"What?"

Rooting Hog licked his lips. "Not many know of this yet, because it concerns only our Clan. But one of the houses on the outskirts of New Camp, where our people mostly are?"

"What about it?"

"Empty. The family of Angry Bear. The tracks led toward the Main Path, then out of the valley."

"You've tracked them yourself? How far?"

"I did. Almost to the mouth of the valley. It didn't make any sense to go farther. The spoor was plain enough. They didn't even make an attempt to hide their trail."

Caribou rubbed his nose thoughtfully. "As if they didn't care. As if they had nothing to fear."

Rooting Hog looked over Caribou's shoulder, at the

snow-humped houses beyond. "I have heard people say that without the Mammoth Stone, Great Maya is powerless. The Stone *or* the Keeper."

"That's bad talk. Wolf has heard it, too. You know why I'm going?"

"Why?"

"Because it may be the truth. Maya is strange now. She spends all her time with the boy, Serpent. And Wolf is worried. He wanted to go, but I talked him into letting me go instead."

"Oh?"

"Yes. You see, if the Chief of the Two Tribes goes, he will take his Mammoth hunters with him. And I don't think Wolf will have much care for the Bison Clansman who stole his daughter."

Rooting Hog smiled sadly. "You may be right about that." Then he took Caribou in a mighty hug. "The Mother go with you, my brother."

"*All* the Gods go with me," Caribou replied, then turned and tramped away before Rooting Hog could ask him what he meant by *that*.

He needn't have hurried.

Rooting Hog watched the lonely figure recede, dwindle, finally disappear. He swiped at the patches of moisture that had somehow appeared beneath his eyes. He wouldn't have asked. He understood. But he was mightily frightened.

Even if all the Gods helped, and he very much doubted that would happen—the Gods, in this case, seemed to be on opposite sides of the matter—Rooting Hog didn't think he would ever see his brother again.

Caribou paused for a moment, not knowing he stood in the same spot White Moon had found for a similar purpose, and turned around. The sky overhead loomed without depth, a flat blue that seemed white at the same time, and somehow ominous. The walls that formed the mouth of the Green Valley yawned like frost-covered jaws. Caribou shivered, suddenly conscious of the great, silent loneliness of the steppe.

The world had turned cold, and even at noon, the light was faded and full of foreboding. In the awesome distance, barely audible, something howled.

It sounded hungry. He slapped his arms together, glanced down to make sure his woven showshoes were still bound securely to his feet, then turned toward the west and began to tramp across the endless frozen waste. The icy crunch of his footsteps was the only sound—except for the wind Spirits, which heard the wolf and bayed their own mournful reply.

The lowering sky had gone gray by noon the next day, erasing the horizon so that Caribou felt as if he were walking in a dream. Or a nightmare, for the wind had risen, and ground squalls of gritty grains of snow whipped at him from all directions.

He had almost decided that he'd lost the way when the first of the jagged river rocks loomed out of the murk in front of him. "Bless the Mother," he muttered as he clambered down into their meager shelter.

"*Snake* Lord," he exploded as his feet went out from under him and he bounced, butt first, down the slick incline that debouched on the boulder-strewn banks of the river itself.

Grunting, he picked himself up and glanced around. Most of the larger rocks held white snowcaps and gleamed with thick coats of ice on the river side. But the bite of the wind was lesser here, several feet below the steppe proper, and with the storm coming on, at least the declivity offered shelter.

He plodded on, turning north, and finally found a likely spot, three craggy boulders tilted against each other to form a small cavelike enclosure at their base. Best of all, the shelter faced away from the prevailing wind, and if he could find some scraps of dry wood, he could hope to keep a small fire going.

Heaving a long, exhausted sigh, he tipped his heavy pack into the little den, and slumped down on top of it until he could catch his breath.

"Getting old," he mumbled to himself.

After several minutes his heartbeat subsided enough for him to think about braving the storm again. The wind might not be able to push all the way into his shelter, but it managed to get its icy fingertips in, and his own hands were starting to feel puffy and numb.

Slowly, he unstrapped his showshoes. Here by the river, the snow was not very deep. There was greater danger from the icy rocks, for if he slipped and broke an ankle, he would never leave this place alive. But a fire would be very good, and so when he was done he mounted to his feet and set out.

Luck was with him. He found a tangle of deadwood not more than a hundred yards away, evidently washed there by the river before it iced over. The top of the pile was snowy and damp, but he unearthed a good supply of dry wood beneath and carried three trips' worth back to his little grotto. It took a bit of work with flint and the fire moss he carried in his pack, but he managed to get a snug blaze going. This accomplished, he unrolled his sleeping fur, wrapped himself inside it, and settled back with his feet almost in the dancing flames.

It seemed to take forever for the feeling to return to his half-frozen toes, and when it did, it came on a rush of needles so painful he almost screamed. But the agony lessened quickly, and within a few more minutes he felt refreshed enough to rummage in his pack for a handful of the hardened paste of dried meat, fat, and ground-up berries that his far descendants would call *pemmican,* and that he thought of as *trail food.*

Why, it wasn't so bad at all. He had shelter, food, a fire, a warm blanket—as good as his own house back in the Green Valley.

Like Snake Fire it is! I'm crouched in a hole next to a frozen river with bad Spirits walking and talking and pounding the blizzard drums over my head, rabbiting off on what's probably a wild goose chase after a crazy man who wants to eat people, a relative who turned out both a traitor and a thief, and an empty-headed girl who probably needs a spanking more than rescuing. Oh, yes, and a talisman that I'm more scared of than anything in this World. I'm too old for this. What am I DOING *here?*

But he knew. He snorted softly. He'd never been very good at fooling himself, had he? No, not really, and while the easy answer to the question was *Maya,* there was a *lot* more to it than that.

Yes, Maya had changed, and not for the better, when White Moon had disappeared with the Mammoth Stone. He didn't understand what was tearing her apart, not exactly, but he knew it had to be connected to that. In some ways, the Mother was as terrible to Her servants as the Father was to His—which was easy enough to understand. They were both Gods, after all, and Maya had told him more than enough about the Gods and Their tools.

Still, it wasn't the complete truth, was it?

Maybe I do remember this Raging Bison a little, as a silent, cold little boy who was more than a little frightening even back then. And now he's a big, definitely frightening man who everybody says is fearless, and he's supposed to be the strongest of the Bison Clan. Just like I used to be. And maybe—even though I'm not the Chief anymore—even so, maybe I'm not quite ready to bow down and kiss Raging Bison's fearless ass. Let alone a plotting little sneak like my brother-son, who did look at me with just the faintest hint of contempt in his pretty black eyes.

So it *was* all a mishmash, and yet all of it true, and even wise men did strange things for stupid reasons. But Black Caribou was old enough not to be surprised at such a thing, even in himself, and so he threw back his head and roared into the teeth of the storm: *"Haw! I'm just a crazy old man, but here I come. Ready or not, here I come!"*

The storm didn't answer him, though, and so he pulled his sleeping fur up around his ears, rolled over, and went to sleep.

4

Gotha lifted his head and sniffed the wind. There was more snow coming, a lot more, but it didn't mean he couldn't still advance his plans a bit. His People had not fought the steppe winter for generations, but the knowledge of it was still in their bones. Besides, he had this fearless lunatic to do his bidding, and it would be a sin against the Lord to waste such a ready weapon, particularly when the weapon was so willing to be used.

Raging Bison's eyes glowed with bloodlust. "It will be easy," he said. "I can lead a party right into New Camp and be out before anybody even knows I was there. I *swear* it, Shaman!"

Gotha thought that in order to feed his lust for blood and still more blood, Raging Bison would swear to an ability to fly through the air like a hawk, and so he turned to the third man crouched around the small fire inside the Spirit House.

"What say you, Sharp Knife?"

The younger man spoke haltingly; after two moons, his facility with Gotha's tongue was not the best, but he could make himself understood. He shrugged. "It's as he says, Shaman. The Two Tribes won't post guards. They don't even know we're out here, for sure. Oh, they know Raging Bison didn't return after the hunting season, and some others, as well, but what happened to them is still mostly rumors. Besides, they don't have enough hunters to guard the whole valley, and even if they did, who would want to crouch in a snowdrift when he could be safe and snug inside his own tent?"

Sharp Knife nodded at Raging Bison. "He speaks the truth. He could probably even get into Home Camp if he really wants to, but that won't be necessary, I don't think."

Gotha listened to this speech in silence, noting the way Bison's eyes flared a bit as Sharp Knife spoke of him. *These two don't like each other,* Gotha thought, not for the first time. It was an interesting situation, potentially valuable, but he would have to be careful that it didn't get out of hand.

The expedition they were now discussing offered a way to assure that everything stayed under control. In fact, the opportunities presented by the raid extended beyond anything so simple as separating two potential rivals.

Like that smelly root vegetable, Gotha thought. *Layers inside layers.*

If these two refugees from the Green Valley were to come to open warfare, and Gotha privately thought it inevitable they would, he had yet to decide which of them he would favor. He thought he knew Raging Bison fairly well—he felt he'd numbered the man's strengths, which were formidable. But Sharp Knife had proved himself a deeper riddle—not to mention the further dilemma of his woman, the Keeper of the Stone.

Gotha's pulse began to throb a little faster at the thought of *her.* But he forced the thought away, lest it color his decision now. The question was simple. He had already decided to send raiding parties into the Green Valley, to lure more recruits to his side. Only who should lead them? If he sent Bison, then he would be able to study Sharp Knife—and perhaps bend him to his will—without disturbance. On the other hand, if he sent Sharp Knife, then he could have a free hand with White Moon. And, of course, he had to consider which of the two were more expendable, in light of his larger plans. Assure him all they might, it was still possible that something could go wrong, that they might be captured or killed. Whom could he most easily afford to lose?

He chewed his tongue lightly while he thought. Finally he came to a decision that seemed good to him. He would be sending mostly hunters of his own Tribe into the valley—and Raging Bison had already well established his reputation with those men. They would follow him readily—he wasn't so sure about Sharp Knife.

"All right, Bison," Gotha said, "pick your men. Take mostly my hunters, though." He glanced at Sharp Knife as he delivered his decree, and thought he saw a spark in the younger man's eyes.

He knows what I'm doing, he thought. *I made the right choice. I want to keep this one close, where I can keep an eye on him.*

Raging Bison grinned a feral grin. "Thank you, mighty Shaman. I will do whatever our Lord wills me to do."

"Yes, of course," Gotha agreed. "Now listen carefully, for I will tell you now what our Lord *does* will for you."

When Raging Bison had departed the Spirit House, his blood hunger almost as strong as the smell of his armpits, Sharp Knife eyed Gotha carefully. "A good choice," he said finally. "I couldn't have done better myself. Bison will be more persuasive. I'm probably considered a coward and a traitor by now—not to mention a thief."

He spoke this indictment of himself more as a question than a statement. Gotha understood the undertone.

"I think," he said slowly, "that what you *are,* and what you *will be,* depends a great deal on who your God is . . ."

Sharp Knife nodded. "My God or my Goddess? Yes, I can understand that." He paused. "It has been my experience that all things can be negotiated between men of goodwill."

Gotha regarded Sharp Knife thoughtfully. *I don't trust this slippery young man any farther than I can spit. But, in the end, I think he will be of great value to me. And, just perhaps, though this boy doesn't know it, he has already taken service with our ancient Lord.*

Gotha smiled. "That has been my experience, too."

5

Caribou peered over the ridge that overlooked the camp of the People of Fire, shocked at the size of it. *This is no gathering of a few raggle-taggle refugees!*

He gulped and slid quickly back down. *There must be sixty or seventy people down there!*

Overhead, the first sun in days blazed down, transforming the steppe into rolling crystal waves. He had rubbed charcoal beneath his eyes and still squinted continuously. For a while, he was afraid he would go snow-blind, but he'd found a bit of shade beneath the peak of the ridge. Even so, he only risked quick glimpses into the blazing white glare beyond his position.

There was some kind of commotion going on down below. Carefully shading his eyes, he risked another look. Yes. A group of heavily clad hunters had gathered near the edge of the camp. They milled about for a while, until a tall, slender man walked over to them.

Shaman, Caribou guessed. He bore a staff topped with feathers, and carried himself with unconscious authority. *This isn't what I'm looking for. This is some other Tribe . . .*

The Shaman began speaking with a heavily bearded hunter that Caribou guessed was at least his own size, maybe bigger. While the two men talked, another man came up to the group. Caribou felt a lump rise into his throat.

Sharp Knife.

As if to confirm his worst suspicions, the men separated, and the big man led his contingent out of the camp. Sharp Knife's farewell was clear on the sharp winter air: *"Good hunting, Raging Bison!"*

Caribou rubbed his lips nervously. Ice cracked beneath his nostrils, where his breath had frozen on the skin there. There was something wrong with the scene, but he couldn't quite grasp what it was. For an instant he almost had it, but then it went away. He shook his head, then narrowed his eyelids so he could watch the camp better.

Sharp Knife was the key. He needed to know which tent was his—for unless something terrible had happened, White Moon would be there.

"Stupid old fool," he mumbled to himself. "And if she

is, what are you going to do about it? Rush the whole camp
yourself?"

He chuckled softly. He hadn't expected to find a whole
tribe out here, but since he had, he would just have to
make do. After all, it wouldn't be the first time he'd
sneaked into the heart of an enemy stronghold and stolen
a woman . . .

6

Raging Bison led his small troupe upward out of the shallow riverside bowl where they had made their winter camp.
The cautious hunter's part of his brain was uneasy with the
planned raid—Bison knew how treacherous the snowy
steppe could be. But the part of him that knew no fear
burned with a consuming fire that urged him on, to strike
yet another blow against those he hated.

"Rakaba, you scout trail ahead. Watch out for soft
spots," Bison grunted.

Today Rakaba found little to rattle on about, and so nodded curtly and plowed on ahead, his snowshoes making brittle scraping noises on the thin crust atop the deeper snow.

About two hours later, midway through the afternoon,
they crossed Caribou's trail, going in the opposite direction. Raging Bison hunkered down and examined the
frozen spoor, his forehead wrinkled in thought.

"One man," he said softly. "A big man."

He stood up. "Turn around," he whispered. Sound carried on the cold air for miles sometimes. "Let's see where
this one is going."

7

Caribou kneaded his cheeks, trying to work a bit of warmth
into them. He glanced at the sky. Dusk was coming on, and
with it a few chilly wisps of cloud that masked the worst
of the glare. He would have to time things perfectly.

Luck, if it could be called that, he thought sourly,
seemed to be with him. The tent Sharp Knife had even-

tually returned to was on the nearest edge of the camp to Caribou's position, just down the slight angle of the ridge, set up near the shelter of a pile of icy black boulders. Even better, when Sharp Knife had exited the tent again, White Moon had followed him out to call some final words to him before ducking back inside.

It just might work . . .

The plan he'd put together wasn't much, but it was the best he could come up with on short notice—and short notice was all he had. He knew he couldn't stay here much longer. The chance of discovery was too great. There might be other hunting parties out—*Something wrong with that, what is it?*—and besides, his toes were already numb and his hands, which he held cupped beneath his armpits, weren't far behind.

He guessed he'd have about half an hour of that weird winter dusk light, a silver-gray glow that turned shadow into mist, and real things into shadow, when he might be able to make his way down that slope to the back of White Moon's tent. *If Sharp Knife didn't come back, if he could club the girl unconscious before she screamed and raised an alarm, if he didn't trip over a buried rock and break his fool skull open, if, if, if . . .*

"Ah, to the Snake with it," he mumbled, glanced around, and slid carefully over the top of the ridge.

He was halfway down, grunting softly, slithering along, when he knew what was wrong with that hunting party. *There is nothing to hunt!*

Not out on the steppe, anyway. Not in the snowy, freezing dead of winter. The nearest prey was two days behind him—beyond the frozen jaws of the Green Valley.

He paused for an instant, then resumed his steady advance. *There's nothing I can do about it now, but when I've got the girl, I'm going to have to move quickly. Maybe I can beat them back, give a warning.*

He pushed the thought away. The rear of the tent was closer now, only the length of a man away. He took out his stone knife, rose to a crouch, and leapt forward, bringing the knife down in a long, sweeping arc.

The thick hide parted beneath the sharp edge of the blade. The hot, smoky air billowed out into his face as he hurled himself through.

The only illumination inside was a small hearth that was

filled with dull red coals. He blinked, trying to get his bearing.

White Moon rose from her furs. "What . . . who—"

He saw her as a looming shadow, and threw an off-balance punch that knocked her back down. He flung himself on her, found her neck with one hand, and squeezed off the scream that was bubbling in her throat. Slammed the side of her head once, twice. She went limp.

He waited rigidly. Then, slowly, he felt the side of her neck. A strong, steady pulse. Good. Working quickly now, he wrapped her in the blanket she'd been lying on. She was fully dressed otherwise.

Luck's still with me. Just a little longer, now . . .

Sharp Knife pushed through the door flap. *"What's—"*

Caribou threw his full weight into the charge.

8

Raging Bison held up one wide hand. "Stop," he whispered.

The party was less than a hundred yards beyond the ridge above the river, with dusk slowly blurring the world with silver.

"There," he said. "Did you see it?"

Agarth, ever taciturn, shook his head.

"Something moved there. In the rocks . . ."

Agarth peered intently at the spot. "Don't see anything."

Raging Bison glanced at him. "I did," he replied.

Agarth's eyes were wide. "A Demon . . .?"

"Come on," Bison said. "I'm not afraid of Demons."

9

Caribou bulled forward and butted Sharp Knife squarely in the belly with every bit of his two hundred pounds behind the blow. Sharp Knife folded in half, air bursting from his mouth in a belching *whoosh!*

They slammed to the earth, and Caribou brought his fist down as hard as he could. Sharp Knife arched under him, strong and slippery as a flopping fish, but he was tangled in his own furry coat.

Caribou slammed him again, then one more time. He heard something crunch beneath his final blow. His fist went warm and wetly slick, and the coppery odor of blood suddenly bloomed in the small tent.

Caribou rolled off Sharp Knife's unconscious body, gasping for breath, sudden explosions of white and pink stars flaring behind his eyes. He steadied himself and waited, crouched, until his breathing was a little more even. Then he floundered about until he found White Moon. He searched at her waist, found the pouch there, and felt the shape inside. He grinned.

Old fool, maybe, but still a lucky *old fool.* Sharp Knife had been a lot easier than he'd thought he would be, but then, he'd surprised the boy. Even so, it had been a near thing—for a moment there, he hadn't been sure he could hold him down.

He checked one more time to make sure White Moon was securely bundled in her blanket, then grunted as he hoisted her to his shoulder. He cast a final look around the dim interior of the tent—Sharp Knife was an unmoving lump on the other side of the fire.

"Let's get going, then," Caribou told himself. He took a deep breath, ducked, and pushed out through his cut into the dusky shadows.

"Who are you?" Raging Bison said as he stepped forward, his great spear pointed at Caribou's belly.

10

Sharp Knife thrashed once, then once again, then moaned softly and clutched at his ribs. The sudden movement brought a harsh, choking gasp of pain. It felt like everything around his waist had been crushed to mush.

He'd been curled on his side, his knees almost to his chest, curled like a baby around the agony in his belly. Now, inch by slow inch, he forced himself to uncurl, to straighten out, and, finally, to lurch to his knees. A wave of dizziness almost knocked him over again, but he fought it, and after a time he stood all the way upright, supporting himself with one hand on the sturdy pole that braced the ridge of his tent.

"Uhh." Still holding the pole, he bent over and vomited a spume of half-digested meat. His belly muscles screamed protest in a series of sudden cramps, but after those lessened and he was able to stand again, he felt better. His head was clear, at least.

He looked around, confused. What had happened? He'd stepped into the tent, and then something had slammed into him and knocked him down, and—

White Moon!

He dropped to his knees and began to search the mound of furs with his hands. Gone!

He snuffled, then snorted a huge gout of half-dried blood out of his broken nose. That was when he noticed the gaping rip in the back of the tent. The wind had blown it open, and in the weird, silvery half-light beyond, he saw moving figures. He grabbed his spear, lurched unsteadily through the opening, and stopped.

His mouth fell open.

That was—

11

Caribou shuffled to his right. His arms felt like logs dangling from his shoulders. He held his spear loosely, ready to thrust or parry. His sweat-soaked hair hung across his face. His breath rasped between his swollen lips, hung for a moment in neat gray clouds, then blew away.

He had passed the first interval of fury, when fear and anger had sustained him in charge after charge against Raging Bison, who had met each advance with tremendous blows and bellowing laughter. Now Bison had subsided somewhat, and his dark eyes were hooded and wary as he sidestepped along with Caribou. A thin trickle of blood etched the side of his face.

Almost got home on that one, Caribou thought, but it was a forlorn consolation. *I could have taken him ten years ago.*

Fleetingly, he thought of Maya. *Will she miss me? I love her so. I wish I could go back to her, see her one more time.*

It was not to be, and he knew it. For some reason, the

knowledge didn't perturb him too much. He thought she loved him, in her own way and as much as she could, but he had always known that her greatest duty lay in something he could never understand.

There was something to be said for a hunter to die with his spear in his hand, in honorable combat.

Mother, this Bison had turned into a monster!

There was a coldness inside Caribou's skull now, as the rush of energy ebbed away. He thought Bison might be toying with him, and he was horribly afraid he understood why that might be. But he would fall on his own spear before he let that happen. In any event, he wasn't dead yet, and he might even get in a lucky stroke or two before the end.

There seemed to be a lull in the fight. Caribou stamped his feet and jabbed out with his spear, forcing Bison backward, but the other man retreated only a moment before parrying with a circular motion so strong it almost ripped Caribou's own weapon from his numbed fingers.

"Good stroke, Bison," Caribou shouted. "You're better than I thought!"

Bison grinned at that, his teeth shining white in the black nest of his beard. "What can you remember, Black Caribou? I was only a boy."

"And now you are grown. But you're still ugly. Come to me, Raging Bison, so I can kill you!"

Raging Bison did a strange thing. He stepped back, almost to the edge of the circle of men who now surrounded them. He planted the butt of his spear in the earth and said, "They always told me you were the best, Black Caribou. I can see what they meant. But you are old now, and I will kill you, if we go on."

He turned, spat on the ground, then grinned. "Return to your own youth, mighty Chief. Take up again the worship of your true Lord, whom you were raised up with. You turned against Him, and brought the downfall of your Clan, but He will take you back. All you have to do is say so, and this need not go on. I will pledge your safety with my own life if you do."

Caribou stared at him. He had no doubt the offer was sincere. "And if I do not?" he said.

Raging Bison shrugged. "Then I will not kill you. *He* will, and I will eat your heart."

So that's how it is. Just about what I thought. Well, at least you won't have that ...

Caribou laughed. "Are you a coward, Raging Bison? They say you are without fear, but I think you are afraid of me. Why hide behind the dirty robes of your filthy God? I wasn't afraid to spit on Him and His unspeakable Meat, but you must be. Do you shit on your heels when He calls you? Do you—"

Raging Bison's eyes had begun to bulge. He jerked his spear out of the earth and twirled it like a twig. *"I fear nothing, traitor!"* he roared, and rushed forward.

Caribou barely ducked under the charge, turned with it, and launched a killing blow at Bison's back as he charged past, but time *had* taken its toll, and his stroke was an instant too slow. The tip of his point ripped a bloody slash in Raging Bison's calf, but this new wound only seemed to invigorate him. He spun on his heel, parried Caribou's second blow, then brought the haft of his spear around and crashed it into Caribou's ribs.

Caribou felt something go in his chest, and suddenly it was hard to breathe. He lurched forward and Bison danced out of his way.

Frantically, Caribou floundered after him, launching blow after huge blow, but Bison only laughed at him.

Finally, the strength ran out of Caribou's arms, and he lowered his spear. All sensation had gone from his legs. He couldn't feel his feet at all. He felt light-headed, and his vision wavered. He licked his lips.

"Kill me, then ..." he whispered.

"Pray to your Bitch," Bison said. "Maybe She will save you."

As Caribou struggled with his own terror—he wasn't afraid to die, just terrified of the manner his dying might take, if Bison was true to his word—he glanced over and saw White Moon's face, as chalky as smooth ice over dark water. For some reason she had taken out the Mammoth Stone, and now held it in her hands.

To Caribou's eyes, the ancient, smooth ivory seemed to glow faintly. He felt a warmth reach out from it and caress him. He smiled faintly.

"You have made a bad choice, White Moon," he said, "but She will forgive you."

White Moon froze as surely as if he'd transfixed her with

his spear. For a moment she reminded him of a rabbit caught
in a trap, and he pitied her. He pitied all of them, all those
caught in the long, incomprehensible weavings of the Gods.

And still the divine heat of the Stone throbbed into him,
filling up his muscles, invigorating his heart, and when he
turned to face Raging Bison, he felt like a boy again, and he
laughed, though blood spurted from his lips with the sound.

He put his head down and charged.

Caribou was halfway to Bison when Sharp Knife
stepped out of the circle and plunged his spear into Caribou's belly. The force of Caribou's charge impaled him,
and the spear point burst from his spine in a gout of blood.

Sharp Knife stepped back. "Now you are dead, old
man!" he spat.

*I see you now, my dearest. Where have you been? I
missed you. Did you come to me because of that? Ahh, I
love you so, I love—*

"Maya," Caribou said, and fell over.

No one else saw the woman who came to him then, and
touched the wound in his belly with her staff, and healed
it, and raised him up. Nor did they see the long white tunnel open before him, or the girl named Spring Flower, who
had been Caribou's little sister in another time, another
place, appear in the Light of that tunnel.

She met him at the end of the tunnel, and with the
woman whose eyes were green and blue, took Caribou's
tired, gnarled hand and led him into a bright place where
the herds always roamed, and the dust rose in clouds to the
never-setting sun.

Nobody, not Raging Bison or Sharp Knife, not even
White Moon who still grasped the Mammoth Stone, saw
these things. All they saw was the fallen hunter.

And the smile on his face.

CHAPTER TWENTY-THREE

1

THE GREEN VALLEY

Maya woke in the dark, a terrible stabbing pain in her belly. She gasped and rolled over. "Ah!"

Serpent, always the light sleeper, was at her side immediately. "Maya. What is it?"

She moaned. After a moment he realized she was sobbing softly. "Caribou . . ." she whispered.

His eyes widened. He touched her shoulder. She didn't move, didn't say anything, only continued that terrible, silent shaking.

After a while he went back to his furs and lay down. Something awful had happened, but he didn't know what it was, or how to help her. It was a long time before he could sleep again.

2

THE STEPPE

Gotha stood on the ridge above the river and watched the ice break. At his back snow still stretched in an endless white blanket, but down below, with booming thunder, another huge chunk of ice broke off and floated down the swiftly widening stream.

At his side, Sharp Knife said, "Spring is coming. Less than a moon, and the steppe will be soft and green again."

Gotha nodded. The time of decision was coming. He turned to Sharp Knife. "How many now?"

"Five more came back with Bison's last raiding party. That makes twenty newcomers this winter. We have almost twenty hands of people in camp now."

Gotha nodded. Bison's raids had been far more successful than he'd hoped. Five times the hero had gone out, braving snow and storm to steal food and people from the Green Valley. But for Gotha, it wasn't the spoils he coveted as much as the information that came with them.

Things were falling apart in the valley of his enemies. According to the latest news, the Clansmen of the Bison were in nearly open revolt. Even the people of the Mammoth Clan were disheartened, fearing that the magic had gone. On one of his earlier raids, Bison had met in secret with some of his Clan Elders and told them of Caribou's death.

Rooting Hog, Caribou's brother, had not been present at the meeting, but the nominal leader, Shaggy Elk, had only shaken his head in sorrow, as if the terrible news was nothing more than he'd expected.

Raging Bison had related the tale gleefully: "He told me that Caribou was trying to regain the Mammoth Stone, that without it, even Great Maya was powerless."

Gotha had a few doubts about that—after all, the People of the Green Valley were still far more numerous than his own growing band—but overall, he was pleased with what the winter had brought him. It gave him no little satisfaction that the Test of Fire had proven—if proof were needed—the superiority of his own Lord over the Bitch, for was not that Power even now showing itself in the disintegration within the valley? Perhaps now was the time to advance the Lord of Fire's cause even further.

"What about White Moon?" he asked. "Has she agreed to your wishes on the matter we discussed?"

Sharp Knife's face changed a bit, hardly noticeable, unless one had keen eyes and a wide knowledge of humanity's talent of evasion. Gotha noticed.

"She is always willing to obey her husband," he replied.

"Yes, of course. But that's not what I asked. Is she ready to publicly acknowledge the Power of the Lord of Snakes, and give over her Bitch's talisman?"

Gotha regarded the younger man closely. The question

was of great importance. There must be no question in *any-body's* mind about the one true Lord, not when Gotha planned for his final killing stroke less than a moon hence. And privately, he had another concern. That Stone had been a shock, for it wasn't a stone, but a carving of ivory, and he had seen its twin. The tentacles of the Gods were somehow entwined between the two of them. Nor did he think it coincidence that just as he'd been given the Keeper and her Stone, he'd lost to his enemy the green-and-blue-eyed Speaker and *his* Stone.

The Gods are playing games, he thought sourly. *The Gods cannot be trusted.*

There was only one way to learn the truth and decipher the divine riddle. Just as he'd tested the Power of the Bitch on the Pit of Fire, he must now test Her Power head on—by ruling Her Stone and Her Keeper first, and then the one he regarded as the ultimate threat—Great Maya, the Wielder of the Stone.

He intended to do both, and as quickly as possible. "It's important," he said slowly to Sharp Knife. "I want that Stone in my hands a hand of days hence, for that is when we *all* will eat that Special Meat. Do you understand?"

Sharp Knife thought of the boy of the Mammoth Clan Bison had brought back from his latest raid, a child barely eight summers old, whose hapless luck had brought him wandering down the Main Path at precisely the wrong time. But Gotha had been delighted—it was almost as if his dread Lord had provided Himself with this sacrifice for His Shaman to serve up to Him in the customary spring ritual.

"Yes, Shaman," Sharp Knife replied at last. "You shall have it."

His answer didn't quite satisfy the older man, for he turned and pinioned Sharp Knife with a burning stare. "You do understand that whether you shall be Chief of the Three Tribes when we take the valley depends on how well you serve our Lord?"

Sharp Knife nodded miserably. "Yes, I understand." *And I hope I can make that wretched wife of mine understand as well.*

Gotha looked away. He didn't mind misery or reluctance or anything else, as long as the will of the Lord was carried out. This youth at his side valued his ambition above all other things—and so was bound in ropes of Power he couldn't even see.

But Gotha could, for he held the ends of those ropes securely in his hands. "See to it, then," he said brusquely, and walked away.

Sharp Knife watched him go, the woeful expression on his face making him look *much* older than he actually was.

3

White Moon sat silently in her tent, thinking about what the Crone had told her. She had grown to like the old woman over the dark days of winter, for only the Crone showed her any real friendship as she patiently taught her the tongue of the People of Fire. *She's an outcast, just like me . . .* White Moon thought.

It was an oddly mature bit of musing for the Keeper of the Stone, but the winter had taught her some hard lessons. Deprived of the almost automatic deference she'd received in the Green Valley, she'd had to learn to think about her world more acutely. And she didn't like what she'd discovered.

Sharp Knife, for instance. Two things—no, three—stood out. The first was her recurring memory of the day she'd gone to the Young Men's House and he'd rejected her. She'd managed to mask the anger and pain she'd felt then, even from herself. And surely she'd been right to do so, for Sharp Knife *had* thrown over everything for her love—or so it had seemed at the time. Indeed, the days after her arrival at the river camp had been a dream of soft kisses and long, passion-filled nights in the sweaty folds of their bedrolls. Then, slowly, things had begun to change.

Her second worry was that now Sharp Knife found reasons to leave her alone, usually to be with the Shaman. His kisses and caresses grew less frequent, and much of the time, her husband simply wrapped himself in his furs and began snoring without so much as a good-night peck.

She thought his behavior had to do with her stubbornness about the Mammoth Stone, but on this matter, her thoughts were even more confused—and her confusion wasn't lessened by the third incident that had changed the world inside her skull.

Even the Crone hadn't been able to make the occurrence entirely clear, but *something* had happened on the night her husband had slain Caribou. The incident wouldn't go away. She replayed it constantly in her thoughts, both waking and sleeping, and the dreams of it were even less helpful than the reality.

Once again, she unwrapped the Stone and held it in her hands, hopeful that somehow merely touching the smooth ivory talisman might unlock the door to the answers she realized she needed desperately—for there was a decision coming, and she was terribly frightened.

"There's nothing important about this old thing," she'd told the Crone the first time she'd shown her the Stone, puzzled at how excited the old woman had become on her first sight of it.

"Oh, yes there is, girl," the Crone said.

"But what? It's only been a burden to me."

Then the Crone had told her about the Speaker, and the Stone he bore, and pointed out that aside from matching Stones, the two of them shared other characteristics—the color of their eyes, for instance.

"You say your eyes are the mark of our Mother," the Crone whispered. "I believe you are right. But what does it mean? The boy always spoke for the God . . ."

At that time, still dazzled by her new life with Sharp Knife, she'd rejected the old woman's musings. Even the rumors she'd heard about Great Maya's intentions concerning her and Serpent seemed ridiculous—Serpent was only a boy, after all. But now, in the silence of her tent, she wondered. There *was* too much coincidence going on—it was almost as if some invisible hand were moving her about, willy-nilly, according to some plan she couldn't even begin to fathom.

It was a new experience for a spoiled, willful child who'd always been in control, always been given everything she wanted—except for Sharp Knife, of course, and that had only been because of Great Maya's return. In the end, even Great Maya hadn't been able to stop her from having what she most desired . . . if this ever more disquieting new life *was* what she wanted. She was no longer certain.

She squeezed the carving, but it remained cold and un-responsive, nothing more than the inert piece of tusk she'd always thought it to be. Yet, on that terrible night, it hadn't been inert, had it? No, as she'd stared pity and terror at Caribou, whose gaze had been locked on the Stone, she'd actually felt it *throb*, hadn't she? She couldn't recall why she'd taken it from its wrappings, why she'd held it so tightly then, but the heat that had suddenly filled her palms as Caribou slowly toppled over had been real enough, hadn't it?

That pulsing warmth hadn't been the only thing, though. There had been something else, something that even now she couldn't explain. But she had *seen* Sharp Knife in that instant, seen the burning core of him, the fire to which he would sacrifice anything, *even her,* and the vision had filled her with horror. It had rocked her world, and though she had tried ever since to push the revelation away, it wouldn't go. It haunted her nights and made her days cold and cheerless.

She'd tried to explain all this to the Crone, and though the old woman had patted her hand sympathetically, she hadn't been much help. She'd told White Moon about Dreams, but this hadn't been a Dream, exactly. No mighty Goddess had come to her with divine commands. It would have been a lot easier if that had happened. But there had only been that one flash of insight, that *seeing,* and it hadn't shown her the Goddess, but only the deepmost hidden part of her own husband.

And that certainly wasn't divine.

"Oh, you awful *thing,*" she muttered in frustration, as if what the Stone had revealed about Sharp Knife were some-how *its* fault, and not his. Then she quickly wrapped the Stone and put it away. Once again she felt an urge to simply throw it in the river. There had been a time when she'd thought that was the answer—throw away the talisman, and all her troubles with it.

Now she was afraid that if she did, her troubles would remain. And she would be left without the only key that might unlock the answers.

What had Old Berry said so many times? That Maya had made a choice. White Moon had no idea what that choice had been, but she knew one thing.

What the Stone had shown her had cracked the founda-

tions of her life and belief. If there was a choice coming
for her, it would no longer be an easy one.

4

Sharp Knife walked disconsolately back to his tent. Nothing was going right these days. Gotha had turned out every
bit as formidable an opponent as he'd feared. In fact,
Gotha could hardly even be considered an appointment—in
this camp, he ruled absolutely. Sharp Knife had no illusions about his own status. He would either do whatever
the Shaman demanded, or he would find himself offering
up his own heart to Gotha's Lord as token of a more final
submission.

Yet hope remained. Gotha needed him. There was no
doubting that, either. The Shaman had made it plain
enough that Sharp Knife was his choice to rule the Three
Tribes, after those Tribes were united in the Green Valley.
Of course, Gotha would rule the Chief, but did that matter?
Gotha himself answered to his own ruler, for Sharp Knife
had finally understood that the Shaman *did* believe in his
Lord, and sought as well as he could to do what he perceived as His divine bidding.

Sharp Knife, on the other hand, was beginning to realize
he didn't believe in *anything,* not even his own natural superiority, the faith which he'd nurtured within himself
since his earliest youth.

Gotha *terrified* him. The Shaman seemed to be able to
read his mind, whether through the Spirit he served, or
through his own magic. Either way, it didn't matter, for
somehow Gotha anticipated Sharp Knife's every move, and
almost every *thought.*

Like now, for instance. How could Gotha, who hardly
ever spoke to White Moon, know of the reluctance Sharp
Knife had sensed growing in his wife? He was hardly sure
himself, and certainly hadn't spoken of his doubts to anyone else. But where had that compliant, pliable young girl
gone to? Now she was withdrawn, silent, even at times re-
sistant to his wishes. She *argued* with him.

He shook his head. What if she refused Gotha's demands? He knew the Shaman frightened her. What if he angered her as well? What if—

Sharp Knife shook his head. There were too many ifs, and such things made him nervous. His steps quickened. He straightened his shoulders. Best not to let her sense his indecision, it would only fuel her own stubbornness.

Besides, in the end, she would have no choice. Somehow he must make her see that. The time for choice was over. She must learn to obey, or die.

5

The Crone stumped restlessly about the camp, muttering to herself. Her ruined feet were an agony to her, but the pain only served to sharpen the pain she felt inside. *That girl.*

Somehow—though she didn't know how—the will of the Goddess centered on that young woman! The Crone's ignorance, and the fear it caused, made her even more irascible than usual. People got out of her way as she huffed and snorted past, her one good eye rolling in her skull like a stone in a cup. They made the sign against evil Spirits at her back, but if she noticed, she paid them no heed.

What is going on here? What is my son planning? He talks to her husband all the time, and I know the look on his face when he does. Gotha is keeping a secret, and it has to do with her.

But what? Great Mother, *help me.* The Crone had tried everything. Fasting, her leaves and berries, constant prayer. Nothing had helped. Her fitful sleep remained Dreamless, and her agitated days without vision. It was almost as if her Mother had deserted her, after her terrible defeat on the Pit of Fire.

I wasn't strong enough, is that what it is? I am no longer a worthy vessel for your Power, Mother?

She paused, not far from White Moon's tent, hawked a glistening wad of phlegm into her throat, then spat it out. It lay steaming on the ground. She stared at it for a moment and then abruptly clapped her withered claws together. The sound was like the slapping of dry sticks on the clear, chilly air.

I must spit it out. He put His fear into me, on the Pit,

and now I choke on it. There is no room for Her in me, not with His fear filling my belly. I must spit it out!

She shivered. She thought she knew a way, an old way, to do it. But it was very dangerous. It might kill her.

She shook her head. It didn't matter, nothing mattered but the girl.

I will be worthy of you, Mother! I swear it!

Maybe.

6

Raging Bison peered over Rakaba's shoulder. The smaller hunter looked up. "What do you think? Sharp enough?"

Bison reached over, took the heavy spear point, and hefted it thoughtfully. "Very good. Sharpen three, though. I want each warrior to carry three spears. There are not so many of us, so we will have to kill more of them, maybe." His eyes glittered as he spoke. Rakaba glanced at him, then turned away.

Raging Bison might be fearless, but Rakaba had no such advantage. The thought of attacking the entire might of the Green Valley made him wake up in the night with his sleeping furs sweated through.

A little raid is one thing, he thought. *But we will need the help of the Lord of Snakes Himself to beat so many.*

Nor was he alone in his concerns. Others had spoken of the same thing. No one doubted Raging Bison's prowess, but he was only one man. That warrior from the Green Valley, Caribou, had even managed to wound him, and though the outcome had never really been in doubt, all had seen Raging Bison's blood glitter darkly in the firelight. Bison was fearless, but he wasn't a God, and it would take the Power of the Lord Himself to vanquish the men of the Green Valley.

Rakaba wanted a sign. He *needed* a sign. So did the rest, except Raging Bison, who carried his own sign inside him.

Rakaba sighed and returned to his work. Maybe the Shaman could give them a sign. The Great Ritual of Spring was two days hence.

We will see, Rakaba promised himself hopefully. *We will see then.*

7

Gotha lifted the door flap of the Spirit House and carefully peered out. All seemed in readiness. The Sacrificial Hearth had burned through the night, and now resembled a smaller version of the Pit of Fire, cracked and scabby with red heat. To the right, six hunters pummeled log drums, sending an ever-rising frenzy of sound into the shimmering spring air. Near the drums, most of the hunters danced with sweat glistening on their chests. Children sucked their thumbs and stared, big-eyed, at the commotion, as their mothers and sisters shooed them hither and yon.

There was an air of joyous festivity to the whole proceeding. Even the small, scrawny boy tethered to the post next to the Hearth clapped his hands to the drums and smiled occasionally.

He saw Raging Bison standing next to the drums, his fists clenched, smile so wide it seemed more a silent shriek, bobbing his head to the rhythms. Not far away, Sharp Knife whispered intently in White Moon's ear. Neither of them looked happy; White Moon's face was set and stubborn. On the other hand, Sharp Knife merely seemed desperate.

Gotha had a good idea what their problem was. *He'd better convince her. Or there will be two sacrifices to the Lord of Fire this day.*

Only one face was missing from the altogether satisfying tableau. Gotha squinted against the soft green-tinted light, but the Crone's raddled, oozing features were nowhere to be seen. *Where is the Hag?* he wondered. He let the flap drop. It didn't really matter, did it? She was only a ruin now, surely no threat since she and her Bitch had bowed to the Fire Lord's power. Nevertheless, he didn't trust her.

I suppose she hates me.

It never occurred to Gotha that his mother might love him more than ever—but it was true. It was the reason for what would come, but he wouldn't know until afterward. When it was too late to do anything about it.

8

The Crone rubbed one finger across the grains she held in her palm. Years before—*When I still had my eyes, my health, my feet . . . my hopes*—the tribe had wandered through a field of wild grain that had stretched for miles across the southern prairie land beyond the river. It had been late in the summer, the grain ripe and golden. There must have been a storm, for here and there on the ground were patches of fallen seed, in places as deep as her ankles. And on some of the patches, dark, damp places that stank of mold and rot. It was these places that drew her attention, for her mother had told her of such things.

The doorway to the other Worlds, her mother had taught her. *Very hard to find, but if you do, gather up a supply, for the spoiled grain will give you the eyes of the Gods Themselves.*

Now, as the Crone stirred the evil-smelling granules, she hoped it was so. She'd never dared use this grain, for her mother had added a warning: *Some never return from the Worlds they visit.*

It is called the Dancing Seed . . .

"Perhaps a dance of death . . ." the Crone murmured to herself, then closed her good eye, brought her palm to her withered lips, and chewed. She grimaced at the bitter taste, but eventually gummed the softened grains into paste, which she swallowed.

Maybe in another World I will find what I need, she told herself, as she settled back to await the opening of the door. *Maybe I will find the Spirit I have lost.*

Outside, the drums pounded on.

9

White Moon jerked her arm from Sharp Knife's grasp and turned away. Two spots of hot color burned in her cheeks. Her eyes flashed with anger, catching the spring light so that they seemed jewels set on the ridge of her cheekbones.

"And what will your precious Shaman *do* with the Mammoth Stone?" she hissed. "I'm its Keeper. You don't think I'm just going to hand it over to him, do you?"

"Yes, that's exactly what I expect you to do. You are my wife, White Moon. You must obey me."

She stamped her foot. "Obey you? I don't have to obey *anybody!*"

Sharp Knife darted a glance at the closed door flap of the Spirit House. The Shaman had not come out yet, but the time was drawing close. Overhead, the sun was only a finger width from high noon, when the ritual must begin.

Spoiled brat! He clicked his teeth in frustration. With any other woman, he would simply have smashed her in the face, taken the Stone, and done whatever he wished with it. But things weren't so simple. Gotha himself had told him, "It must be of her own free will, or nothing. Either she submits willingly, or she dies—there is no middle ground."

Worst of all, Sharp Knife understood the reasons for Gotha's stricture. Within days, they would launch an all-out attack on the Green Valley. But Gotha's goal was not a massacre. He wanted a victory, but more than that, he wanted to rule in the name of his God. Piles of bodies would not accomplish that.

Yet, in order to rule, Gotha needed submission. And Sharp Knife knew that submission was far more a matter of belief than of naked force. If those who worshiped the Mother—still the large majority of the Two Tribes in the valley—were to be effectively controlled, they must believe that their Goddess had been defeated by a greater Power. Just as the Bison Clan had seen the defeat of *their* Lord at the hands of Great Maya and the Mother.

But it had been Maya *and* the Stone who had defeated Broken Fist and the Shaman Ghost that day. Now Maya no longer had the Stone. It had remained with the Keeper. If the Keeper could be induced to hand over—to *submit*—the Mammoth Stone to the Lord of Snakes and Fire, then Maya was effectively rendered harmless, and the primacy of the Fire Lord established once and for all.

Sharp Knife knew that Gotha had visions of leading his warriors into the Green Valley bearing the Mammoth Stone in his own hands as talisman of the Snake Lord's victory. But if the Stone he bore had been taken from its Keeper by brute force, then those who sought a reason to doubt the

Power of the Lord and his Shaman would have one. Gotha couldn't allow that. *Nor,* Sharp Knife thought, *can I. I will be his Chief, and my authority threatened, too.*

He sighed. *Oh, you wretched brat, don't you understand what's at stake here?* Even as he thought the words, a faint, bitter smile twitched at his lips—for *she* would be at the stake if she couldn't understand. *Tied* to the stake, and screaming.

For that was the other side of the choice. If the Keeper refused to relinquish the Stone of her own will, there was only one other way to show the Power of the Lord, and that was to destroy the Keeper herself.

If the Mother couldn't protect Her own Keeper, then what Power over the Lord of Fire could She have? Either way, the point would be made, the example clear.

There was no middle ground. White Moon must choose, and choose now, for part of that choice was her very life!

I will make you see, he thought. *For your sake. For my sake.*

I don't care which choice you make, but you must choose!

10

THE RITUAL OF SPRING

Gotha stalked from the Spirit House bearing his great staff of cavern snakes. He felt a wild surge of triumph. The scene laid out before him was essentially unchanged, though the boy tied to the stake suddenly began to cry, and White Moon and Sharp Knife now stood nearer the stake than they had before.

White Moon looked angry, Gotha thought, but her husband appeared calm, though his face was pale. Evidently whatever decision they'd made had soothed his earlier anxiety. As the Shaman approached the stake, the drumming ceased, and only the boy's thin wails sounded forlornly in the silence.

For one moment Gotha remembered another boy tied to the same stake, but that boy was gone now, in the hands of the enemy.

Not for long, though, he thought, and again that terrible current surged through his body. It was all he could do not to throw his head back and roar with laughter.

He reached into the belt of his long robe and withdrew a knife chipped from quartz so clear and red it was as if he wielded a tongue of flame. He raised the knife above his head and let the light of the sun drip from it, the awed murmur of the crowd like a soft breeze in his ears.

Slowly Gotha bowed to the homes of the four wind Spirits, and then took from his belt pouch a bit of powder that he sprinkled on the fire. Aromatic odors of pine and roses suddenly filled the air with sweetness; even the boy stopped crying and stood looking up at the Shaman, his eyes round and full of wonder.

Then Gotha stamped first his right foot, then his left, down hard on the earth before the stake.

"Ah! Ah!" he chanted. "Ah! Ah!"

Slowly the drums began to beat. After a moment the Shaman's chant was taken up by the rest. "Ah! Ah!"

Now the smell of sweat, damp and hot, began to mix with the sweetness of the fire. Flesh jiggled up and down. Breasts slammed against rib cages, hips jumped and fell.

"Ah! Ah! Ah!"

Surging from the tip of the knife he held over his head, Gotha felt burning flows of power jolt his hand, his arm. He jumped higher and higher, as if to leap above, beyond the appalling energies that filled him.

His eyes turned back in his skull until nothing showed but blank whiteness, and the people began to moan and shout in frenzied ecstasy.

"Ah! Ah! AH!"

The drummers lifted up their eyes. Their tongues lolled from their mouths. Their faces glistened. The movement of their arms became a continuous blur as thunder issued from their instruments.

"Save us from the Winter, Mighty Lord of Fire!" Gotha screamed.

"AH! AH! AH!"

"Bring us safely into Spring, Great Lord of Snakes!"

"AH! AH! AH!"

"Take our humble gift, Father of Breath and Power!"

"AH! AH! AH!"

"Our gift, this Special Meat partake!"

"AH! AH! AH!"

Gotha grasped the boy's black hair, jerked his head back, and with a single downward stroke slashed his throat from ear to ear.

"AAHHHHHHH!"

Blood gushed high into the air, fell splashing on the Shaman's face, arms, chest. He leaned back and opened his mouth and caught the hot stream and drank deep as the crimson fountain spurted, ebbed, died. He followed it down, and finished with the ritual kiss that turned dead flesh into meat blessed in the eyes of the God.

The boy dangled from the stake, twitching. Gotha stood upright. He cut the bonds with the bloody knife, grunted, picked the body up, and cast it into the fire. It lay upon the coals, smoking, sizzling, charring. A hot, fatty stench erased the smell of roses.

Gotha faced the crowd and smiled a bloody smile. "It is good," he said. "The Lord of Snakes and Fire loves your gift. Once again Spring returns to us."

He raised both hands. Gouts of blood dripped softly from his fists. "And in token of His love, he gives you a talisman of great triumph to come. On this day, the Lord of Fire shows you his Power over the greatest of His enemies."

Gotha turned to the side then, arms outstretched. *"Give it over!"* he roared. *"Give unto me the token of the Bitch Goddess! Submit to me now, who submits to Him Who is the source of all Power!"*

He paused, then inhaled deeply. Blood sprayed from his lips as his shriek split the noonday air. *"FALSE KEEPER, GIVE THE MAMMOTH STONE TO ME!"*

Sharp Knife pushed White Moon forward when she hesitated. Her features were drawn, set, pasty-white. Slowly she fumbled in her pouch, took out the small, fur-wrapped object, unwrapped it.

When she hesitated, Sharp Knife's hiss was clearly audible: "Go on, *give* it to him!"

As if in a daze, White Moon lifted up the Stone, stretched out her hand.

Gotha's smile screamed upon his lips as she reached forward—

"Wait."

There was an almost audible *snap* as every eye there jerked in its socket. Somebody moaned.

Gotha turned with the rest, a fierce light in his eyes. But when he saw what was stumbling, shambling, lurching toward him, all he could do was gasp one choked sound: "*You!*"

11

The Crone's single eye blazed as brightly—and as redly—as the knife that dangled slackly from Gotha's hand.

"*Me,*" she agreed, though it wasn't entirely true. Thousands of years later, half of Europe would dance through the Middle Ages to a tune played on spoiled grain—which was a perfect culturing medium for ergot, whose chemical structure was nearly identical to LSD.

The Crone had indeed opened a door, but instead of passing through, something from the other side had stepped through to *her*.

From the looks of it, something huge. The Crone was truly destroyed now. Gotha, frozen with horror, couldn't imagine how the apparition before him could *breathe*, let alone walk and talk.

But somehow she did. She staggered right up to him, and involuntarily, he drew back. The thought of her actually *touching* him made him want to scream.

Aside from the moment his father had died in his arms, Gotha's most ghastly memory was of a bison he'd found as a youth. For some reason predators had not scavenged the carcass. It had lain undisturbed beneath the scorching summer sun until he'd found it.

In that torrid furnace, gases inside the carcass had expanded until the rotten flesh had burst apart in black, oozing holes where maggots crawled so thickly the meat seemed to possess a horrid life of its own. The one eye Gotha had seen had been parboiled, so that part of it had turned white, and the rest dissolved into a smooth amber jelly.

The Crone reminded him of that. But worse. She was naked. Her belly hung like a great basket beneath her withered breasts, although her left tit had swollen; something white leaked from its nipple. Her ruined feet seemed even more twisted than before—skin sloughed from her ankles as she walked, leaving a clear, mucus-slick surface that slowly turned pink.

Her good eye resembled the eye of the long-dead bison, except that it blazed with demonic intensity—not dead, no, hideously *alive*. The blind socket didn't blaze at all. It oozed blood, puss, tiny wiggling white things—

Maggots? Gotha thought, his stomach heaving.

The side of her head, now completely bald, bulged crazily, as if the gray stuff inside her skull had suddenly grown too big for its receptacle. Blood and liquids far more disgusting seeped from her ears, her nose, her mouth.

As she walked, she dribbled shit and piss and appeared not to notice. In fact, the Crone seemed to see nothing at all. Nothing except Gotha.

you want the motherstone?

Gotha stared at her. Her lips had not moved—how could they? They were mostly rotted away. Then he realized that somehow he was hearing her voice *inside* his head. The voice was soft, flatly, deadly.

"Go away," he whispered hoarsely.

She only smiled. *you want the motherstone, my son? very well. all you have to do is take it.*

She brushed past him and he shuddered at the nearness of her passage. If that pustulant flesh touched his own, he would die. He knew it. What awful Spirit had taken her?

She shambled to White Moon, who seemed not to fear the apparition at all. The girl waited with her head high, her shoulders back. She ignored Sharp Knife, who was down on his knees at her side, retching violently.

daughter?

"Yes, Mother?"

give me the motherstone.

"I am Its Keeper!" White Moon replied, and there was a certainty in her ringing declaration that sent shivers down Gotha's spine.

so shall you keep it again, daughter. but for now, i take it back. give it to me.

Wordlessly, White Moon handed over her burden.

The Crone turned and lurched back toward Gotha, who raised his knife before him.

Don't let her TOUCH me! he thought wildly.

A horrible, wordless chuckle filled his mind. *go ahead. use it. it will not protect you.*

Terrified, he saw that his blade had gone dull, opaque. People were beginning to scream now. Some ran away. Others simply fainted where they stood. The rest stood as if they'd been turned to stone.

you want the motherstone, my son? all you have to do is take it. show me your power now.

And, with that, the Crone clambered up onto the Sacrificial Hearth and walked, her broken stride suddenly ponderous and sure, right into the middle of it.

come into the fire and claim your talisman of victory, o shaman gotha.

Smoke billowed around her, but she did not burn. She held the Mammoth Stone out to him, beckoning, mocking, but he hid his eyes from the sight.

After a while the Crone sighed and lowered the Stone. She bent down, picked up the body of the little boy, and threw it from the coals. It landed with a dull thud on the earth beyond the Hearth, almost at Gotha's feet.

there is your sacrifice, mighty shaman. but who will take the motherstone from me? if you will not, my son, who will?

"I will," White Moon said softly. And without a further word, she crossed to the hearth, mounted it, and walked to the Crone's side.

ah, daughter. i told you it was yours to keep. Then the Crone lifted her head and spoke aloud for the first time. *"SHE WHO TAKES THE MOTHERSTONE IS ITS KEEPER. NO OTHER COULD BEAR THE TEST BUT HER, FOR THE STONE IS HERS TO KEEP. MARK IT WELL!"*

In the yawning silence, the sound of White Moon's footsteps crunching across the white-hot coals—unhurt, unburned, untouched—was a more terrible sound than any they had ever heard.

The Crone's single eye now sought Gotha, found him. She smiled a final time, as blood gushed from her throat with her departing words. This time the voice was her own. The dread, dead thing that had lived in her was gone.

"I do this because I love you, my son. But I am the Special Meat," she said. "Eat of me if you dare."

With that, she lay down on the embers, and the fire took her at last.

12

The Shaman Gotha remained true to his plan. Two days later, the armed might of the People of Fire and Ice, together with the warriors of the Bison Clan, Raging Bison at their head, set off for the Green Valley. And if Sharp Knife led his wife, bound and gagged, at the rear of the straggling march, he did so fearfully. Hostage though she might be, she still Kept the Stone.

No one, not even the Shaman Gotha, dared take it from her now, for she had Chosen.

CHAPTER TWENTY-FOUR

Everything that rises must converge.
—Flannery O'Connor

1

THE GREEN VALLEY

Maya's gaze drifted away from Wolf's anxious features. Her brother was terribly worried, but then, that was an old story. The winter had brought him only bad news, and now that spring was coming on, he'd begun to hear rumors that something worse might be approaching.

He ticked off the variety of potential dooms on the fingers of his right hand as he spoke. "First, it seems that the Tribe from which Serpent fled *did* manage to track him here. Second, the Shaman of that Tribe makes sacrifices to the Forbidden God. Third, Raging Bison and his people have joined up with this new Tribe. Fourth, Sharp Knife has also joined, taking my daughter and the Mammoth Stone with him—and both are now in the control of this Shaman, who is evidently very powerful. Finally, almost four hands of people from the Green Valley *also* ran away to the enemy Tribe."

He paused. "It's not very good news, I'm afraid."

She nodded glumly. "I'm afraid I can offer you worse, brother. From what I hear, if this Shaman should decide to attack us here in the valley, at least half the Bison Clan warriors would defect to his side. Rooting Hog blames us—well, blames *me*—for his son not marrying White Moon, and is now telling everybody that none of this would have happened if Sharp Knife were leading the Two Tribes."

Wolf sighed heavily. "Well, he isn't. And thank the Mother for it—at least *that* one showed his true colors." He shrugged. "Any word from Caribou?"

She stared at him. "My husband is dead, Wolf."

"But we've only heard a few garbled rumors—"

She waved him off. "I knew it the moment he died, brother." She seemed about to speak further, but tightened her lips and said nothing.

"Maya?"

"Mm?"

"Are we cursed? I mean, nothing has ... uh ..."

She smiled tiredly. "Nothing's gone right since I came back?" She rubbed her eyes. "I guess a better question would be am *I* cursed? I don't know, Wolf. Everything that has happened seems almost like it was *planned*—I feel the fingers of the Gods all over us, pushing, moving, plotting."

His expression grew troubled. "Even the Mother? But I thought we were Her People. Wasn't that the Promise?"

She patted his knee. "Perhaps the Green Valley was the Promise, Wolf—and the keeping of it, and our People within it, left up to us."

He raised his head and stared across the Jumble at the houses in New Camp beyond the sward. "The Bison Clan still outnumbers the People of the Mammoth," he mused softly. "If too many of them go over to the other side ..."

She stood up. "Only time, and the Gods, will tell, brother."

"Cold comfort, sister."

She rubbed her shoulders against the ache that seemed to ride in them constantly now. She'd never felt so old, so tired, so *helpless*. But what could she do? Nothing. Nothing but wait for the convergence of mighty forces she sensed building around them. And to what purpose?

She couldn't begin to guess. "Serpent is doing well, at least."

The observation didn't seem to cheer her brother much. "I guess," he replied. "He's certainly sprouted up over the winter."

"Eats like a cave lion," she agreed.

"I almost wish you hadn't brought him, Maya. I mean, I'm sorry, but—"

"I know. Because I brought that Shaman, Gotha, along with him. I didn't mean to, Wolf."

He nodded somberly. "I know you didn't. But I wish we still had the Mammoth Stone. It would make me feel a lot better."

Maya exhaled softly. "Perhaps it will return to us."

"Perhaps. But by then, I'm afraid it will be too late."

She glanced up at the sky, found it as empty as her own hopes. "I don't know, brother. I just don't know."

There seemed nothing more to say. They regarded each other for a long moment. Then, silently, they each returned to self-appointed duties: Wolf to keep on trying to rally support among the Bison Clansmen, Maya to her unceasing education of the boy Serpent in the ways of the Spirits.

He was a quick pupil. Why, then, did she feel as if she were only wasting her time? But what else could she do? He bore a Stone—somehow, he must be brought to use it.

But how, Mother? *How?*

2

Gotha raised his right hand and brought them to a halt just inside the jawlike place where the Green Valley spilled out onto the steppe. At his back, an ocean of grass waved silently beneath the blazing sun.

Gotha turned and looked at the small army gathered at his back—all his own hunters, plus three hands' worth of defectors from the Bison Clan and the Green Valley. Raging Bison, his eyes the color of cherries, stood like a giant in front of these men. His bulk dwarfed Sharp Knife, who followed with White Moon—whose wrists, Gotha was pleased to note, were still securely bound. There was only enough play left in her hands for her to grasp the Mammoth Stone, which was unwrapped and glowing softly in the morning light.

A leather leash was noosed about her neck. Sharp Knife led her like a tethered animal. Her features were pale, her eyes dull.

I won't take your Stone, bitch, Gotha thought. *I don't have to—it should be plain enough to those fools in the Green Valley how much Power you have left.*

Still, he would rather have carried the Stone himself—but the Crone—*Burn her forever*—had fixed that. Mentally, he shrugged. Dragging the Keeper of the Stone and her puny talisman along like a slave would do well enough, he guessed. And he had one more card up his sleeve, in case anybody still doubted who was the stronger of the two. Unconsciously he rubbed the right-hand sleeve of his robe, and the red crystal knife hidden there. Its light might have dulled a bit, but he thought it would still suffice to cut a fallen Keeper's throat.

Raging Bison came to his side and pointed at the rocky rim of the jaws. "If they put somebody up there to watch, it's too late to keep them from raising the alarm."

Gotha glanced at White Moon. "It doesn't matter. Today we will have victory—"

"In His name," Bison finished. His face was red and bloated with fever—not illness, but something hotter, more fearsome.

Vengeance, Gotha thought. *This one lusts for blood.*

That might become a problem later, but for today, it suited the Shaman's purposes well enough, and so he smiled. "Yes, in His name," he agreed.

Raging Bison nodded. "Shall I lead the way?"

Gotha nodded. "With your Clansmen—especially Sharp Knife. But I will take the woman."

Bison's eyes flashed at Sharp Knife's name, but he understood the need for the younger man to be seen in the van, if they were to encourage the Bison Clan defections they hoped to receive.

"I don't trust that one," he whispered.

"In good time," Gotha replied. *Nor do I trust you, my friend. You don't belong to me, nor to our Lord of Fire— only to your own dark urges.*

"In good time," he repeated. "Now bring me White Moon, and let's get on with it."

She came sullenly, her head down, and refused to look at him when he took up her leash. "What's the matter, Keeper? Not so proud today, eh?"

Her lips worked. She spat on the ground next to his feet, but he only threw back his head and laughed. Then, sobering abruptly, he jerked the leather thong so hard she almost lost her balance. "Come on, bitch," he hissed. "We'll see if you're still as insolent when the sun sets on this day!"

Sharp Knife watched all this with an amazed expression

on his face—a sickening blend of humiliation, lust, greed, and fear that twisted his features into an inhuman mask.

Gotha saw, and approved. Let them all see who held the true Power! As abruptly as his mood had lowered, it rose again, and a vast, bubbling glut of cheer filled him up. "Lead on, Bison!" he called.

The warriors behind him raised their spears and cracked them together with a sound like bones splitting, and let out a cheer that sounded strangely thin beneath the vastness of the sky.

Thin, Gotha thought, *but deadly.* And if the tiniest part of him shivered once again at the smallness of men upon the immensity of the World, he did not show it.

"For the Lord of Snakes and Fire!" he roared suddenly, and raised the staff of Snakes and its grisly cargo.

"For our Lord!" echoed Raging Bison.

They crossed over to the Main Path and began to run, the shrieks of their battle cries like a promise on the wind before them.

3

Wolf rested his elbows on top of the barrier of brush the men of the Mammoth Clan had built to protect the Home Camp. The thorny wall stretched as high as a man's chest from the Jumble on one side, along the top of the stream's steep bank, all the way to the edge of First Lake. He peered out across the stream at the smoke rising from the charred husks of the New Camp, and listened to the screams.

"It's a slaughter," he said to Maya. "And we're next."

She stood next to him, smoke-smudged, the tracks of dried tears marking her cheeks. In her arms she held a baby boy she'd rescued from the carnage. "Can we hold out here?"

Wolf shrugged. Now that his worst fears had come to pass, he seemed almost cheerful. "I don't know. It depends on how persistent this Shaman is. If he is willing to wait, we can't hold out forever."

He turned and glanced up at the top of the Shield Wall, which arched out over the narrow plateau on which Home

Camp was built. "If they get up there—and I don't know how we can stop them—they can drop rocks on us." He squinted. "Not if we get back under the overhang, but then we couldn't defend the stream bank, and they could come right across."

"Serpent has spoken much about this Shaman, Gotha. He is an impatient man, he says. Perhaps he will not think to climb up to the top."

Wolf grinned faintly. "If he doesn't, Raging Bison or Sharp Knife certainly will."

The baby made a soft cooing sound. Maya touched his nose with one grimy fingertip. "What can we do? Is everything hopeless, then?"

Now Wolf's grin widened, though there was bitterness in the twist of his lips. "I was just going to ask you that, sister. The Mother is supposed to protect *us,* isn't She?"

"Oh, Wolf . . ."

"I'm sorry. I know it isn't fair. You can't make Her do anything She doesn't want to. But She doesn't seem to want the People of the Mammoth to survive. A lot of our People died across that stream today, and those who didn't—" He shivered as something no longer human began to screech mindlessly near the hidden center of New Camp. Noxious smoke rose from that spot. No doubt the Forbidden God was happy with His sacrifices.

"I don't know *what* She wants," Maya said dully. "Why should I? I'm only a tool."

Wolf glanced at her. "Well, I'm not. If She means for me to die, then I will die. But I will take some of *them* with me, if I can."

"Oh, Wolf! What are you going to do?"

He hefted the heavy spear in his right hand. "I'm going to try to kill Raging Bison and Sharp Knife. I will challenge them to battle, and if they accept, I will kill them."

She stared at him. "There may be time yet. Has anybody seen White Moon?"

He shook his head. "My daughter? No. But if she is helping those monsters, I hope I never see her again."

Gently, she touched his shoulder, but his eyes were bleak, and he turned away from her comfort. "Can the boy help us?" he asked.

"I don't know."

He turned suddenly to face her. "Maya. He is the reason

this terrible Shaman has come here. Maybe we could trade him for White Moon and the Mammoth Stone." He paused, and then, his anguish plain on his face, added in a low voice, "Or just the Stone. If that would be enough to save us."

She stared at him for a long time, then nodded once. "All right. I will bring the boy here, so this mighty Shaman can see him. Then we will see."

For the first time, a shadow of hope flitted across Wolf's face. "Yes. I will call out to them for a parley. You bring the boy. Best we do it now, before Raging Bison puts some warriors up above us."

"All right," Maya said. She turned to go.

"Maya?"

"What?"

"Are you all right?"

"No," she replied. "Nothing is all right anymore."

4

Gotha turned to Sharp Knife. "What's he yowling about?"

Sharp Knife, streaked with smoke and blood, grinned triumphantly. "He wants a parley. He wants to talk."

"To surrender?"

Sharp Knife moved his shoulders. "Wolf? I doubt it. It's possible, though."

Gotha sighed. He stood in the center of New Camp, next to one of the great community hearths. Bodies lay strewn about, pathetic in their bludgeoned silence. White Moon crouched at his feet, sobbing. He had tethered her to a nearby tree trunk. She refused to look at him, and flinched whenever he came near her. She turned the Mammoth Stone over and over in her hands, as a terrified infant might clutch at a straw doll.

Nothing more to fear from that *one,* he thought. But the task remained unfinished, and though he was not pleased by the prospect of further carnage, he would not shrink from it.

But what a massacre it had turned out to be! The ferocity of Raging Bison's attack still shocked him. In the end, more than half of the Bison Clan, led by Rooting Hog and

Shaggy Elk, had defected. They had joined the invaders not far from Maya's house beyond Second Lake and then, retracing their path, had murdered everybody they found, man, woman, or child.

Only a few had escaped to the shelter of Home Camp. Unfortunately, Maya and the brat had been among them. Gotha had seen her himself when Sharp Knife had pointed her out, running through the smoke, carrying a squalling infant in her arms, accompanied by a young man who looked vaguely familiar.

From where he stood, he could see the top of the Shield Wall. "Have you sent any men up there yet?"

Sharp Knife shook his head. "Not yet. Bison wants to go himself, but he's still . . . busy . . ."

A bone-quivering howl split the air, as if to underline his words, and Gotha grimaced. "When this is done . . ." he said slowly, "perhaps our mighty warrior will not be as necessary as he has been today."

A brick-red glow rose up in Sharp Knife's cheeks. "Perhaps," he replied, just as carefully, "something will happen to him."

"Perhaps," Gotha agreed. Then, curtly, "but that is for later. Now, O Chief-to-be, I want that woman and the brat. Go find out what that shouting is all about. If they want to talk, I'm willing."

Sharp Knife nodded, then turned and trotted away. Gotha glanced down at White Moon. "Your husband doesn't seem very attentive, my dear. What a shame. Maybe you should use the great Power of your Bitch's talisman to make him love you again."

She didn't answer, and after a moment, Gotha uttered a short barking laugh. Then he went off to find Raging Bison. He didn't look at White Moon. After all, where could she go?

Bitch of a fallen Goddess, there was no place left for her to hide.

5

Serpent looked up as Maya entered the Chief's house. "Are you all right?" he asked anxiously.

Maya didn't reply immediately. Perhaps she hadn't heard him through all the noise. The Chief's house was crammed with frightened, wailing women. The children weren't sure what was happening, but had picked up the terror of their mothers and now squalled along with them.

She saw Old Berry crouched by the far wall, carefully rubbing a sweet-smelling paste into a savage cut on Red Hair's breast. Berry raised her eyebrows, but when Maya shook her head, the old Root Woman went back to work, as calm as if she were out strolling on the Main Path.

Maya smiled grimly. At least Berry would never give in to the panic that throbbed within Home Camp, an ever-rising tide that at times threatened to overwhelm even Maya's hard-maintained poise. But did it matter? Old Berry might keep her stoic demeanor even unto death, but would that delay her death so much as a single instant?

"What?" she said absently.

"Are you *all right*?"

Now she looked down, responding to the raw fear in Serpent's voice. "Oh. Yes, I'm fine. Here, hold him." She handed the crying infant over before Serpent could refuse. Maybe if he had something to concern himself with besides his own terror, he would calm down. Why not? It had worked for her.

He took the whimpering bundle into his arms and jiggled it until the tiny boy's face lost its swollen redness, and his sobs trailed off into a series of liquid bubblings.

"Actually, I came to see if *you* were all right," Maya told him. She crouched down on her haunches and rested her fists on her knees. He *looked* well enough—though as smoke-streaked as she was, for they had escaped their house just ahead of the invaders, then hidden at the edge of New Camp until they could sneak through the conflagration and reach the safety of Home Camp.

A sudden thought struck her. "Do you have it?" She looked for the small pouch he usually carried at his waist, and when she didn't see it, she felt a wad of dread swell in her throat.

He joggled the baby and stared at her. "Have what?"

"*The Fatherstone!*"

"Oh. Yes." He glanced down, then hitched the pouch from where it had twisted around to his back. "Here. Inside." He paused, then said more slowly, "Why?" Abruptly his eyelids widened. "*He's* here, isn't he? He's *come* for me. I . . . ah . . ."

He made to rise, but she took his shoulders and forced him back down. "No, Serpent, he hasn't come. Not yet."

"What are you going to do?"

I don't know. What I'm wondering is, what are you *going to do?* What little hope she had was bound up with this boy she'd saved, and the Stone he bore. She couldn't believe it was only coincidence that her life had brought her to this place, this time, this *moment*—no, surely it was something far more powerful than mere happenstance. But if there was purpose behind the coincidence, that purpose was incomprehensible to her. What divine madness would place the Keeper of the Motherstone, *and* the Motherstone, beyond her reach just when she needed the Stone most dearly?

And why was she left with the Fatherstone and *its* Keeper instead? What awful game were the Great Spirits playing at? It was almost as if the Spirits plotted to destroy *everything*—but no. She pushed *that* thought away. It was too horrible even to consider, for it would mean that life itself was only a pointless exercise.

No. Better to continue as if there was hope, purpose, some sort of plan for the Mother's tools. To think otherwise was to court the great void, the endless nothing within which she'd once seen a turtle.

She patted his arm. "Right now, I'm going to see if there's anything left to eat. Then I'm going to help Old Berry. And you can help us."

He nodded gravely. Once again she was astonished at the changes a single winter had wrought in him. He'd grown a good two hands taller; smooth, hard muscle now covered his once bony frame; his voice had deepened into a clear, pleasing baritone. He was no longer a boy. He'd become a strikingly handsome man, and all in the space of the two or three moons since White Moon had departed the Green Valley. More evidence of divine handiwork? It was as if Serpent had been *changed* just in time for this confrontation.

She couldn't begin to know how, or why, this might be so, but that didn't bother her. She'd spent a whole life in ignorance of Her workings, made only one single *choice* of her own free will—and she had doubts about *that* at times, too.

"Come on, let's get something in our bellies. It will be a long day, I'm afraid, and we may not get another chance to eat."

Still carrying the baby, Serpent clambered to his feet. Outside, despite all the horror of the day, someone was cooking meat. It smelled delicious.

He couldn't help himself. Though he looked the man, somewhere inside was still a boy for whom meat had been an unobtainable luxury. He licked his lips, and followed her out the doorway.

6

White Moon watched Gotha prepare himself for the parley. He paid her no attention as he donned a long white robe, although she looked away when he took up his great carven staff with its hideous freight. In fact, she almost managed to pretend that he wasn't there, that none of this horror had anything to do with her, no, not at all—until he jerked on her leash and half choked her.

"Get up, you stupid bitch," he growled. "Do you still have your pitiful talisman? Good. I want to show it to somebody. Someone who will know what you—and *it*—mean now." He chuckled. "Maybe then she will understand what sort of doom *I* bring for *her*."

Head down, mute as a dumb animal, White Moon followed without a word. Her hair hung lankly across her face. But she still turned the Mammoth Stone over and over in her fingers. Gotha wondered if she were even aware of the vacant, ceaseless movement.

He yanked her leash viciously, noticing but not caring that the noose around her neck was throttling her, that a bluish tinge was beginning to color her slack, drooping lips. "Let's go," he said, and led her away.

That even with the Crone's treacherous help she'd been able to resist still amazed him. But he didn't intend to kill her, though he would if it became necessary. He hoped it wouldn't. She belonged to Sharp Knife, and he wanted to keep Sharp Knife happy, so the boy would have her again.

Once she'd been suitably tamed, of course. It mattered not at all if she *could* resist—only that she *didn't*. He thought she would never defy him again, not this broken, pathetic lump at the end of the leash, and that suited him perfectly.

The other one, though. Maya. That might be a different story.

The Shaman Gotha smiled and continued on his way.

7

Old Berry helped Maya don her robes. By rights, the Shaman Muskrat should have accompanied Wolf to the verge of Home Camp for the parley with the invading Shaman, but he sulked inside his tent, his envy of Maya evident in the distasteful expression he'd worn when Old Berry taxed him on his seclusiveness.

"Let *her* go," he said. "She's taken my place anyway."

"No, she hasn't. She doesn't want to be Shaman here. Why do you think she left in the first place? And remember—she trained you to succeed her."

"Then why," he whined, "did she come back?" He raised his hands and shook his head. "Because her own Tribe kicked her out, that's why. And she had no other place to go. So she came back here, and she brought that devil-child with her."

Berry crossed her arms atop her massive breasts and stared down at Muskrat's bald skull. He seemed almost childlike in his hunched posture and whimpering protests.

"Oh?" she said ominously. "And what is that supposed to mean?"

He wouldn't look at her. He mumbled something she couldn't make out.

"What?" she said.

"Maybe the Shaman Ghost was right . . ."

Quick as a striking adder, one of Berry's meaty palms made jarring contact with the top of Muskrat's head. The blow knocked him half sprawling.

Tears filled his eyes. *"What did you do that for?"*

Disgust dripped from her words like rancid honey. "And you call yourself a Shaman. You are dirt beneath my feet."

Feebly: "Get out. Get out of my Spirit House."

She spat. "Gladly. And when this is over, I will remember your words."

He stared up at her, but said nothing further. After a moment she spat again, turned, and lumbered away. Outside the doorway she paused, rubbing her chest, and muttered, "*His* Spirit House?" She shook her head and took several deep breaths. She felt exhausted.

She had labored most of the day on the wounded, applying the fruits of her vast lore, as well as the storehouse of her berries, roots, and ground-up pastes, trying to help those who could still be helped. Maya had worked at her side, and the old bond between the two women, once teacher and student, now equals in skill and knowledge, had sprung up again.

And where was the ratlike Muskrat during all this? Cowering in his *Spirit House!* She snorted.

She intended to do something about *that* when this was finished. The thought warmed her as she plodded through Home Camp, past the Men's Mystery House, now crowded with the remaining warriors of the Mammoth Clan, then past the Chief's house, where women and children sought refuge. Oh, yes, she would cook Muskrat's goose if she could.

If I'm still around when it's finally over . . .

But even that thought didn't fully dismay her. She'd lived an extraordinarily long and busy life, during a time in her Tribe's history that was equally exceptional—and if the Mother called her home this very instant, she would go willingly, even eagerly.

"Stupid old woman," she muttered to herself as she trudged along. Yes, she would go, but she hoped she wouldn't have to. Her part was not yet done, she thought, for the great tapestry of which she'd lived more than any other, even Maya herself, was not yet complete. Maya had spoken of her suspicions, of the great net she felt being cast about them, and Old Berry agreed. She, too, felt the whispery fingers of destiny touching them all, though to what purpose she couldn't imagine.

Something greater than the Promise of the Stone, though. Maya was She Whom We Have Waited For, and the Green Valley was the Home at the End of the Journey. Berry was ancient, but something bright and new had begun to quiver gently in her heart. She didn't know how to express the feeling, beyond two simple words: *Something coming.* Perhaps it was hope.

So if the little fart-smeller Shaman would not stand with Maya in her time of need, Berry would. She smiled a secret smile as she came up to the barrier of bracken and thorns where Wolf and Maya and the boy, Serpent, stood waiting for the enemy Shaman.

Something coming, and whatever it is, I think I'll have a better view from here.

And so, with Berry's arrival did all the living players, pawns, pieces, strands, and tools of a long and very strange weaving finally come together at the End of many Journeys, beneath a cloudless blue sky in the springtime of the World.

8

Maya looked over the shield of thorns, shading her eyes against the sun. Most of the fires had died in New Camp, though a horrible, lingering stench hung in the listless air. She saw occasional figures flit among the destroyed huts, but too far away to make out details. Except for fitful gusts of wind, the afternoon had turned dreadfully silent.

They're all dead over there now, she thought as a wave of ineffable sadness bloomed within her. On her right, Wolf stood straight and stern, while Serpent, hiding the terror she sensed within him, waited as well. She glanced down and saw that his fingers were clenched in bloodless claws around his belt pouch, and wondered if he was the salvation she so devoutly hoped for.

In the end, her strategy was a simple one. Serpent had been sent to her, bearing the other half of the Mammoth Stone. In many ways, his life had paralleled her own, and she hoped this wasn't mere coincidence. He was a tool, but then, so was she. So perhaps, in the end, the parallel would hold, and Serpent, whom she had rescued just as Caribou had rescued her, would make his own choice, as she had on a similar day of blood and terror so long before.

She had taught him what she could. He knew the Stone was more than he had ever guessed, and over the winter he'd come to appreciate—or so she believed—a little of the great winds of destiny that blew round his shoulders.

But he'd never been able to wield his Stone. He'd tried—tried with everything he knew, but the small carving remained inert in his hands.

First you have to choose, she thought. *I did.* But he'd never been faced with an inescapable choice, so she had to create one. Perhaps, when faced with the ultimate terror of Gotha, just as she had when faced with the Shamans Ghost and Broken Fist, something inside him would rise up to grasp the Power she believed was in him.

She sighed. They would know soon enough, all of them. And if she was wrong? If the Fatherstone was as inert in his hands as the Motherstone was in White Moon's, then they were doomed, and the People of the Mammoth with them.

But she had seen him in a Dream, mighty beyond reckoning, wielding the terrible Power of his Stone even as he claimed it for his own.

It is mine! he'd said then, and she thought it was true. She had *seen* his Stone glow with the light of a thousand stars, had *seen* his face—

But she hadn't, had she? She hadn't seen his face. He had turned to her, and the light—the fear—

Oh, his *face!* What was it about his *face*? *What had she seen?*

This seizure of vision passed as quickly as it came, though she grabbed Wolf's arm and squeezed, hard. He turned to her and saw how gray her features had become. Alarmed, he slipped his arm about her waist to keep her from falling.

"*Maya!*" For one instant she was dead weight, her eyes rolled back in her skull, and he almost staggered. Then she snapped back, and a bit of color bloomed in her cheeks.

"No, I'm all right, brother. A little dizzy, it's been such a long—"

"*Ho, tame bitch of the Bitch Goddess! Are you here to face your doom?*"

Abruptly she straightened, for beyond the stream on the green meadow the Shaman Gotha faced her at last. She was astonished to see he looked nothing like she'd imagined. Her only description of him had come from Serpent, who had described a monster, but this was no monster.

There was nothing of the Shaman Ghost's pale malevolence to him, no whiff of the Shaman Broken Fist's dark deformities.

He stood straight and tall, garbed simply in a white robe that hung to his feet. His dark hair fell loose to his waist, and shone in the sunlight. His black eyes, bisected by a proud hatchet of a nose, seemed almost mild.

She barely noticed the rest as she numbered those who accompanied him. On his right stood Raging Bison, whom she had never met, but whose size and fearsome glower made unmistakable. On Gotha's left was a far more pitiful tableau—her niece, White Moon, pale and shaken, tethered by a leather cord that her husband, Sharp Knife, held in his hand.

Before she could speak, Wolf stepped forward. "I am Wolf, Chief of the Two Tribes! Speak to me, invader!"

Gotha stared at him. Maya was entranced by his eyes, his dark eyes. They seemed serene, like pools to drown in. She could look at nothing else.

"What do you want of me, vanquished Chief?"

"Not vanquished!" Wolf shouted back. *"Not by you, and not by all the traitors with you!"*

Gotha smiled faintly, and made a motioning gesture with his free hand. Sharp Knife stepped forward, his movement almost reluctant. "This traitor will be your new Chief, before the sun sets on this day."

Wolf's mouth worked. He spat across the barrier, then laughed coldly. *"That* one, the coward? The little boy who ran away? The thief? He will be Chief over the dry bones of my body."

This seemed to afford Gotha considerable amusement, for his smile broadened into a wide grin. "Yes, I guessed it would be that way. So will you fight with this man, Sharp Knife?"

"I will."

Gotha nodded. "Let us see your bravery against my cowards, mighty Chief." His voice oozed with disdain. "I will make you a wager. If you can defeat my heroes in battle, I will leave your Green Valley forever. What say you?"

"Heroes? What other cowards have you for me to kill?"

Gotha shrugged. "Raging Bison, of course." And the big man stepped forth, no hesitation at all, and waved his spear fiercely at Wolf.

"I need no help to destroy the destroyer of my People," Bison roared, "and though I would rather do this thing alone, if you fight to save your valley, Wolf of the Mammoth Clan, you must fight us both!"

"What say you, Chief? Two of my cowards against your bravery? It should be only a *little* test for you and your Bitch Goddess."

Then he brandished his carven staff of snakes, and his voice rose clear and piercing across the meadow. "Though you must be stronger than the other mighty warrior you sent. I have brought him back to you!"

Wolf gasped. Maya managed to tear her gaze from Gotha's face, for the Shaman had turned his staff around, and the shapeless lump impaled on its crest now became discernible as a human head.

Caribou's head.

A low, moaning sigh swept through the Mammoth warriors gathered along the barrier at the grisly sight. But Wolf was made of harder stuff. He threw his head back and roared defiance.

"Cowards, all of you! You think to frighten me with that? Come, I will kill you, too."

But Gotha only shrugged and lowered his staff. "I don't think so," he said. Then, "Do you accept my bargain, Chief?"

Wolf was already clambering over the thorny barrier. "I do!"

Gotha took White Moon's leash from Sharp Knife. "Then come ahead," he called, and tugged her back.

Wolf reached the stream below and clambered splashing across. At the verge of the meadow he paused to shoulder his spear. Then, uttering his war cry, he charged.

"Stop!"

The single word was so powerful the very air seemed to shiver with the sound of it. Raging Bison pulled up his own joyous advance and stood blinking, confused. Wolf halted as if he'd run into a wall. And Sharp Knife, who was diffidently bringing up the rear, slowed as if relieved by the interruption.

All trace of indifference vanished from Gotha's face. He stepped forward again, jerking on White Moon's leash to follow. It was almost as if he'd expected something like this. Now his eyes blazed like dark coals.

"What is it, bitch?"

Maya didn't glance at Serpent, though she could feel him quivering at her side. Her chest was aflutter with cold dread, but her face was calm as winter ice. Her eyes flashed reply enough; two gemstones, one of blue, one of green, twin fires burning in her sockets.

"It's me you want, Shaman. You speak of bargains. Very well, so shall I. Will you and your foul Lord Big Dick face me? Now, in this place, in this time?"

"I will." Gotha's reply tolled like a great iron bell.

Maya nodded. "Bide a moment, then, and we will come to you." She turned to Serpent. "You understand what is about to happen?"

The boy's tongue rasped across his lips. He nodded slowly.

"Good. I have told you what I believe. There is a choice. You will know it when it comes. You must make your choice, and then use the Power within you. That is our only hope. I can't wield your Stone. Perhaps, though, I can still bear the other, if it should come to me."

He nodded once again, and she squeezed his shoulder in reply. Then she walked the length of the barrier, stepped out onto the Jumble, and made her way to the meadow floor, Serpent stepping light-footed at her rear.

Only Maya, perhaps, understood what it cost the boy to once again come face-to-face with the horror of his life— but he followed, and a great joy filled her heart.

Some still stand, she told herself. *Some do.*

The soft brush of her naked footsteps across the grass was the only sound in the aching silence. Calmly, slowly, she marched up to a position no more than an arm's length from Gotha, who towered over her, smiling grimly.

"We meet at last, bitch," he said. "I see you've brought my Speaker back to me."

Her answering smile could have cut through the hardest flint. "You poor tool," she replied.

It wasn't the greeting he expected. His face slowly turned the color of fresh-fired clay. But he rallied quickly. "Yes," he said, "I am a tool, of Him who is greater by far than the Bitch you serve."

"At least you know," Maya told him softly. "I was afraid you didn't."

Gotha's shoulders stiffened. "Be careful, woman. I am not those dead men you once faced."

She nodded. "No, you are not. You are greater, for you believe in Him who is greater than you. They did not believe, they only lusted. But it still won't help you, for in this time, and in this place, all things come together. Can't you feel it?"

Gotha stamped his staff on the ground. Caribou's half-rotted skull teetered precariously. "I feel your death, bitch. Enough of this! Will you match your Dreams against my own?"

Rage bubbled in Gotha's voice now, and he reached forward with his left hand as if to grab her neck, but the motion died still-born. Perhaps he remembered the Crone's challenge.

Maya smiled gently. "No, not that way, O Shaman. You must face me beyond the World." Then, ignoring him, she reached into her pouch and withdrew her elixir. She brought it to her lips, tasted, swallowed.

"Dare you follow me, mighty Shaman?"

He sought in his own pouch and brought forth a handful of dark green berries. "I follow to your destruction, bitch," he snarled as the juice of the berries trickled shining down his chin.

They stared at each other, waiting, until—

CHAPTER TWENTY-FIVE

The old order changeth yielding place to new,
And God fulfills himself in many ways.
                              —Alfred, Lord Tennyson

1

Maya lowered her arms, a despair so bleak she could not
bear it pressing down on her. Where she had expected at
least the vague disorientation that accompanied a normal
dosage of the drug, she felt nothing. The World remained
before her, sharp-edged, cold, cruelly real. "I cannot
Dream," she said. "The Way is closed to me."

Gotha stared at her, a puzzled expression on his handsome features. "I can't, either." His glance slipped away
from her. "That's never happened before."

He was silent a moment. Then he shrugged. "It seems
neither of our Spirits wishes to commune with us today.
Perhaps because there is nothing to commune about."

He looked over at Raging Bison. "Kill him," he said,
and pointed at Wolf. Then he reached into the sleeve of his
robe, withdrew the crimson knife, and pulled on White
Moon's leash. The girl lurched forward.

"You have no Power," he said to Maya. "And now you
have no Keeper." He took a fistful of White Moon's hair
and dragged her head back, exposing her throat.

(an itch, a tingle.)

The sound of spears clashing came from where Raging
Bison and Wolf threw themselves at each other again and
again. She was conscious of a low, gurgling sound issuing
from White Moon's mouth as Gotha tightened her leash so
he could hold her and his staff in the same hand. The girl
tossed her head wildly back and forth, but the Shaman

pulled the soft flesh of her throat inexorably closer to the glittering edge of the blade.

Maya turned to Serpent. "If you have Power," she said, "use it now, or all is lost."

The boy had taken the Fatherstone from its pouch, but his face was empty. Tears ran down his cheeks. "I can't," he said.

Gotha uttered a short barking laugh. "Hold still, you little bitch," he muttered as he struggled with the girl.

(fingers itch. tingle. hunger . . .)

Maya stared deep into his eyes, the green, the blue. *His eyes—I saw his eyes, and they weren't—*

Wolf grunted as Raging Bison bore him backward beneath the sheer weight of his charge. Maya quickly judged the battle, and felt sick inside. Wolf had experience, and much of his old skill, but Raging Bison was younger, bigger, and almost as fast. Unless Wolf could get in a lucky stroke, he was doomed. And now Sharp Knife found his courage, raised his spear, and began to circle around to Wolf's back.

Gotha cursed and lowered his knife, to get a better hold on the gagging, thrashing girl. He held both White Moon's hair and his staff in his right hand while he sought to gain purchase with his left, which still grasped the killing blade.

The two of them heaved back and forth. The violent motion dislodged Caribou's death-skull, and it, leering horribly, toppled from its perch. The gruesome thing struck White Moon squarely in the face. She uttered a choked shriek. Her hands, still bound, jerked up and the Mammoth Stone flew from them.

Maya caught it in her left hand.

(ahhh.)

It was as if the touch of the Stone, so long forgotten, turned a rusty key in a forgotten lock. Once again, she saw the face of the boy in the Dream, saw it full on, and her heart rang inside her chest like a great bell.

His eyes weren't marked. They were black, the color of winter ice. Not green and blue. It wasn't Serpent who wielded the Fatherstone, but another, on Serpent's behalf and hers, for in that Dream the Wielder had saved both of them!

But if Serpent had not used the Stone, then who had? It

was the Fatherstone. *Could the Father have saved her, He who was the enemy of old?*

Yet though she tried to grapple with the crazy thought, her mind wouldn't let her. It fizzed and bubbled with frantic energies, thin strings of light, sudden jitters. The drugs were beginning to work at last!

Gotha paused, momentarily disconcerted by the sudden entrance of Caribou's skull into the action. Then his mouth fell open as he realized Maya now held the Mammoth Stone. Slowly, he lifted his head and stared at her, consternation arching his eyebrows, widening his eyes. But Maya paid him no attention.

She had turned back to Serpent, who regarded her fixedly, his miscolored gaze beginning to glow.

"Give it to me," she hissed at Serpent. *"Give me the Fatherstone!"*

With that, his eyes rolled back. Only the whites showed. His lips worked with horrid slowness as she reached for him. Then, in croaking gasps, the words in the Spirit tongue issued forth, as the Speaker Spoke at last.

2

SERPENT'S CHOICE

Serpent stared at Gotha and felt horror twist his insides, for before him stood the man who represented all pain, all terror. He thought he'd escaped, and he'd sworn never to go back, but what did that mean now? Merely the ravings of a fevered boy—because he hadn't escaped, not at all. Before him stood the post, the whip, the knife, and there was no escape, just as there was no escaping his own past . . .

What?

But I don't want *to remember that.*

(Yes, you do.)

No! If I remember, I'll die!

(Yes, you will. *You* must die, to live again. Remember!)

No!

(Yes.)

Serpent's eyes rolled in his skull. The World fell away, and he felt himself slipping . . .

* * *

"This is yours, baby boy. Here, take it." The tall man whose eyes were sapphire and emerald unwrapped the small object and pressed it into the chubby fingers of the small child he cradled in his arms.

The child, whose eyes were identical to the man's, cooed softly at the smooth feel of the Fatherstone. Automatically he grasped it and began to smile.

"It is yours, my son, to Keep. Never give it up, for it is mighty in the World."

The tot stared uncomprehending into the man's face. He didn't understand the words, but he remembered them. For a time . . .

Smoke filled the small camp. Men roared in battle and women screamed. The dark invaders—so many of them!—slew without quarter. The boy, four years old, cowered in his father's Spirit House, shaking with terror.

"Father . . ." he moaned, but nobody came. He hugged himself and then, without thinking about it, took the pouch that rode at his waist and squeezed it.

For some reason this comforted him. He didn't have much, but the thing inside the pouch was his to Keep. His father had told him so.

The tent flap crashed wide! He stared up at the man who towered over him, then began to cry. His father's face was covered with blood. Without a word, the tall man scooped him up and carried him from the tent. His lips rode close to the boy's ear, and as he raced for the edge of the encampment, slashing his way through clots of bloody, screeching warriors, he whispered urgently, "You must Keep the Stone. Let no one have it, for it is yours. *Remember!*"

The last word was spoken in such a horrid, croaking rasp that the boy began to wail even louder, but the man paid no attention. They reached the camp's boundary and the tall man threw him to the ground.

"Run!" he roared. *"Run for your life!"*

And at first the boy did, but a few yards beyond the camp he stopped and turned. Saw his father face another man, whose black hair dropped to his waist. He watched, frozen with panic, as the two Shamans fought, but when his father's blood gushed out onto the ground, he closed

his eyes and charged at the Shaman who had destroyed his
world forever.

But he couldn't hurt the Shaman, though he tried, and finally his rage overpowered him and he fell into merciful
darkness. When he woke, there was a cord bound tightly
around his neck, and he *remembered* nothing. Not the
Stone, not his True Name, not the secret tongue of his ancestors, not *anything*.

The awful Shaman turned the Stone in his long, graceful
fingers, a quizzical expression on his face. "What is it, little boy?" He looked down at it, then up again.

The boy stared at him. A trickle of drool traced its way
down his chin. He didn't answer, because he *couldn't*. He
couldn't *remember* anything.

The Shaman examined the boy's blank eyes carefully,
and saw nothing there that might be a threat to him. He
shrugged and tossed back the harmless little talisman.
Some hunting amulet, he supposed. Let the boy keep
it—he would have little else.

"I can't call you boy all the time. What's your name?"

But the boy couldn't remember *that,* either, and so the
Shaman rubbed his chin a moment, and then, recalling the
strange Speaking the boy had worked when he felt pain,
Gotha knew what he would name the brat.

"Your name is Serpent," he said, "for you belong to Him
now."

Serpent felt as if a mighty wind blew through his skull,
and he wandered lost within it. Voices screamed and
howled at him. Without knowing he did so, he took out the
Fatherstone and clutched it, just as he had on that day so
long before.

Suddenly the cacophonous darkness vanished: he hung
in a place with no name, a vast emptiness that seemed
somehow familiar.

"Are you there?" he whispered, and his voice was lisp-
ing and infantile.

"i am here."

The voice seemed to come from everywhere, and nowhere. It too, was familiar.

"I'm afraid," Serpent whispered.

"look. see. remember," the voice replied. Then there was

Light in the Void, and Serpent saw the Fatherstone before him, and from it stretched a long and twisted line, and somehow he understood that the line stretched not only into the past, but far beyond him, into the future as well.

"remember," the voice urged him softly, and Serpent began to weep. His tears hung about him like silver bubbles, and through their shifting glow he saw the man who had first placed the Stone in his hands, and the moment of the placing.

Then his eyes were lifted up, and he saw the One who had orchestrated that moment, as surely as It had woven every other strand of an impossible long and complicated weaving.

Then did Serpent know his past, and understand his Choice.

No walls broke. No lightning flared. No thunder rolled.

Into the utter silence, Serpent spoke. "I know the purpose. I have Kept the Stone as you willed. Now is the time. I Choose to *remember!*"

(i love you.)

"Yes," Serpent said, and then woke up, as the Power who guarded his Stone—though not the Power who had Made it—roared through his lips, on the heels of his Choice.

"I YIELD THE STONE TO THE JOINER, SHE WHO WE HAVE WAITED FOR!

His hand moved with mechanical jerkiness as he offered the Stone to her. Maya took it in her right hand. Overhead, the sky began to split. A great darkness issued forth, and a mighty wind.

Maya felt Power arc between her hands, more than she'd ever known, Power that dwarfed the Force that had destroyed the Shaman Ghost, the Shaman Fist, Power that eclipsed even the potency she'd felt when the Gods Themselves had entered that long-ago fray.

Naked bolts of lightning sizzled between her fingers. She arched her back and summoned every bit of strength remaining in her arms, her hands. Sweat sheened her forehead. She ground her teeth in aching jaws as, slowly, slowly, she brought the Motherstone and Fatherstone together for the first time in eight thousand years.

A mighty flash scorched the clearing. In its center stood the Wielder of the Stone Rejoined, the single talisman held above her head, as with a cosmic groan, the Great Spirits pried apart the sky of the World to pay her homage.

3

WHAT THEY SAW

Raging Bison saw the sky split open. From that hideous wound bulged forth the Void, which squirmed and crawled and festered with manic energies. And written upon the Void in suppurating lines of force was a face. The sky wept at that face, for it was far older than the World, seamed and wrinkled and leaking unnameable fluids, crawling with the putrefaction of centuries, oozing with the sounds of Time itself. And from sockets of utter darkness within that cosmic horror burned two eyes.

Bison couldn't look at those eyes, for they were abomination, and so he looked down to find the spear he held against Wolf's throat had turned into a writhing snake. The eyes of the Snake were rubies, and the tongue of the Snake was Fire.

"My son," said the Snake, *"look up, for I bring you the Gift you thought to have earned in My service."*

And Raging Bison looked up and saw the face of Him Whose Face Was Fear, and his joints turned to water and his nerves sizzled and his heart burned in his chest.

"But you forgot your way, and served a false Spirit, who lived inside your breast and ate your guts. You, in all your fearlessness, served Death, and I am not Death, O worthless servant!"

Bison shrieked, and tried to raise his spear, but it squirmed and twitched in his hands. He began to sob as he fought his own weapon. The Voice ground on like an avalanche falling from the sky above him.

"Just as I took fear from you, now I return it full measure," the Snake said. Then it struck at his eyes, and blinded him to his old life, and in the terrible darkness of his new existence, Raging Bison spun into the pit that had been prepared for him.

That was the last Raging Bison saw of the real World, before the madness took him.

Sharp Knife looked to his own spear, and his mouth fell open and his jaws creaked with terror, for his spear was no longer a spear but the tusk of a great Mother Mammoth. A green eye regarded him from above with cold, insectile calm.

"No!" Sharp Knife howled beneath the furious sky.

A long pink tongue dripped slowly from Her mouth. Blood leaked from the surface of it. It hung before his face, bloated, pendulous, and then snapped back between her great grinding teeth, coating his face with pink spray.

"Who do you serve, O slippery one? Me? My husband father brother son? Or just yourself, and the unspeakable lust you have nurtured like a rotten plant inside you?"

"Ahhh! I have served you, you alone, only you—" Sharp Knife shat himself, and peed himself in his terror, but he could not look away from Her green eye.

It judged him, that eye did.

Her tongue flicked out, touched him, and he gabbled in the madness of Her touch, but he could not turn away.

And She said: *"Receive your reward, O Chief of treachery. You want power? Then you shall have it in full measure. Feel it now, know my Power deep in your belly, be lifted up by My Power!"*

Then the gigantic beast tossed Her head once, disdainfully, and the tusk plunged upward. That was the last thing Sharp Knife saw, deep in the eye of his mind, as he impaled himself on his own spear.

Serpent looked at Gotha's face, a wondrous expression transforming his own features.

"Father?" he said hesitantly, but Gotha only stared at him, not understanding what Serpent saw that day. For it was not Gotha, but another, a tall, bright-skinned man whose eyes were green and blue. And click-click-click, in a hundred glimmering pictures, Serpent saw his past, heard the words of the Fatherstone chanted to him like a lullaby: "Keep the Stone, you are its Keeper, Keep it safe, Keep it long, always *Remember* . . ."

And behind the face of his father he saw another, a greater Face, but that Face was dark and terrible, for it promised a test, and torture beyond bearing, to be borne in His name.

Then Gotha's features swam as if swift-running water

washed over them, until that same Face rode upon the Shaman's shoulders, but it was no longer terrible.

Now it smiled upon him, and a great love burned in its multi-colored eyes. *"You have borne My trials and Spoken with My tongue and Kept My talisman until the time to give it up. You have done well, O Keeper. Receive now My gift."*

Serpent turned away from Gotha, and saw only the face of White Moon, and smiled into the light of it, for White Moon was the gift to him, that together they might make a much greater Gift. The scars that had bound him fell away as if they'd never been. A mighty heat began to burn in his loins. He stepped forward and took her hand.

White Moon gazed upon the transfiguration of the Serpent, and found it good. The boy's skin glowed gold. Sparks shot from his eyes in green and blue showers. A fire kindled in her belly. She stepped forward and received his hand.

She saw nothing but him that day, for her Keeping was far greater than simply the Motherstone. She would keep another in her belly, until His time was come, for so she had Chosen when she Chose at last to Keep the Motherstone.

The Shaman Gotha watched as Caribou's rotted skull rose up from where it had fallen. The vacant eye sockets turned slowly to face him. The jaws of the skull began to creak. Words dropped like stones.

"You are what you are," the Skull said. "And you have served as well as you could, though you had not choice. For you are a tool, Gotha—but I will set you free.

"You had not choice!" the Skull thundered. "That is the heart of your matter! Murder was done at the behest of the Great Ones, not once, but a hundred times. For They had not choice, either!"

Then, more softly, the voice soothed him, for Gotha had begun to weep. "They who have no choice can bear no blame, O Shaman. And if the Gods bear no fault, for They are Gods, then you cannot bear fault either. That would be to question the Gods Themselves."

Gotha put his hands over his eyes, for he felt the weight of invisible chains rising from him, floating away light as feathers, and for the first time in his adult life he wept for the Crone, for his mother, for the fate of tools.

But somehow, even in the shadows of his soul, the Skull found him and said, "You are free of the nets of the Spirits, Gotha. Stand up! Stand!"

Gotha raised his staff, but to no avail, for the meadow fell away and he found himself in a long tunnel. The Skull floated in front of him, glowing gently. In the far distance, a Light began to grow.

Maya gazed slowly about the meadow. She watched as Raging Bison fell to the ground and lay there twisting and screaming. She watched when Sharp Knife, his face an empty mask, leaned slowly onto the point of his own spear. She watched Wolf lay down his weapon, a sheen of wonder transforming his features. She saw Serpent step forth from her side to take White Moon's hand, and she saw the Keeper of the Stone move forward to join him. As their fingers touched, a soft radiance surrounded them and then they were gone. She watched Gotha weep, and then vanish.

Still she stood, the Stone Rejoined held above her head, while the sky split apart as the Gateway opened fully at last and the Gods Themselves spilled endlessly into the World and changed it forever.

She looked at Old Berry, who stood to the side, her eyes shining with fear and wonder and joy.

"You are the oldest of those who remain," Maya said to her. "You have earned the right to See, and so you shall. Come with me."

Then did Maya brandish the Stone Rejoined, and shout, *"Make way, make ready, for She Who Is Waited For!"*

One final thought: *A tool, yes, but even tools may be lofty upon the World.*

4

So they all came together at last on the vast plain beneath the mountains. The air lay like crystal all about them. In the distance, the great animals of the World began to issue forth, and at their head the woman whose True Name was

Ga-Ya, Mother of the People of the World, and at her side the man Named She-Ya, Father of the People of the World.

Slowly they approached, majesty trailing from them like music, and when they were close, Ga-Ya called out, "Welcome, She Who We Have Waited For."

And She-Ya echoed, "Welcome!"

Serpent gasped out, "Father!" The locks fell from his mind, and he knew his true destiny, and knew the Stone was not for him, but he mourned not, for his was the greater gift yet to come.

She-Ya smiled on him, and said, "Know your True Name, Morning Star, for you are the Light at the Dawn of your People."

Nor did White Moon weep, for she also was given the truth in that moment, and saw her destiny in the joining of the Moon and the Star, and what would come.

Maya stood in the center of all, and in this Place Prepared, the Stone Rejoined blazed with the light of a billion suns.

"I made a choice long ago!" she called. "I chose Life! For I am Maya of Many Names, She Who Is Waited For. I am the Key to the Lock, the Joiner of the Stone, the Bearer! Know now the Power granted me!" For only then, after all her life, did she understand the Gift that she had received, and the nature of the tool she was.

In the Light of the Stone Maya unlocked all gates, sundered all barriers, and opened the Ways to and from the World. Then did She Who Steps Down From Stars and He Who Burns Endlessly enter the World They together had made for the last time.

Maya watched them come with wonder glowing in her eyes. They came down from the mountains and walked across the grass as two children, skipping hand in hand, laughter both terrible and joyous upon their lips. And when they came to the Place Prepared, only Maya saw their true glory, and felt the shifting and groaning of the World as it sought to encompass, if only for a moment, Their eternal weight and breadth.

In Their Presence, even the Stone Rejoined dimmed, though it throbbed in her hands with invisible fire. But Maya felt no fear; if one must be a tool, there was no dishonor in fitting the hands of the Gods.

The Boy and the Girl bowed to her, and with Them also

the Animals, and the Mother and Father of the People, who had made the Stone.

The Children spoke: *"GREETINGS TO SHE WHO WE HAVE WAITED FOR! GREETINGS TO SHE WHO BEARS THE STONE! GREETINGS TO SHE WHO BREAKS THE BONDS!"*

Now Maya bowed in reply. *I have Chosen,* she thought. *I thought I Chose Life, and Chose Her. But what have I truly Chosen?* Then, once again, she remembered her Vision, when she fought the beast for Serpent's life, and saw the eyes of the boy who had wielded the Fatherstone.

All around her she saw the marks of the Mother—in the eyes of Ga-Ya and She-Ya, who were the Mother and Father of the People, in Serpent whose name was Morning Star, in White Moon, in the Girl and the—the Boy?

But the Boy was the Father! How could He bear *Her* marks?

And though she had spoken this in the silence of her own mind, the Boy and the Girl heard her, and smiled, and spoke as One.

"NOT OUR MARK, BUT THE MARK OF—"

The Two named no Name, but turned slowly, and gestured with awful majesty at the distant mountains. Then all veils were lifted, and Maya saw at last the Uncreated Creating One, for the mountains were not mountains. They were only the highest tip of the back of the Turtle, rising, rising over the Worlds.

Now even the Place Prepared shattered beneath them, and she saw once again the Mammoth that danced upon the back of the Turtle, and the Fire-tongued Snake that issued from the vagina of the Mammoth and twined about Her, and was held gently in Her mouth, the Circle Without End.

And from the fiery mouth of the Snake floated the gem of green and blue that Maya finally saw for what it was: the World the Gods Created.

In her mind she asked the question, and the Turtle turned his head to gaze upon her, and spoke in the softest whisper.

i did. i created the gods. i create all the gods.

Maya shivered, for she knew that the whisper was heard in all the worlds that were, or are, or will be, and though she knew now whose tool she truly had been, the knowledge filled her with fear.

do not fear, for you are the one they have waited for. know now the true lineage:

> *i swam alone in the void*
> *and was lonely*
> *so i created them, the great spirits*
> *and filled them with my own power*
> *and they created the world*
> *and were bound to it*
> *but they grew lonely also*
> *and created the beasts*
> *and then the peoples*
> *to fill the world.*

The Turtle's eyes flashed, and a vast light of green and blue filled the void.

> *yet even gods grow weary*
> *and wish to lay down their burden*
> *so i granted their wish*
> *and laid upon them a task*
> *that they must prepare the way*
> *for the one to come*
> *who will take up the world*
> *in their place.*

Maya felt the Stone twitch in her hands, as if it were gathering itself for some enormous outpouring of Power. She held tight, and waited for the Turtle. Again, that awesome Light flared, and she realized the Turtle was blinking its eyes.

> *this, then, the lineage:*
> *the mammoth and the snake are*
> *the father and the mother of the world*
> *She-Ya and Ga-Ya*
> *are father and mother of the people*
> *and with my power*
> *they made the stone.*
> *then come the Moon and the Star*
> *and from them*
> *the one to come*
> *who inherits the world.*

Maya floated. A vast sadness suffused her, for in the end, she *had* only been a tool, for her name was nowhere in the Turtle's lineage. Nor were the nets of He Who Creates Without Being Created fully woven. Another was to come after her.

But before her desolation could fully take hold, the Turtle spoke again.

> *you are not of them, daughter, for you are mine*
> *and you have chosen well.*
> *now make way for Him To Come*
> *the Gift, the Promise, and the Test*

A third time the infinite Light flared, and in its gleam, Maya raised up her face in joy, for in that moment she knew that she *had* looked upon the eyes of the One to Come, and they bore the mark of the People of the World, and that he was a Promise, a Gift, and a Test.

And though it was not her fate to see the One to Come in His flesh, without her, He could never have been. And so she raised up the Stone Rejoined one final time, and Spoke for the One Uncreated Who Creates All.

"*All locks are broken, all doors open. Go now, Great Ones, for Your task is done!*"

Thus were the Gods of the World unbound, and returned to the One Who Created Them. Thus was the World unbound from They Who Created The World. And thus was the future unbound, for Him To Come, and for a Promise, a Gift, and a Test.

Then Maya sailed in the void alone. "And me?" she whispered at last.

But the Turtle remained silent, and closed his eyes, and the endless Light vanished. Only when the void had spat her out, and she stood trembling on the familiar meadow beneath the Shield Wall, did she think It might have spoken, for a thought hung unadorned within the perfect emptiness that filled her mind.

do not fear, for i am with you always.

The Shaman Gotha stepped forward and took her in his arms to keep her from collapsing. His face was transfigured, cleansed of all anger, all frustration.

"Do not fall, Maya," he whispered in her ear. "If the Gods are gone, then you and I have much work to do."

She looked up into his eyes. Finally she nodded. "Yes. We do," she replied.

But when he led her to White Moon and Morning Star, who waited for her with radiant faces, she turned to him and said, "For a time, at least. For a time."

5

Maya took Old Berry's withered hands in her own. The two women stood at the mouth of the Green Valley. Beyond, the steppe had turned golden with the fullness of summer.

"Must you go?" Berry asked, though she knew the answer.

"Yes. White Moon will soon begin to grow a fat belly. My task is done. The way is ready for the One To Come."

Berry nodded. "Do you think the Gods are really gone?"

"Yes," Maya said. "What you saw that day was a true thing. Do you still remember it?"

"Why, of course I—" Then a perplexed look crossed Berry's features. "I mean, well . . ."

Maya patted her cheek lovingly. "Don't worry, old friend. All things pass away, and some things aren't meant to be remembered. You were there, though."

"Yes," Berry whispered, awe in her voice. "I was, wasn't I?"

"You keep an eye on Gotha."

Berry snorted. "That one! Though I have to admit, he's a great improvement on that bald-headed mouse, Muskrat."

"The Three Tribes will need a good Shaman," Maya said. "Gotha will serve better than you think. He wasn't a monster, you know, only a tool. Like me." She sighed. "He loved his People. He'll be fine. Help him if you can."

"Yes. I will." Then the old woman swept Maya into a bone-crushing hug. "Oh, daughter, I will *miss* you!"

"And I, you, Mother," Maya whispered in reply. She disentangled herself and stood back, the wind running silent fingers through her hair. Her eyes were jewels in the light. It was how Berry would remember her for the rest of her life.

"But I must go. My time is done, really done. And I am

tired. Even the Gods were allowed to lay down Their burden."

"They were?" Berry looked puzzled, then shook her head. "It doesn't matter. I love you, dear."

"I love you, Berry."

They parted. Berry watched her go, as she had watched her go in what seemed to her now another age, before the World had changed. But there would be no return this time.

After a while, Berry's old eyes could make her out no longer. She wiped her nose, sniffed, then turned and trudged back up the Main Path to the only World she knew.

6

Maya walked all through the summer and into the fall. The winds of autumn ruffled the great forests and tossed the surface of the long waters and made her feel light as the air itself. She felt herself growing *thinner,* as the rivers began to throb and thunder in her ears.

Autumn was growing to a close when she reached her destination. Beneath a gray, snow-kissed sky she found a hollow in a rocky place and lay herself down and listened to the pulse of the rivers, in the place where the waters of the World joined together. It seemed fitting that her story should end here.

The rocks felt soft as a thick pile of mammoth skins beneath her. She placed the Mammoth Stone Rejoined upon her breasts and sighed, and it seemed the sigh went on until all the air was gone from her lungs.

"Maya."

"Yes, what?"

It was very dark, but then a faint light began to grow, and she saw him above her, bending down to take her in his arms and lift her up.

"Oh, Caribou," she said. She rose to meet him, free at last of all the Great Bindings, free to float in the endless Light of the Love that was her final reward.

"I love you, Maya," Caribou said.

i love you, too, the Turtle whispered, his Voice sighing through all the Worlds. *come home to me now and forever.*

Then Maya who bore the Mammoth Stone left the

World. But her bones remained behind, and on them the Stone Rejoined, for it awaited yet another who was to come.

Stone and bones, bones and Stone.

A gift. A promise.

A test.